The Water is Wide

ELIZABETH GIBSON

The Water is Wide

A Novel of Northern Ireland

Zondervan Books
Zondervan Publishing House
Grand Rapids, Michigan

THE WATER IS WIDE
© 1984 by Elizabeth Gibson

First U.S. paperback edition 1990

Zondervan Books
are published by
Zondervan Publishing House
1415 Lake Drive SE, Grand Rapids, Michigan 49506

Library of Congress Cataloging-in-Publication Data

Gibson, Elizabeth.
The water is wide.
1. Northern Ireland—History—1969- —Fiction.
I. Title.
PR6057.I246W3   1984   823'.914   84-12023
ISBN 0-310-31821-1

Printed in the United States of America

90 91 92 93 94 95 / AK / 10 9 8 7 6 5 4

To my friends on both sides
of the narrow and wide waters

I gratefully acknowledge the help and encouragement of Sr. Patrice McCabe, Fr. Cornelius Welch, O.F.M., John Darby, the Londonderry City Council, Cindy Lastoria, Judi Mollenkof, and my husband.
Though the historical events and almost all the places of this novel are real, the characters are fictional.

Many waters cannot quench love;
neither can the floods drown it.
Song of Solomon 8:7

For locations, see maps at end of book.

Londonderry
September, 1969

The eyes lift from the paper. The blue irises dilate. Against the dusty yellow-white light of September, the black pupils contract. The eyes are sharp, coldly blue, focusing here and there with a quick motion.

Only since 1949 have blood and brain sung and snapped behind those eyes. Eyes that saw in the flesh and on the black and white screen the dizzying legacies of war: coupon books and meager rations on her father's table; shell-shocked men on the doorstep begging for soup, shelter, or a job; the blackened, timber-charred ruins of Coventry where only the high altar stood untouched. Eyes that saw in the flesh, and on the searing screen of memory and repeated nightmare, fragments of a war within a war: gray, litter-strewn streets and the barrel of a drunk sniper's random rifle; her own frightened crying spilling out into the deserted Belfast street like her mother's and sister's blood—its sound as red and terrible as the blood itself, as red and terrible as her mother's scream— *"Get down, Katie! Get down! It's dangerous. Get down! It's dangerous."*

The same eyes saw through the frosted glass of her father's preaching the beckoning, concave glory of heaven in its narrowness, its boundlessness: burning blues, fluttering doves, fold upon fold of cloud and angel wing, echo upon echo of trumpet and song, a shattering blast of light and sound that would carry the chosen into eternal bliss with God.

All these she has seen in flesh and spirit.

The universe, her brain instructs her, is simple, clear, and purposeful. Death equals black markets, black banners, black congealed blood on a Belfast pavement, baleful sirens shrill as banshees. Life equals white-hot light, white wings, white robes washed in the blood of the Lamb, soaring choirs sweet as thrushes.

At twenty, she still believes it, though the child of thirteen had spoken of it and had been laughed down by a classroom full of scornful girls—*God will not let us destroy ourselves in civil or nuclear war.* A debate on nuclear war and weapons. Her uncle, a brilliant physicist, whom she trusted, had worked at Aldermaston then. *God will not let us be destroyed. . . .*

Her eyes unfocus, drifting out beyond the immediacy of her round-rimmed glasses, beyond even desks and chairs. *God will not let us. . . .*

Unconscious of all but sight, she misses the slight scratch of fountain pens, the rustle of paper, the click of a cigarette lighter, the rise and fall of the old man's voice.

Her eyes pass down the row in front of her. Arrow-straight black hair. Coal black and glossy. *Catholic.* A long, narrow face and jutting chin. Pale eyes. Sandy brown hair and sunken cheeks. *Protestant.* Bright, freckled cheeks and a freckled snub nose. Tangle of red curls. *Catholic.* Thick, untidy flaxen hair—a thatch in County Donegal. Rounded shoulders and a cigarette between thin lips. *Catholic.* Straw-colored hair. Long face. Gray eyes that catch hers without expression. *Protestant. No. Catholic?* She hesitates, staring a little longer than usual, but then her eyes waver and skip across the room. Pale skin except in the cheeks. Wavy, reddish-blond hair. *Catholic? No. Protestant? No. . . .*

The old man steps out from behind the podium, his voice changing as he opens the window with a laugh. "Ireland doesn't know we have to work."

The breeze rushes in and blows a flurry of papers from the podium. He stoops awkwardly to retrieve them, then continues. From beside the wooden platform, the flag of the province ripples out above his head. The bloody hand appears and disappears into its folds.

"Dorothea Brooke, we see, is so proud that she's completely blind. She's almost literally blind. Notice the repeated mention of short-sightedness. She's also metaphorically blind. Notice her refusal to see Casaubon for what he is, her inability to recognize love when she sees it in a real, fleshly form."

[10]

Kate hesitated. "Thanks." Then she added, grudgingly, "Have you just arrived here?"

The girl's eyes went down suddenly, no longer laughing. "Yes I'm a—what d'you say? 'Fresher'? Is that it?"

Kate smiled with forced brightness, wanting to be gracious. "My name is Katherine Hamilton." She tightened her arms around the books, her right hand glued to *Middlemarch*. She would not shake hands.

Catching this slight rebuff, the girl's voice became unsure. She pushed her hands into the deep pockets of her robe. "I'm Deirdre McAvoy. . . . Do you live up here?"

Kate jerked her head toward the corridor. "Yes, just along a little."

"Well, I'm just around here. The room at the end."

"Oh, yes. That's a good room. Someone I knew had it last year." Kate's tone was indifferent.

"You're third year?"

"Second."

"Doing what, if you don't mind the asking?"

"English. What about you?"

"French."

"Ah, well, good-night . . . Deirdre."

The girl's soft slippers shuffled back toward her door, but stopped just as Kate was turning away.

"Oh, wait a minute. I think you've got my Bible with your books."

Kate stood very still. "Your *Bible?*" she repeated dully.

Deirdre came back toward Kate. She was flushed now. "Yes, I was sitting out here reading." She gestured toward her room. "The girl I share with has gone to bed."

Kate shook slightly as she fumbled with the pile of books. *The Great Tradition. A Short History of the English Novel. Essays in Nineteenth Century Fiction. Holy Bible . . . Her Bible. A Catholic called Deirdre McAvoy is reading a Bible. A Catholic . . . reading a Bible?* She passed it back, murmuring an apology. Then, "Listen, if Sheila's not in bed yet, you could read in my room if you want. I'm going out again. It's not very comfortable out here, is it?"

[13]

Deirdre's face brightened again. "Not at all." Still, she hung back, a little shy.

Kate rattled the key in the lock and edged the door open. No sound of breathing. Both beds still made. A clutter on Sheila's desk etched in the dull light from the corridor. "No, Sheila's out yet."

As Kate snapped on the lamp between the beds, then another on her desk, Deirdre still hovered uncertainly near the door.

Kate gestured abruptly to her own desk and chair. *Why can't she just sit down and stop looking so nervous?* "You can sit here. I'm going for a walk."

Deirdre padded in. "Thank you very much. But what if your friend comes back?"

"Sheila? She won't mind. She'll probably talk your ear off, though." Kate looked at her quizzically. "So you'd better read now if you want quiet. . . . What are you reading, anyway?"

"First Corinthians. It's a New Testament letter," Deirdre said slowly, almost apologetically.

Kate stopped in the doorway, her arm half into the sleeve of a light coat. The muscles around her mouth and eyes relaxed slightly. Almost a smile. "I know."

"You're a Christian?"

"I am."

Deirdre's face lit up. "So am I!" She rested the gilt-edged Bible on her lap. "Ah, that makes me glad. I didn't expect to find many Christians at university."

"And you won't, either. . . ." Kate stepped back into the room, sliding out of the coat again. A good talk, not a walk, would lull her tonight. "Maybe I'll not go out after all. We could talk a little, if you'd like."

"Oh—yes. I would."

"But I'll not keep you from Corinthians." The smile was genuine now. "I'll have a bath, and *then* we can talk. All right?"

"What church do you go to?" Deirdre leaned forward to take the cup of cocoa Kate was offering. Her eyes were warm.

There. Now Kate would find out. "Presbyterian. I go to Great

[14]

James Street while I'm here. At home, I go to my father's church. He's a minister."

Deirdre did not mistake the pride in Kate's voice. Her own was deferential, hesitant. "I'm Church of Ireland."

"Oh? There's a good Church of Ireland on the Wall near the Diamond. St. Augustine's. Have you heard of it?"

"Not likely. I'm from Armagh. This is the first I've been up here."

Kate leaned back on the vinyl padding of her chair. "You know," she began slowly, "I mistook you for a Catholic."

Deirdre smiled. An old joke. The light danced in her eyes. "Everyone does. It's the name. My father's a Catholic."

Kate stared. "You were baptized—christened—Catholic?"

Deirdre shook her head. "No. My mother's Methodist. My father—well—he's not a strict Catholic. Only goes to Mass a few times a year. I found myself at home in the Church of Ireland. A sort of compromise, I suppose."

A mixed marriage. But Deirdre was a Christian. How could that be? What would her father say? *"Two unequally yoked can't pull well together, Katie. Remember that."*

Remember that! . . . The indirect lights and brown furnishings of her father's study in England and herself at his side. Fourteen years old: the year she first fell in love. The choice she made was inappropriate—an older boy from down the street—a Catholic, as it turned out.

"But what difference do beliefs make, Daddy?"

"All the difference in the world, Kate. A Roman Catholic wouldn't accept many things in Holy Scripture—if he knew about them, which he doesn't, of course . . . but that's God's Word, as well you know . . . and besides, your mother. . . ." His voice had trailed away painfully, and she had turned away with a set mouth.

A mixed marriage. A room of glib seventeen-year-old girls at a race relations conference in Westminster. *"Would you ever marry a colored man?" "Yes, if I loved him." "I wouldn't." "Oh, I would." "Why?" "Why not?" "Marry in your own class." "What difference does skin color make?"*

Kate shifted, turning her attention back to Deirdre, laughing

[15]

nervously. "Your parents . . . I mean, are they still . . . well, how are they getting along these days when there's fighting?"

Deirdre shrugged. "Oh, just as always. Armagh's not been affected much—except last November when Paisley stopped a civil rights march there. Dad's quiet, not the belligerent type. Always kept to himself at work. He let us all go to church as we pleased. Mum's kept us all going. She's a good little woman." Her voice softened. "I miss her already."

Kate said thickly, "I know. I do know." And her eyes filled.

Beside them, Kate's alarm clock crackled and hummed. A quarter to one. Both sipped their cocoa. Kate began to feel weary; it was an effort to keep her eyes open.

Deirdre watched her steadily. "Do you have brothers or sisters?" she asked.

"No—" Kate bit her lip but forced herself to look straight at Deirdre. "No—none."

That pixyish smile again. Real *joie de vivre*. "Oh! Well, I'm the last of six."

"Six!" *Of course. A Papist father.*

"They both wanted babies," Deirdre said quickly, defensively. "Dad wasn't young when they married. He was discharged from the army in 1944—wounded at the Somme in France. When he got back to Belfast, all the young women he'd known before the war were married with weans already, or gone away. He met my mother when she was cooking for returning soldiers—with all the other Methodist women. She was thirty-two herself."

Kate listened with a mixture of fascination and disbelief. "And how—you're the last of six?"

Deirdre laughed. "Yes," she said. "Born in 1951, I was. I don't know how Mum put up with us all. Bridget in '45. Ann in '47. Jim and Patrick in '48—they're identical twins. Sarah in '50. They thought she was the last. Dad was fifty by then, and the doctor told my mother she'd be foolish to go on. And I came along." Her voice had a sing-song quality as she made this declaration of names and dates. A liturgy often recited. "Dad sometimes says the doctor was right; they *were* foolish to have me." She laughed with delight.

Kate smiled a tight smile. Her own father never made jokes, especially about sacred matters like childbirth. And sometimes she found it hard to know whether someone was joking or serious. Now she was beginning to feel too tired to think clearly anyway, though a question nagged. *Barricades. Molotov cocktails. Kick the Pope. Orangemen go home.* "How on earth did they get to know each other?"

"Oh, things were different then. The war, you know. Not so many 'troubles' then. And Mum had her eye on him from the start. Saw he was clean-living and decent. Found out he liked children. Liked his jokes. That was it." Deirdre shrugged. "Very matter-of-fact, my mother. And, you know, she loves him yet."

Another question was stirring in Kate's brain. How could Deirdre's mother go on living with a man who had not converted? And love him? What could they possibly have in common? On this matter, she now shared completely her father's strict view. "Do you mind if I ask one thing more?"

"No. Go on."

"Well—did she ever bring him . . . did he come to know Christ?"

Deirdre's face told her she had trespassed too far. Kate felt the reproach. She looked down, sorry she had destroyed the tenuous connection between them.

"If you mean," said Deirdre carefully, "did Mummy convert Dad to Protestantism or even to a kind of evangelical Catholicism—if such a thing exists—then no, she didn't." Her eyes flashed. "But Daddy has his own sort of religion, and I'll not be the one to say if he'll go to heaven or not."

"Oh—no—no—" Kate stammered. *He won't though,* she thought. *What on earth will James say if Deirdre starts talking like this at a CU meeting?* What would she herself say? James mustn't find out, that was all. It would complicate things. And Deirdre might get hurt. Not by James—oh no—but somehow. She shook her head. Too awful to think about.

"And he and Mummy long ago reached a consensus. They live and let live," Deirdre continued.

But Kate still wondered what they said at night in front of the television when an IRA man had blown up one of the mother's friends, or when some wee girl had been tarred and feathered for going out with a fellow from the wrong side of the barricades. She

[17]

couldn't even imagine what they had to say to each other. How terribly sad. Aloud, all she said was, "I see."

Deirdre drained the dregs of her cocoa and glanced at the clock. "It's getting late," she said.

"It *is* late."

Even so, neither of them moved.

"And how do you come to be studying in Ireland?" Deirdre asked. "You seem to know what's been going on over here. With the situation and all, why would you come?"

Kate looked amused. "You think I'm English?" She was relieved their conversation was taking a lighter turn.

"I'm not sure. I've been trying to decide. Sometimes I hear BBC English, or better—" Deirdre's eyes twinkled. "And sometimes I catch a glottal stop or a trilled 'r' that's surely Ulster-Scots. A minute ago you said 'airth' for 'earth'—as I do. Not 'urth'—with the 'r-less' dialect the way the English say it. And 'late.' You had a diphthongized vowel—as if the vowel sounds 'a' and 'y' were quite distinct. That's Ulster, too." She leaned forward. "So tell me, which side of the water *are* you from?"

"I'm impressed. You're a linguist."

Deirdre colored. "I've a *good* ear, too good for my own good. 'Better mind you do some good with that good ear of yours,' my father says." She laughed again.

In spite of herself, Kate said, "He's right. Hence the French, no doubt."

"Well now, which side?" Deirdre insisted.

"It's hard to say. This side, I suppose. Both of my parents were born here—I was, too. Lived here . . . in Belfast . . . until '53. Of course I was too little to remember—much. Then we went to England. Ever since I can remember, I've wanted back over here. When Daddy heard of the New University—the New U—he said I should think of applying. So I did. Daddy studied here, too. It was Magee Theological College then." She gripped the handle of her mug tightly. "He's Northern Irish, you see."

"Ah, now it makes sense. And the 'better than BBC'?"

"Boarding school."

Deirdre smiled. "I was thinking so. And an outstanding academic record no doubt."

[18]

Kate had come back to Ireland proud of her academic distinctions, but she had learned the first year to wear them lightly. "Well, actually—" she stopped, cringing inwardly. Was Deirdre making fun of her? Or was it just her way? "Not in French," she countered.

Deirdre chuckled. "For me, it was *only* in French."

"Mine was a spurious French," Kate admitted. "Schoolgirl French. Are you fluent?"

Deirdre nodded. "Yes, but it was easy for me. I lived in France for a while. I'd heard from Dad about the beautiful countryside— he was at Caen and Falaise and said even in wartime with all the bombing, Normandy was lovely. I'd always wanted to go. The way you wanted to come here."

"When were you in France?"

"A year ago. I spent a whole summer there before 'A' levels. Went with *ma famille* to market and learned to haggle in street French. I even learned to talk French baby talk to the children—I was *au pair*. I loved it." She stopped, seeing Kate covering a yawn. "But that's another story, and you're tired, I'm thinking."

Kate nodded. "Yes—all of a sudden." She smiled a lopsided smile. "My brain's funny. It churns away for hours and then stops dead. After that I'm good for nothing." Still seated, she stretched, her arms and fingers reaching almost to the top of a disused fireplace built into the middle of the wall.

Deirdre stood up to put the empty cocoa mug on the mantelpiece. Tightening the tie of her dressing gown, she looked down at Kate. "You've been very kind, Katherine. Thank you."

Kate waved her hand in acknowledgment of Deirdre's gratitude and in dismissal. "That's all right. Let me know if you need anything. I'll look out for you. And please call me Kate."

"I will. I feel I've found a friend," Deirdre murmured. The wooden door closed softly behind her.

Tuesday, September 30

The creakings and squeakings of the floor outside her room were already familiar to Deirdre. She drowsed over the comic dialogue of Molière, the print appearing and disappearing on the page until at last she gave up and rested her head on her arms. She drifted to her mother's cluttered kitchen.

A knock and a voice roused her. "Deirdre?" She jumped up to open the door, still rubbing her eyes.

A tall, slender girl in a white raincoat stood outside, blue umbrella in hand. Her fine, gold hair was pulled back off her face into a knot so that every curve, every hollow of cheeks, eyes, and chin was accentuated. The blue eyes, so cold the first time she had seen them, were bright and alive.

"Oh—Kate."

A smile—a little crooked but wide, with good teeth. "Yes, remember me?"

"Of course! Come in." And she stepped aside.

The radiators had begun to bubble and click that afternoon, so the room was warm and shadowy in the fading daylight. Kate's spotless white coat struck a dazzling contrast.

"I came to see if you'd like to come to a prayer meeting with me. . . . Would you?"

Deirdre looked over at *Le Tartuffe*. "Well—"

"You're reading?"

"Yes. I should finish this for tomorrow."

"There'll be time tonight, won't there?" Kate urged, "Do come. You'll meet all—almost all—the Christians here if you do. It's the first prayer meeting this term."

"Well, if you put it that way—" but she still hesitated, frowning slightly. "What sort of group is it? Not Paisleyites and the like, I hope."

Kate looked shocked. "It's the Christian Union—part of InterVarsity Fellowship, you know."

"That's good," Deirdre said as she rattled coat hangers and pulled her cloak from the old wooden wardrobe.

Their shoes clattered down the stairs, and they went out into the early twilight and heavy drizzle of autumn. Gray clouds rolling down from the mountains. Lights going on. Seagulls flapping aimlessly over the treetops. The cathedral clocks faintly chiming the hour. Umbrellas up, they trudged along past the drenched rhododendrons and then up the broken cement steps of the theological building. A dim sodium lamp illuminated their way.

Deirdre shook her umbrella just inside the door so that the droplets shot everywhere. The hall was drab and quiet. Heavily framed portraits of nineteenth-century ministers with black robes and starched white collars were the only adornments. She sniffed. The dry, warm smell of old radiators just turned on, chalk dust, musty books.

The front door suddenly opened and a thin young man in a long gray mackintosh cannoned right into Deirdre, who was standing with her back to the door.

"Oh, sorry," he mumbled.

Kate was instantly at her elbow. "James—hello!"

Deirdre understood immediately. As Kate lifted her chin to smile at this James, a faint pinkness spread from neck to hairline while her intent, hot eyes took in his every detail. Kate's voice had changed, too, dropping to a lower register.

James barely returned the smile as he hastily shrugged off his wet coat and hung it on the rack against the wall. His face was narrow and somewhat pinched, lined across the forehead and over the bridge of his nose. Otherwise, though, the skin was perfect, smooth and slightly tanned; no hint of beard or blemish. And the eyes—Deirdre was struck by his eyes—were a startling, hypnotic blue, the kind she would not find it easy to look away from. But there was something about him that she wouldn't trust, that she would fear. What was it? A kind of intensity and earnestness—like

[21]

Kate's, but much more severe. She looked away, ashamed that she was judging so quickly. *Bide and see,* she told herself.

"Hello, Katherine," he was saying. "What were you doing over the summer holidays?"

"Oh—I had a job at home. But never mind that," she said quickly. "I want to introduce someone to you. This is Deirdre, a fresher, from Armagh."

Deirdre caught a hint of pride in Kate's voice. Pride that she was bringing a first-year student to the first prayer meeting? But defensiveness, too, as if she expected disapproval.

James appraised her but didn't offer to shake hands. "Ah—that's where Reverend Paisley was born."

His voice was toneless. *What does he mean by bringing Paisley into the conversation?* Deirdre shivered slightly and looked at Kate questioningly. The older girl returned the look with an expression of utter bewilderment. Was she remembering what Deirdre had asked her in the room?

"Well," James said stiffly, "we're all a little late, I think. Let's go in, shall we?"

Kate nodded vigorously. "Yes, yes, let's." Her ardent face made Deirdre indignant.

"Is Sheila back?" James asked as he led the way down a narrow corridor.

Following directly behind, Kate answered brightly, "Yes, but I've not seen much of her so far."

"And Roger?"

"Yes, I hear he's back. Perhaps that's why I've not seen much of Sheila!"

"Good. I thought I'd seen him—on Shipquay Street. Oh, by the way—" and he stopped so suddenly that Kate almost fell against him. "I gather I am nominated to be president of the CU this year. And you have been nominated to be vice-president. Will you run?"

"Will you?"

"Of course."

"Well, I'll have to pray about it. I didn't know a thing about it."

James shrugged. "I hope you will." He sounded petulant. "If I'm elected, I don't know of any other girl in the CU who could help me."

Kate flushed again. *She's pleased*, Deirdre observed, *but she doesn't want him to know.*

From a room ahead of them she caught a soft murmur of voices and laughter. Laughter. What a relief. Not all as sober as James.

A door abruptly swung open. "Katie! James!"

Deirdre glimpsed a high-ceilinged lecture hall and a circle of students. Then Kate was again introducing her, this time to the person who had opened the door, Roger Forbes.

Roger's hand immediately stretched toward hers. There was no mistaking the English accent this time—Eton, or Harrow? Home-knitted sweater and neatly combed brown hair. Compact build—not even as tall as Kate, and stocky. Laughter lines at the corners of his eyes.

"Deirdre! Oh, yes, the lass for whom 'the greatest amount of blood shall be shed that has ever been shed in Erin since race and time began.'"

She stared at him.

"The story of Deirdre and Naoise. Don't you know it? Here I am, a Sassenach, yet I know all your old tales better than you do."

James tutted impatiently. "Pagan nonsense, Roger."

Not in the least nonplused, Roger beamed back. "We're glad you're here, Deirdre. What, has Kate taken you under her proverbial wing already?"

Deirdre looked quickly at Kate, whose mouth was still turned up at the corners. "You might say that," she answered cautiously.

All the chatter had subsided as soon as they entered, and now a ring of expectant eyes was turned on them where they stood in the doorway. The faces were friendly but curious.

Kate surveyed the circle of students. "Sheila's not here?" she asked Roger.

"Afraid not. I left her in the library. She's presenting a paper in 'Pope to Crabbe' next week."

"Already?"

He nodded, drawling, "And not doing very well at it."

"Oh—"

"Kate, you'd better introduce your friend to everyone, and then let's start," someone instructed.

"Come on, Deirdre, we can sit here," Kate said, leading the way to two empty canvas chairs.

"All right, everybody, welcome back!" Deirdre presumed the speaker was the outgoing president of the Union. "Kate Hamilton has brought someone along to our meeting today. The first of many freshers, we hope. Kate?"

Again, Kate introduced her, and Deirdre felt rather overwhelmed and conspicuous. She began to wish she had waited until the freshers' squash; according to Kate, that was the first meeting to which all new students were invited.

One by one, the students introduced themselves. There were about thirty present, with a few stragglers still coming. Most were Irish. And most were men, she noticed—a change from her church in Armagh, where women made up the majority of the congregation.

The solid male presence unsettled her. For some reason, it conjured up old men and young with the Orange sash, the flutes and the drums. Belfast. July the twelfth past. She had grown up fearing such parades because of her father and nowadays was the more afraid because of the Bogside riots of August in Londonderry, her memory still bruised by unforgettable television images. Rock-and-bomb-throwing crowds. Houses burning on Bombay Street. Screaming women and terrified children. *I pray I'll fit in here,* she thought, *that things won't be hard on me on Dad's account, that Kate will prove a good friend to me.*

The room fell quiet; heads bowed. Every sound was intensified: Kate's quiet, even breathing, the hum of an overhead fluorescent bulb, the minute rustle of a skirt or trouser leg. Gradually, though, the silence deepened until she could hear even her own heartbeat, the steady pulse and pump of her own blood and veins. The sound frightened her, loud in her ears while her eyes were shut; she felt as if she were somehow lifted out of her chair. Her head felt light, unattached.

Across the room, a low voice began. When it finished, there was another. Irish or English made no difference; there was a kind of power and rhythm in the words that Deirdre had never heard in common speech. An utterance somehow ordained by God.

The prayers washed and rolled over and around her like great

[24]

waves. She was drowning in an uncharted sea of strangers' voices. The Church of Ireland had few prayer meetings. Any she had attended were with her Methodist mother, and there she had heard only the simple, homebound prayers of housewives and linen-factory workers. No rhetorical flourishes.

At last, a voice she recognized. James. Beside her, Kate's breathing quickened.

"Great God and Father, Judge and King eternal, Thou knowest that we dare not come before Thee, that all our righteousness is but filthy rags in Thy sight. And yet, Lord God, Thou hast sent us Thy Son to be our Mediator, and so we make bold. We pray Thee for our country, that Thou wilt raise up men mighty in loyalty to Thee and to Thy servant the Queen; that Thou wilt purify our land of all the wiles of Rome. Help us to do our duty to love our Catholic neighbors and to show them the error of their ways, the lostness of their lives. Let us keep the faith of our forefathers undefiled. We pray Thee also for this university, that Thou wilt make us unashamed to proclaim Christ, and Him crucified; that we will not cringe under criticism and hatred, but that we may boldly declare Thee and thus be Thy instruments of delivery for those that walk in darkness. O God, hear us through Jesus Christ our Savior."

As a faint murmur of "Amen" rippled round the room, Deirdre opened her eyes and sat back, her mirage of pure spirituality dissipated. *I do not belong here*, she thought coolly, moving her eyes slowly round the circle. Doctrinal orthodoxy infused James's prayer, but where was love? Why did she hear hatred in this calling down of damnation and duty? Why were the groveling words of approach arrogant rather than humble? Was this what she would find among the Christians here? Then she noticed that Roger, too, was open-eyed; and, catching her eye, he winked.

So, she thought, *James's vision is not shared by everyone here.* But what of Kate—this half-friend beside her. Mesmerized by James, would she befriend or betray?

Kate had known James would pray, had longed for his prayer. It would bring her the same security, the same comfort as her

[25]

father's prayers from the pulpit. His prayer would bring the same reassurance, the same sense that the world was ordered and designed by God, that with Him all things were not only possible, but probable. His prayer would bring balm to her bruised soul, balance to her lost equilibrium. It would eradicate his coldness in the hallway, his comment about Paisley's birthplace. For if James could not live with passion, he could pray with it.

She had listened with Deirdre's ears to all the prayers. Already she felt a tug of loyalty to the younger woman, a desire to protect her as she would have protected her sister Jo. In Deirdre she saw some of the qualities she knew she herself lacked: a lively, spontaneous spirit, a warmth and sense of family that seemed to have died with her mother and sister. All last year she had searched among those she knew at the university for a friend close enough to tell about that day in Belfast, for a friend who would listen but not pity. She had found none. Even Sheila, who knew her better than anyone and who tolerated her occasional sleepless nights and black days without complaint (at least not to her), was not the person she wanted to confide in.

Now James was praying. She waited for the comfort, the balm and balance. Listening. . . . *What is this?* Even with eyes shut, she frowned. His voice was different. Why? Had she changed or had he? No birds sang when he prayed. *A thorn in the roses of Eden. What clichés! Concentrate . . . in God's presence. . . . But, Lord, what has happened? He sounds angry, vituperative, almost strident. . . . James— strident?* ". . . *wiles of Rome . . . do our duty . . . will not cringe . . . those that walk in darkness. . . .*"

She felt a mountain of tension and indecision thrusting itself between her growing desire for Deirdre's friendship and her full-blown desire for James's love. Then Deirdre began to pray.

Kate was awed by her courage. She herself had not dared pray aloud until her third or fourth week in this august group of theological students and future missionaries. Yet Deirdre was speaking out with barely a quaver in her voice.

"Dear God, thank you for bringing us here. Thank you for Christian fellowship and friendship. Thank you for everyone here. Help me here to serve you and to grow—" She paused. "—help us all to accept one another's differences, to see that we can still serve

[26]

and love you even though you ask us to do it in different ways. Help us to love one another truly. I pray through Jesus. Amen."

A murmur of surprise and rustle of faint movement passed round the circle. Kate heard Roger say a loud "Amen" and mechanically repeated the word herself. But to what she had said "Amen" she barely knew.

Hubbub as the meeting ended and the members dispersed. The narrow, dark corridor again. At one end, Kate and James, intent and intense. Deirdre watched, waited, then trailed away to supper by herself, disappointed.

"Well, Katherine?"

"Well what?"

"Are you going to run for vice-president or not?" His voice grated.

She looked at him, afraid yet hungry. His eyes were just as clear as she had remembered, and they still sought hers with their direct blue gaze. His skin was just as smooth as she had remembered. His face was still alert and frank—the face she had summoned up night by night in half-dreams before sleep. Nothing was different, surely.

"I don't know, James. I need time to think."

"It's only a week away, you know."

"Oh, I'll decide before then."

"What's the difficulty? Don't you think we'd get along together?" His tone implied that this was only a remote possibility.

"Of course we would." Her eyes went down, and she repeated the words more slowly. "Of course we would."

"You seem unsure," he insisted, probing. "Not like you."

She put her hands into her pockets. "Well, and if I am?" She raised her eyes to meet his again.

For the first time since she'd known him, there seemed a division between them, an invisible but real barrier. The difference, once realized, was painful, frightening. And the discrepancy between her fantasies about their first meeting this term and the present reality made her ache. In her dreams his voice had been warm, his

[27]

eyes searching only for her. As it was, he spoke impatiently, abruptly, and his eyes looked through her coldly. In her dreams she was his equal—a woman who could stand beside him, a woman prepared perfectly by upbringing and faith to be his wife. She had been certain that this year her dream would become his. What had happened?

Now he laughed dryly. "What *is* the matter? You're so—so—" He shrugged. "What can I say?—defensive?—all of a sudden."

"And you—" she blurted, seizing the opportunity, "you've changed, yourself, James. Something must have happened this summer. What was it?"

His lips twisted slightly. "Come, come. Don't turn this back on me, Katherine. No, I haven't changed. Though you're right, something *has* happened—as you put it."

"What, then?" What an odd turn this was taking. How did she dare say all this? She swallowed. "If some of your beliefs have changed, I ought to know, don't you think?"

His blue eyes narrowed on her intently. "If you mean my fundamental Christian beliefs—then nothing's different. In fact, if anything, I'm all the more convinced of what I've believed all along, and of the importance of bringing others to that truth, too." He twisted the handle of his umbrella round and round as he talked, periodically stopping to make a small dent in the linoleum with the tip of it.

Kate smiled, relieved. "Then, what—" Her hands moved aimlessly in the air. What could she say? Impossible to put into words precisely how his prayer today was different from other prayers, how his prayer betrayed not just scorn (she was used to that, after all), but hatred.

"I came to some conclusions about the Catholic Church last year. . . ."

"Yes—of course. We've all done that, I'm sure." She was placating her own fears, trying to forestall any further divergence between them.

He was annoyed by the interruption. "Wait a minute . . . and I tested their validity this summer. It was a good time to do it, with all that's gone on. Shameful. Be thankful you weren't on this side of the water in August."

[28]

She shuddered. BBC television news was as close as she wanted to get to that travesty of the law and order for which Prime Minister Chichester-Clark had so loudly called. Derry—Bogside: stone and bomb throwing, riots and tear gas, snipers and "B" specials beating rioters with cudgels. Bernadette Devlin organizing the Catholics of Rossville Flats. Little children cursing and name-calling from behind barricades. Belfast: houses burning on Conway Street. Police firing machine guns on Divis and Brookfield Streets. . . .

"In some ways I was here," Kate said firmly. "It *was* terrible." At last, something they definitely agreed upon. "What do you mean, though, 'tested your conclusions'?"

"I mean that I've joined with some others who share my views on Papists. I've joined the Free Presbyterian Church—you know—the Reverend Paisley's church."

He might as well have struck her. She shrank back. "No—no, James, surely not!"

"Why not? It was the most logical step for me to take. Within that denomination I'll have every opportunity to work for the loyal Protestants of Ulster. It's time to let the Papists know that Protestants are here to stay in the North and that we *will* remain in control." His eyes glittered.

This was not her James. This was a stranger, a man she neither knew nor understood. At last she managed weakly, almost bitterly, her voice very low, "How did this come to be?"

"Don't look so horrified. You look as dumbstruck as if I'd told you I'd changed to Popery."

"James!" she gasped, then recovered quickly. "Mr. Paisley's a mob orator. His ideas are extreme, inflammatory. How can you associate with them? I just don't understand."

"And you—what's come over you suddenly?" he flashed back angrily. "Not a sympathizer with Papists, I hope?"

She stared at him in brief silence. "You shock me. How can you speak that way to me?" She was choked with emotion. "I don't want to talk to you any more just now."

"Wait—" He arrested her with a jerk of his hand, though he didn't actually touch her. "I'm sorry. Let me explain a little."

Kate leaned back against the peeling paint of the wall and

sighed. She longed to run out of the building, to fling herself on her bed and sob in proper Emily Brontë fashion—anything to wash away the ugly words that had passed between them, to make them no longer true. Still, they hung as heavy between them as summer mist by the River Lagan.

"This August," James began slowly, still turning his umbrella, "I found myself angry and disillusioned with the government but—of course—powerless to do a thing. When Chichester-Clark called for British troops, I felt ashamed. Why should loyal Protestants—and God knows there's a million of us in this province—need an army, of all things, to stop the madness of the Papists? All that burning and looting. Why, they even burned down some of their own houses! It seemed like a disgraceful capitulation—the calling of troops, I mean."

Letting down her guard a bit, Kate nodded slowly. "I know. I felt it too, when I read the paper."

"So I was in Belfast on the thirtieth—last month—and it so happened a man I knew told me about a rally outside Stormont where people were protesting all the concessions being made to R.C.'s. It was timely for me. I'd even begun to think of politics rather than the ministry. That was wrong, but now I can combine both."

Kate stared at him, knowing what he would say, yet hoping he wouldn't. "So you went to the rally?"

"I did, indeed. And I know what you think—how could I? Well, I was surprised—never had had time for Paisley myself. But he was erudite, brilliant. He spoke with such energy—the way I'd like to preach one day."

The way Daddy preaches, Kate thought. Erudite, brilliant, energetic. All the words applied. *But my father's no fanatic, no man of hatred, though he has reason to be. He might criticize, might pity, but never hate. He's no pulpit politician.*

"And so I came back determined that if I could hold office in the CU, I'd try to help others see things the way I do now. There must be Protestants to stand up against people like Bernadette Devlin."

"Aren't there already?" Kate asked mildly. "Didn't Paisley himself follow her all the way to America to denounce her every word?"

[30]

He nodded. "Yes, and that's the sort of thing we need to be doing. Paisley needs supporters—people who will see him into Parliament to speak against her Communist lies and baseless accusations."

Kate was surprised at how the Paisley jargon saturated James's speech. "And you intend to gather support here? To use the CU as a base for political activity?"

"No—not exactly."

"It sounds like it, right enough, though." She licked her lips, choosing her words carefully. "James—I agree that Bernadette Devlin is wrong; I agree that Ulster should always be basically Protestant and governed by Protestants. But I don't agree with the kind of hate-mongering that Mr. Paisley engages in. And if—if you're going to propagate his ideas here, then I will not run with you."

His face darkened. "Your final answer?"

She stared at the floor. Her eyes were swimming. How different things should have been. "It is."

He jammed the point of his umbrella into the skirting board. "Then I'll not be elected myself, Katherine."

She looked up, surprised. "Why not? Of course you will. Who else could be?"

"Forbes. Roger Forbes is also being nominated."

She laughed in disbelief. "Roger? But he's only a second-year student."

"And so are you. That makes no difference."

"Are you sure Roger's nominated?"

"Absolutely."

Kate tried to imagine Roger as president of the group—a position that demanded a certain charisma, a great deal of dedication, and—usually—a strong theological background. Affable, disorganized Roger? Never. . . . And yet . . . ? Might he not restore a little lost gaiety to the Union? Perhaps erase the CU's reputation for being dull, dowdy, and rather gloomy—a reputation she felt was undeserved and unfaithful to the image of Christ?

James was watching her closely. "I suppose you'd run with him, would you? The old public-school tie and all."

She averted her gaze, unable to reply.

[31]

"He's far too liberal, anyway. He dances, you know, and goes to the cinema, even drinks on occasion. Told me so himself, he did. And you know how much time he spends with Sheila. Could he really be president? Think now."

For once, Kate saw herself wiser than James. "Oh—as if those things make much difference!"

"You're telling me, then, that you'd rather run with Roger than with me?"

"No, oh, no, I'm not saying that at all," she said slowly, sadly, every fiber of her being denying what was happening. Before, the only sorrow she had known in her love for James was that he neither knew of it nor returned it in the way she wanted return. Now there was the terrible pang of a deep rift that would only widen if he stayed in Paisley's church. She wanted desperately to say, "Look, James, I cannot agree with you. But I love you. Running or not running as your vice-president—that's all entirely irrelevant, utterly separate from my feelings for you. Don't you see?" She didn't say it, of course.

James muttered in exasperation, "This is all so foolish, Katherine. You'll be throwing away such a chance to witness, to help the other girls—all the things you've said you want to do. No one else has the influence you do over people like—what's her name? The one you brought today who sounds and looks as if she's straight from the Catholic ghetto?"

"What a terrible thing to say!" she almost shouted, her cheeks reddening. "Deirdre—she's a solid Christian, James."

Ignoring her, he went on. "The girls here look up to you. You've a basis for talking to any of them—Irish or English. You're just the person to start prayer cells and lead Bible studies."

"And just the person to lead the girls into the Free Presbyterian Church?" She shivered. "Never. I'll not use my 'influence,' as you term it, for any such thing."

The corridor was quiet, echoing their silence. At last James said, "So you're determined? You'll not budge? You'll forget our friendship because I've changed my outlook a little?"

"That's unfair, James. And not true," she said hotly. Quickly she looked away from him, afraid he would now scorn her for her lack of reserve, for her sudden display of feeling.

"Then—look at me, Katherine." His voice was soft, dangerous.

Unjust! He was using her. *He knows how I feel, after all. But he's wrong—wrong to use that against me.* All the same, she looked up, and his eyes forced her to remain as still as if he held her with his hands.

"Will you, or will you not, run with me, help me in the CU this year? I won't ask again."

Tears welled and ran down her face. "You know I will," she said. Then she was running blindly. Doors, walls, steps—all a blur. He knew now, and he had her completely under his control—a position she had vowed never to be in—not for any man, even the man she loved.

Loyalty . . . she had been schooled in it on both sides of the water.

Sunday, October 5

Dawn over Rosemount. The sun turned the arch of sky from deep blue to green, gold, then white. It outlined in gold the tarnished oak and beech leaves. The green and brown ferns in the stone wall around the university suddenly showed, now vivid among the slate and mortar. In the shrubbery, rhododendrons that had drooped in the night imperceptibly lifted their leaves toward the light. A car swished by, scattering the pigeons. The cathedral bells began to ring: Sunday in Rosemount.

Above Northland Road a square of well-kept, tall Victorian houses looked out onto a railed-in area of grass and shrubs. Two of the houses, though, were more worn than the others. The first of these stood to the left of the square, the so-called Presbyterian Hostel. The second stood at the very top of the square next to a narrow alley. Its bow windows faced downhill toward the university wall and the city beyond. On its gatepost a small sign read, simply, "McCrae." One window on the top floor was curtained by a thin ivory-colored muslin that covered only the lower part of the sash. The glass reflected the walls and towers of the city; the room within was shadowy and dim.

The sun climbed higher, pushing long yellow bars into the shadowed room. A desk haphazardly piled with books, papers, and journals adjoined the window sill. Over a chairback, a white towel hung limp and damp. Below it, several days' worth of clothing lay where their owner had dropped them. A bulging, open suitcase spilled shirts, socks, and records onto the floor by one of the beds. The name "Forbes" was scrawled on the suitcase in heavy black ink.

On the other side of the room, a small, neatly ordered bookshelf stood on top of a table which obviously served as a desk. The tabletop was clear of all but a mug of sharp pencils, an opened packet of loose-leaf paper, and a family photograph. Beside this desk, a spotless sink and small wall mirror above gleamed in the eastern light. Razors, shaving brushes, and a cracked china cup cluttered the glass shelf over the sink.

One of the two sleepers turned over, groaning softly. His eyes blinked open and shut. Particles of dust hung and swirled in the sunlight over the bed. He screwed up his eyes and frowned, pushing his hand through his brown hair.

Sunday, he thought, stretching. His mouth moved silently as he woke to habitual morning prayer. *Thank you, Father, for today. I need it. I don't feel ready for this term yet. Help me to rest in you, to set work aside. Communion today. . . . I'm not ready for that, either. "Love the Lord your God with all your heart, and with all your soul, and with all your mind." All. Father, I haven't. Forgive me, Lord, but she's so beautiful and I do want her. Purify my love for her so that it's a small part of my greater love for you, my longing to do your will . . . including your will in relation to her. Also, help me if I'm elected to the CU presidency—help me to change things. Help me to have a right balance of tact and—Tact! You know I don't have much, Father—and boldness . . . and graciousness. Especially toward James. Help me to love him more even if I dislike him. Lord, I'd like it if everyone in the CU could be more open, less concerned about what others think and more concerned about who we are and what we need to do here . . . "Love thy neighbor" . . . James again. I simply have to learn to love him more. Who else is my neighbor at the moment?*

He stopped, looking across the room at the form hunched under an old gray eiderdown. Jack Monaghan. Speaking of neighbors . . . How strange to have lived with someone for a week, yet to know so little about him, to have seen so little of him.

He'd been at Queen's University in Belfast last year, he'd said, waiting to see if the New U would actually survive. Older than the usual second-year student, apparently. Twenty-five perhaps? Used to be a carpenter for Harland & Wolff. Here to read English—like Sheila.

Roger studied his roommate, half willing him to wake. Straight, straw-colored hair. A long nose, generous mouth. Day-old beard.

[35]

Rather as Roger imagined a medieval peasant—though much bigger, he recalled, remembering that on one occasion when they'd met briefly in the room he'd had to look up to meet Jack's eyes. Steady. They'd get along.

He slid quietly out of bed and walked barefoot to the window. Leaning over the mess on his desk, he drew back the muslin and looked down the square. Few leaves were left now, but the square, the university, the whole city that he could see glowed in autumn light. Everywhere towers, trees, and—today—bells. *Towery city and branchy between towers; cuckoo-echoing, bell-swarmèd, lark-charmèd, rook-racked, river-rounded* . . . Sheila had quoted that—Gerard Manley Hopkins—once when they stood together at a window in the tower of the library. Apt words for Derry. He had said them over and over until he knew them. He said them, softly, now.

Not far down the square two young men—Roger knew them slightly—left the Presbyterian Hostel. Walking briskly. Gray flannel suits, tightly rolled umbrellas. Going to church. A bit early, though, wasn't it?

He moved some papers on the desk and unearthed his watch. Half past ten.

Groaning, he dashed across the room and turned on the light above the sink. He was supposed to have met Sheila at breakfast— well before church. She was probably waiting in the refectory right now, sitting with Kate, joking about his lateness. "Typical," she'd be saying.

He splashed water on his face, lathered the shaving soap, and began to shave. His fingers seemed stiff and awkward. A trickle of blood spread out into the lather.

"Damn!" he said. "Oh, no!" He saw his mouth in the mirror, a pink slash amid the white foam, uttering a curse. "Heaven forgive me," he added under his breath.

"Amen to that," said a low voice. "A minute ago I heard you quoting 'Duns Scotus's Oxford'—the good words of a godly Jesuit—and now you're polluting the clean air of this room with foul invectives."

Rebuked, Roger turned to see Jack Monaghan sitting up, grinning. The V of his half-buttoned pajamas framed the curling blond-brown hair on his chest.

[36]

"Sorry—I don't usually . . . it's just that it's half ten and I'm hopelessly late for church. Supposed to meet a friend first, as well."

"Half ten, is it!" Jack sprang out of bed. "Well, then, I'll be late with you. Where do you go?"

"St. Augustine's—up by the Wall." Roger paused to wash away the last of the lather. "It's right near Bogside. Eleven o'clock is when we usually go."

"Right you are. I'll be with you." Jack grimaced in the mirror at his unshaven face. "I've a car. Too bad I left it up at the library the other night. Shaving'll have to go by the board today."

The two men scrambled to dress. Roger was hunting for his umbrella when a soft knock came. Jack, knotting a thin tie at the mirror, reached over to open the door.

A young woman of medium height stood on the threshold. Her brown eyes sparkled as the door opened, but then a quick frown appeared when she looked up into the face of someone she didn't recognize.

"Oh—hello! Good thing we were dressed."

Roger turned round with a big smile. "Sheila."

"I should say it is a good thing you're dressed," she laughed, making a face of mock severity. "Come on, we're terribly late. Ten minutes to eleven."

Roger grasped her hand. "I'm glad you came up. I'd never have made it to the refectory for you."

"No—of course. I thought you must have overslept." Sheila stepped into the hall again, a hand to her brown hair. "We'll have to run, you know."

"Introductions as we go," Roger agreed. "Ready, Jack?"

Roger and Sheila ran hand in hand down the square in front of Jack. Sheila was laughing all the way, protesting that Roger was dragging her. Her shoulder bag bounced against her coat, as though weighted with a heavy object. Roger ran with the long strides of an athlete, Sheila with the smaller steps of self-con-sciousness. Her high heels clacked on the paving stones.

They reached Northland Road, breathless.

"Shame!" Roger called back to Jack. "I'll never be able to play rugby this year at this rate. Lost all my wind."

[37]

A familiar jolting sound accompanied by the grinding of gears greeted their ears. A bus labeled "Altnagelvin" was gathering speed down the road.

"Let's try to get across, shall we? We might just catch it." Roger was already waving his arms at the driver.

"Don't!" Sheila complained. "You look silly."

"Better silly than late," he returned.

The driver had seen them and was slowing the bus. They stepped onto the platform and, breathless and laughing, fell into the back seats.

"So much for introductions," Sheila said, looking across the aisle to Jack.

He smiled at her. "I'm Jack Monaghan."

"And this is Sheila Russell," Roger said, putting his arm around her to clarify the situation. He thought Jack was looking at Sheila's round, happy face with something warmer than approval.

"Glad to meet you, Jack," Sheila murmured. Her eyes were quick and watchful, though not cold, as she looked back and forth from Jack to Roger for a few seconds. "And how do you come to share a room with Roger? Must be hard, isn't it?"

Hearing the lightness in her voice, Jack replied dryly, "I don't know yet. We'll see."

Roger feigned glumness. "Now, you two, don't gang up agin me already."

Sheila turned warm eyes on him. "Of course not. But he'll have a lot to put up with."

Jack turned away to look out the window. The bus stopped and started. Clarendon Street. Great James Street. The buildings were drab and gray but looked in better repair than he had expected, in better repair than the streets at home. It was all so ordinary and serene: men and women dressed for church, their faces calm and cheerful, their Sunday-morning eyes turning inward. Surely these were not the same souls who had hurled bricks and bombs a few weeks before. Surely not.

Now they passed Guildhall, its red-gold sandstone a Gothic wonder facing the walls; then the unnatural steepness of Shipquay Street, up which the bus labored as if it had no hope of ever gaining the top.

[38]

"We'd never have got to church on time on foot," Jack commented.

Roger stood up. The bus was pulling over to the left of a monument in the Diamond. The three stepped down together and hurried across.

"No—but there is a shortcut the bus can't take." Roger pointed down toward Butcher Gate. "See? There's another part of the wall. Bogside's down that hill. We could have come up that way on foot."

Jack looked intently. All he saw was a line of chimneytops and gray smoke curling upward. "Bogside? I'm curious to see it."

"You haven't been watching the news?"

"Oh, indeed I have. I mean, see it in the flesh."

"And see," Sheila was pointing diagonally across a small, open square where a few cars were parked. "There's St. Augustine's. When we get up to the churchyard, you'll be able to see right down into Bogside, then over and across into Creggan—almost all this side of the city except the walled part."

Jack was walking ahead of them toward the church. The west door was open, but he quickly passed it to look over to Bogside. Sheila and Roger hesitated by the door, waiting for him; Sheila removed her Bible from her bag.

"He seems nice," she said in a soft voice.

Roger nodded slowly. "Yes. I'm looking forward to talking more with him."

"What's he reading?"

"English. I thought I told you."

"I don't think I've seen him in any of the lectures. What courses does he have?"

Roger shrugged. "I'm ashamed to say, I don't even know."

Jack was strolling back toward the church. His face wore an odd expression. Surprise? Amusement? He said not a word about Bogside. Instead, he was peering into the darkened vestibule of the church. "We'd better go in, don't you think?" he said.

The service over, the worshipers lingered outside the grayish-black walls of the church. Few uncovered heads among the women; most wore pastel straw hats discreetly trimmed with artificial cherries or flowers and the occasional ribbon. The men stood stiffly in gray and blue flannels, chins high over the unaccustomed bulge of a tie-knot; they all carried umbrellas, though on this mellow-warm Sunday there was not a cloud in sight.

Roger led Jack among the crowd to introduce him to other young men: a few from the naval base, and even a couple of Americans from the U.S. Naval Communication Station.

"Sheila!" A young woman she didn't know was coming toward her. "Excuse me, aren't you Sheila Russell?"

Sheila smiled. "Yes, but I—"

"I think Katherine may have told you about me. My name's Deirdre McAvoy."

"Ah—Deirdre. Yes, Kate told me about you." Sheila smiled again, liking what she saw. Deirdre's face looked fresh and alive, her dark blue eyes meeting Sheila's a little shyly.

"Kate told me last night to look for you and Roger if I came here today." Then she laughed, a silver laugh like a small bell. "And what did Kate tell you, I wonder?" Deirdre, too, felt immediately at ease. None of Kate's first aloofness in Sheila.

"Oh—not a lot. Just that you're Irish, and that you actually prayed at the first CU prayer meeting. She was rather struck by you, I think."

"Well, then, it's mutual. Kate's rather striking herself."

Sheila nodded with amusement, her voice tinged with light irony as she replied, "Yes, she's quite amazing."

Deirdre assessed Sheila's tone but said nothing.

"I mean—she's such a brain." Sheila qualified her remark. "Takes a First in every course. She's a good person to share a room with—helps me with lots of things I can't understand."

"And she's been nominated to be vice-president of the CU, too."

"Yes, she's going to be busy this year. But that's Kate—she's always doing something or other. Works terribly hard, she does. . . . And Roger's nominated to be president. You met him, didn't you?" She gestured toward where the men were talking.

"Yes, at the prayer meeting. I met James McQueen there, too." Her eyes twinkled. "Does he come here to church?" she added.

[40]

Sheila's mouth curled. It was hard not to laugh. "No, indeed; he's probably off to Great James Street. That's where Kate goes, too." Her direct gaze added meaning to the last words, but Deirdre ignored the insinuation, having come to her own conclusions about Kate and James. Sheila continued carefully, "James is also nominated."

"So I hear." Deirdre looked over at Roger. "I hope Roger's elected. Somehow, I don't think James would be so good." She remembered his prayer. "I'm trying not to judge prematurely, though, because I hear good things about James from Kate."

"Yes, Kate always has generous words for James." Again the fixed, meaningful look. "And you're right, it's just as well not to decide yet. Two days left till the election, anyway."

"I know." Deirdre scanned the crowd again, then asked, "Who's that with Roger—next to him, I mean? The tall one. I've seen him in the Students' Union, I think."

"That's Jack Monaghan. He and Rog are living together this year. I don't know him at all. Roger hardly knows him yet either. He's reading English I understand, so I'm sure I'll get to know him. Are you in English, too?"

Deirdre smiled. "Oh, no. French."

"Oh, dear. I got a terrible mark at 'O' level French."

"That's what everyone says to me. Well, don't you tell me what happened to you in French, and I won't tell you what happened to me in English Lit, fair enough?"

"Fine," Sheila laughed.

Deirdre was still watching Jack as he and Roger talked. "Jack looks older than Roger—quite a bit. Is he third year?"

"He does, rather, doesn't he? But this is his first year here. Not a fresher though. Rog said he went to Queen's last year, but I don't know what he was doing before that." She eyed Deirdre curiously. "Do you want to meet him?"

Color spread through Deirdre's freckles. "Well, yes, of course. Does he belong to the CU?"

"I really don't know. Roger didn't say. But we've not had a freshers' squash yet, so one never knows."

Roger and Jack had turned toward them, and the two seemed to

[41]

be joking as they made their way through the crowd. Sheila watched, glad that Roger had found a roommate he liked.

Two little boys were playing in front of Deirdre and Sheila. Dressed in suits that were too small for them, their thin wrists protruding from their cuffs, they reached into their pockets for marbles. They grinned conspiratorially, looking quickly toward their parents, then began to roll the marbles near Deirdre's feet. Caught between her desire to meet Jack and her initial unsureness whenever she met anyone who seemed superior to her, Deirdre stooped to watch the marbles, her face level with the little boys'. They accepted her immediately, seeing she was young-looking and pretty.

"Here, have a go," one said, handing her two marbles. "See if you can knock us off the stone."

The marbles were round and new, clear like cats' eyes. She rolled one and missed.

"Playing marbles, are you?" Roger asked scornfully, his face deadpan. "And right after church, as well."

Deirdre looked up, forcing a laugh, but Sheila said, "What, is there a new commandment: Thou shalt not play marbles?"

"No," said Jack. "An old one. Thou shalt keep holy the Sabbath." He bent down. "But as for myself, I think marbles are a grand way of passing away the Sabbath."

The boys stared at him, then sheepishly began to put away their game. But Jack stopped them, and soon he, too, was down on his knees on the sparse grass rolling marbles on a gravestone. Deirdre was not as intimidated as she thought she'd be. He had none of the haughtiness she associated with tall men.

When the boys tired of marbles and the adults of talking, Roger and Sheila, Jack and Deirdre walked down the hill through Bogside and back toward the university. They hardly talked as they passed along Waterloo and Rossville Streets.

People stared at them, knowing they didn't belong. Deirdre felt oppressed by the ugly row-upon-row houses, the narrowness of the streets, the obvious poverty. Old men and women sat outside their houses, deck chairs on broken pavement. The incongruity was sad, depressing. Sitting in deck chairs by a road. Not a blade of grass, even, and only an occasional leafless sapling to brighten the grayness of everything. Had these people ever seen the sands and strands of Portrush and Portsteward, the islands and inlands of Donegal?

And only two months ago—less—the people of William Street had been fighting with the Royal Ulster Constabulary and the "B" Specials: barricades against armored cars; stones and petrol bombs against clubs and pick handles. The barricades were down now, but for how long? The white-painted words FREE DERRY, emblazoned on several house walls, reminded everyone of enmity past and present. Perhaps she should have gone to Queen's herself—or even to Trinity College in Dublin.

At the foot of Crawford Square, Roger and Jack left their companions to return to the university by themselves. Roger wanted to clear up his side of the room before dinner, and Jack said he'd go along, too.

"About time we talked, anyway," Jack said as they entered McCrae.

"Yes," Roger admitted. "I haven't been much of a roommate this week. I promise to reform."

"You'll not promise anything of the kind. With Sheila around, I don't see how you could keep your promise."

"Jealous, are you? She's lovely, isn't she?"

"For an English girl, I suppose."

Roger made a mock fist. "Watch that tongue. . . . Deirdre's got her eye on you, anyway. Didn't waste any time, did she?"

"Well," Jack murmured as he pushed open the door, "she'll not be keeping it there for long, I'm thinking." He sat down on the side of his bed, hands on his knees.

"Why not? Girl friend at home?"

Jack smiled a slow smile. "No, not at all."

"Then—what?"

"Well, there's something you'll need to know about me first off."

Roger straightened up from pulling the bedclothes across his bed. His eyes turned quickly to Jack's. "What?" he asked, a little afraid.

"We misunderstood each other completely today," Jack began. "You said St. Augustine's and mentioned Bogside in the very next breath. It never occurred to me that you weren't talking about a

Roman chapel. I should have known, you being English and Sheila with her Bible and all."

Light broke on Roger's face. "Oh!" He, too, sat down.

"I'm a Catholic. More than that. I've a vocation—I'll be joining the priesthood in a few years."

Wednesday, October 8

A quarter to ten. Kate had sat in the Students' Union for almost three hours with one of the CU girls whose boyfriend had written her a "Dear Jane" letter from home. Now she felt drained, abstracted. She had always believed she could distance herself from the emotional tangles of others, but empathy would creep in. Their grief became hers. For "John" she heard "James"; for "I" she heard her own name. And it always made her angry, this intimate spilling of sorrow, this identification of her own feelings with those of others. Only a week ago she had raged at James, cried for several hours, and vowed not to be his vice-president after all. She would *not* submit; she would *not* give in to her own weakness or to his will; she would work harder than ever on her essays and would renounce him (were he hers to renounce).

But her resolve had crumbled yesterday at the CU meeting. There would have been too many questions if she had refused to stand for office. She must just do what had to be done and bury her sadness. She must never betray herself to James again. And perhaps—just perhaps—James would come to respect her, love her even, not just as another Christian soul, but as a woman.

Kate toiled up the stone steps to the library building. What a place of consolation! She looked up at the gray towers, pointed windows, and elaborate stone tracery. "Looks like a huge cathedral," Deirdre had said a few days ago. For Kate, it was the happiest place at the New University. She would sit by a window, facing out, from supper until long after dark. The cargo cranes down at the docks were silver and still at twilight, the water of Lough Foyle a pearly blue-gray. With the night, often, came wind

[45]

and rain, the wind bursting on the windows and the rain writing a queer Chinese script down the glossy blackness of the panes. Or, if the evening were clear, she watched the lights come on over in Waterside, their reflections like luminous stalactites hanging from the far banks. And the Foyle lights in the middle of the river—to the right the Aberfoyle light and to the left the St. Columb's light—both red.

Tonight the wind was blowing hard enough to take the last leaves, but no rain fell yet. Kate was glad to enter the warmth of the Great Hall underneath the library.

She checked her pigeonhole before going up the stairs—no letters tonight. As she pushed open the swinging door of the main reading room, a few heads automatically bobbed up, then down again. A hand went up, too—beckoning—Sheila's. Kate picked her way round the tables and chairs and an occasional pair of long legs propped on a radiator. Sheila watched her all the way down the room.

"I promise not to talk after this," she whispered to Kate, who rarely sat near Sheila in the library for just that reason. "But I just can't sort this all out."

Kate reluctantly lowered her books to the table where Sheila was working. She sighed. Three hours gone, and she did need to read at least a hundred more pages of *Middlemarch*. But she had always helped Sheila, and she would now.

"What?" she asked as patiently as she could.

Sheila pointed at her cluttered array of papers and open books. "Well, I've done most of the reading on this poem—"

Kate looked at it coldly—*The Essay on Man.* "I don't know much about Pope, myself," she said.

Sheila waved her hand, dismissing her disclaimer. "That doesn't matter. But there's a reference here to an article that would help a lot if I could find it. But I can't." And she pointed to a footnote in one of her books.

"*Essays in Criticism?* Where did you look?"

"Oh—I hunted around in the journal stacks until I found them. But there were so many volumes, and this doesn't give a date or volume number."

"Here, let me see." Kate took up the book, an edge of

exasperation in her voice in spite of her intention to reveal none. Sheila's work was always so haphazard; it was amazing she ever finished an essay. "Do you remember precisely where this journal was?"

"No—somewhere down in the small stacks."

"Well, look—I'll show you."

Kate led Sheila out to the circulation room and showed her how to use the card catalogue to find journals.

"Ah—you're brilliant. I thought this was just for books."

"No. Now I'll show you how to use the indexes. Then—" and she looked and spoke pointedly, "you won't need my help doing this sort of thing again."

"All right," Sheila said meekly.

When they had located the article, Kate picked up her books and with a polite smile moved to another table. It was round a corner and out of sight of Sheila and most of the other readers, away from the windows—a corner she didn't like. At least, though, she'd be left alone for a while.

She opened *Middlemarch*. At the table next to hers, someone else was reading the same novel. He looked up with a fleeting, vague smile, then back again to the page. Kate stared at him for a minute. Straw-colored hair. Long, attractive face. She'd seen him at some of the lectures and at a seminar. He usually sat down the row from her and said nothing, but wrote as fast as he could whatever Kennedy said. *Catholic? Protestant?* It was hard to tell.

Kate lost herself in the complications of the novel and its characters. How bitter and heavy their lives seemed. Dorothea's warm spirit snuffed out by the cold grasp of a dead man; Lydgate's creative brilliance quenched by the pettiness of a vain wife. Lydgate belonged to Dorothea. They belonged to each other, but not in the sternly moral world of *Middlemarch*, not in the narrowly circumscribed boundaries of early Victorian England. Funny how the novel made her suspend her judgment, change her views, even on marriage. Was it possible that the best relationships crossed the sacred boundaries of social position and marriage? The notion was something she dared not think about much, for it challenged her old beliefs, her father's teaching—it challenged her faith itself.

[47]

Somehow, she must separate the fictional from the real, yet learn what she could about the one from the other.

The library was quiet and warm with only an infrequent foot-scuffing or suppressed laugh, until she heard footsteps round the corner near Sheila's table, followed by a conversation between Roger and Sheila that was just loud enough to distract. Her stomach tightened in mounting irritation.

Her neighbor looked up after a bit, gray eyes catching hers, smiling again. "They'll not get much reading done, I'm thinking," he whispered to her.

"Probably not," Kate said dryly. She looked down at her book again, but could not absorb what was on the page. Was she supposed to know this man's name? He had spoken to her as if he knew who she was.

"Surely you've done enough by now," Roger was saying, making no effort to talk quietly. "You've been in here since supper."

"Not quite finished yet," Sheila insisted. "I've got to finish this article before the place shuts. And I ought to make an outline, too."

"Ah—come on—I particularly need to talk to you tonight."

"Can't it wait? Don't you have any reading to do yourself?" she begged.

"None that can't wait."

Kate heard Sheila rustling paper. "Let's compromise . . . I'll come out with you in a few minutes. Look, I've got just three pages to go."

Roger sighed. "For love, I'll wait."

"Roger—for goodness' sake—!" Sheila was whispering now, but loudly. "Oh, I do wish you'd been elected. Would have kept you out of trouble for a while."

Kate scraped back her chair. Couldn't she have peace to read even in the library these days? Was there no place free from inane chit-chat? Snatching up her coat, she ran down the side aisle and out of the building.

Back in the room, she felt ashamed that she had lost her temper. She sat down at her desk, trying to reckon with her own behavior. Since her outburst in front of James, she had forgiven herself more impatience than usual, feeling she had grounds for it because of him. She had allowed herself more display of emotion, had lost some of her self-control. She was not herself.

Hardly thinking about what she was doing, Kate pushed off her shoes and stood up. The floor was warm under her damp, rather cold feet. She stood in front of the mirror. *Well*, she thought, *I don't look any different.*

A strand of hair had come out of place, so she unpinned it all. A stream of pale gold rippled down over her shoulders and back. She was glad she had grown her hair, in spite of what her father had said last Christmas. . . .

They had been getting ready for the Christmas Eve service. She had just washed her hair, but it was not quite dry. Her father was calling her from the hall. "Are you ready, dear?" So she had gone down quickly, hair flying. He had stared at her, cleared his throat. "Kate, your hair is very pretty, but it's not appropriate that way, I think. Have you a ribbon or something to tie it back with?"

"No," she'd said. "Just pins. But it's too damp for me to pin it yet."

"And you won't catch cold if it's still wet?"

"I doubt it, Daddy; colds come from virus, you know."

He'd looked at her reproachfully. "Are you sure it's not out of vanity you're letting it grow long, Kate? You'd better consider your motives."

She rarely disagreed with him or resented anything he demanded of her. He was always right. But that time she had just stood there looking at him, defying his reproach. Finally he'd looked at his watch. "We'll have to discuss this later. But I don't like to see your hair loose that way. It makes you look like a—" he had waved his hands irritably, "like a Beatle fan or something. We'll talk about it tomorrow."

But he had never raised the matter again. And out of deference, she had kept her hair pinned up when she was at home. For the sake of convenience, she also generally pinned it when she was studying; otherwise, she wore it down.

[49]

He was right, she admitted now, looking in the glass. *I am proud of it. I do have the wrong motives.*

Setting her glasses on the mantelpiece, she peered closely at her reflection. In the rather poor light, shadows accentuated her fine features. Except over her cheekbones, her skin looked pale, without a single freckle. Of that she was glad. Freckles she associated with Catholics—a sort of mark of Cain. But her cheeks were pink, pinker now because she was still angry. And her eyes were wide and clear, almost fierce looking.

She brushed her hair this way and that to see how it looked best. Pulling it back off her face, she noted the width of her forehead. *Yes, that's best.* But then she thought of Chaucer's Prioress, who'd worn her wimple so as to display just that feature—out of vanity. She brushed her hair down over her temples and set her mouth severely. *There. That's how she should look.*

Then she thought of Genesis: *"In the image of God, created he them."* She stared again at her reflection. *In the image of God. Severe? Harsh? Yet the Father created beauty to glorify Himself. "A thing of beauty is a joy forever: Its loveliness increases; it will never pass into nothingness. . . ."* Who said that? Oh, yes, Keats, of course. So was it wrong to think herself beautiful? Was it sinful to be vain? Yes, but was she? Perhaps. No one had ever told her she was beautiful.

She turned away, impatient with the internal debate. Her eyes fell on her Bible, which always rested on the stand between the beds. She picked it up and sat on the edge of her bed. Opening it, she started to pray silently. She gave up almost immediately, however.

Why was I so angry about Sheila's talking in the library? This had happened many times before. Was it that she herself had truly wanted Roger to be president of the Christian Union? No, not really. But it was no consolation that James had been partly right about him: that he was too happy-go-lucky to do the job. And she could have worked with Roger if she'd had to. Evidently others thought so, too, for James's electoral margin had been small. What a choice! Stern orthodoxy versus equally important warmth and friendliness. She herself had abstained from voting, unable to choose. So why was she so angry?

Was it possible she was jealous? No, she couldn't be. She smiled at this absurd notion. Never—she'd never wanted Roger. But it was painful to lose James even as she was winning the election with him. Ah—James: the man of clear eyes and—or so she'd believed until he'd become a Paisleyite—clear vision. So utterly good, so utterly right in his theology and decorous in his behavior that he might one day be Moderator of the Presbyterian Church in Ulster. And, in her daydreams, she'd be beside him.

Dreams. Like James's vision, they were clouded now. Once the election was over, he had barely acknowledged her. At their first committee meeting, last night, his voice had been businesslike and cold as he'd given her directions for organizing the freshers' squash. Would he wear down her emotions week by week with his indifference? Or would he try to use her, knowing her weakness?

Again she tried to pray. *Deliver me, Lord, from mental confusion and bitterness. Turn this time to joy in the service of others in the Union. . . .*

Upstairs, heavy feet marched across the floor; several people had come into the room above. She heard loud laughter and talking, then all other sound was drowned by the blast of a record player: *Sgt. Pepper's Lonely Hearts Club Band*—the Beatles at their best and worst.

> *We were talking—about the space between us all*
> *And the people—who hide themselves behind a wall of illusion*
> *Never glimpse the truth—then it's far too late—when they pass away.*
>
> *We were talking—about the love we all could share—when we find it*
> *To try our best to hold it there—with our love*
> *With our love—we could save the world . . . .*
>
> *We were talking—about the love that's gone so cold and the people*
> *Who gain the world and lose their soul—*
> *They don't know—they can't see—are you one of them?*

Kate gritted her teeth, pulling back her lips in anguish and frustration. The whine of an Indian sitar and the hypnotic and insistent voice of George Harrison seemed to be crushing her brain.

She opened her wardrobe and took out the same battered tennis shoes she had worn on the courts at boarding school. No distinction there, but she had loved tennis. And the shoes . . . she had learned an even better use for them than tennis: a trick she had learned from her father. "When I was up at Magee," he'd said once, "I'd get to thinking about your mother down there at Queen's and I'd be lonely. So I used to run. I'd go a mile, two— however long it took—until I forgot my aching heart and became just an aching body."

She'd laughed at the time, unable to think of her father having sexual longings, of having anything but a purely spiritual or intellectual nature. (Hadn't she raged at James for thinking of her in the same way?) Then last year, before comprehensive examinations, she had discovered the rightness of her father's idea. Now it was habit. She would walk or run through the streets whenever she felt crowded in by her own conflicts. Just seeing the real conflict— the hatred leaping from every daubed wall and boarded window— was usually enough to still her.

Her head felt light, her whole body too. The gravel road past the library was wide and even under her feet. She synchronized her breathing with her feet: one-two-three-four-five-six . . . in; one-two-three-four-five-six . . . out. Not down Northland tonight. One never knew, these days, if it would be safe. So she left the university back gates and Claremont Church behind her and ran onto the Buncrana Road.

A light rain had begun to fall. It soaked through her sweater. Under her body, her legs pumped harder; her breathing became painful. Her hair—she had forgotten to plait it—gradually flattened into a tangled wet mass that sent lukewarm rivulets down under her collar to the skin of her back.

Reaching Glen Road, she turned to cross it. A car was approaching, its lights a blur in the wet darkness. She hesitated on the edge of the pavement, her breath coming now in sobbing gasps. The car seemed to slow, but then it jolted into a pothole, sending up a muddy spray that instantly splattered her.

She shouted indignantly. Someone yelled "Sorry" from the driver's window; then the red tail lamps vanished up the Buncrana Road.

Overhead the rhythmic bass thump of Ringo Starr's drums had given way to the plaintive voice of Joan Baez. Probably only ten people upstairs, but their dancing had sounded like a hundred. The feet were quiet now, but under the lament of the folk songs, Kate could still hear the low voices of men and women—drinking, she supposed.

> *The water is wide—I cannot get o'er*
> *Neither have I wings to fly*
> *Give me a boat that can carry two*
> *And both shall cross, my true love and I.*

She turned over, groaning and burying her head in the pillow. Her hair, still damp, stuck to her cheeks. Why—on a Wednesday night when she would have to be up early next day for a prayer cell, and when her upstairs neighbors no doubt had classes first thing in the morning—couldn't they leave off?

The run had left her sleepy and more at peace with herself. No more introspection. Instead, she had stood in front of the bathroom mirror not even seeing herself, just fighting with the tangles in her hair. Now, though, she was wide awake again because of the music. She might as well read *Middlemarch*, she decided, switching on the light.

She had read about forty more pages when the record player finally stopped. Laughter. Loud whispers. Heavy boots clattering down the stairs. Peace. Kate snapped off the light, pulled up her eiderdown, bent her knees to her breasts, and fell asleep.

It might have been an hour—or two—or more. She awoke suddenly, adrenaline rushing into her blood. Someone was opening the door. A key rasped out of the lock; the crack of light around the door widened, then narrowed. Sheila, finally.

Kate squinted at the luminous dial of her clock. Quarter to three. Sheila, trying to be quiet, was fumbling her way in the dark. Then she stubbed her toe and let out a cry of pain.

Kate sat up, all her anger flooding back. "It's all right, Sheila. I'm awake!" she said, her voice harsh with sarcasm. "Absolutely no need to be quiet. Who needs sleep at three o'clock anyway?" And she switched on the light.

Sheila was standing by her desk, coat over her arm and shoes in one hand, her face puckered against the sudden light. Something in her hand flashed in the brightness.

"Kate, I am sorry, honestly," she said contritely.

"Well, I've just had enough, that's all!" Kate's voice quavered with indignation, verging on tears. "I couldn't finish reading in the library tonight because you and Roger talked so much—"

"Talked? He was in there for five minutes!"

"—and then Heather and Grace had a party upstairs until half past one. This is just the last straw!"

Sheila sighed. She hung her coat over the chair and dropped her shoes on the floor. Even without glasses, Kate could see the unhappy blur of her face.

She immediately regretted her anger, especially as Sheila came and sat on her bed and apologized again. "I promise not to crash around again. We should leave the angle light on in the corner—it would be enough to see by. But I'll try not to be so late again." Her hands knotted and unknotted in her lap.

Kate lay back against her pillow, shutting her eyes for a moment. "That's all right. I'm sorry I snapped at you. You have every right to come in when you want to. I've disturbed you sometimes, too. This is a free country, after all."

Sheila smiled. One of Roger's favorite clichés. "Kate, can you stay awake just a little longer in spite of it all?"

Kate scanned Sheila's face; she had something to tell. Her eyes were full of entreaty. "Oh, yes, what is it? What's the matter?"

"Nothing's the matter." She extended her hand toward Kate's face. "Look, can you see without your glasses?"

A small white light on Sheila's ring finger. Kate stared. A diamond with two minute sapphires.

"Oh—Sheila!" Abruptly she sat up, taking Sheila's hand to look at the little ring. "Oh, my dear girl!" Kate hugged her, all anger melted away. "You're going to be married!"

"Roger said he couldn't wait any longer to ask me. Didn't want me to get snatched up by someone else, he said. He took me over to Fahan—to a pub there. That's where he asked me. Oh, isn't it wonderful?" Her joy spilled out over Kate, even as another's sorrow had a few hours earlier.

"I'm so glad, Sheila. So glad! It's just right. I saw it coming—just didn't see when, that's all. So—" She drew back, her eyebrows curving. "So, when will you get married? Not before you finish here, will you?"

Sheila's eyes danced. "No, we can't. We would lose all our grants. We can wait, I know."

Kate looked at her steadily. "Yes, I think you'll do fine."

Sheila made a wry face. "I'll have you to keep me in order—this year at least." She set her mouth in determination. "And I think we both need another year or two, anyway."

"That's what your father will say, for sure."

Sheila laughed, standing up to peel off her stockings and unzip her skirt. "Oh, yes. That's exactly what he did say. We rang my family a little while ago."

Kate laughed. "In the middle of the night? I'm sure they were pleased!"

Smiling happily and ignoring Kate's irony, Sheila nodded. "Oh, they were."

Kate watched her. Curling brown hair. Brown eyes. A certain quick neatness about her, though she wasn't a particularly tidy person; a certain liveliness, though it was tempered by a cheerful, easy-going nature. Her body was compact, small. She would be Roger's *wife* in two years. Pope, Crabbe, Milton—none of these would matter any more. She would put her books behind her quickly. Instead, there would be love, children, stability, laughter.

Kate looked away, her thoughts churning dully. Sheila was so terribly ordinary—not very bright, not very pretty. But almost everyone liked her, and someone was in love with her. He wanted

[55]

her—spirit, mind, and body. And for all his lightness, Roger wouldn't dishonor her. He'd wait. They'd have their two years— two years to grow together before they were together. How absolutely perfect!

She turned her face away so Sheila would not see her tears. Soon the light was off anyway, the room completely quiet except when Sheila sighed or turned over in bed. Kate lay stiffly under the bedclothes in the again-darkened room. Lines from *A Midsummer Night's Dream* drifted into her sleepless mind.

> *O happy fair!*
> *Your eyes are lodestars, and your tongue's sweet air*
> *More tuneable than lark to shepherd's ear*
> *When wheat is green, when hawthorn buds appear.*
> *Sickness is catching. O, were favour so,*
> *Yours would I catch, fair Hermia, ere I go.*

Hot tears began to run down into her ears and pillow. She made no sound. *Joy*, she told herself. *I'm rejoicing that Sheila has found her place in the scheme of things.*

Sheila's breathing came faintly and steadily, so she surprised Kate with her sudden whisper. "You still awake?"

Kate lay quiet, not wanting to betray her tears. She coughed. "Yes," she said.

"It's hard to sleep."

"I'm sure it is."

"For you, too?"

"Yes." Kate was glad the room was dark.

"Would you like to get married one day, Kate?"

Kate half smiled to herself as she wiped her damp face against the pillow. How typical of Sheila, who in spite of her cheerful nature was not insensitive to others' sadness. "Oh—I don't think much about it, really. I'll be studying for so much longer yet . . . what's the point?" She was pleased by the steady indifference in her voice.

"Oh—I always thought—"

"Thought what? Thinking's dangerous, you know."

[56]

"Katherine Hamilton!" Sheila laughed. "You of all people say that?"

"It's true."

Silence again. Kate was uneasy about pursuing the conversation further.

"Well," Sheila began again, "the girls in the CU are forever speculating, as well you know."

Kate froze. "About what?"

"Oh ... about you—among others. They gossip, just like anybody else."

"Then that's something I'll have to help them with this year."

"Yes." Sheila's voice held a touch of irony.

But Kate couldn't bear to let the hints rest. "What—what do they say?" she asked guardedly.

"It's just gossip, but I've heard some of the girls say that you must be in love yourself or you could never be so sympathetic about the end of relationships."

Kate knew Sheila was dangling a carrot before her, trying to extract information. And Sheila would spread it, too. But what if she spread misinformation? That would be even worse. Finally, making her voice light, Kate said, "Well, now, you'll have to tell me what all the juicy rumors say."

"Sam McGowan. Some think you have your eyes on him. You're always joking and laughing around him." Sheila hardly hesitated. She must have waited a long time to say this.

Kate laughed easily now. "Oh—Sheila, what utter nonsense! Of course I am! Sam makes everyone laugh."

"Well, that's what I thought—and that's what I said, too, on your behalf," Sheila put in defensively. But she must have been emboldened by the laughter that had broken the tension, for she came back to her original thought again. "Then is there no one— special?"

Kate suddenly remembered boarding school. The after-lights-out conversations and guessing games in the long, hospital-like dormitories. The giggling in corners, the furtive discussions of who had a crush on whom, of what it was like to be kissed, to be held, to be made love to—awful, awful conversations! She had shut her

[57]

ears then, ashamed of the profaning of what her father called sacred.

She had that same feeling now about Sheila's guessing game. Carefully, she said, "There is someone I care for very much." She rushed on. "But it's not to be talked of. He doesn't love me except as a sister." Her alarm clock hummed more loudly than usual in the dark.

"I think I know, then."

"Do you?" She held her breath, hating the conversation and yet longing for the fresh openness it could create between them—the sort of frankness that had existed for a short time at the beginning of their first year when Roger had only just entered Sheila's life; when Sheila had agonized with Kate over and over about Roger's feelings for her and hers for him.

"Is it James McQueen? That's my own guess—I just thought of it."

Kate nodded dumbly; then, realizing that Sheila couldn't see her, she said, "Yes." Her voice was small.

Sheila sighed. "Oh, Kate! It just came to me, honestly."

Kate sat up and hugged her knees. "Methinks the lady doth protest too much," she murmured. "Are you sure *others* haven't talked about him and—and—" She stammered into silence. Impossible to speak of what for so long she had admitted only to herself in dreams.

Sheila came right back with a definite "Yes, I'm sure," and Kate believed her. "Don't worry. It's my idea entirely. You've been very discreet, Kate. That's just like you."

Kate hesitated. Could she ask Sheila to keep her secret? Yes. "But, Sheila—please, please don't talk about it—not to Roger, not to anyone. James suspects my feelings, I think, but no one else—no one except you. If you want to talk about it, talk to me—please!"

The room was quiet for a minute; then Sheila asked, "Well, then, how did it all happen, Kate? Your caring so much for him, I mean?"

"Oh, I don't really know. Very gradually, I suppose." Now that it was out in the open, she wanted to tell Sheila more. "He was the first man in the Union who ever talked to me. I began to look up to him right away. . . ." She stopped, trying to recall the beginning of her love that seemed to have been there forever. "Don't get me wrong, though. He never gave me any encouragement. He was just acting the way any mature Christian should: considerate, helpful—"

"Yes, yes," Sheila murmured, though she did not sound convinced.

"He showed me all round the library, for example."

"And he took you to the first rugby game of the season?"

"Sheila! You're laughing at me. You know very well James couldn't care less about rugby." She sniffed. "Nor could I. . . . But he was kind. I loved his directness, his no-nonsense ways."

"Well, that hasn't changed," Sheila said tartly.

"Oh! I'm not going to talk about him any more."

"Sorry, Kate. I can't help talking that way. I've never really liked James. There, you like directness, don't you?"

Kate herself had always been outspoken but had rarely been on the receiving end; it was painful. "No," she finally said, slowly. "I've seen that. A lot of people misunderstand James, I think. But why? And if they don't like him, then why is he in the position he's in?"

"They respect him, Kate. They see him as a steady Christian. Listen, I don't mean to hurt your feelings. Least of all tonight. I don't begrudge you your love for him—not at all. Not for a minute. But—"

"But what?"

"But I think you're too good for him."

Kate laughed hollowly. "Don't be absurd. How can you say that after sharing a room with me for a year? You know what I'm like—so angry and impatient and critical and—"

"Stop! You're always too hard on yourself."

"There you are! Another fault."

"Well, now, for heaven's sake! Who ever said anyone was perfect?"

"Not Calvin," Kate laughed ruefully and settled down under the covers. "Sheila—?"

"What?"

"We've not talked like this since last year."

"No. It's good, isn't it? But I can't get engaged every day just to start a talk like this, can I?" They both laughed a bit, then grew silent again.

"Sheila?" she said again.

"Yes?"

"Please remember. Don't tell *anyone.*"

"I'll be careful, I promise," Sheila said softly.

The covers lay warm and heavy over Kate's cold arms and aching body. She was sleepy again at last.

Friday, October 31

A month gone, and the need for a break gave every excuse for a weekend at home in Belfast, Ballymoney, Ballymena, or Antrim, though not all chose to go home. Under the lengthening shadow of the library tower, students clustered around half a dozen cars: two Minis, three Volkswagens, and a Morris. Scattered around them were small suitcases, bulging duffel bags, piles of books, and two guitars. The sound of animated voices and idling engines was deadened by a fog that had moved in quickly from the lough, its tentacles curling over the trees and up the long lawn to the ha-ha. It hung low in thickening clouds just below the gravel driveway where this group of twenty students was gathering.

Kate stood among her friends, her back to them as she looked eastward into the mist. From deep within it came the harsh grinding and clanking of the dredger working at the mouth of the river. It was joined now by the booming moan of a foghorn. She shivered, though the evening was mild, tightened the belt of her white raincoat, and turned up her collar.

Thin, pink sunlight filtered through the clouds above the library, glistening on the uneven wads of fog just below. As she watched the subtle color changes of the invisible setting sun, she thought of Thomas More's Utopia. The university seemed an Aircastle on the Island; a city within, and yet without, a city; a community rising above the brutality of war and greed for property and power. Utopia. A kind of perfection—with inadequacies, certainly, but nevertheless a kind of perfection.

The dirty wharves and the rundown houses of Waterside were lost to sight now, while the distant horn droned; the dirt, division, and corruption of the city swept away by a foggy hand. The university floated high above in the ivory twilight of the clouds. Utopia. A place of freedom from the stifling concerns and groveling doubts that bound the small city-dwellers below.

She thought of the Transfiguration of Jesus and the apostle Peter's impetuous desire to remain forever on the mountain: *"Lord, it is good for us to be here; if thou wilt, let us here make three tabernacles...."* But then, she remembered, Christ had led His friends down from the mountain, down into arguments with the scribes, down into the suffering world of sick children and brutal crucifixion. Down.

Behind her, Sam McGowan was wrangling with Roger about who was going with whom. She heard her own name spoken, so she turned.

Sheila was sitting in the back seat of the Morris, leaning out to listen to the two men. Trevor's Mini was parked directly behind the Morris, and he and Sam evidently wanted to take Kate and Deirdre. "But of course Kate will go with us," Sheila said imperiously to Sam. She was impatient to leave.

Kate smiled vaguely and walked over to the Morris. "It doesn't matter who I go with—" She looked at her watch. "The good people will burn our supper if we don't leave soon."

"Kate's right," said Sam, turning to Roger, who was lounging against the back of the Morris. "Anyway—why should you blokes garner all the pretty girls? You've Sheila already. Give someone else a chance."

Kate looked away. That sort of talk annoyed her. Were she and Deirdre cattle to be haggled over? And where was Deirdre? They had agreed to travel together.

"Well, Kate me dear," Sam went on in an exaggerated Irish sing-song, "choose for thyself. Wilt thou go with us in the peasant Mini?" He bowed low. "Or wilt thou go with Roger and his friend in the royal Morris? Or—should we have a duel, Sir Roger?"

Kate laughed in spite of herself. And then she heard Deirdre's laughter. The younger woman now joined them, duffel bag over her shoulder. Her black hair was newly cut and washed, and her rose coat showed off the warm color in her cheeks.

[62]

"Deirdre—you look nice," Kate said. She spoke in an under-tone, but Sam picked up her comment.

"Oh, yes, indeed. Not often Trevor and I have the chance to take *two* pretty CU girls away for the weekend."

"No," Kate stated sourly, "there aren't many of us, are there?"

"All the worse for us, it is," Sam agreed with a grimace, insensitive to the edge in Kate's voice. "You girls'd better do something about that this year."

Kate flung out her hands irritably. "Sam—that's terrible talk." She looked quickly at Deirdre. "We might as well go with Roger and Sheila, don't you think?" She wasn't sure she could stand Sam's bantering all the way from Londonderry to Dunfanaghy.

Out of the corner of her eye she noticed someone come down the library steps and open the door of the Morris. She turned her head and saw that the man she knew now as Roger's roommate was getting into the driver's seat. She hesitated, surprised. Wasn't Roger driving the Morris? And why was Jack Monaghan going? She had heard he was a Catholic. Why on earth was he going on a CU retreat?

Deirdre, too, was watching Jack and seemed not to hear Kate's question.

Jack rolled down the window. "Come on, Roger," he called. "The girls can go with the others. Let's be going."

Deirdre stepped forward as Roger, saluting Sam and Trevor and grinning foolishly at Kate, ducked into the front of the Morris. "Oh—we'll go with you, Jack, if you've room," she said.

Kate flashed a look at Deirdre, whose face was almost as pink as her coat. Then she stared back at Jack, but his face was half hidden inside the car. Did Deirdre know that Jack was going to be a priest? She herself had heard it from Sheila just a few days before.

Jack made himself visible now by leaning out of the window. "No, Deirdre," he said with a smile. "I think Sam won the debate. We'll see you and your friend over there." Then he turned the ignition key and the car lurched away.

Deirdre's face looked wistful for a moment, but Sam and Trevor were soon shepherding them both into the back of the Mini.

The little car seemed cramped. Kate's right leg was jammed

[63]

against Trevor's guitar. There was little talk. In the half-light they all became quiet and watchful. With Lough Swilly on their right and the fog-enshrouded blue hills the Irish called *slieves* on their left, they took a back road toward Letterkenny. The higher they climbed out of the Swilly Valley, the scarcer the fog, until the long hills looked like dark, sleeping animals crouching along the pale horizon.

Beside the car, yellow gorse burned among the heather and scrub brush of the uplands. Below, neat haystacks shaped like rounded cottage loaves surrounded the farms nestled among the little valleys. The dank smell of peat oozed up with the damp, green smell of moss on boulders. From among the farms and tumbled stone walls came the singing of grasshoppers, the last bickering of sparrows, and the bleating of sheep. Now the sky, like the hills, became completely dark.

Always a lover of the sea, Kate kept the wing window open to listen for the first sound of the waves. She smelled the water long before she heard it—a faintly brackish scent tingeing the cold air that burst in through the little window. Seaweed on the strand. Then the salt—she could already taste it on her lips.

The rutted lane that led to the farmhouse was like a long tunnel. The car's headlights searched the darkness, and on either side the overgrown hedgerows rose above them, alive with moths, grass-hoppers, and frightened birds. Twigs brushed and scratched the car.

As they rounded the last curve, dim outlines of cattle sheds and chicken coops appeared, then a bright rectangle of light from the front door. In front of the rambling farmhouse, Jack, Roger, and Sheila were unloading the Morris, their figures silhouetted against the yellow light.

Deirdre lightly touched Kate's arm. "This retreat is going to be such fun, Kate! I'm so glad to get away from Derry for a bit, aren't you?"

Kate returned the smile. "Oh yes!" She had looked forward to it for weeks. Dunfanaghy made an ideal place: isolated, quiet, wildly beautiful.

"Did you bring books—work to do?"

"I brought a novel, but I doubt if I'll read it."

Trevor pulled the Mini in behind Jack's car. The air was utterly silent for a minute after the motor was cut, full of the scents of sea salt and fresh soda bread. No rumbling buses. No chiming clocks, clanking dredges, or wailing sirens. The quiet was overwhelming. Peace. Kate sat still, pressed down by it, flooded by it.

The farmer's wife and daughters, their faces flushed and intent, served supper. In and out of the kitchen they tramped, the door swinging to and fro behind them. The steam from the plates they carried curled up round their eyes and dampened their hair.

Kate watched them move awkwardly among the crowded tables. She felt lazy and comfortable. Here there would be no need to wonder about what others thought of Christian talk and behavior. Here they were all Christians. All except one.

She flashed a quick look to the other side of the room where Jack Monaghan was having an animated conversation with Roger and Sheila and some of Roger's friends. What would *he* think of it all? And why was he here? Was Roger trying to convert him? She had never spoken to Jack by choice—except that time in the library before she knew who he was. He was in a class with her, but even there she avoided him. Somehow his presence unsettled her.

She looked down at the food before her: hot beef stew with mounds of potatoes and carrots. Far more than she could eat, but the sight of it warmed her. Soda bread like round, flat stones dusted with flour was piled on a plate in the middle of the table.

Deirdre caught the slight smile as Kate slid her hands under the plate to warm them. The rooms upstairs where they would sleep were chilly, but down here a fire roared in the stone hearth and the room glowed with red faces and heat from the kitchen.

"Bliss," Deirdre said happily.

Kate looked round the table: Deirdre, Caroline, and Ruth—all girls she loved to be with. "Bliss," she agreed. "And I don't think I could touch Dickens this weekend."

"Dickens?" Caroline repeated, having to speak loudly to be heard above the hubbub in the room. She was a small, mousy English girl who was studying classics. Kate had known her at boarding school, and they had traveled to the university together the first year. "Which novel do you have to read?" she asked.

"*Hard Times.*"

Deirdre pulled a face. "What a dreadful title. Is it as bad as it sounds?"

"Not really. Haven't you read it?"

"No. Should I?"

"Probably."

"What's it about?"

"Industrialism. A machine-minded father bringing up a girl alone—her mother was out of the picture—" Kate stopped, hearing herself.

"And what happens to the girl?" Caroline asked, perhaps noticing Kate's change of expression.

Kate turned her hands in half-shrug. "I've not finished yet. But the heroine has no moral basis for her life—she's a pawn of evil partly because she can't distinguish it from good. I'm curious to see what happens myself—"

Loud shushing came from across the room. James McQueen was standing, trying to gain everyone's attention. As the noise diminished, Kate's voice had sounded clear and ringing; it drew the group's attention to her, not to James. It seemed they were all looking at her, some with laughter, some with mild exasperation.

James, too, turned his eyes on her. Then, folding his hands, he said, "Let's ask the blessing, shall we? Katherine, will you lead us?"

Kate stood, covered with confusion. Her chair scraped loudly on the wooden floor. She suddenly felt gauche, ill-prepared to take any position of leadership this weekend. Unwilling, too, for she wanted just to be at peace: to study the Bible, to pray, to walk on the strand, to shed the coil of daily vexations. But here was James calling on her already. And there was that outsider Monaghan staring at her with such a droll look.

She prayed, however, her voice sounding subdued in the overcrowded space. A low-beamed ceiling and twenty warmly clad bodies absorbed all the sound of it. Yet there was, as always, a calmness, a stillness in her voice when she prayed.

Immediately afterwards, the clatter of knives, forks, and plates began. Jugs of milk passed round each table, tea was poured, and the ebb and flow of loud talk started again.

"Kate, there was something—" Ruth, who sat beside Kate, wore an anxious, even agitated expression. Her voice was low.

Kate looked at her quickly, sensing again that she would have no peace this weekend. She thinly buttered a wedge of soda bread. "What is it?" she asked mildly.

Ruth was from an old Loyalist family in Lisburn. Kate's father had known Ruth's people years ago. She was a shy girl, but pretty in a kittenish way; her blond hair fluffed round her face like baby's hair. She was much sought after by the men in the Union, though she had declined all comers (according to Sheila, who supposedly knew such things).

Deirdre and Caroline weren't listening to Ruth; with all the clatter, they probably couldn't hear anyway.

"I've been—something's happened." A strange half-smile played around Ruth's mouth, but her eyes were still anxious.

"Go on—it's all right. No one's listening."

Ruth flashed a glance across to Caroline and Deirdre. Then, "Last afternoon we were late out of Meyer's class. One of the men in the class—I've often sat next to him in the lecture—he stopped to ask me out."

"Oh?" Kate's response was carefully neutral.

"It was Steve Lenehan—do you know him?"

Kate shook her head.

"He doesn't belong to the CU. He's a Catholic."

"Oh!"

Deirdre and Caroline looked up quickly. They would listen now, Kate thought. She wished Ruth had cornered her after supper. "So, what did you say?" she asked, her fork poised in mid-air.

"I hardly knew what to say—how to reply. He knows I'm a Christian. I don't know why he would even ask me. But I like him. Once or twice—" Ruth hesitated, watching Kate's expression change from neutrality, to concern, to disapproval. "Once or twice after a lecture he's helped me get my notes right—you've never heard anyone like Meyer—goes so fast. And Steve takes such good notes. He's been kind, friendly."

[67]

Kate was shaking her head. "That's good, Ruth." She sighed. "But that's not good enough for you."

Ruth laughed nervously. "But I have no great sense of myself. 'For *all* have sinned and come short of the glory of God,' remember? Would it be so terribly wrong to go out with him a time or two?"

Kate thought for a minute. "Not wrong, perhaps."

Ruth rushed on, indifferent now to the ears of Caroline and Deirdre. "I could witness to him. He has some fine qualities. The Lord could use him if he became a Christian."

Deirdre was alert, her eyes fiery. "What do you mean, 'became a Christian'? What makes you so sure he isn't one already?"

"B–but—he's a Catholic—he can't—" Ruth spluttered.

"So's my father," retorted Deirdre. "And I'd not dare say he isn't a Christian." Her voice was emotional, growing louder.

Kate cringed. She had hoped the subject of Deirdre's parents would never enter into a conversation; this was the worst possible timing on Deirdre's part.

In a low, controlled voice, Kate begged, "Wait, let's not get sidetracked into that old argument—please." She looked around their table. "It's somewhat beside the point anyway. Ruth wanted to know if it's wrong to go with a Catholic—" She stared pointedly at Deirdre, eyes commanding her to silence. "And I'd say that it may not be wrong, exactly, but pretty dangerous."

"Dangerous?" Ruth echoed, her eyes dazed.

"Of course," Kate snapped, her control slipping. *"Get down, Katie! Get down! It's dangerous!"* "Think of what's been going on! Think of all the violence—what will happen to us if the "B" Specials are disbanded. And all the fuss about the British Army no one wants. The searches for bombs. . . . People flocking to Paisley's new church on Ravenhill Road. The pot's just simmering now. It could boil over any time." She turned to Ruth. "Do you want some sick fanatics in Derry to tar-and-feather you—or worse? Are a few outings with this Steve worth that? And think of your parents, Ruth." Her voice was hard now, full of warning.

Ruth quailed. Slowly shaking her head, she said, "No, no. If you put it that way."

"So did you tell him you'd go out with him?" Kate asked more gently, seeing the effect of her words.

Ruth shook her head. "I told him I'd have to see," she said. "But I wasn't discouraging him. He'll ask me again, I'm sure."

Deirdre still listened to their exchange with hot eyes. As much as she cared for Kate, she could not remain silent. "Katie, you're right, it's dangerous. But are you sure you should persuade someone into or out of a relationship? That's a big responsibility you're taking on yourself."

If anyone else had said it, Kate would have turned on her. To Deirdre, though, she said only, "Yes, but I think that's part of being vice-president of this group."

Deirdre shrugged. "Perhaps—it depends. But doesn't Ruth have a point? About witness, I mean? Steve may come to know Christ much better from seeing Him in Ruth, whatever his spiritual state."

Kate smiled. "That's an old rationalization, Deirdre. I've heard it many times—but I doubt it works. It might if the man were a committed Christian. But the woman?" She shook her head. "A man takes the lead in any relationship, usually." She stared at her friend. *It doesn't matter that Deirdre's parents have a relationship that works*, she thought. *What matters is the principle of the thing.*

Ruth's head was bowed. Like most of the young women in the Union, she admired Kate's purity and strength of purpose. Ruth dreaded Kate's disapproval or condemnation. "Then what shall I do?" she pleaded.

Kate took a sip of tea. She didn't want Ruth to suffer, but did want her to do the right thing. Exchanging another glance with Deirdre, she said, "Next time he speaks to you—if he does—just tell him you've thought about it and decided it wouldn't be right just now. He'll understand, if he's as nice as you say." Her voice was soft and slow, patient as a mother to a child. "And meanwhile ... I know you're much admired in the CU—" She stopped, desiring to remain above the level of mere gossip. "The Lord will have someone else for you, I'm sure. Get involved in more CU activities. You could join our Thursday prayer cell. The extra fellowship would help."

Ruth nodded, but she looked unconvinced.

[69]

The kitchen door swung open for the farmer's wife, and with her came the blare of a radio and the voice of James Callaghan, Home Secretary. "The British Army is doing a vital job in Northern Ireland, though we do regret the necessity of keeping so many troops in Ulster. There cannot be any return to normality until they are willing to live with each other without barbed wire and British soldiers." Then the voice of the news announcer: "A time bomb exploded today at the grave of Wolfe Tone at Bodestown, County Kildare. No one was injured—" The door closed again behind the farmer's wife.

Jack and Roger climbed the narrow carpeted stairway to their room. From below came the soft murmur of conversation and the quiet plunking of Trevor's guitar; he did not play well, so only a few were singing. They had just concluded an hour of hymn-singing from the *Billy Graham Songbook*, and James had led closing prayers. Then everyone had drifted away: some to chat, some to walk in the lane, and some to bed.

The room where Jack and Roger were to sleep had never been intended for two men. In order to shut the door, they had to pass directly into the middle of the room first. Once the door was shut, they had to move the only chair in the room against it; otherwise, they could not open the chest of drawers—a tall, narrow piece that scraped the gabled ceiling. A small casement window set deeply into the gable let in the only air, while its sill provided the only shelf in the room.

For all the cramped conditions, however, Jack delighted in the homeliness of a carpet on the floor and proper curtains at the window. He surveyed the room with pleasure as he undressed.

It was rare for the two men to spend as much time together as they would this weekend. Jack spent most of his days in the library; Sundays he closeted himself in their room at McCrae. Roger, on the other hand—usually with Sheila—frequented the coffee bar in the basement of the Students' Union or the table tennis room downhill from it in a prefabricated hut built for billiards, darts, and ping-pong. And on Sundays he went to St. Augustine's, then out with Sheila.

Roger dropped his clothes on the floor as usual, leaving the chair for Jack's things. He climbed straight into one of the two narrow beds and relaxed back against the pillow. "Are you still glad you came? You'll have some uncomfortable moments, I'm afraid."

Jack smiled as he buttoned his pajamas. "It won't be the first time if I do." There was no bitterness in his voice.

"You must have been on retreats before, right? Is this the same sort of thing you're used to?"

"Not at all." He shook his head.

"Then what's the difference?"

Jack sighed. "Oh, lots of differences. This seems very well . . . well . . . intimate. So much talk, and we're all crowded together in this place. And the informal prayers—it's all strange to me."

"I'm sure it is. And is that why you didn't say anything tonight?"

"That, and other reasons."

"Oh?"

"I don't want to start an argument with anyone. I didn't come just because you invited me. I also wanted to look . . . observe. And I hope no one minds."

"I doubt if anyone does."

"Not even the fellow who did most of the talking tonight? Who is he anyway? He seemed rather . . . domineering."

"McQueen. James McQueen. He's president of the CU."

"Aye, now I remember you mentioning him." Jack sat down on his own bed, facing Roger. "What about him? Do you think he objects to my being here? Not that it matters if he does, you understand." He grinned.

Roger snickered. "He'd mind if he knew you were Catholic. But I doubt if he does, or he would've made some comment by now. But since the CU elections, he's not had much to say to me. Leaves me alone, pretty much. So he wouldn't know a thing about you."

"But your friends know about me."

"Yes, *my* friends. Not James's."

Jack looked at Roger curiously. "The man is a trifle bigoted, I take it." His eyes twinkled.

[71]

"Ah—you'd better not get me started talking about him. I'm always praying I'll learn to love him as a brother. But it's hard. We're totally different."

Long dimples appeared by Jack's wide mouth. "You are indeed. Well—but I'll not tempt you any further."

Roger opened his mouth to say more about James, then closed it again, his face breaking into a smile. "So what else is different here?"

"Partly what I already mentioned," Jack explained. "The intimacy, the informality. And there's no silence here. You sing and you talk and you pray. There's no lecture about self-examination or penance. And there's no pastor here, either."

"Does that make you uneasy."

"Yes—and no. I like the warmth. I like the feeling of closeness among everyone. There's nothing put-on about it. You're genuinely concerned about each other. But you're all so—pardon me, this will sound scornful—so young. How can you know enough to teach and instruct each other the way you all seem bent on doing? That's where you need a spiritual counselor, I'm thinking."

"Well," laughed Roger, "here *you* are, Jack."

"Not yet! Not yet! And you people wouldn't be wanting what I'd be offering anyway."

"But you were wondering how we know enough to help each other, weren't you?" Roger was thinking back to Jack's earlier question. "There's one of the differences between us right there. You've read history, and you know how we emphasize Bible reading and lay ministry much more than you Catholics do. The Bible—" he paused a moment, "we start to read it very early on. We teach ourselves, if you will, by the light of the Holy Spirit."

"Then why not dispense with priests and ministers altogether?"

"Like the Quakers, you mean? Well, that's all right, too, I suppose. For myself, though, I like the cohesion a clergyman brings. We might go wrong if we went too much on our own. And an ordained man can spend all his time in service. . . . He's not doing another job as well, usually."

"There you are!" Jack slapped his hands on his knees and leaned back with a triumphant smile. "We're not too far from each other in our outlook after all."

Roger grinned. "You and I may not be. But I'm a 'liberal' according to James. To get a fuller view of things, you'd have to talk to some other people . . . to James, for example."

"True," Jack agreed. "So tell me, will there be no minister here tomorrow? I'd hoped there would be. It's not—I repeat, it's *not* that I want to criticize. Not at all. But I've a lot of questions. Certain things are puzzling me."

"Not a minister, no. But one of the InterVarsity Fellowship secretaries will be here instead. That's the usual thing at a retreat."

"The tradition," Jack laughed, teasing.

"Yes, the tradition," Roger agreed. He shifted so that he, too, leaned against the wall. Then, waving his arms as he talked, he went on, "Before I came over here, I used to call Protestants who didn't belong to the Church of England or the Church of Ireland 'nonconformists.' That was the word we used at school. But that was before I came to Ulster, where the Church of Scotland is establishment . . . practically."

"What are you driving at?"

"Just that Protestants have far more 'traditions' than they'd own to. Almost as many as you people, I'm sure, though quite different." Roger shifted his gaze from Jack's face to the curtains. "I've been to Masses, and I've been to Baptist assembly halls, and I can see tradition in both: an order of worship that stays the same Sunday by Sunday, a certain litany in the prayers—and the testimonies, too."

Jack looked amused.

"The Baptists'd never admit it, mind you, but it's true," Roger added.

"And this secretary, she'll lecture?"

"*He'll* lecture. If you can call it that. It'll actually be more like a seminar, with plenty of discussion. And it won't be all theology either. A lot of talk about application of Scripture . . . to all sorts of things. Sex, for example."

"Ah."

Roger glanced sideways at his friend. "Of course, that subject won't interest an old celibate like yourself."

Jack gave him a strange look. "On the contrary—it raises some

[73]

interesting questions. Celibacy brings its own set of problems . . . but that's beside the point."

Assuming from Jack's expression that he would rather leave the subject, Roger grinned puckishly and said, "All right, I'll not make you expand on that for now." Then, fidgeting a bit, he became serious again. "And do you sense a different view of God from your own? Here, I mean?"

"Entirely. The same God, but seen from another side. Your Presbyterian friends are very Calvinistic, aren't they?"

"A little too much, even for me," Roger conceded.

"They make it sound as if salvation's so hard to come by. As if heaven is impossibly narrow and sparsely populated." He couldn't help adding, with a smile, "Mostly with like-minded Protestants."

Roger nodded. "It's awful, but you're right."

"But things are different for us," Jack said, leaning forward, his face earnest. "Salvation's a gift given by God at christening. It's renewed through the Mass and through belief in Church dogma. Aye . . . there are other sacraments, but those are the essentials."

Roger was nodding again. "I know. And I'm sure you know that things aren't quite the same for us." He spread his hands and arms in a half-shrug. "Jesus died *once* and for all."

"As I believe, too."

"Yes, but Protestants emphasize it to argue that all we have to do is believe and act on that truth—then we're redeemed. So the sacraments aren't as central for us."

Jack was warming to the discussion. "Well, while we're on this subject, here's something else. The way you talk about God, the way you talk to Him—it's almost as if you could put Him in your pocket, like a genie in a lamp, and He'd be at your beck and call."

"I wouldn't go quite that far," Roger said uneasily, "but, yes, God is personal to us. We talk about knowing Him in person."

"Don't you think something's lost, though?"

"To us, you mean?"

"To you, certainly. Not to God, who's not diminished by anything we do or think."

"Yes," Roger replied slowly, "you're probably right. The theology about God's omnipotence and glory isn't emphasized much. We like to be 'familiar' with God."

[74]

"That's what I meant when I said 'intimate' a few minutes ago."

Roger regarded Jack affectionately. "But listen, Jack, I won't push my convictions on you. Some of the others will try, you can be sure."

Jack smiled. "They won't get far. I don't change my beliefs quickly."

"Yet you don't seem like a conservative, either."

"I hope not." Jack's eyebrows rose. "Especially about the faith."

"Then you should read this with me, systematically," Roger said, pointing to his Bible, which had been lying on the bedclothes beside him.

"Ah, no, that's too fast, you see. Perhaps sometime, but for now—I'm not used to the idea. The Holy Scripture is for the priest to read in church and interpret there for the people."

"Checkmate!" Roger shouted. "Then you'd better get started with *your* study."

Jack nodded in amusement. "In time, O rash youth, in time."

Roger tossed his pillow at him. "Rubbish. I'll have you a good Protestant before we get our degrees."

"Never! I'll see you a Catholic first," Jack laughed as he threw the pillow back and settled under the blankets.

Wednesday, November 12

Deirdre had noticed him before. Funny . . . usually he slouched in a seat at the back, his coat on, as if in a hurry to leave. Yet today he had dropped into the seat beside her, right down in the third row of the philosophy lecture. He smoked nervously, his hand jerking up and down from the inkwell he was using as an ashtray. He would puff out a small cloud of blue smoke, set down the cigarette, then jot a few more notes on his paper.

She stopped listening to Dr. Andrews as she looked more closely at her neighbor. He did make an interesting study, for he fit her stereotype of the world-weary, unkempt university student. His long, untidy hair fell almost to his shoulder blades in thick, muddy yellow waves that thinned out over his ears and below his collar. His eyes, deepset by a small, sharply cut nose, moved as quickly as his hand, and with the same sort of jerking motion: from paper, to lecturer . . . to herself. Her eyes skipped away; she didn't want to be caught staring. But he seemed amused, so she scanned his face again. His eyes were a luminous green: striking, but not large; bright, like a cat's, and full of wit.

He blew out a pale ring of smoke and mouthed "Hello." Surprised, Deirdre answered the same. He reached for a blank piece of notepaper and began writing furiously.

Deirdre again tried to turn her attention to the lecture. Dr. Andrews droned tonelessly, his face turned upward like a washed-out full moon, as though reading his notes from the ceiling.

A few moments later, her neighbor pushed his paper across the desk so that it covered her own notes. He had written several lines to her. She lifted her eyes again, a puzzled frown flitting across her

[76]

face. He drew on his cigarette, inhaling the smoke and narrowing his eyes slightly as he watched her read.

"Who are you? I know who I am. I think, and therefore I am Liam Donnelly. Isn't this class terrible? Why is it you know so much about French philosophers? You're always answering his questions about them. Are you Irish or English? Irish, I think, but I'd like to be sure."

The writing was uneven, almost childish. What a strange way to introduce himself. If he wanted to talk to her, why hadn't he caught her after the lecture? She should be listening. Ah, yes, she should, but she wasn't. Glancing up at the podium, she quickly scribbled a reply.

"Deirdre McAvoy. And I'm not enjoying this course either, except the French philosophers. I've read them before. I'm from Armagh."

Liam smiled as he pulled the paper back toward himself. Deirdre watched him for a minute, but now he seemed unaware of her, seemed actually attending to Dr. Andrews. She resumed her own note-taking in a desultory way. It was hard to concentrate though. She liked the way he had looked at her, his eyes appraising and frankly admiring, his smile satirical, yet not mean or cold.

Once or twice she caught him out of the corner of her eye, his face turned toward her, but she resolved to ignore him. First essays were due at the end of the month, and she needed information from this lecture to make a point in her essay on Descartes.

Dr. Andrews paused for a moment, once again staring at the ceiling for inspiration. "Spinoza learned from Bruno that mind and matter were integrated; that philosophy's goal is to pursue contradictories to find unity. Knowledge of universal unity, Bruno said, was equal to a love of God. . . ." Deirdre's watch said twenty minutes till eleven. Ah, she could soon escape to the coffee bar for a warm drink. Her feet were cold and her mouth dry.

Just then Liam nudged her with his elbow. She turned her head, frowning a little. He was holding something toward her. Thinking

[77]

he was offering her a cigarette, she shook her head. He screwed up his face as if affronted by her refusal; then she saw a half-full packet of Polomints in his hand. He passed the roll to the student on the other side of him, and they went hand to hand under the desks, causing a titter of laughter and a momentary release from boredom.

Oblivious to all, his head tilted back, Dr. Andrews continued to fix his eyes on an asbestos ceiling tile. Deirdre smiled inwardly at the man's eccentricity, at the same time pitying him for his complete lack of connection with his students.

The mints had come back to Liam. He held the packet out to her once again. "Go on," he whispered. There was only one left in the roll of green paper.

"No, it's yours," she whispered, hesitating, for he had not taken one for himself.

"Here," he returned, dropping the mint onto her notes. "I don't want it."

She put it in her mouth, her dimples appearing and her eyes crinkling into a smile. "Thanks."

His eyebrows lifted slightly, and he winked at her.

". . . Descartes, as you know, also exercised deep influence on Spinoza with his notion that philosophy has to begin with the self, since the mind knows itself first and knows externals only as they impinge on the mind through sensation and perception. Hence, *Cogito, ergo sum. . . . . .* "

"There. What did I tell you?" Liam scrawled on Deirdre's notebook.

". . . Spinoza, however, took over where Descartes left off. He was excommunicated from his synagogue and his faith at the age of twenty-four for his supposed claim that God had an actual body, among other claims—ah—" Dr. Andrews actually looked toward the clock. "We shall pursue this further on Friday."

Sighing with relief, Deirdre gathered her notes and her copies of Spinoza and Descartes. She pulled her wool cloak around her shoulders and turned to move to the end of the row of desks.

"Can you not wait for a fellow after eating his sweets, Miss McAvoy?" The voice was rough as gravel, but not rude.

She turned, laughing self-consciously. Liam was clowning as he walked down the row toward her, his head back, his eyes fixed on the ceiling in a burlesque of Dr. Andrews.

"Wisht, you look perfectly foolish," she remonstrated. Others were staring at them with amused curiosity; she wanted no part in his theatrics. His face fell, but he moved so close behind her that she had to step out into the sloping aisle to avoid being pushed.

"Excuse me. Could you spare a minute, do you think?" he asked.

"I should think so," she answered gently. She did not want to be discourteous. Besides, the lecture hall was almost empty now.

"Are you after getting a cup of coffee?" The lilt of his voice carried an accent like her own, only more pronounced; he must have grown up somewhere near County Armagh.

"Well—yes. I am, as it happens."

"Then I'll treat you," he said grandly, pushing his hand into his pocket. "That is, if I've anything left in here."

She nodded. "Thanks, but I'll pay for myself, if you don't mind."

He held the door for her and they stepped into the cold air together. "But you'll deign to talk to me, I hope."

"Of course," she answered, laughing. "But please don't talk here." She shivered. "Come on, let's get down there before we both freeze."

"You call this cold?" he jeered as they quickened their pace. "Ah—you should feel the cold in America. My sister's out there. It's minus thirty sometimes, or worse—fahrenheit."

"Is it now?" she said, only half believing him.

When they reached the bottom of the stone steps into the coffee bar, Deirdre quickly glanced around the L-shaped room. No one she knew, but the coffee bar didn't usually fill until right before eleven. She was ashamed of her desire not to be seen with Liam. But neither did she want the women in the CU to be clacking their tongues about her. (She'd learned early that gossip was a main source of entertainment in such a small university, even for Christians who avowed themselves above such things. Sheila, particularly, always had a tale to tell about someone or other.) She was quick to push fourpence across to the cashier at the counter before Liam could pay for her coffee.

[79]

"Miss Independence," he muttered, following her as she made her way round the corner to a recess in the long wall at the far end. They set down their coffee and slid into seats opposite each other. Deirdre panicked. What had she allowed herself to begin? Reason told her: *Nothing. I'm merely drinking a cup of coffee with another student.* Emotion countered: *Yes, but he's not my kind of person. And the way he looks at me is reason enough to run.*

Liam stirred two well-heaped spoonfuls of sugar into his coffee. Now that they were actually facing each other, he, too, seemed unsure. He sipped his coffee, shutting his eyes for a moment. "Ah, I needed this."

"Me, too, after an hour of Andrews," she said automatically. The flippancy of her reply sounding in her own ears surprised her.

"I've seen you hanging about with some of those Christian Onion types," he said bitingly.

Deirdre inhaled quickly. "Ah—yes." She looked down. "I do belong to the Union."

Her emphasis on the last word halted him for a moment. "Oh, do you now?"

She took the initiative then, reasoning in a way that Kate often did that under his badinage he might be veiling a spiritual hunger. "I gather from your tone you're not a professing Christian?"

"Well now, that depends on your definition, I suppose," he said evenly. He lit another cigarette and leaned back in his chair, laughing. "I sound just like Andrews, don't I? My parents, y'understand, would be shocked to hear you say that. I'm no heathen. Baptized, confirmed . . . the whole lot. As far as I know, that makes me a Christian."

Deirdre swallowed hard. She had argued that way herself, just a few days ago, in defense of her father. "It makes you a Catholic, anyway," she conceded.

"Right enough. Not a very good one, perhaps—" he blew smoke out across the room, "but there's time enough for reform when I'm older."

"You hope."

"Well, I do hope. I'm not after getting myself blown up like some of the mad IRA men I know, all for the sake of a little bang at some power line or monument. No thank you."

[80]

Deirdre slowly set down her coffee cup, swallowing hard. "You—you have friends in the IRA?"

He narrowed his eyes; it seemed an habitual expression with him. "Not friends, perhaps. Fellows I knew at school. Men I've known all my life."

"You're from Armagh somewhere, aren't you?"

"Almost—Newry. And you?"

"Armagh itself. And how did you manage to avoid getting pulled into the IRA if you grew up with these fellows?"

He shrugged. "My dad's a pacifist. Drove ambulances in the war and was spat on because he wouldn't fight. I grew up sure he was right. I'm still sure. Of course—" and he smiled quickly, "that doesn't mean I'm not politically and socially activist. But I still believe in peaceful means."

Deirdre thought of her own father: he had been proud to fight in France, even if by tradition he owed no loyalty to the crown. And she herself had never committed a political act other than expressing a willingness to vote in the next general election. And as for social activism . . . .

"Can you explain what you mean by politically and socially activist?" she asked carefully.

He shrugged again. "Oh, I won't trouble you with all the details. They probably wouldn't interest you anyway, you being a Prod and all." He winked.

She laughed. "Oh, come on. No—I want to know."

He seemed to measure the sincerity of her tone before he said, "Well, to start with, then, I joined the Northern Ireland Civil Rights Association—NICRA—right at the beginning, in '67. I came up to Derry last year on the fateful fifth of October. Remember?"

"You marched that day?"

"I did."

She shook her head. "And look what you got for your pains. Blood and bruises no doubt—and a whale of troubles to follow after."

"It had to be done. It was long coming. There are no rights for Catholics up here."

She looked away. "I don't know enough about that to say." She

[81]

had deliberately softened her tone, for Liam had begun to raise his voice; she did not want to be drawn into a pointless argument. Neither of them would win, and others now drifting into the coffee bar would soon be listening or arguing too. "And did you march at Burntollet, too?"

He nodded grimly.

"It was suicide, surely."

"Could have been."

"Then you'll not live long to 'reform' after all."

He shrugged, watching her face. Then, shaking his head, he dropped his voice lower. "Well, see, we'll not talk about it now, shall we? I didn't bring you here to talk religion and politics, anyway."

Deirdre was silent, staring down into the hot brew that was sending a slow warmth through her at last. Even her feet were warm again.

Liam stubbed out his cigarette. "I suppose, though," he said off-handedly, "there's at least one political question I ought to ask—or religious—that is, if you don't mind."

"What, then?" she said.

"You're not of Mr. Paisley's flock, are you?"

Her head went up and her eyes sparked. "No, indeed I'm not! Whatever makes you think so?" Color spread through her freckles.

He smiled winningly now. "I didn't think so. Just making sure, though. I didn't want to—" He hesitated, his teeth resting briefly on his lower lip as though uncertain how to go on. "Well—"

Deirdre guessed what was coming. Her hand moved nervously where it rested on the table beside her cup and saucer.

"The fact is—" He had collected himself, and was looking directly at her now. "I think you're quite lovely. You've distracted me in the philosophy lectures more than you know." He raised a hand as if anticipating a rejection. "I know," he went on, "our faiths are different." Then laughed. "Should I say, you've a faith and I have none? Still, we've some things in common, I'd suppose. And if you're interested—as the *Union* professes to be—in doing things for others, I could get you involved in some projects in Derry—housing, child care, and the like."

All this came out in a disjointed rush, so that Deirdre warmed to him. The appeal in his eyes was hard to ignore. Yet she held back, hearing Kate's warning words. *It's not wrong, exactly, but pretty dangerous.*

Deirdre had been thinking seriously about Kate's views on "mixed" relationships. Perhaps her parents' relationship was the exception that had worked. It was not likely in these times that such a friendship would survive.

Very softly, but awkwardly, she said, "You're kind—I mean thank you for the compliment. I'd like to do some of the work you mentioned . . . but I don't think—" Her voice trailed off, and she looked at him uneasily.

He nodded slowly, his mouth twisting slightly. "Well, fair enough. That's what I thought you'd say."

She suddenly remembered that Jack was involved in a housing survey in the city. She'd never thought of asking him about it, but perhaps she could help if Liam knew about it. Quickly she said, "I really meant what I said about wanting to work on something in the city, though. I don't want to live in an ivory tower for three or four years."

He smiled approvingly. "Well, that's good. Ironically enough, I do things with the Student Christian Movement. I could take you down to the Derry Development Commission some time and you could help with the survey. They've been surveying and building since April." His voice was hopeful and enthusiastic.

"Yes—I'd like to do something like that."

"You'd go with me?"

She hesitated. "Well—I—I don't know. Someone else I know is doing the survey, too."

"Oh?"

"Jack Monaghan. Do you know him?"

"I don't think so. Wait—does he live in McCrae?"

"He does—lives with Roger Forbes."

"I've heard of him. Another Onion type, right?"

"Roger is, yes. Not Jack. Jack's a Catholic." Deirdre spoke as evenly as she could, not wanting to betray herself. Sheila had told her the weekend of the retreat that Jack was going to the seminary at Maynooth after his degree. She had tried to look at Jack with different eyes since then, not without difficulty.

[83]

"A big fellow? Older than the rest?"

"He's the one."

"Then you could go with him."

She gestured helplessly. "Or by myself, if I knew where to go."

He laughed, his head flung back. "Oh, no. You've no idea what it's like. It's not a volunteer job for womenfolk by themselves, especially not a pretty young girl like yourself."

She put out her hand to still him. "Listen—stop."

His warm, dry, rather thin left hand closed over hers immediately. "Forgive me, Deirdre, but I can't help it."

She stood up crossly, wrenching her hand away. "Oh, what blarney. You could sweet-talk half a dozen girls that way, Liam Donnelly, but not me."

He sat back, laughing easily, surveying her hot blue eyes and pink face. "Well, I needn't have asked if you were English, I'm thinking. You're Irish as they come, Deirdre McAvoy."

She had turned away in disgust, so his voice followed her up the coffee bar. Hardly looking where she was going, she let out an exasperated sigh and turned the corner as fast as she could. The hem of her cloak swept over one of the coffee tables by the door, and she looked down in horror to see that in her haste she had knocked over someone's cup.

"Deirdre! Whatever's wrong?"

She stood still as a guilty child. Kate, Ruth, and Caroline were looking up at her in surprise; it was Kate's cup lying on the table in a small pool of coffee.

"Oh! I'm sorry, Kate!" She dropped into the fourth chair at the table, half-laughing in relief, back with the comfortable, the familiar. She began to mop at the coffee with a paper napkin.

"What's the matter?" Kate urged. "You were all flustered. Never mind that coffee, either. I'd almost finished."

"Oh, nothing at all—someone making a bit of a nuisance of himself." How else could she explain Liam Donnelly?

Caroline smiled wanly. "What did he do?" she asked.

Deirdre hesitated. She would rather Kate not know about any of it. "Oh—never mind it now." Kate searched her face, but Deirdre pressed to change the subject. "Where are you three off to now?" she asked, looking at her friends.

[84]

Ruth looked at her watch. "I've a lecture in two minutes," she said, bending to pick up a pile of books from the carpeted floor.

"I have, too," said Kate. "Well, a seminar actually."

"I'm going to the library," Caroline said. "You too, Deirdre?"

"What? . . . Oh, I don't know," she said vaguely, still preoccupied with Liam.

"Wake up," laughed Kate. "You're in a daze."

"He must have been a handsome fellow," Caroline teased.

"Oh, he was that," said a harsh voice.

Startled, the four looked up. Liam was passing their table, his face twisted into a ferocious scowl, which Deirdre knew was all pantomime. Still, her hands flew to her face in dismay, and she caught her breath. Liam, however, stalked directly up the steps and out of sight.

Kate stared at Deirdre in disbelief. "*He* was the one bothering you?"

Deirdre laughed a tight little laugh. "Not to start with—we had quite a conversation. But then—"

"Heavens, Deirdre! He looks completely wild. Hair that's never seen a comb in weeks, half down his back. However did you get mixed up with him?" Kate frowned her disapproval.

Deirdre regarded her friend steadily for a moment, her sympathies wavering back to Liam. She loved Kate, but was annoyed with this penchant she had for quick pronouncements about people she hardly knew, or about people she didn't know at all. Deirdre herself always tried to suspend her judgment. She had even raised the matter once, gently trying to remind Kate that no matter how a person looked or what his faith or lack of it might be, he was beloved of God. Kate recognized this truth intellectually; in practice, however, Deirdre found she usually ignored it.

Now, therefore, Deirdre was careful in her reply. She laid her hand lightly on Kate's arm. "Kate, I'm not 'mixed up' with him as you put it. His name's Liam Donnelly, and he sat next to me in philosophy just now, and we got talking afterward. That's all."

"But you said—"

"Never mind it, Katie," she said, and tapped her watch. "It's eleven already."

[85]

Kate and Ruth jumped up, Kate laughing. "All right, Deirdre. We'll see you later. And you, Caro."

Kate ran up the steps, her long legs flying. She would be late for her seminar—a rare thing for her.

As she ran down the hillside pathway, she tried to focus her thoughts in preparation for the course that had absorbed most of her time and enthusiasm this term. Nineteenth-century fiction. *Middlemarch, Wuthering Heights, Jane Eyre, Hard Times* . . . one by one the novels had gripped and held her. And now she was reading Hardy, for her a puzzling and rather modern writer whose ideas disturbed her because of what she saw as his challenge to Christianity.

Colm Kennedy, who taught the seminar, seemed to relish the contradictions and controversy each novel brought to his class. At first, Kate had dismissed this characteristic in his teaching as merely disputatious. She had even accused him of moral fence-sitting. Recently, however, she had begun to appreciate the creative tension. Kennedy was expanding her mind, making her think in ways none of the other lecturers had, challenging traditional views by undercutting them, prodding her to see the other side of every issue. She left his classes as stimulated as if she had just drunk several cups of coffee. Others felt this excitement, too, she knew. No one ever fell asleep in Kennedy's classes, and students always left amid much loud discussion.

Feeling conspicuous, Kate slipped into the side door of the cramped seminar room. Her confusion magnified as she squeezed her way round chairbacks to the far side of the table and the only empty chair. Her efforts to be quiet were futile; she stumbled over books and coats.

Jack Monaghan sat beside the vacant seat; as usual, he was completely absorbed in the discussion. Without looking up, he drew back the empty chair for her.

Colm Kennedy occupied the seat at the end of the table, just two chairs down from Jack. Kennedy's bright eyes were seemingly the only live thing in his sallow face; their blue fires danced and sparkled behind the thick glass of his pince-nez, a contrast with the lined, leathery skin of his cheeks and forehead, with the thin, austere line of his mouth. *All this man's soul is in his eyes*, Kate often thought. She wondered at that, having learned he was a Franciscan. His thinking was radical; it spawned not only further thought, but action. He never pressed his students toward partisan views, however. She thought of him as a sort of mystic, respected him, but knew little or nothing of the Franciscan Order or his theological views.

Kate knew as soon as she picked up her pen and began to listen that Kennedy was going to question her. Intolerant of tardiness, he battered latecomers with extra questions. Now his eyes rested briefly on Jack, then focused on her. She looked quickly at Jack's book; they were discussing the early part of *Far From the Madding Crowd*. Then, calmly confident that she could respond as well as usual, she met Kennedy's piercing look; she had never yet felt intimidated by any of her university lecturers.

"Ah, Miss Hamilton—" His voice was mild, a slight crack in it. "What would you say Hardy is trying to do in this scene when Gabriel Oak loses his sheep over the cliff?"

Kate had read the critics, and she had finished the novel. Without hesitation, she said, "He's introducing the reader to his idea of the universe."

"Which is what?" Kennedy enquired blandly, but as quickly as a swordsman in a fencing match.

"Well—that fate is utterly amoral. That no God intervenes to change circumstances. That man is a mere toy to fate. The same sort of view Shakespeare expresses in *Lear*. 'As flies to wanton boys, are we to th' gods—'" She wondered fleetingly what had been said before she entered the room. "It's a completely pessimistic view."

Kennedy's eyes were fixed impassively on her face. "Oh—do you think so?"

She smiled slightly, undaunted yet uneasy, sensing his challenge was imminent. But she knew he would like her comparison with *Lear*. "Yes—it's the same thing that's operating later in the book when Fanny goes to the wrong church."

"Well, I'm not sure. Is there another way to read this novel? Is fate utterly indifferent, as Miss Hamilton asserts? Is God totally

[87]

absent?" Kennedy's eyes traveled round the table, piercingly bright.

No one answered. Kate fidgeted in her chair. "I can't see how else we can read the book," she insisted. "We know about Hardy's life. He completely rejected Christianity. This book is just the beginning of his rejection, and I think his writing is spoiled by it."

"Oh? Have you read the later books as well?"

Kate curled and uncurled the corner of her paper. "No–o, but I've read about them."

"Then let's confine ourselves to one novel at a time, shall we?"

Touché, thought Kate irritably. But then she rallied, determined to prove her point by examples. "All right," she said resolutely. "I'm thinking about passages like the one in which Joseph Poorgrass is talking . . . and later when Matthew Moon is talking," and she quoted.

A faint groan sounded from the other end of the table. Kate always had an answer for Kennedy, so most of the students regarded her with a mixture of envy, dislike, and admiration.

Kennedy beamed at her. "You make a good case for your argument, Miss Hamilton. But I'm still not convinced. What you're saying might hold water if we were looking at—say—*Tess* or *Jude*, but in this novel, is the universe really quite so fatalistic as you seem to think?"

She frowned, annoyed at his persistence. "Yes—it's totally unpredictable."

"Is that the same thing?"

Kate sat back. "Not exactly," she conceded.

Kennedy raised his finger. "Aha! The crux of our argument!" The students laughed after a brief hesitation. "It is somewhat unpredictable," he went on, "but can man resist it? Is he a mere victim?"

"Yes," said Kate, "according to Hardy."

"No!" said Jack, suddenly interrupting. "At least, I don't think so." He glanced at Kate, who had turned her head toward him in surprise. His face was pale, his gray eyes intent.

Kennedy looked at him. "Someone of my persuasion, perhaps? Not victims? Then what?" His eyes were twinkling again.

Kate stirred. *Here he goes again*, she thought. And then, irritably, *Of course Jack Monaghan would agree with him.*

"In this early scene," Jack began, his voice slow but precise, "Gabriel can't help the loss of the sheep. But he fights back for the rest of the novel. He fights fire and he fights water. His name gives him away."

"And his booklist," added another student. "He's reading *Pilgrim's Progress* isn't he? He's Christian slogging away against 'fate' and winning."

"We–ell . . . it may not be quite that simple," Kennedy replied, "but you're right—" he nodded down the table, "Mr. Monaghan. Gabriel understands the universe, so he's equipped to deal with it, rough or smooth. He's not vain, like Bathsheba, or—how shall we describe Troy?"

"Heartless," someone said.

"Heartless like Troy, or introverted like Boldwood. He's naïve about women, but he understands sheep, and weather, and so on. His world. He is, if you will, an agent of God."

Cut and thrust! He made his point so quickly that Kate felt dazed. She met the old man's eyes. *He likes to throw me off balance. Why?*

"Well," said Kennedy, "we won't settle this, as usual. What we can say, though, with some assurance, is that many of Hardy's contemporaries misunderstood his work because he was not an orthodox Anglican. They rejected him for his peculiar kind of beliefs instead of examining his work for its fine literary qualities. The old fallacy of ad hominem. We should be careful—" and here he turned his eyes to Kate, though not unkindly, "not to do the same." He laughed suddenly, his hand to the throat of his brown habit. "You all know I'm no Anglican, but I have no trouble appreciating Hardy. I want you to do the same. All of you."

Sunday, November 30

Roger eased back into the well-worn overstuffed chair and stretched his legs onto the empty chair in front of him. The dark television lounge, stuffy with smoke, was lighted only by the black and white flickers from the television set across the room. With several other McCrae men, he sat watching the ten o'clock news. The door of the lounge opened, framing a first-year student Roger had seen both in McCrae and at rugby practice. The fellow usually held a cigarette; this time he held a guitar. The room darkened again as the door closed behind him. His small, angular face was gray in the pale light of the television screen, and his mat of flaxen hair and his sparse reddish beard faded to almost the same tone. He crossed the room and leaned his guitar against the wall, then dropped into a chair beside Roger.

"Smoke?" he asked, and Roger heard the rustling of cellophane.

"No thanks."

"But you don't mind if I do?" The voice was rough but polite.

"No," said Roger absently, his attention focused on the BBC news. A lighter flicked and flared.

"The Reverend Ian Paisley, self-styled Moderator of the Free Presbyterian Church, today said that people were blackening the name of the Ulster Protestant Volunteers by linking them with the outlawed Ulster Volunteer Force. The Ulster Protestant Volunteers is a group associated with Mr. Paisley that has pledged to 'take whatever steps it thinks fit to expose unconstitutional acts . . . when the authorities act contrary to the Constitution of Northern Ireland.' Mr. Paisley, who is also chairman of the Ulster Constitution Defence Committee, has made this claim exactly one

[90]

year after leading a group of one thousand Protestants against a civil rights demonstration in Armagh. The Ulster Volunteer Force was previously banned by then Prime Minister Terence O'Neill in 1966 after the Malvern Street murders. Mr. O'Neill at that time called the UVF 'a sordid conspiracy of criminals against an unprotected people.' "

The newscaster's voice was typically neutral, but Roger heard his neighbor curse under his breath at this last remark. "That it bloody well was—is—and the UPV to boot." Roger shot a wondering look at him, and the face behind the cigarette grinned back disarmingly. "You're Protestant, I suppose."

"I'm English," Roger answered dryly.

The student exhaled slowly. "Ah, that says it all."

"Shut up, Donnelly!" snapped a voice from the other side of the room.

"Sorry." He rustled paper again, this time passing Roger a packet of mints. "Here, have one. It's Sunday, so we can live at peace."

Roger laughed. "Oh—I can live at peace with you any day. I quite agree with you."

"Not you too, Forbes?" howled the voice across the way. "Can't we watch in peace, never mind live in peace, you idiots?"

"Oh—surely you may," Roger said mildly. "I'll leave you to it, I think. I've got friends coming up anyway."

A lewd laugh came from the darkened corner, then a falsetto voice. "Oh, hello. Yes, this is Sheila Russell. Can you look and see if Roger's in his room, please?—Get to her, Roger boy."

Roger laughed good-naturedly. "Ah, but I'm entertaining three ladies tonight."

"Some blokes have all the luck. Who else? Sheila's frigid roommate? Katherine the Great?"

Roger opened the door. "Enough, Lenehan. If you mean Kate, yes; and one of Kate's friends, too."

Lenehan's feet slid off a chair and thumped to the floor. "Ruth?" His voice sounded odd.

"Ruth who?" Roger asked. "Graham? No. Anyway, it's Deirdre McAvoy—not that it's any business of yours. And don't be bothering us."

[91]

Lenehan growled, "Kate-the-Great Hamilton has a friend named Deirdre McAvoy? Ho, that's ironic!"

"Shut up, the both of you," the chain-smoking newcomer yelled.

"Enough of this brawling, you cases," a voice complained from the other side of the room. Grinning, Roger banged the lounge door shut behind him.

The girls hadn't arrived yet, so he ran upstairs to see if Jack would come down and join them. He bounded straight into the room as usual, then paused on the threshold with a muttered, "Oh—sorry, Jack."

Jack was asleep, one arm thrown out of the eiderdown and his relaxed face turned toward the ceiling. His wide mouth was open and he snored lightly. Roger looked down at him affectionately in the dim light from the lamp left burning on his own desk. He had come to respect Jack's particular habit of quiet contemplation on Sundays. His own morning prayer times, weekly prayer meetings, and Bible study somehow paled before Jack's disciplined self-examination and his ability to find inward tranquility no matter what the noise around him. And McCrae was no quiet place, least of all on a Sunday—for most students a day of loud recreation.

The peel of the front doorbell recalled Roger. He shut the door softly and ran down the stairs to admit Sheila, Kate, and Deirdre. His eyes were for Sheila only, trim and pretty in the brown dress she had worn to church that morning. "We'll have some cocoa, shall we?" he asked as he shut out the November damp. "I was hoping Jack would join us, but he's asleep already."

"Cocoa sounds good to me," Deirdre replied.

"Not unless I make it, it won't," Sheila commented. "Roger would scald the milk!"

Kate laughed. "Oh, Roger's got more sense than that. You don't give him much credit, Sheila."

Roger twisted his face into a mock scowl. "If you womenfolk are going to argue over me, you can all go home again." But all the same he led the way past the television room and down the half-flight to the kitchen, a spacious room with high windows and ceilings, bare wooden counter tops, rows of dusty upturned pots and pans, and a slight smell of gas. The sink was filled with a

[92]

motley collection of dirty mugs and pans. A firedoor with an uncurtained window opened out onto an alley.

"Does this room get much use?" Deirdre asked.

"Not much," said Roger. He rinsed a small pan and poured milk into it. "Now and then if someone has a party."

Deirdre perched herself on one of the high stools and stared round, her eyes moving swiftly, alert and expectant. "Well, I think this is a great kitchen," she said. "It has all sorts of possibilities. Just look at those lovely wooden counter tops."

Roger grinned at her enthusiasm. "Don't look too closely. They probably haven't been cleaned for ages."

"But if they were, what a wonderful place to roll out bread and scones and—"

"Stop! I'm getting fat just listening to you. You mean you actually know how to make all those things?" Sheila looked impressed. The milk hissed and bubbled to the brim of the pan, and Kate caught it before it could boil over.

"Yes, had to learn," Deirdre muttered, embarrassed to have everyone looking at her. Almost apologetically, she explained, "I've a big family at home. My mother couldn't—and wouldn't—do it all. We all learned to cook."

"Hmmm." As Sheila stirred the cocoa, Roger turned around and opened the cupboard over the stove. "What do you need to make bread?"

Deirdre laughed. "Oh—only about three hours."

"Well then, scones?"

"Self-raising flour, buttermilk, a little sugar and margarine and salt."

"Do they take long?"

"Not very. D'you have all those things?"

"Here's sugar and salt . . . wait, here's some flour."

"Buttermilk?"

Kate opened the small refrigerator and peered into its greasy interior. "No—just plain milk, and some butter."

"Ordinary milk would do if there's some vinegar or a lemon to make it sour."

"We don't have either of those."

"Well, we can try them with ordinary milk and see what

[93]

happens. Does the oven work?" Deirdre slid off the stool and turned the oven door handle. "Ugh, it's dirty!"

"I don't know if it works or not."

"With all that grease it'll probably catch fire," Kate said gloomily.

"No, it won't. All right, I'll make some scones if you all promise to help clean this place up a bit and to eat the things—even if they aren't quite like your mother's!" Deirdre's eyes sparkled.

"Promise!" said Roger. "Here, let's have some cocoa to fortify ourselves for the great cleaning and cooking lesson from Miss McAvoy." He looked around at the girls. "But you're all too well-dressed to clean. You don't want to dirty your Sunday best, do you?"

"Never worry," said Deirdre. She'd found a ragged linen tea towel, tucked it inside her waistband, and rolled up her sleeves; now she took a knife to the crusted black floor of the oven. Kate and Sheila reluctantly followed her example and, with Roger, set to washing the counter and table.

"Is it really worth all this trouble?" Kate grumbled after a few minutes of impatient scrubbing.

"You can judge for yourself, Katie." Deirdre turned to look at her friend. "But that's fine. You don't need to do any more. Look for a rolling pin and a sieve and spoon."

Five minutes later, the oven was turned on, smoking slightly, but apparently working; and Deirdre's hands were wrist-deep in flour. The other three watched as she worked butter into the flour until the mixture was as fine as bread crumbs.

"What's all this?" a gravelly voice asked from the doorway— Liam Donnelly, with his guitar in hand.

He hesitated slightly, then crossed to the sink and stubbed out his cigarette in a dirty cup. Deirdre's jaw set tightly. Even though Liam had said nothing more to her in the last two weeks, he had shadowed her in and out of philosophy classes until she felt hunted. Now she would not meet his eyes. *Let the others talk to him,* she thought.

"She's making dropscones for us," Kate answered in a severe tone that excluded the newcomer from the group. She recognized him from that day in the coffee bar, though Deirdre had been resolutely silent about him.

Roger and Sheila, knowing nothing of what had passed between Liam and Deirdre, blithely invited him to join them and share some scones.

"Well, I don't know," Liam answered sulkily. "The cook mightn't like it. And I mightn't like them anyway."

Deirdre's eyes flashed up, provoked. "Nor you might," she replied tartly. "And anyway, you didn't work for yours as these good people did, so you'll maybe not be getting any anyway, Liam Donnelly."

"Then I'll sing for some," he laughed, liking the quick way she said his name. He held up his guitar and smiled winningly.

"Yes, sing, by all means," Sheila urged, leaning against the table and folding her arms.

He perched on one of the stools and picked out the melody of "Black Is the Color."

Kate was surprised by the sureness of his voice. Harsh, perhaps, but perfectly in tune. She couldn't help frowning, however, for the song was plainly directed to Deirdre.

> *Black, black, black is the color of my true love's hair.*
> *Her lips are something rosy fair,*
> *The purest eyes and the bravest hands.*
> *I love the ground whereon she stands.*

In spite of her will to the contrary, Deirdre's mouth would turn up at the corners. She could imagine Liam singing at a ceilidhs at home; his voice was just the kind for soft Gaelic love songs and for drinking ballads. She caught Kate's eye and winked. Kate pursed her lips, but a smile wrinkled the corners of her eyes, too; even a scorned singer could not mar her love of folk music.

The song over, Liam propped his guitar in a corner and began talking to Roger. "So what kind of an Englishman are you to be agreeing with me about the UVF and the UPV?" he asked out of the corner of his mouth as he lit a fresh cigarette.

"An honest one, I hope," Roger said. He twisted his face grimly, half shutting his eyes. " 'Loyalist' is one of the most abused words

[95]

in the Queen's English; Paisley's a rabble-rouser, and no mistake. You don't have to be Irish and Catholic to see he's dangerous."

"You're bloody well right. And what sickens me is that this— this so-called Ulster Defence Regiment isn't going to be any different from the "B" Specials. A wolf by any other name still stinks and slinks its way around. No different from the UVF either."

"It's a terrible truth, but I'm afraid you're probably right."

"Amazing! A Prod, and you agree so quickly! Where's the hot debate I love so well?" Liam glanced at Deirdre.

Ignoring the provocation, Roger frowned and asked, "The UVF is still going—even now?"

"Of course it is," Liam said with scorn. "Soon as word got out that the government'd disbanded the "B" Specials, those guys were building up their arsenals as fast as the UDR will, too, illegal or not."

"How do you know that?"

Liam shrugged. "Brian Walker says so, and I see no reason to doubt it myself, knowing history."

Deirdre looked up as she laid the cut dough onto a baking tray. She tightened her lips, resolved on silence.

"Anyway," Liam went on, "I'm in NICRA. We've come out publicly against the UDR. It's not going to be the above-board bipartisan force people said they wanted. Look at the loophole already open! They can keep arms in their houses 'in an emergency.' Now, I ask you, lad, who's going to define 'emergency'?" He grimaced. "Too much philosophy lately! But this whole country's in an emergency. The laws for the UDR are just tokens to appease the ignorant. The men'll be the same. Do the same."

"No—Catholics can join, surely!"

Liam scoffed. "You're naïve if you think they will. What self-respecting Catholic would join a Protestant army—whatever they call the bloody thing—and be tolerated by his neighbors? He'd not be able to hold up his head. And he'd be dead in no time—shot by his own brother or by the Prod vigilantes who're supposed to be his comrades-at-arms. It's absurd!"

Roger stared at Liam, half-afraid of his vehemence. Then the sound of footsteps and the rustle of a raincoat cut the tension.

[96]

James McQueen hovered in the doorway, uncertain and frowning. Roger thought he was probably a bit disconcerted by Donnelly's presence in the otherwise familiar group. James took off his cap and turned his eyes on Kate, who met them with an expression of frank pleasure.

"Er—Katherine—someone told me you were here. So I thought I'd come up for a minute—" he nodded toward Roger curtly, "instead of looking for you tomorrow morning. There's something I want to talk to you about."

Roger winked at Sheila. Was James finally coming cap in hand to Kate? "No business now, there's a good chap," he said to James. "We're having a jolly time here cooking scones." He glanced at Deirdre. "Do stay and have some, James." His heartiness sounded forced, even to his own ears.

With a wave of his hand, James dismissed the invitation. "No, I won't, thanks. Katherine—I really—"

"Oh, leave her alone," Liam growled.

James turned his head sharply. With swift appraisal, he took in the matted fair hair, mocking green eyes, and rumpled windbreaker.

Kate, meanwhile, slipped off her stool. Her stocking snagged on a rough edge and instantly laddered. "What is it?" she asked, made impatient by her own awkwardness.

"Oh, don't be going, Kate," Deirdre begged.

"No—the conversation's just warming up," Liam drawled, deliberately puffing smoke toward the middle of the room.

"Oh?" James's eyes darted back to Liam.

"We were just talking about the UDR," Roger interposed, trying to sound casual. Dangerous ground, but the damage was done. Liam had thrown out a challenge to James, and James would take it sooner or later.

"Yes," Liam intoned, directing his remarks to Roger but his intent to James. "Bernadette's right. Westminster had better think this UDR through carefully. Your countrymen in London haven't a notion of what's really going on here. Nor have the absentee-landlord ruling classes."

Sliding the scones into the oven, Deirdre slammed the door shut.

Brian Walker! Bernadette! Was Liam name-dropping or did he really know these people?

Roger blinked. "You know Bernadette Devlin?"

Liam drew slowly on his cigarette. He was acting a bit now, and both of them knew it; but acting or not, he believed in the stance he had assumed. "A little. I've been to some of the People's Democracy meetings."

"You belong to the PD?" James asked in a horrified tone.

"No—not yet."

Deirdre's head jerked up. Of course he knew Devlin. He'd been at Burntollett Bridge when Protestants had stoned and beaten the PD. So had Bernadette Devlin. January the fourth of this year! The brutality of that attack had deeply shamed her. But the People's Democracy . . . wasn't it almost entirely a Marxist group? Was that where Liam was heading? To find his faith in politics that claimed religion an opiate? To make grand, meaningless gestures against an enemy that was in reality within, not without? *"No—not yet,"* he had said.

"And you'd be a fool to join it," James said bluntly. "The PD, and NICRA for that matter—they're all the same. Just want to cause trouble. Cover for Communist subversion. Bernadette Devlin—huh! She's a subversive if ever there was one! Just when there's a chance of peace with a new defense force—concessions to Catholics just written right into the provision—what does she do? Comes out against one of the most generous moves in a long time." James stopped, his eyes glittering. "Now surely it's obvious she's not in favor of anything that'll strengthen the country."

Liam smiled. "Unionist propaganda." His voice was silky, patronizing. "Don't you know that every high-ranking man in the "B" Specials has been promised a place in the UDR? It'll never be a representative group, if that's the case. The PD may not be right about some things, but they're right to complain about the UDR."

"You're not answering my accusations," James said, a smirk of victory dawning in his eyes. "Bernadette Devlin admitted herself that she threw petrol bombs—"

"Oh, no, she didn't. That's a gross misrepresentation of the facts—a lie, in plain British," Liam snapped. "She admitted she

[98]

had organized the throwing of bombs in Derry. But that's different altogether."

"Not to my mind," James replied righteously. "If you're right."

"Right? Look at the Scarman Tribunal records for yourself."

"Wait up, fellows," Roger put in nervously, glancing from one to the other. But they ignored him.

"Aye—she was charged with breach of peace and riotous conduct. Organizing others to throw bombs or throwing them yourself—what's the difference? She's just more intelligent than the poor Bogside Taigs—too clever to be caught with a bomb in her hand. She betrayed her own people—the dupes."

James's tone was strident now, ugly. Deirdre stared at his livid, harsh face, and her own flamed with indignation. *Taigs? Dupes?* How dare he talk so?

Kate's hurt eyes flashed from James to Liam to Deirdre and back. It was agony for her to hear James talk this way.

"I'm not the only one who thinks so, apparently." James couldn't let the matter rest. "Some people have no idea what's best for them. Thank the Lord for men like Paisley. At least he has the courage to speak out for good. The Protestant Volunteers are just what the province needs. God bless them, I say!"

"And I say, God damn them all to hell!" Liam shouted, his face contorted with rage, and he spat on James's polished black shoes.

Kate and Sheila gasped. Deirdre covered her face with her hands and cried hysterically, "Stop it! Stop it! Both of you! In heaven's name, stop it!"

Kate gripped Deirdre's shoulder with her arm, steadying her as her whole body shook. A lump rose in her own throat; she couldn't look up. Roger edged over to a pale and anxious Sheila. Was Liam going to fight? His head barely came to James's chin, but James was thin, not strong. Liam could wrestle him down in an instant.

Instead, Liam turned his back and stalked to the firedoor, hesitated, then pushed it open with a brutal shove and was gone.

Deirdre wiped her eyes and glanced around quickly. James stood awkwardly by the refrigerator, his face averted. Sheila was crying silently into Roger's wool sweater. Kate stared at the floor, the corners of her mouth down, her eyebrows knitted.

Roger met Deirdre's eyes, then faced James. "You should be

[99]

ashamed, James McQueen. Forcing an argument like that. You push too far. You'd better go." His voice rang with a trace of Eton arrogance.

James opened his mouth in surprise, then closed it again with a snap. *Like a reptile,* thought Deirdre. Kate started toward him, then stopped, gesturing hopelessly; he turned a bitter look on Roger and walked out. They heard the front door slam; then the only sound was the whir of the electric clock above the stove.

Suddenly Roger broke the shocked silence; he leapt across the kitchen and jerked open the oven. "The scones! Oh!" And he began to laugh. A small billow of smoke clouded the room as he rushed the blackened tray out onto the counter. A dozen charred lumps lay smouldering on the metal surface.

Then they all began to laugh hysterically. Tears rolled down Kate's face, her emotions wrung and twisted like a wet towel. Deirdre looked over at Liam's guitar. *He'll have to come back for it,* she thought. The acrid smoke choked her for a minute, and her eyes ran again.

Friday, December 5

Kate sat hunched over the small handmirror she had propped on her desk. Having folded her hair into a neat chignon, she was now plucking her eyebrows. Sheila came up behind her, leaned over with a laugh, and stuck out her tongue. "You're awful, Miss Hamilton. What could possibly be wrong with your flawless face?"

Kate clicked her tongue, half smiling, but kept her eyes on the mirror. "My eyebrows are too bushy."

"What nonsense! You look lovely." Sheila stood back a bit, still grinning impishly. "Anyway, why worry? I thought you were just going to, quote, pick bodies off the floor?"

Kate sighed with annoyance, smacked the mirror down on the desk, and half turned toward her roommate. "Well—and I am."

"By yourself?" Sheila teased.

Kate screwed up the corners of her mouth. "No, if you must know; it was James's idea." Her color heightened and she rushed on. "James sometimes goes with some of the other men from the Hostel. But most of them have gone home for the weekend. He was telling me about it, and I—I said I'd go too—to help him, I mean."

Sheila began to bounce a brush through her curls. "That's good, Kate."

Without her glasses, Kate couldn't see whether Sheila was serious. To test her, she said, "And you and Roger can help, too, if you see we need help."

Laughing again, Sheila opened the wardrobe and pulled out a floral print dress. "Oh, yes, dear Kate, you—or rather James—definitely need help."

[101]

"Sheila!"

"Well, for heaven's sake, stop being so earnest. You're going to the Rugby Club dance, aren't you? With James, aren't you? You might as well admit you'll probably have a lot of fun. And I hope no one gets drunk, so James will actually have to pay attention to you for a change."

Kate swung round. "You mustn't talk that way. You're so—"

"Oh, you want someone to get drunk?" Sheila asked mildly.

Kate reached for her glasses with an exasperated groan and an angry look. It was lost, though, for Sheila was pulling her dress over her head. Kate was irritated with herself, too, especially as she turned again and saw her flushed cheeks in the mirror. Of course, Sheila was right. She did want James to notice her tonight. Not that there was a possibility of their dancing—not at all. Only a few members of the CU, mostly the "liberal" English ones, ever danced. But it was a CU tradition to "pick up the bodies" at the dance: to help the drunks get back to their rooms without bloody noses, cut hands—or worse. Kate had only a vague notion of what it would be like to help someone in that condition, but she knew it was right for her to support James. She wanted to be with him, and perhaps—just perhaps–he would see her differently. So she resigned herself to Sheila's banter.

"Well, will I do?" she asked with pretended indifference.

"Kate, you'll do well," Sheila flourished her hairbrush above her head. "Probably be elected Rugby Club queen or something."

"No thanks."

"But it would look better if you wore a dress, I think. Your petticoat's pretty, but—"

"Enough, please," Kate laughed ruefully.

A few months ago, even, such a conversation would have been impossible. But since her engagement, Sheila had often assumed the role of the experienced, wise one—a role formerly Kate's. And now Sheila was staring at her afresh and frowning. "Seriously, Kate . . . you look beautiful. But you're awfully thin, aren't you? Haven't you been feeling well?"

"Thin?"

"Yes. I noticed when you were doing your brows that your shoulder blades stick out like chicken wings."

Kate smiled. "Oh, but I'm sprouting angel's wings, don't you know?"

"And a halo, too, with your hair up that way."

"Sheila!"

"All right—all right—now let me see your dress. Roger'll be here soon and you ought to be dressed."

Kate glanced at her watch. "Eight o'clock already! So he will. But doesn't the dance begin now?" She reached to search for her dress in the wardrobe.

"Probably not. These things never start on time. And Roger won't be on time either. Oh, is that what you're wearing?"

Kate held up a dark blue shirtwaist dress she sometimes wore to church. "Yes, it's all right, isn't it?"

"We—ell. No one wears short dresses to this."

"No one who's going to dance, perhaps," Kate replied, resolutely tugging the dress over her head and wriggling her arms into it.

Sheila marched to the wardrobe. "Wait—don't you have anything long? What if you do decide to dance?"

"I won't."

"But you might meet the man of your dreams."

Kate frowned. "At a dance? Not likely!"

Sheila was still rummaging through Kate's skirts, blouses, and dresses. "Ah! What's this?" She pulled out a red dress encased in a clear plastic bag.

Kate hesitated. "That's something I'm saving for a special time."

"Wow! It's fabulous. Oh, why don't you wear it tonight?" Sheila lifted the plastic and held it up.

"Don't be silly. I told you, I'm saving it—for the formal next spring."

"Aha, Kate Hamilton! You're going to that?"

Kate avoided Sheila's eyes and shrugged. "How do I know? But I bought it on sale—rather on impulse. Not the sort of thing I usually get. I just thought sometime—"

"Oh, do put it on—just let me see how it looks."

"No, it's too late."

"Please?"

[103]

"Oh—all right then. Just for a minute." Soon Kate was standing self-consciously in the middle of the room looking as brilliant as an Oriental poppy, the red of the dress accentuating her gold hair and the pale skin visible above the scooped neckline.

"You look like a queen, Kate!"

Someone knocked on the door.

"Just a minute," Kate called out, fleeing back to the bed to retrieve the blue dress and change again.

"No—Roger? You can come in."

Kate moaned, "Sheila Russell!"

"Come in or not?" Roger called, rattling the handle.

"Yes!" Sheila said loudly.

"No!" cried Kate.

But Sheila had opened the door. "Just look at Kate, Roger, will you?"

Roger whistled, then beamed at them both. His arm round Sheila, he murmured, "You both look as if you stepped out of *Vogue*." He offered his other arm to Kate. "May I escort both you beautiful ladies?"

"Yes," said Sheila, quickly. "We're all ready, aren't we, Kate?"

Kate was paralyzed with amazement. It was completely against her judgment to wear anything that would draw the wrong kind of attention tonight. But Sheila had somehow taken charge. And she herself was just excited enough about everything not to insist on changing. Roger and Sheila were so admiring. . . . She shot a bewildered look at each of them. Should she just give in? "Oh, I don't know," she wavered.

Roger took her arm. "Kate, you look wonderful. Come on."

She let herself be carried along by the tide of their enthusiasm. She wouldn't think now about what James would say. He would—no—she would not think about it. And the other CU girls? They would not be at the dance, anyway, most of them. Except Deirdre. She'd said she was going. Kate snatched up her black cape, throwing it round her bare shoulders, and the three of them swept out. *Like a queen*, she thought. Skirts rustled and frothed down the stairs. She caught the scent of Sheila's perfume and vaguely wished she had some of her own, but her father had always condemned it. Her father—what would he think? The thought sobered her, so

[104]

that by the time they reached the steps of the Great Hall, she was already regretting her rashness.

She must have slowed her steps, for Roger turned to her solicitously. "Are you all right, Kate?"

She held up her chin. *Like a queen,* she thought again. "Yes, fine. But I was just thinking—I was supposed to meet James out here."

"Oh. Shall we wait with you?"

She wished James had come for her at the room so she could have faced him alone—in the blue dress. "No, I'll wait here for him. You go along."

"Are you sure?" Sheila persisted. "Listen, if he doesn't come, you come in and find us. We'll be sitting near the door."

"Sitting?" Kate could not imagine what this dance would be like. Her only experience of university dances was the rhythmic throb of bass guitar pounding through the Saturday night air when she was trying to sleep or study.

"We'll look for you, Kate," Roger assured.

After Sheila and Roger had gone into the hall, she hung back in the shadows of the Gothic gargoyles below the building. Students passed her singly and in couples, but she tried to show by her direct gaze and aloof stance that she was waiting for someone. At last a familiar, tall figure materialized out of the darkness. By now her feet, in light shoes, were pinched with cold, so she gratefully stepped down to meet him.

It wasn't James, however. *Jack Monaghan.* She drew back into the shadows again, not wanting him to see her. When he was almost even with her, just a step below, he glanced up and saw her.

"Hello, Katherine," he nodded, then passed on, his arms full of books.

Cringing, she tried to answer, but her voice seemed to have disappeared. She swallowed hard, flinging a look back up at the library windows above her. Of course, it was Friday. She was usually studying, too. But how could anyone concentrate with all that noise coming from the first floor? *Ah, I've done it many times myself!* She looked down at the red dress hanging in folds below her cape. *This is all so silly,* she thought. And her feet felt numb. She would go back and change, then look for James. She crunched down the graveled driveway toward the Woodburn.

"Katherine!"

She stopped dead. A film of sweat formed beneath the thin stuff of her dress. "Hello, James." Was that her choked voice?

"I was looking for you."

"Oh?"

"I thought I'd come up for you, but you weren't in your room."

Was she imagining that look on his face? And she was puzzled by what he had just said: James rarely set foot in the women's hall, and then only to see her on CU business. His apparent lack of attraction to her had always hurt. But something was different tonight. She frowned, speechless, and tried to fathom the change. . . .

In the dimness his eyes traveled up from the folds of rich red over her feet, up the long lines of her legs, then rested on the curves of her breasts and shoulders, which were only half-concealed by the cape. He blinked. "You look . . . very . . . er, very nice, if I may say so."

Unconsciously she pulled the cape more closely around herself. Something in his eyes unsettled her. For a second she glimpsed the same intentness she had noticed in McCrae a week ago when he thought he had cornered Liam Donnelly: that same hardened certainty, that same hint of superiority, even cruelty. It was the look of a hunter closing in on something weak. It made her shiver.

His eyes came up to her face at last. "You're cold," he said firmly. "Let's go in. It sounds as if it's already in full swing."

She grasped at his cliché. "Yes, in full swing is certainly a good way to put it."

He smiled vaguely and offered her his hand. "We've an important job to do together," he said.

She hesitated, seeing again the alien glitter in his eye. *His hand,* she told herself numbly, *he wants me to take it.* She had waited for months to do that, and now she was delaying.

"Together," he repeated, holding her with his eyes.

She mumbled an incoherent answer and gave him her hand. He crushed her cold fingers in his moist ones, and they went up the steps, together for the first time.

[106]

"You're here, Deirdre!" Sheila gushed as the younger girl slipped into the canvas seat beside her.

Deirdre smiled self-consciously. "Yes. I'm glad to see you two."

"We're just here to chaperone, don't you know," Roger drawled, leaning toward her. "To keep an eye on pretty girls and see they behave themselves." He leered at her in jest.

"Rubbish," said Sheila. "We should be dancing."

"We will, we will, Madame Impatience," Roger said. "Do you want to do a solo tap dance while the group's taking a break? Deirdre, are you here to help James and Kate?" He smiled broadly.

By now Deirdre was accustomed to the sly comments about her friend, but she knew Roger intended no malice.

"No–o. I like to dance, that's why I'm here."

"A girl after our own hearts," Sheila murmured. "Oh, Deirdre, have you seen Kate yet?"

"No, why?"

"She's over there, see? Near the bar, where James is handing out tracts."

"I can't see her." The hall was only dimly illuminated from the footlights under the band's platform, but white splashes of light reflected off the double bass and off the copper-colored drums.

"She's wearing a red dress with white—"

"Oh—now I can see her. Why, she looks marvelous, so she does. She's not dancing, is she?"

Roger laughed. "No, not yet. But we're working on it! I think James is absolutely smitten tonight. That dress is what did the trick!"

"About time, isn't it?" Sheila added.

With surprise and a strange sense of regret, Deirdre watched James hovering like a bumblebee over a large, colorful flower. Here a tract. There a tract. Back to Kate, his mouth moving incessantly, his hand resting on her arm at times. Kate looked quiet, withdrawn, but happy. Should she wave? No, Kate saw only James.

A sudden crash of cymbals and loud chords from the electric guitar and the group began to play *Good Day Sunshine*. Someone tapped Deirdre on the arm. With only a half-glance back at Sheila

[107]

and Roger, she was up and dancing. It was the movement she loved, never mind the partner. In fact, she hardly looked at him until a slight pause between songs.

"What's your name?" he asked, bending his fair head toward her dark one to shout above the music already beginning again.

"Deirdre."

"Mine's Raymond—Ray. You like to dance, don't you?"

"Aye," she said.

"Right enough!" He swung her round, laughing. "And you like the Beatles?"

"Have to, around here."

The pulsing rhythm of *Lovely Rita* sent them quickly across the floor among the other couples until the song ended and the haunting melody of *Eleanor Rigby* changed the mood of the dancers. Deirdre looked around and saw that now most other couples were dancing close, arms round necks, heads on shoulders. She suddenly felt hollow, empty. She had wanted to dance but had given no thought to any possible consequences or entanglements. She did not want to begin an artificial relationship that would lead nowhere. Nevertheless, she went through the motions mechanically, avoiding her partner's eyes and periodically catching a glimpse of Sheila and Roger holding each other closely, or Kate and James circulating among those around the bar. She began to feel wistful and withdrawn. At last, the band took a break and she could excuse herself.

"Look—d'you want a drink," Ray asked.

"No thanks," her smile was fading. "I don't drink. But thanks." She backed away, hoping to let him know by her tone that she did not want to dance any more. Then she turned and hurried across the hall toward the door, eyes down so no one would attempt to stop her. She just wanted to get back to her room.

She grabbed her coat from the cloakroom and left the Great Hall. Outside, Liam Donnelly was rushing up the steps, his face so intent that he almost collided with her. "Deirdre! Are you after going to the dance?"

"I went," she said tersely. "Please—" She stopped, really seeing him. The beard was gone, and the thick mat of hair was cut

[108]

shorter, close around his ears and collar. She had not seen him since Sunday night. She had missed him.

Now his sharp green eyes took in everything at a glance: the droop of her shoulders and mouth, her glazed eyes. "You're tired and upset, aren't you." It was a statement, not a question.

"Yes," she murmured, scuffing her foot on the dirty steps.

"Will you be letting me walk you back at least?"

"Yes," she said softly. "You could do that." The cold mantle of isolation dropped from her shoulders; her blood was running hot.

As they walked slowly along the loose gravel, she was keenly aware of the man beside her: the pungent smoke from his cigarette, the rough wool of his jacket, the supple leather of his brown moccasins. Near the bottom of the steps that led up to Woodburn, they stopped under the lamppost.

"You look different," she observed, not even looking at him as she said it.

He shrugged. "You thought I should reform. So I tried." He drew deeply on his cigarette.

She laughed, suddenly, her head tilting back and her eyes meeting his at last. Behind them the music drummed and throbbed again.

"Are you sure you're too tired to dance any more?"

Her eyes went down again. In a small, embarrassed voice, she said, "I don't know."

Now he laughed at her. "And if I dance with you—? That is why you went, isn't it . . . to dance, I mean?"

"Oh, yes." She knew he was enjoying her confusion.

"Then . . . will you?"

She hesitated. Unconsciously, she had waited for this moment. And now he was waiting, too, staring at her, his face serious again. She could not meet the directness of his gaze.

"Of course," he muttered, lightening his tone, "we could always dance here, if you prefer. We can hear the music almost as well, so we can."

She laughed, letting down her guard. He flung his cigarette toward the shrubbery. It made a pale yellow arc in the darkness. Then he held out his hand. She was almost won over. She took two

[109]

steps toward him and tripped as her foot caught in the hem of her long dress.

"Now, now, you don't need to be that eager," he chided as he caught her. His hands rested briefly on her waist where he had broken her fall. She laughed again, nervously, half afraid. But he released her, caught her hand, and tugged her back along the way they had come. She remembered his hand, which she had once rejected: dry, warm, hardly bigger than her own. It was comforting around the cold dampness of her palm.

"So you like to dance?" he asked as they entered the dim warmth and noise she had so recently fled. His voice sounded awkward, as though he was still not sure of her.

"Yes," she answered.

He hung her coat and his jacket on the same hook by the door. *Can't Buy Me Love* was shatteringly loud, saving her from further comments, and he swept her into the whirling, seething crowd of dancers. The band soon moved them into a slow, quieter mood with *Hey, Jude*. Though the hall smelt of sweat and beer—*Where are Kate and James?* she wondered fleetingly—Liam's shirt was fresh, with only a hint of cigarette smoke in the collar. He held her lightly, his green eyes all the time on her dark blue ones. After a while she let her head rest on his shoulder so that her cheek brushed the warm skin and soft stubble at the base of his neck. As if he had been waiting for some kind of signal from her, he drew her closer, one arm round the hollow of her back.

She did not pull away, but she was afraid—afraid of her own response, afraid of her blood flowing faster and the lazy warmth spreading throughout her body. Afraid of the consequences.

But wait. She was merely dancing with Liam. This probably meant nothing to him. Just a dance . . . just another girl. What did a casual encounter like this mean nowadays? Nothing.

A passing couple jostled them. Deirdre blinked out of her daze and saw Roger and Sheila beside them.

"Hello, Deirdre," Sheila said, the gleam of a giggle in her eyes. Roger beamed, nodding at Liam, but within a few seconds the dance had separated them again.

"They're the ones you were with in McCrae the other night. Your friends, are they?" Liam asked.

[110]

"Not close friends. Sheila is Kate Hamilton's roommate. Kate was with us then, too. Kate's probably my best friend here." She had to force herself to talk, when all she wanted to do was lose herself in the dream world suspended somewhere above the dance floor.

"Oh, then that will let me out after tonight," Liam grumbled.

"What do you mean?"

"Kate Hamilton has a reputation. I've heard her name before."

Deirdre's feet slowed and she drew back a bit, carefully examining his expression. *I'll not get caught in the middle,* she thought steadily. *If things go forward with Liam, Kate will have to learn to let be. And so will he.*

Aloud, she said, "Let's not be talking of my friends now."

His arms tightened round her. "So you like me, after all. I thought I was doomed to pine away for you."

"Not so fast. You still might have to."

"I don't think so."

"Arrogant, aren't you."

"No. Persistence and patience are my two trump cards. Arrogance? Well—"

"That's what I said."

"You're absolutely beautiful, that's what I say."

"Away with the nonsense, Liam Donnelly." The song was ending.

"It's the gospel truth."

"Shame on you. Such blarney." He pretended to look contrite. "There's no 'gospel' about it, my lad, and—" Something arrested her. A scuffle at the far end of the hall by the bar. A fight?

Liam followed her gaze. "Someone probably passed out, that's all."

"That's all? No, wait, there's Kate. Oh, something's wrong."

Leaving Liam to follow, Deirdre began pressing through the dancers toward her friend. But Kate was running for the door. Flinging past Deirdre without seeing her, she ran with skirts in hand and disappeared. Bewildered, Deirdre turned back to Liam. "Did you see Kate's face? Something terrible must have happened."

[111]

"Whose face? No . . . I was looking . . . look, isn't that the fellow who was disputin' with me Sunday?"

"Where? On the floor? Drunk? James? Oh, it can't be."

"It is, but—"

"Oh, Liam, can we do something?"

James McQueen was on the floor, oblivious to music and dancers alike. His tie and shirt were flecked with vomit, and in the pale light his face was cast of alabaster. A small circle was gathering, including Roger and Sheila. Someone rolled up an aran sweater and placed it under James's head. A jabber of voices demanded to know what had happened.

Liam pushed through the crowd and knelt beside James. "Someone get a glass of water. What happened?"

"No one seems to know," Sheila volunteered anxiously.

Someone snickered and pushed a glass of beer toward Liam. "Here, give him that. That'll wake him up."

Liam struck the glass away. "Don't be a bloody fool. Deirdre, get some water."

But Roger was there now with a cup from the janitor's office downstairs. Liam raised James's head onto his own knee, loosened his tie and collar, and chafed roughly at his face and hands. Deirdre looked on, struck by the absurdity of the scene. Kate had vanished. Liam was the only one with enough presence of mind to do anything to help.

"Maybe some idiot put something in his glass," Liam said and looked up around the circle of deadpan faces.

Now there was a commotion beyond the circle. Two CU men were making their way toward the spot: Trevor and Sam. "What's going on?" Trevor demanded, his voice as strident as a police sergeant's. "Here—" and he elbowed Liam out of the way. Deirdre frowned, angry at his rude interference, yet thankful that responsibility could be shifted. "We'll look after McQueen. Don't all stand and stare. Go and dance your silly dances. Forbes, what on earth—"

"I've no idea what happened." Roger shrugged helplessly, then threw out his arms in a wide gesture. "Donnelly thinks someone might have doctored whatever James was drinking."

"What was he drinking?" Trevor snapped.

No one knew.

"Kate was with him. She would know," Sheila said. "But I doubt if anyone would do anything like that."

Everyone looked around for Kate.

"She's gone," said Deirdre. "He looks to me," she added distastefully, "as if he's just got a bad case of the flu or something."

James's eyes flickered open, shut, then open again. He made a gurgling moan and turned his head slightly. His mouth moved, all awry.

"Are you all right?" Sam asked gently, trying to get him to sip the water.

"I felt . . . so . . . sick all of a sudden," James said, hardly above a whisper. "Where's Katherine?" he asked, his eyes searching for her.

"She . . . went out," Deirdre answered slowly.

"It's my fault. It's my fault," James cried, his voice cracking.
"What is?"

His eyes went round the circle of faces again. Slowly, he said, "I wronged her."

"He's hallucinating," Liam muttered, half-joking. No one laughed.

Picture yourself in a boat on a river
With tangerine trees and marmalade skies.
Somebody calls you, you answer quite slowly,
A girl with kaleidoscope eyes.
Cellophane flowers of yellow and green,
Towering over your head . . .
Everyone smiles as you drift past the flowers,
That grow so incredibly high.
Newspaper taxis appear on the shore
Waiting to take you away
Climb in the back with your head in the clouds
And you're gone.
Lucy in the sky with diamonds . . .

[113]

The psychedelic tune followed her out of the hall and down the endless steps. In the darkness she was reliving some old childhood nightmare that had come to her night after night: a door falling open and herself falling or flying down an eternity of broken, dark steps. No sound, no scream, no pain—only everlasting, empty, descending stairs.

She did reach the gravel, though. Without looking back, without even feeling the sharp granite nuggets under her thin shoes or the sting of rain on her bare arms, she ran as she had never run before, blind to all but her own swinging movement. More than once she stumbled. At first she ran aimlessly, conscious of nothing but the running. Direction was immaterial. But then she came to the gates by Claremont and stopped, breathing hard.

The red dress clung to her limply. She looked down distractedly. It was ruined. She must wash and be clean. She felt soiled. Turning, she ran, more slowly now, toward the gymnasium-swimming pool complex. No one would be there at this hour, and it would be warm. In the open shower room, still fully clothed, she turned on the warm water. The stinging droplets pricked her cold flesh like hot needles. Her hair unraveled and fell down her back.

Full awareness returned with the shock of water and stillness. She stood immobile under the spray, her mind working painfully over the last hour. *He liked the dress—that was it.* She should not have worn it. They had done so well, she and James, giving out tracts and talking to the other students, but the dress had aroused him. . . .

She tried to remember the sequence of it all. What had happened first? "I feel a bit funny," he'd said. Then he'd wanted to walk outside with her for some air. His head had come so close to hers when he said it that she had felt the slight prickle on her skin as his hair brushed against her face. He'd pulled her arm through his and led her toward the door. And when her body had betrayed her so that she sank against him, his arm had closed round her, tugging her against him so hard that she almost fell. She had pulled away, about to say, "Do you really feel terrible— we'd better get out of here—" when she had noticed that contorted look on his face: the same intent, intensely grim expression he'd worn earlier.

[114]

"Yes, let's," he'd said. Then, in sudden warning, he'd blurted, "Oh, I'm going . . . to be sick." And he'd reached for her again, toppling forward.

He reached for my shoulders, she said to herself over and over again, *for support. For support—because he felt so ill? But I didn't see that.* No, she'd seen repugnant ugliness, hate, as if he'd wanted to hurt her. . . . His hands had slid down below her shoulders and the vomit had risen from his mouth, the sourness dripping down her ' dress, her hands, her feet. As she relived it all, she screwed her eyes shut against the images and raised her face to the insistent water; her breath came in short, agonized gasps.

Even in the twilight of closed eyes, she saw clearly for the first time that she had not loved James at all. She had loved the illusion of status he might have given her had she become his wife. She had loved his zeal and spiritual fervor. But she had not loved him as a man. All the time she had been bitterly bewailing his blindness to her as a person, she had blinded herself to her own ignorance. He'd finally pushed himself on her because of the provocative dress. But it wasn't her fault he'd acted so strangely. With revulsion, she defended herself against him. *He could have said, "I'm not feeling well. I'm going back to the Hostel—excuse me." He could have said, "You'd better change that dress. I'll wait for you downstairs in the reception room. I need some air, anyway."* Instead, he'd used her, she realized; used the dress as an excuse to paw at her. Should she have known . . . ?

She tried to think back further. Was there some pattern? Had anything warned her? Several images floated into her mind: James in the hallway as he disdainfully ignored Deirdre; James in the prayer meeting, his voice harsh and vengeful, his face frowning as he spoke of Catholics; James outside the meeting, talking with her in rapt enthusiasm about Paisley, his eyes gleaming, his face obsessive; James in the kitchen, his superior assumption of impeccable spirituality, deliberately rousing Liam's hot temper *Why, he's unstable,* she realized with deep shock. *He's a fanatic.* He would have oppressed her, not respected her as a partner and equal. He would have snuffed out her soul.

Had she known these things subconsciously? Was that why she had suddenly wanted to reject him tonight? She hadn't wanted his hand, she recalled. She hadn't wanted his kisses, either, though he'd bent his mouth to her face more than once. She had recoiled, disgusted, chilled to the marrow. Was it the smell of his breath, sour even then? Or was it simply that he had repelled her altogether, that there was no real attraction between them after all, and shouldn't be? The old illusions were shattered. She saw that she had made a cardboard god of him and had worshiped at his shrine.

Opening her eyes at last, she looked down at the ceramic floor to see a slow red stain seeping from the soaked dress. It feathered out into tiny vein-like tributaries across the floor and toward the drain grid. *Ruined,* she thought. *All ruined.* She began to cry.

"I must find Kate, " Deirdre said.

James had been half-carried, half-dragged away to a waiting car that would bear him back to the Hostel, and the dancers had drifted back to the floor. Liam pushed his hands into his pockets. "You want me to help you?"

"Would you?"

"Right enough," he said.

Coats on, they descended the steps into the cold rain. They looked in Kate's room, in the coffee bar, in the Students' Union lounge: everywhere Deirdre could think of. Finally, they gave up and sat together in the empty reception room of Woodburn Hall. If Kate came in, she would have to pass them.

"She'll not do anything foolish, will she?" Liam asked.

"No—but she's sometimes impulsive. She might walk into something that would hurt her."

"Like what?"

"I don't know."

"She won't go far. Remember—you found her cape. She probably just wants to be by herself."

"I would think she'd rather be with James if he's ill."

Liam's mouth drew into a tight line. "Maybe. But something changed her mind about him, I'm thinking."

"No. Kate's too steady in her feelings for people. Too intense. She wouldn't change that quickly."

"Love and hate are close, you know."

"That's just a platitude, Liam. You don't believe it, do you?" She felt suddenly as if she had known him a long time, as if she could say anything to him.

He was silent, frowning. The clock on the wall clicked past the hour: only ten? "What's she like anyway?" he asked slowly, reluctantly. He did not want to spend his first evening with Deirdre talking about another woman, but he knew she was too preoccupied to think of anything else.

"You really want to know?"

"Sure—oh, can I smoke here or not?"

"I think so."

He struck a match on his shoe and lit a cigarette, then offered her a Polomint. She took one, half-smiling.

"Kate's been very kind to me," she began. "She cares deeply about what happens to all the girls in the CU. Regards it as more than a job."

"A job?"

"She's the vice-president of the group. James is the president."

"Oh, I wasn't aware there was such a political hierarchy in these religious clubs."

Ignoring his playful tone, she went on. "She'll go out of her way for us . . . do anything, I think. Of course, she's brilliant anyway, so it doesn't hurt her if she misses some of her reading to sit up half the night with someone. She's like that."

"That's good. I'm glad to hear it, honest I am."

"Then why don't people outside the Union like her."

Knocking ash into an empty teacup beside him, Liam stared at the worn carpet. "Perhaps people don't understand her. She seems to keep everyone at a distance . . . that's easily interpreted as a sense of superiority."

"True, true, but she doesn't set herself above others as far as I know. She's more vulnerable than anyone knows."

He laughed softly. "Is that right, now."

"I'm not joking, Liam. Something terrible—something really terrible—happened when she was very small, in Belfast. I don't know what it was, but she's hinted—" She was torn between loyalty to Kate and her desire that Liam understand and like her. "Anyway, she grew up alone with her dad, who apparently's very bigoted. I think she's had a hard time of it, Liam." Her eyes were smarting.

He moved closer to her, his arm resting along the back of the sofa behind her. His tone softened. "Deirdre, you shouldn't fash yourself so about her. She's stronger than you think, I don't doubt."

"But not as strong as *you* think," she said. "Some of the hardness—I know what people see because I saw it myself at first—is just put on. The shell of a tortoise . . . so she can retreat."

"Well, she does a good job of hiding any fear she has."

"You'll see, you'll see. When you get to know her."

"Get to know her? I probably won't."

"You will if I have any say in it."

"Oh, you can certainly wield influence with me, Deirdre, my girl." He blew smoke across the room and dropped the butt into the cup. She was silent, looking up from under her lashes— provocative without meaning to be. He bent toward her and eased his arm round her shoulder. The gesture was both protective and possessive. Hot color flushed her face.

"Well, go on," he said, grinning at her obvious confusion.

"What?" she drew back.

"Hit me," he laughed.

"Hit you?" she echoed stupidly.

"For being in such a hurry with you, I mean."

"Oh." She smiled and shook her head.

"You almost did one morning in the coffee bar."

"Don't remind me."

"See, I told you. Patience and perseverance. They always pay off."

They sat still together for several minutes without a word. The room was quiet except for the steady hum of the wall clock and the faint sound of music from the dance.

"Deirdre? Can I . . . I want . . . "

"What?"

[118]

"I'm Catholic, love. You know that's going to make it hard for us."

"I'm Protestant, Liam. I know that's going to make it hard for us."

"So it doesn't matter to you?"

"Yes, it matters," she said wearily. "But not as much as people think."

His face was very close to hers now. She ached somewhere inside, wanting to laugh and cry at once. He kissed her, a slow, warm kiss that left her shaking slightly. "You're so beautiful," he said simply, brushing her hair from her cheeks.

"So are you," she said, her voice unfamiliar, low and far away.

He laughed. "It's hardly a word that applies to me."

Her eyes rested on the sharp, lively lines of his face. "Oh, it does, though."

"I'm glad you've changed your mind." And he kissed her again.

Kate shivered with cold and stared sightlessly toward the cloud-covered lough. *Penance. This is how people used to do penance. "All have sinned and come short of the glory." I have. James has. Lear did. He lived in the storm for his sins* . . . . She shivered again. Reason clamored for her to get off this bench, find her cape, and go to bed. Anyone seeing her now would judge her mad, sitting out in the rain in a thin, drenched dress. Mad to run away when James needed her. Mad to hate when love was most required.

The crunch of gravel behind her warned her that someone would pass by in a few seconds. Fast, long strides. She would not look around.

The feet stopped. "Katherine?"

She knew the voice. "Yes?" She was deliberately hostile. *Please go away. Please.*

"In heaven's name what are you doing sitting out in this rain. You're drenched." Jack Monaghan stood watching her from the shadows cast by a lamp some twenty yards away. "You'll catch pneumonia if you sit out here. Here—" He shook off his jacket and

offered to put it round her. "Let me walk you back to your room."
He put down his books and tried to help her.

She turned away; her head felt light, hot. "I'll be all right, thank
you," she said haughtily, stood, and walked away.

Jack followed a few paces behind her all the way to the steps of
Woodburn. He did not turn away until she had shut the front door
in his face.

Saturday, January 24, 1970

Yesterday's light snowfall had left the Duncreggan playing field raw and muddy; the whiteness had gone, but everything lay sodden under the cold, heavy air. The creosote-stained fence around the rugby pitch was swollen and dark from humidity. Even the wind failed to dry it out. Players and spectators alike tramped ankle-deep through the churned turf.

The black and yellow jerseys of the British Army team dodged and dived everywhere. Clumsy bumblebees in a swarm. University players, in blue and red, looked smaller beside their muscular opponents. But the play had gone good-naturedly so far—no serious contest. The two teams regularly played together.

A flock of rooks clattered out of some leafless elms in one corner of the field and wheeled above the game, cawing and cackling. Below them, the green, red, and white scarves of the University; the black and yellow Army shirts; the dark coats and brown mud—all mingled in splotches of moving color.

Deirdre stood among the crowd, flanked by Jack and Sheila; they had come to watch Roger and Liam. Deirdre wore two coats: Liam's old black one and her own cloak. Even so, she was cold. Fingers of damp curled round and clutched her toes. She wished she had two pairs of thick socks like those the Army team wore.

The crowd roared as the game hurtled toward the nearest touch-line. Insults, curses, yells, and cheers went up. Everyone backed away from the line as the ball rolled out of play. Liam, his shirt, shorts, and socks plastered with mud, was playing wing three quarters. He shouted and heaved the ball over his head to the lineout. The catcher passed it straight to Roger, who as scrum-half

[121]

had to run away from the lineout as fast as he could. He dodged, passed, and kept running for a try. Sheila gripped Deirdre's arm in excitement. She jumped up and down, screaming, but four Army players piled on top of Roger before he reached the line. The play then veered off the touch-line on the far side of the pitch.

"Where's Kate?" Deirdre asked Sheila. Jack looked around, his gray eyes searching over the dark colors for a light head of hair.

"Kate?" Sheila asked, her eyes leaving the game. "Oh, you ought to know by now. She never watches rugby. Poor Kate. Misses all the fun."

Liam had the ball again. He was passing back and forth down the near wing to one of the other University players. Deirdre called loudly to him, even though she knew he wouldn't hear. Sheila followed Deirdre's gaze, then let her own attention wander. "By the way, Deirdre, what has Kate had to say about you and Liam?"

Deirdre resented the question but tried not to show it. She shifted from foot to foot, pulling her cloak closer in a gesture of defense. Through Sundays at St. Augustine's she had grown to like Sheila, but the older girl's inclination to talk too often about others was one trait that always made Deirdre wary. "Oh, very little," she answered carefully, refusing to meet Sheila's eyes. She hoped she sounded noncommittal and final enough to forestall further questions.

But Sheila's curiosity was aroused. "You mean she hasn't made any comments at all?"

Jack watched Deirdre's face and understood her dilemma. In turn, sensing his eyes on her, Deirdre felt all the more uncomfortable. She remembered the night before they had all left for Christmas holiday; Liam had already gone, and she had spent the evening with Kate.

"You must be careful not to discuss your relationship so openly," Kate had warned.

"But why?"

"No harm will come from me. But what about in Armagh, over Christmas? Not everyone will be delighted about you and Liam. Your talking about him might even cause trouble. There are Paisleyites in Armagh."

[122]

"And here," Deirdre had said, then immediately regretted her comment, knowing it had reminded Kate of James.

"Aye, true," Kate had said, "but most people at the university wouldn't think twice about a mixed relationship."

"But you do?"

"I still think it's dangerous." She had spread her hands. "Look, I've given up saying 'stay away from him' because I know you won't, and because I don't want to lose your friendship. I'm only saying, be careful. He's not a . . . he's Catholic. And maybe Marxist."

"Those are big, loose words, Kate. Don't think you've got him pigeonholed."

"I don't. I like him."

"Good! But that seems irrelevant. You don't like him for me."

Kate had looked away, unable to contradict. And Deirdre had forgiven her, aware of Kate's father's maxim on which she built her attitudes: "Two unequally yoked don't pull well together."

"Katie, he's not what you think," she had begged.

"It doesn't matter in the end what I think, Deirdre."

But Kate's opinion did matter to her, and Kate could not deceive her. Deirdre knew well enough what she must think. And she understood why, but that understanding did not lessen the tension she felt, pulled between two people she loved.

Talking now to Sheila, Deirdre felt torn between truth and loyalty. All she said was, "Well, she warned me to be careful, but hasn't seemed to want to talk much about Liam."

Jack observed this interchange without comment. His watchfulness made Deirdre squirm. Didn't Sheila know he was listening?

"It's hard to talk to her about some things," Sheila persisted, either oblivious of, or deliberately ignoring, Jack. "She puts up a wall around some subjects. Take what happened at the dance, for example. She never did tell me what went on. I had to find out from other people so I knew how to live with her for the last few days of term. James? We hardly mention his name any more."

"Gossip," Jack interposed. He sounded, but didn't look, amused.

Deirdre silently thanked him with her eyes. Kate had told her about that night, but she would never betray the revelations to

Sheila, who would spread them round the Union within a few days. Deirdre had kept to herself all Kate's outpouring of feeling: her sense of guilt, of sorrow, of the sudden realization of her own foolish infatuation.

Sheila laughed at Jack. "Oh, Kate's such a dear, really, but she gets herself into such impossible situations! As if she likes to sit in the middle of some huge jigsaw puzzle just to see if she can piece it together all by herself. And when she can't—well, she literally turns and runs. Spends days depressed, thinking and praying."

"She could do worse," Jack said dryly.

"Oh, and you know about James and Ruth, do you?"

Jack moved off with an exclamation of mild disgust.

"No," said Deirdre, feeling helpless, trapped by Sheila's prying.

"Ruth won't even speak to Kate any more. It makes our prayer cells pretty difficult."

"Sheila—I'd rather not—" How could she politely tell Sheila that she really didn't want to talk about Ruth or James or Kate?

"James is going with Ruth all of sudden. One of Kate's oldest friends, no less! What an eye-opener for Kate! But they're perfect for each other . . . deserve each other, they do."

"Sheila, please, I really don't want to hear about it, honestly." She tried to get her full attention. "Please, don't talk about Kate, or James, or Ruth. We have better things—"

"What better things, fair Deirdre?" A muddy arm suddenly went round her shoulder. It was half time. She hadn't even heard the whistle. Liam and Roger had come over together. Their legs were red from running in the cold; their faces were bright and laughing.

"How can you stand all the mud?" Sheila grumbled.

"What mud?" Liam asked innocently, daubing a little of it on Deirdre's nose.

"Don't even notice it!" Roger exclaimed. "You women ought to have a team. It's exhilarating play. Gets the blood running."

Sheila shuddered. "I'd rather play hockey. But you're probably warmer than we are, even with all our woolies."

"For a while anyway," Liam said. He was looking around. "Did anyone bring oranges?"

Sheila pulled a plastic bag from her shoulder bag. The oranges

[124]

were cut into thin segments that fell open as she unwrapped them.
Liam, Roger, and several others ate them in proper style, the juice
spurting over their chins, the empty peel flying backward over
their shoulders. They made the appropriate lip-smacking noises
and wiped their hands on their shirts.

Jack strolled back to his friends now, lightly patting Roger's
back. "Good play."

"Thanks. We're not going to win, but it's a good game. Can you
stay for the whole thing?"

"Probably not. It's been good to get out of the library for a wee
while, but I should wend my way back to the books, I suppose."

"Such discipline!"

Jack smiled. "Partly, partly. But I need time for other things as
well."

"Tell me. What now?"

"Oh, Liam will tell you."

"Tell him what?" Liam asked.

"About St. Jerome's. Remember?"

Liam thought for a minute, frowning slightly. "Oh—yes. When
Jack was down at the Commission last week, he got talking to
some people from Creggan. They said that children's home up
there—St. Jerome's—is looking for students to go up and do odd
jobs now and then."

"Like what?" Sheila asked.

"To play with the weans, mostly, I think," Liam said.

Jack added, "But also to do some of the heavy outside work the
sisters can't do."

"You should ask Kate to go, Roger," Sheila put in.

"For the heavy outside work?" he laughed.

"No, silly, the children. She likes little kids so much. If she could
screw up the courage to set foot in a Roman orphanage, she'd love
it."

"Why should I ask her?"

"She's more likely to do it if you ask her," Sheila said. "Liam
and Jack would hardly—"

"I could ask her," Deirdre volunteered. "And I'd be glad to go
myself."

"You could go together," Liam said.

"Well, that would help," Jack said. "If you two girls would go up now and then."

"And you?" Deirdre questioned.

"Now and then, too," he said.

"You'll chat up the pretty sisters," Liam laughed.

"Right," said Jack sourly.

"Do you really think Kate would go?" Sheila asked.

Deirdre thought for a moment. "She might. She's been talking quite a bit recently about what's going on in Derry. She's as concerned as anyone, I think—especially about the children. Let me ask her. I'm glad you told us about it, Jack. If I'd waited on Liam—"

Liam suddenly swung her around in a muddy polka and in full view of everyone—players and friends alike—kissed her full on the mouth. "There, that'll shut you up. I'll see you later."

"I can't wait," she laughed.

"Time to go at the Army lads again," Roger commented, squeezing Sheila's arm.

"Ugh, you're so muddy!"

"Make sure you beat the Sassenachs, Liam," Jack called lightly.

Friday, February 6

Deirdre had parted from Liam in the basement of the Students' Union where he was to rehearse with some of his friends for a folk club night on Saturday. She envied him. When he worked on a philosophy essay or an economics problem, he worked with a furious intensity and a tight, self-imposed discipline that left him time to do so many other things: the housing survey, folksinging, rugby, time with her. . . .

How different from herself! She worked so slowly. Compared with Liam, she was desultory and dilatory. Her reading dragged on all day; she had to drive herself to be finished in time to go out with him on a Friday or Tuesday . . . or whenever. Sometimes she wondered if she should have come to the University at all.

A collection of Maupassant's short stories demanded her time now. Under her desk, she scuffed her feet. She rocked back on her chair and craned to look out of the small, high window. She often wished for Kate and Sheila's great bow windows that faced the lough and the docks. Hers was mean and meager. She often wished, too, for the airy rectangle of her bedroom window at home. Even there, in the crowded row-house back streets of Armagh, she could look out onto small squares of lawn with an occasional greenhouse, neat shrubs, snapdragons, sweet williams, rows of scarlet runner beans tied to bamboo poles, banked mounds of potatoes in white flower. No matter what time of year, there was color. Here, however, there was nothing to see but the slatey lines of skylight and rooftop; the ugly red-brick vertigo of a Victorian chimney top; the gray turrets and gables of the library's back wall;

[127]

the empty and incongruous tennis court surrounded by crisscross chain-link and two inches deep in dreary snow.

Students passed in and out of the back door of the Great Hall. Perhaps she should go down there herself and look in her pigeonhole to see if any letters had come from home. No, it was too much bother to put on her boots and coat just for that. And Maupassant would still be lurking in the corner when she returned.

Down below, two students she didn't know were lobbing snowballs at each other. The man tried to hide behind a tree as he rolled the snow expertly. It was too light for a well-packed ball, but he aimed so accurately that he hit his girl friend with a splatter of white almost every time. Her cries of indignation and helpless laughter floated up to the window as she scooped up her revenge, but she was losing the battle. After a few more minutes of shouts and laughter, the two went rolling over and over in the snow down the slight incline from the tennis court. When they stopped in the mess of dead grass, mud, and snow at the bottom, she pelted his face with snow and he bent to kiss her.

Deirdre turned away wistfully and started reading again. Once she was drawn into the story, she didn't find it hard to go on. How would Maupassant twist the tale to surprise her this time? He always had a trick to play on the reader.

Coming to the end of "La Parure," she smiled to herself, rocking back in her chair and letting her attention wander again. *Liam.* An inner light radiated through her at the thought of him, a sense of completeness. How he'd laugh and tease if she ever said she thought he was God's gift to her! But that's how she saw him. Kate, Roger, Sheila, Caroline . . . these friends had filled voids left from church and home in Armagh. Pascal, Descartes, and Comte . . . Maupassant, Molière, Balzac, Proust, Baudelaire, and Mallarmé . . . these writers had filled voids left from grammar school. And Liam . . . he filled the emptiest void of all: that filled usually by brothers, sisters, parents. She did not miss home any more. Like her parents, Liam took her at face value. He did not seem to want to change her or rearrange her life. Nor did he veer from his consistent feeling for her. Love it was, and no mistake. If he had loved other women before, he appeared to give no thought to them

[128]

now—no reminiscence, no comparisons. *Comparisons*, her grandmother Douglas had always said, *are utterly odious.* She had all his attention, and she basked in its warmth and light.

She questioned now whether she loved him as unreservedly and with as much commitment as he loved her. He had made some changes for her, not because she had asked him to but because he knew they might be important to her; he had cut his hair and slowed down on the beer and cigarettes. Externals, right enough, but in doing so, he showed a respect for her, an understanding of her inevitable sensitivity to what her friends would think. In fact, he seemed more concerned about some of those matters than she was at the moment; she was still caught up in the excitement and magic of their first weeks together. Only recently had she started to allow her mind to travel ahead on the path of consequences; the early glitter of their new love was only just beginning to be tarnished by anxious thought about spiritual differences, about what her mother thought, about what God thought.

Suddenly she saw the strange contradiction between her idea that Liam had been given her by God and her new suspicion that He might not endorse their love. How could He approve a love that was not going to grow into marriage unless Liam changed deeply? Was she supposed to change him herself? Something told her that she wasn't. And anyway, she didn't want to change him.

Uneasiness had thus begun to dull the shine of her joy. It had started at home with her parents' reaction to Liam. Not that she had taken him home; she wasn't ready for that yet. But she had told them about him almost as soon as she was in the door. Her father had received the news with a nod and a subdued, "Well, that's nice, Dee." But her mother had gone quiet, and for three days offered no comment at all. When she did, her comments surprised and hurt, and sounded eerily like Kate's. So she had given her mother an I-don't-know-how-you-of-all-people-can-say-this challenge. And her mother, more stone-faced and gray than Deirdre had ever seen her, had said, "Love, there's a whale of difference between 1944 and 1969—a whale more than just twenty-five years. A difference of marches, bombs, and barricades. I hope you both know what you're startin'. It's dangerous."

If Kate and her mother—her two highest standards of womanly

perfection—both doubted what she was doing . . . should she back out now? *No*. Vehemently her heart and mind rejected the idea. She loved and was loved in return. There could be no wrong in a love like that, even if it did cross some barbed-wire borders. Like Liam, she had chosen. And now she would follow her choice to its conclusion.

She turned the pages of her book despondently and began to make small notes on what she had just read. Out in the hall, the telephone rang, though she was hardly aware of it until one of the women thumped the door and shouted, "Deirdre? Phone."

It was Jack. Would she like to go over to St. Jerome's again this afternoon? A pang of doubt. Would Liam mind? She had gone there with Jack once already. No, Liam would be glad she was helping the sisters and the children. She pictured them now: the nuns with their serene faces, severe headpieces, and solemn black habits; the orphans with their passive, empty expressions and dispirited play. The children at the convent home needed so much more than an afternoon of her attention. The sisters were devoted, but there were just too many children to love.

"Well . . . Jack . . . I'm not sure."

"You're studying."

"Yes, but I might be glad to leave the books awhile. You're going up now?"

"In a few minutes."

"What do they have for you to do this time?"

"Move some boxes—that's what they mentioned. But the children and the sisters liked you. They'd be happy if you'd come back."

"All right. I'll come. I'll see if Kate'll come, too. Is that all right with you?"

Soft laughter on the other end of the line. "Aye, you can ask her, I suppose. She was too busy last time, wasn't she?"

"Yes, she was. But it's Friday afternoon. She might be glad to go."

Deirdre listened briefly outside Kate's door a few minutes later. Silence. She knocked lightly. Sheila's voice called her in. Watery sunlight filled the room, which was tidy, as usual, only on Kate's side. Balls of wadded paper dotted the floor around Sheila.

[130]

"You're looking for Kate?"

"Yes."

"In the library."

"Is she writing an essay? I see you are."

"She's not," Sheila groaned. "I am. For some reason I seem to get the first seminar paper every term. She's over there reading."

Deirdre found Kate in the tower of the library. She was holding a book on her lap and staring absently over the lough.

"Katie?"

"What? Oh, Deirdre."

"Are you working very hard?"

"Not terribly. Why?"

Deirdre noticed in Kate a certain stillness and withdrawal. Had she perhaps been praying rather than reading? She asked the question as she took the chair opposite.

"Oh—unconsciously maybe."

Deirdre leaned forward. "Kate, I'm going up to St. Jerome's again. Jack has to go, too. They want him to move some heavy cartons or something. Would you be coming with us?"

Still the quiet, introspective gaze. "Well, no, I don't think so." Kate shifted her eyes, but seemed to avoid Deirdre's. "But thanks for asking me again."

"Are you all right?" Deirdre reached out to touch Kate's hand.

"No . . . yes . . . no. Oh, I just have cramps, that's all."

"Oh, that's enough."

"I shouldn't complain. I can read, at least."

"But wouldn't you feel better if you got up and did something? Exercise helps a wee bit, doesn't it?"

"Sometimes. But today I'd rather just sit." She hunched forward slightly. Her face was paler than usual.

"If you're sure, then." Reluctantly, Deirdre slid out of the chair and stood.

"Sure."

"But will you come some time?"

"Oh, I will. Though actually I'd almost rather do something outside—like that survey you said they were doing. It would be more . . . neutral somehow. I wouldn't have to talk to—" she

[131]

stopped, her eyes moving out to the lough again, her forehead creasing, "to the nuns, I mean."

Deirdre smiled at Kate's inability to hide her bias. "You're scared of the sisters?"

"Not scared, of course not."

"What then?"

Kate shrugged. "What would I say? I wouldn't know how to talk to them, Deirdre."

"But they're just women like you and me. Some of them not much older, in fact."

Kate tapped her head. "I know that up here. But there are some old inhibitions I'd have to overcome first. In here." Her fingertips touched her breast. "What could I possibly have in common with them?"

"As much as I do. They're ordinary women, Kate. Just ordinary women who love God—"

"Who are Catholics," Kate broke in.

"Catholics, Kate," Deirdre said gently, "not lepers."

Kate covered her eyes with one hand. "Oh, let's not start this old debate again, please." Then she looked up, her face tinged with regret. "Honestly, I don't mean to hurt your feelings. I know how you see things. I know the differences mean less to you than to me. But I can't change overnight." Her voice dropped. "And anyway, I really do have cramps."

Kate's tone told Deirdre that the subject was closed.

With stained linen aprons over their habits, some of the younger sisters moved in and out of the wide circle of occupied highchairs in the convent refectory. In the center of the low-ceilinged room was a large table spread with a frayed oilcloth and covered with an assortment of bowls, spoons, jugs, and open dishes of food. A crucifix gazed down from the wall.

Sister Celestine was in charge today. Sister was small—not even as tall as Deirdre. The white facepiece accentuated the roundness of her freckled face and the intelligence of her bright, bespectacled eyes. That she loved the children, Deirdre saw immediately. Her

[132]

small feet moved quickly back and forth from table to highchair and back again. She did not seem to notice either the heat or the noise in the room; she was as unperturbed by tears as by food dropped, spilled, or thrown. She had directed Deirdre to fill two or three bowls at the table and to feed several children at once.

"One spoon will do, darlin'," she said. Sister Celestine called everyone "darlin'" except the Mother Superior.

Sitting in front of three highchairs, Deirdre doubted that one spoon and two hands were enough. Of the three children she had chosen, the two boys had runny noses. She looked around for paper handkerchiefs but saw none. Some gray dishrags lay on the oilcloth, so she got up to fetch them. They reeked of sour milk.

The dark-haired baby began to cry, his face puckering; tears spilled out and his mouth opened into a red cavern. Frustrated, she ran out to the stone sink in the adjoining scullery. The hot water seemed slow to come. Behind her, all three children now began to wail. One of the sisters tried to hush them, but they went on crying. Back she came with the dishrags and wiped their faces.

Again, she picked up bowl and spoon. The food looked flat and uninviting: chopped beef in a gummy gravy with lumpy mashed potatoes and overcooked cabbage greens. But the babies were hungry. They opened their mouths greedily, like baby birds.

Once the hunger pangs had subsided, the room became quieter. Deirdre could hear the low murmuring of one sister talking to another. Some of the babies banged spoons, giggled, and leaned over to poke each other's arms and faces.

"What are their names?" Deirdre asked a nun who was sitting a few feet away.

The sister looked over vaguely. "That one is Sean—the one you're giving the potato to just now. In the middle? That's Josephine. And the other one's Peter."

Deirdre looked back at the babies, wishing she could take them home to her mother. There would be no more weans at home until Bridget or Ann brought the first grandchild home. All three had eyes as fragile and blue as cornflowers, but there any similarity ended. A mop of unruly black hair flopped over Sean's small ears and forehead, and he noisily slapped his hand on the tray. Josephine was blonde, fair-skinned, and finely made—a bit like

Kate, even, with her skinny little legs hanging down from the highchair and her eyes so intense and serious. Of the three, Peter was the least lively. His body seemed limp, his eyes dull and vacant. There was no joy in him.

"Why are there so many children here?" Deirdre asked Sister Celestine later when the two of them were washing dishes in the scullery. The other sisters had taken the small children off to the playroom while the older children were fed.

Sister Celestine sank her hands into a soft mound of soapsuds and vigorously rubbed at the bowls and spoons; her hands looked red and chapped. She did not look at Deirdre as she answered, "There's the pity of it. God save them, we have too many."

"But why?" Deirdre persisted.

"Lots of reasons, darlin'. Some weren't born to married girls, mind." She paused. "Some came late into families with fathers out of work and too many to feed already. Some came from broken homes or abusive homes, the poor wee darlin's. Some were abandoned, left right here for us to take in." Sister Celestine's sing-song revealed she was up from County Kerry or thereabouts, and Deirdre warmed to her.

"How do you manage them all? And what about the other children?" She pointed back to the dining room where fifty or more children were now eating.

"It's hard sometimes. We manage by the grace of God, Deirdre. And with lay workers. And with help from kind souls like yourself and . . . what's his name . . . the one you came with?"

"Jack Monaghan."

"Ah, yes—John. He's been coming for several weeks now. A hard worker, he is. Has a vocation too, God bless him. I wish all the fathers would care as much for the poor as this one will."

Deirdre realized the sister presumed she was a Catholic. She would not disillusion her. "Yes, Jack's unusual. Everyone likes him."

Jack, meanwhile, bent his back for another box of apples. The crates were heavy: layer upon layer of fruit rested on gray corrugated cardboard. He heaved them out of the cool woodshed behind the convent and staggered down the ten-yard pathway across the end of the orchard and so into the back door of the storeroom. From the crates came the sweetish scent of slight decay. The apples had kept well since last autumn, but brown spots and wrinkles were now beginning to mar them.

Inside the windowless, apple-scented storeroom, five sisters stood clustered round a bare, scrubbed table under a single light bulb. One sister lifted each layer of apples out of the crate and onto the table; another wiped each piece of fruit with a cloth; another pared with silent efficiency; two others cut out the cores and brown spots and dropped the apples into a large aluminum kettle that stood beside her on the uneven flagstone floor. They were enjoying the work. He could hear snatches of their conversation as he went in and out of the door. "Sister Theresa said we should . . . no, this one's no good . . . and Father Clement asked him if he'd see fit to let him give him the last rites, but he wouldn't hear of it at all . . . ugh, there's a maggot in this one . . . Peter's lookin' terrible pale these days . . . I shouldn't think she should! . . . she's a little better than she was."

"You don't need to bring us any more, Mr. Monaghan." The silent sister spoke suddenly as Jack deposited another crate on the end of the table. Four other pairs of eyes rested on him simultaneously. He stood there for a moment, feeling slightly foolish. His arms and shoulders ached.

"You're a big help," one of the sisters said.

He found a handkerchief in his jacket pocket and wiped his hot face. "Thanks," he murmured, turning aside for a minute. The cold outside had made his eyes and nose run, too. "Is there anything else I can do while I'm here?"

The sisters exchanged eloquent glances. Then, one said, "Aye, if you know anything about machines."

"Machines?"

"Washing machines."

"Well—I could look."

"We've an old Hotpoint. Been used every day for years. Run to death. Finally gave out today."

"I don't know a thing about them." He looked doubtful. "I might do more damage than good. But I could try."

[135]

"He might do more damage than good," one sister repeated. "Let him try."

"Wait up, though," Jack said. "Haven't you phoned the shop it came from?"

They looked at each other again. "They take so long to come. And charge so much."

Jack thought quickly. "I met a man on Fahan Street last week— I've been helping with a housing survey—who's been out of work for weeks. Laid off. He's your man." And he gave them the name.

"Then you can help with the apples now."

"If you wash your hands first."

"There's a tap outside on the wall."

Jack worked beside the three who were peeling and coring. Their conversation ebbed, temporarily restrained by his presence. But they were curious about him. Why would he want to help up at St. Jerome's? What was he doing at the University? Where was he from? They'd heard he was studying to join the priesthood— was that true?

He began to smile. "Oh—I didn't know this was the Inquisition up here or I wouldn't have come."

He looked around the table and stopped himself—just in time— from winking at one of the more attentive sisters. He didn't find it hard to distinguish them, now that he stood among them. The uniformity of their habits accentuated rather than diminished the differences in their facial features. It was hard, though, to tell their ages; their faces were smooth and bright. Mentally, he nicknamed them: "the silent one," who pared as if the Second Coming were in an hour or less, and who seemed to be in charge; "the strong one," who lifted out each layer of apples; "the round one," whose smile never left her face as she wiped off the winter's grit, dead flies, and dust; "the talker," who talked more than she cored; and "the tall one."

They seemed at ease with him now, and he knew they would not have talked so freely with an ordained man. But because he was going to be ordained, because he had already chosen the celibate life, he was accepted as a little brother who understood them and who, in turn, could expect understanding.

He found himself talking much more than usual, thinking they

[136]

might be hungry for ideas and words from another, less narrow world. He told them of his childhood in West Belfast. The tall one, it turned out, had known his older sister. He told them, too, how his family had singled him out—from the time he was confirmed at seven—for the priesthood. "Jackie's the one to be called," they had all said. "Look at how he reads. Such a deep thinker. Prays longer than Dermot and Vincent and Eugene." Jack laughed, recalling it. "At first it made me feel special and important. I loved serving up at the altar. Then when I turned sixteen and left school, I rebelled. I was sick of hearing about it. I wanted out. My mother was so disappointed. 'You'll break my heart,' she said. I took to drinking. I got in trouble—well, I suppose I can't tell it all."

The sisters blinked. Then one of them laughed. "You don't need to. We've all known wild fellows like yourself."

Someone hushed her.

"It's all right. I can take it." He looked down at the apple he was peeling. The work was awkward and slow for him, but no one noticed.

"Then, tell us," said the silent one, "what brought you back to God? And what you're doing up in Derry, of all places."

"I was working for Harland & Wolff. Started out as carpenter's apprentice. I liked the job and seemed to pick it up quickly . . . so if you ever need any carpentry done here—"

"We have a carpenter, a lay worker from Creggan . . . bless you . . . that's nice of you to offer, but . . ."

"Well, I worked there six or seven years till I got restless again. I'd not been living at home most of the time—usually with a friend—" he did not meet their eyes, "but I felt—oh, now how can I explain—" He shrugged. "Something was missing. Life went on in a routine that seemed meaningless. Get up. Pack a lunch. Work all day. Read the paper or see a film or go to an evening class. Fall into bed. Then start again." He scanned the sisters' faces. Two of them nodded in understanding. "So I moved home. By now my mother'd learned to hold her peace about the priesthood. Never said a word. And—funny—that got me thinking more than if she'd started on me again. Dermot, Vincent, Eugene—all married and gone by then, they were. My sister was

[137]

at home, Eileen, and we spent a lot of time talking. Eileen—now there's a good Christian girl for you. Very deep, very gentle."

The sisters smiled. "Go on," they urged. "You tell it well."

"Well, Eileen's married now. But being the last to leave home, she'd had time and inclination to grow into a woman of prayer. More than my mother, even, who herself never missed a single Mass or parish retreat. Used to go to Mass every morning. Eileen got to going with her as a wee girl while the rest of us, all boys we were, went out and fought on the school playground. What a bunch!" The storeroom was dead quiet except for the scrape of knives on apples and the soft drop of fruit into the kettle. He was enjoying his tale. Roger had heard it with as much enthusiasm as these sisters, but even Roger couldn't fully understand how everything had fallen into place for him. "But then, when we'd all left home, Eileen kept going to Mass anyway. Like my mother— never missed. So when I moved back in, she was the one who talked to me the most. 'Have you thought about your vocation, Jack?' she'd say. 'Not much,' I'd say. And in her gentle way, she'd say, 'Now how do you think you're going to shut God out like that? Do you have to be stubborn like Paul the Apostle until God blinds you into seeing what He wants?' After a year of that kind of talk with Eileen—about the time she got married—I went down to see the priest—" He nodded to the tall sister. "You'd know him, I'm thinking—Father Maurus O'Hanlon?"

She smiled, "Oh, aye. Christened us all, and said the Christian Burial for both my grandfathers. Father Maurus now, he's in parish work yet?"

"Oh yes."

"He's seventy-five, surely?"

"I don't know. Ageless, he seems. Anyway, he'd been keeping an eye on me. Said I should start out in classics and philosophy at University College." Jack laughed suddenly. "But I hadn't a mind for such meaty stuff just yet. I wanted to go to the New University instead."

"You must have come when it opened, then?"

"No. Father Maurus wouldn't hear of it. Didn't think the University would survive. He seemed to have an inkling that Derry was going to 'blow up,' as he said it. Told me I should start out at

[138]

Queen's if I'd not go to Dublin. As it turned out, I might as well have started up here."

"You might, aye."

"I prevailed on him to let me come up here this past September."

"Reading classics?"

"Oh, not at all. Literature."

"English?"

"English and Irish both."

They began to ply him with questions about the New University; few people knew much about it in these early days. He told them all he knew. Then they began to ask about the rest of his training.

"Father Maurus wants me to go down this summer and spend some time talking with the rector at Maynooth to see if I'd really be wanting the seminary down there. I'll do that, I think."

"You'll be down there by the end of next year, then?"

"Yes."

"And be ordained by 1975? Dear Lord, doesn't that sound far away?"

Jack smiled. "Too far, sometimes."

"And your vocation's to the secular priesthood, is it? You'll not be going into a religious order?"

He shook his head. "No, not unless something changes. God wants me in different work than that, I know . . . social service of some kind . . . out in the world with young people or in the slums. God knows."

Because Jack wanted to see if the University bookshop was still open, he and Deirdre got off the Creggan Heights bus in the Diamond and went together on foot down Shipquay Street. Deirdre disliked Shipquay Street. *There'll never be peace in Ireland until blood has flowed down Shipquay Street*, Roger had once said on the way to St. Augustine's. The street lent itself to such doomsaying. Running steeply downhill from the walled part of the city that overlooked Bogside, it ended abruptly opposite the Guildhall, not too far from the British Army barracks. *Blood would flow fast down those gutters,* Deirdre thought in horror. She could never even come up to buy a book at the A.P.C.K. without a shiver.

Halfway down the hill, Jack hesitated. The street was strangely empty. Alerted by Jack's stillness, Deirdre looked around; several shopkeepers were boarding up their windows.

They could not yet see into Guildhall Square; ash-gray walls and ancient cannons blocked the view, and dusk was falling. The square was always busy: buses revving and pulling in and out, people hurrying in and out of the Northern Bank, cars honking, boats in the Foyle waters blowing warning whistles, cranes whirring over the hoppers down on Prince's Quay. But the sound ascending to Deirdre and Jack as they stood in the middle of the pavement was none of these; it was the roar of a crowd.

"Wait here, Deirdre, till I see what's happening." Jack started down the hill without her.

She glanced around frantically. "Oh—no—please, let's turn back. Don't make me stay here by myself."

He turned. "I didn't mean to frighten you. Come on, then, if you want to stay with me."

She hurried to catch up with him. "Shouldn't we go back up and around the other way?"

A sharp bang in the Diamond made them both jump.

Jack swung round. "Oh—it's just another board going up. . . . But I don't know if it'd be any better going the other way. If a riot starts down here, all Bogside'll be up in arms." He steadied her with his hand on her arm. She had begun to shake. "Here—would it make you feel better to take my arm?"

"No, of course not," she flashed back. "How would it be looking to anyone who knows us?" She set her jaw. "We'll do whatever you think best, though . . . I mean about the way we should—"

Suddenly male voices, yelling and cursing, and the tramp of feet sounded behind them, beyond the crest of Shipquay Street. Twenty or more youths, one of them displaying a small Tricolour, emerged from the darkness on the west side of the Diamond and came marching down the hill in military formation. They were gangly, wiry fellows with heavy boots. The Tricolour appeared luminous in the twilight.

[140]

Jack saw no sign of weapons, but was not going to wait for a confrontation with them. He grabbed Deirdre's arm. "Like it or not," he said, "we'll be safer this way . . . in the square . . . more anonymous . . . hurry . . . let's get down there."

They fled ahead of the small battalion under the arch of the wall and into the square. The place teemed with people. Opposite them on the lighted steps of the Guildhall and below it, Protestant crowds waved Union Jacks and chanted, "Paisley. Paisley. No surrender." Nearer to them, at the back of the crowd, enraged Catholic men and boys surged forward with fists raised in fury. Skirting the edge of the crowd, Jack led Deirdre along in the shadows of the city wall by the Magazine Gate and out toward Strand Road. Over the roar of the mob, he yelled, "All we want is the British Army. Then there'll be a full-scale riot."

Deirdre stared back in terror. She caught a glimpse of a big man in clerical garb coming out of the Guildhall with his hands raised as if in victory. Holding a bull horn in one hand, he was silhouetted in the yellow light of the wide door behind him. Below the steps, the crowd stilled somewhat to listen.

"There are one million Protestants in this country, and half a million Catholics. We will not bow to Rome."

Again the front of the crowd shouted, "No surrender, no!"

He went on, warmed by their response. "We must let the agents of Rome know that we intend to stay in Ulster—and to stay in charge. . . . We will not talk peace with the Scarlet Woman as long as she doesn't accept the Northern Irish Constitution. Until then, the Catholic Church is the enemy. Ulster will be Protestant! Ulster will be free!"

"Burn the Union Jack. Burn it! Burn it!" screamed a man's voice a few feet away from Deirdre and Jack. The fury erupted again.

Is Liam here? Deirdre suddenly wondered, her stomach muscles tightening in fear. If he had known Paisley was having a rally, surely he'd be down here with other civil rights men to protest. Had he truly been rehearsing for folk club—or was that just a cover? She looked around again, wildly this time, as if expecting him to rush out of the crowd toward her.

Jack pulled her along. "Don't turn round, Deirdre."

[141]

They had almost reached the edge of the square when a man staggered out of the crowd just ahead of them; a torn Union Jack dangled limply from his left arm. For a minute, Deirdre thought he was wounded. He clutched at his stomach with his right hand and stumbled forward in front of them, swaying, and blocked their path.

"Hey, big boy! Got a fancy little piece there, ain't ya?"

Jack stood still, holding Deirdre tightly. "Get out of the way. You're drunk," he said, his voice low and menacing. Deirdre hardly recognized it. Her heart thudded.

The drunk spat. "Filthy, whoring Taigs!" He lurched toward them, his hand out to grab Deirdre's coat.

Breaking free of Jack, she dodged to the side, ducked past the drunkard, and began to run. Jack shoved the man against the wall and sprinted after her. They did not stop running until they reached the back gates of the University.

Breathlessly they leaned against the wall at the foot of the path that would lead them up to the Students' Union. Deirdre began to cry, great sobs of relief and release.

"I should've given him a good beating," Jack gasped.

"No—no."

"I should have," he said between his teeth. "No one should talk to a woman that way."

Deirdre's crying suddenly turned to broken laughter. "Indeed you shouldn't. What sort of a priest will you be . . . if you get in a fight with a drunkard . . . for wee Protestant girls mistaken for Catholics?" She looked up the wooded hill. "But never mind, we're safe." In the quiet of falling darkness not a sound came but the swish of a passing car.

Jack's breathing had slowed. "Aye, for now."

She was silent as they trudged up the dark pathway, sobered by his long, sorrowful face. Light snow had begun to fall. Dimly, the sound of singing floated out of the Students' Union into the darkness. Then, in a warm pool of light that spilled out of the coffee bar's back door, she saw Liam, hunched over his guitar.

Come all you young rebels and list while I sing,
For love of one's land is a terrible thing.

[142]

It banishes fear with the speed of a flame,
And makes us all part of the patriot game.

The mad hysteria of Guildhall Square seemed almost a world away.

Friday, May 8

Snow had given way to snowdrops; crocuses and tulips to billowing clouds of blackthorn and apple blossom in the shrubbery. Kate sat on a dry-stone wall outside Woodburn. She swung her legs lightly. How good to feel a light wind and dry, warm air on her skin. The University lay quietly under the blush of mid-afternoon spring sunshine. Many of the students had picked up their open-book examinations from their tutors and gone home for the weekend or to the beach at Fahan. Deirdre had invited Kate to Armagh, but Kate had refused and was waiting to see Father Kennedy to pick up her own exam. She had gone to his office once, but, hearing two male voices inside, had decided to wait outside the lecture building.

A cuckoo called from somewhere in the trees down by the Strand Road gates. Then she heard a squeaking sound as someone pushed open a door. It was Jack Monaghan. He came quickly up the steps, a sheaf of papers in hand. Seeing Kate, he nodded, slowing slightly.

"You're waiting on Father Colm?"

"Yes." She slid off the wall. "He's free now?"

"He is, yes."

She passed him and descended to the building. Jack still made her uneasy. It was odd. Her friends—Roger and Sheila and even Deirdre—spent a great deal of time with Jack, yet she did not know him. And it was odd, too, the curiosity he had about their faith, their particular brand of Protestantism. He swerved around it like a hypnotized moth around a burning candle. *But he's not getting himself burned yet*, Kate thought. She knew from Roger and

Sheila that he went to Mass at the Roman Cathedral, St. Eugene's, every week, and that he regularly traveled home to Belfast to see his spiritual mentor. No, he was sticking to his traditions. Traditions of a religion, like Father Kennedy's, that was as alien, obscure, and mystical to her as Hinduism or Buddhism. And she saw it as no more that that: religion—not faith or the practice thereof.

As she entered Father Kennedy's office, she glanced around the room. She had been here but a few times, and had never examined it closely. Her incipient interest in the lecturer made her curious about his environment. The walls were bare of all but a small brown crucifix. The desk was empty of books and papers—just a pen and an ashtray full of used matches and bent cigarette stubs.

Father Kennedy was leaning back in a swivel chair, seeming somehow smaller—frailer—than he did when commanding his students' attention from a podium or the end of a seminar table. Kate noticed that his skin was slightly yellowed, more parchment-like than ever. His habit was wrinkled, falling in disheveled folds to the floor and twisting partly around the base of his chair. In his right hand, white except where stained by nicotine, he had the habitual cigarette, and as Kate entered, he leaned forward to stub it out, though he did not rise to meet her.

"Ah, Miss Hamilton, come in."

"Thank you." She closed the door carefully, snapping it tightly behind her, and sat down facing him.

"Have you your essay there?"

"Yes, I have."

"Let me see."

She passed it across the desk.

He riffled through it. "It's longer than I asked you to write."

"Is it?" Kate watched him closely. Did he mind?

Now he flicked the pages one by one. "This looks thorough," he said. "I'll get it back to you by the end of the exams." A brief pause, then he looked up. "Do you feel ready for them?"

"Only partially," she said. "I never feel ready enough to satisfy myself."

"Perhaps you expect too much of yourself." Leaning forward

[145]

again, he put the essay to one side and said, "Now these are your questions for the exam."

Kate stood up and stretched across the desk to take them from him.

"No, wait a minute," he said, and drew them back.

She sat down again, embarrassed.

"I want to add one question. I'd like you to look into some of Graham Greene's novels. Have you read *The Power and the Glory* or *The End of the Affair?*"

"No," she said coldly. "No, I've not."

He cocked his head and looked at her with a sly look. "Do you think you'll have time to read some of his novels this week?"

She shrugged. "Perhaps. It depends how many you want me to read, I suppose."

"I want you to read at least the two I mentioned. And I want you to consider this question." He took the paper and scrawled down on it in his large, uneven script, *"Is it inevitable that we read Greene's novels in the context of his Catholicism?"* He pushed the sheet across the desk to her.

She read it unhappily. "I don't think I can answer this," she said, chewing her lower lip.

"Well, of course you can't yet. You've not read the novels."

"But I don't know enough about Catholicism," she objected.

He smiled a benign, polite smile, looking out at her through his pince-nez with his eyelids only half open. "Then you'll learn," he said evenly.

"Are you requiring this question of me?"

"Yes. I want you to do this first. When you've done it, choose two of the others."

"Why are you making me do this? You know where I stand." She was pale, shaking a little.

Kennedy put his hands together, the tips of his long fingers touching, almost in an attitude of prayer. "Katherine . . . may I call you that? . . . you've done very well in literature this year. But I think you'll not stop with just a B.A. Honors, even if it is a First. Am I right?"

She nodded, but with reluctance. Concession to him was usually dangerous.

"You'll go on, probably to Oxford for the M.A. . . . or perhaps even further, I don't know. But I want you to have a more liberal education . . . in the best sense of that phrase. Sometimes I wish I could send off all you students to the States for a liberal arts education to broaden you out a wee bit. Some of you are so limited to your own interests; you've not read widely enough."

Kate frowned. "Oh, I don't know if that's true."

"If it's not," he made the thrust swiftly, "why haven't you read some of the Catholic writers? It's time you broadened out, Katherine. You've determinedly avoided, at least since I've been your tutor, reading in the Catholic tradition. Joyce and Synge, O'Casey, Hopkins . . . you've neglected them all. You can't leave out a whole realm of English and Irish—even American—literature. You can't ignore them, as if they don't exist. You won't even begin to understand world literature until you've read some of their work. That's why I'm giving you this question."

Kate looked down at the paper before her; she shifted in her chair. "Well, I have no choice, have I?" Her voice sounded small, even in the small room.

"No, that's right. You don't. Understand, Katherine—I'm not trying to make you do this just because I feel like playing devil's advocate," he went on, pinning her with his fierce blue gaze. "I want you to do it for your own good, your own scholarship, your own growth. I told you at the beginning of this year that I wanted you to read Gerard Manley Hopkins." His voice dropped to a whisper of urgent enthusiasm. "You'd enjoy him so much. His work is startlingly beautiful. But you held off, wouldn't read him. Now you may find you want to."

"After I've read Graham Greene?" she laughed bitterly.

"Yes, after you've read Graham Greene," he repeated, ignoring her sarcasm. "Greene's vision is—" the long fingers parted, fluttering as he searched for the words, "—almost a Calvinist vision." He laughed suddenly, without humor. "He doesn't miss for a minute the human depravity that you Presbyterians are always talking about." He shrugged. "Hopkins, on the other hand, looks at the glory of God. He sees the wonder of God's creation. The wonder of salvation and redemption."

[147]

Kate averted her eyes. How could he talk so glibly of salvation and redemption? What did he know about either?

"Well—you see what you can make of those novels." He drew her eyes to his. Leaning forward again, intent, he said, "Katherine, you are one of the most . . . ah . . . how can I say it? . . . intellectually able students I've had the privilege of teaching. And I can't bear to see you stifle that acuity with the narrow-mindedness that so often stifles intellectual activity in this country."

"Why should this country be more narrow-minded than others?" She was indignant.

He smiled. "You should know. You've lived in England. And whether we like it or not . . . or whether Ulster-Scotsmen like it or not . . . there's a vast difference between this and that side of the water. There's a different view of things over there, is there not? Oh, how you love England but hate the English!"

She nodded slowly, unwilling again to concede too quickly.

"Then—to get back to our point—do you think you can pick up the gauntlet I've thrown you? See if you can make sense of those novels? Do some outside reading on Catholicism and come up with an essay answer for me? I think you'll do a masterful job."

"It may not be the answer you want to read," she warned.

"It may not be the answer you want to write," he parried.

Kate reflected for a moment. She wouldn't show it, wouldn't admit it, but she was pleased, surprised by the compliment. Never had he encouraged her before; always he had come out with his rapier—probing, cutting open her comments. Oh, certainly he had argued with other students, but it always seemed that he had been quicker to criticize her than the others. She was so taken aback by the praise that she found herself for the first time almost wanting to read Greene and Hopkins just to please him. Haltingly then, she said, "Is there other reading . . . perhaps . . . perhaps I could do over the holidays . . . that you think would 'broaden' me?"

He smiled. "A dangerous question, Katherine! You're opening Pandora's box."

"I mean it," she urged. "Do you have anyone else to recommend?"

He opened the top drawer of his desk and removed a clean sheet of paper on which he hurriedly began to write a list of names. "I want you to read Evelyn Waugh's *Sword of Honour* trilogy. Have you read any Waugh?"

"Oh, snatches. I read *A Handful of Dust* . . . let's see . . . I can't remember what else. Oh, yes, *Decline and Fall.* . . . He was a Catholic then?"

"When he wrote *A Handful of Dust,* aye. He converted to Catholicism in 1930."

"Is there anyone else?" she asked carefully, her enthusiasm already flagging.

He caught her slight retrenchment. "Yes. I'd definitely like you to dip into Hopkins. There's a paperback containing both his journals and his verse. You'd do well to read it. And try Yeats . . . you can't tell me you've come this far without reading Yeats. Have you?"

Her face grew hot. "I've read some of his early poems, the romantic poems."

"Did you like them?"

"Yes, in a way, but they seemed awfully like the aesthete-decadent school at the turn of the century. I didn't see that they were particularly as noteworthy as everyone around here seems to think."

"No, perhaps not. But didn't you read further?"

"No."

"Then I want you to read more. And keep a log for me with your impressions." He went on writing as he spoke: "Yeats, Joyce, Synge, O'Casey. . . . An afterthought," he said suddenly. "You can read some Robert Lowell and Flannery O'Connor. They're both Americans—he's a poet, she's a storyteller. Have you heard of them?"

"Yes."

"Read them?"

"No."

"Then you will—this summer. Anyway," he said, putting down his pen, "this list'll be useful. Didn't I say a minute ago that I'm thinking you'll go beyond university here?"

"I'd like to."

"Have you thought where you might go—what you'll do?"

"I've thought of applying to London University. I like the look of the postgraduate study there."

He nodded. "That might be a possibility. Perhaps you wouldn't be altogether comfortable in Oxford or Cambridge. Have you considered an American university?"

She shook her head.

"Then I'd like you to give that some thought. You might have to go on beyond an M.A. there . . . get a Ph.D. It's a different system. All this reading will help."

"Are there any other American writers you'd suggest?" she asked.

"Fitzgerald. *Tender Is the Night, The Great Gatsby,* and some of his short fiction. Perhaps *The Diamond as Big as the Ritz.*"

She nodded. "I'll try to read whatever you suggest." Was she truly saying these things? It dazed her to think how he had won her over. "I'll be at home for the whole summer, with plenty of time."

He knew she was exaggerating slightly, but pressed his advantage. "And when you get back I want you to come and see me right away, so we can arrange a more balanced academic timetable for you. I'd like you to make a formal study of some Irish literature."

"I don't know if I want to."

"You may change your mind by then. I think you will. Try to read the writers for their work, rather than for who they are or what they believe. Now that sounds strange, coming right after that question on Greene, but some critics, I think, carry the tradition of criticizing literature on a biographical basis a wee bit far. And if you come to me in the autumn, I'll help you get out your application to London and perhaps for scholarships abroad. Would you like that?"

"Thank you."

"Is there anything else?"

"I can't think of anything . . . except . . . well, one thing."

"What's that?" His voice had softened now.

Gripping the arms of the chair, she asked, "Is this the sort of thing you say to everyone? That they're too narrow . . . that they need to read more?"

"Oh . . . not to everyone. I was just talking to Mr. Monaghan a few minutes ago. I said . . . well, you know what he's going to do when he's finished?"

"No, except I heard he's going to be a priest." She couldn't say "has a vocation" the way Roger now did.

"He's going to have a pretty rigorous training ahead of him, too. Intellectual training. Four years of theology at Maynooth. Or perhaps he might even go to St. Isadore's in Rome. Or Louvaine in Belgium. He has to start reading in the classics. I told him to take Latin and Greek next year. . . . So, what I try to do with all of you is help you get absolutely the best you can." He gestured. "I can't talk to everyone like this. And I don't think it's right for me to make too many comparisons between you and my other charges."

"No—I didn't mean to lead you into that." She moved restlessly in her chair.

"Any other questions?"

"No, not now."

"Well, I'm here if you have any. And if you get into a blind alley with Greene, let me know. Bring me your answers in two weeks. Then I suppose you'll be finished."

"Yes, I will."

"You'll be glad to get home?"

"Oh, indeed—to see my father." She realized suddenly that she had hardly expressed a word of interest in this man who had shown special interest in her. "And you—what do you do in the holidays? Stay here?"

"Aye. Oh—the summer's a great time for reading." He spread his hands expansively.

She groped around for what she might remember of monastic history. "And are you—I mean—do you have anything to do with the parish priest? Do you help with the services—or do any social work—or . . . ?" She fumbled for words, having no idea what the proper terms might be.

"Oh, yes. We can administer the sacraments. We're priests, too, you know." His eyes were smiling in faint mockery.

[151]

"I'm sorry. Am I saying it wrong? I don't know much about monastic life—especially modern monastic life."

"I suppose you learned history as far as the Reformation and then stopped?"

"Well actually, we did." She looked down ruefully. "But we read beyond it a little."

"You didn't read about the Roman church beyond it, though?"

"No, we didn't."

"Then I'm glad I gave you this question on Greene. Off you go now and do the best job you can with it. And—Katherine?" He closed his hands again as if in prayer.

"Yes?" She paused in the doorway, her curiosity aroused by the soberness of his voice.

"Leave the past to the mercy of God, and the present to the love of God, and the future to the benevolence of God." There was no mockery in his eyes now, only warmth.

She nodded, hardly able to absorb his words, yet aware that she must remember what he was saying, that it would be important. "Thank you, thank you," she muttered, almost stumbling out of the door.

"Remember," his voice followed her, as he repeated, "the past to God's mercy, the present to His love, and the future to His benevolence."

Somehow, she thought, as she went up the steps and out into the spring sunshine, *somehow he does know God in a way I don't understand yet.*

Father Kennedy's words had left Kate in a meditative mood. She didn't want to go back to her room and face Sheila's gossip. She didn't even want to go to the library and start *The Power and the Glory.* Nor did she want to wander aimlessly or go running. Instead, she would do what she sometimes did when she felt quiet and thoughtful: holding her cotton skirt close to fend off the sticky, clinging brambles that infested the path, she made her way to one of her favorite places, a bench in the shrubbery that was surrounded almost completely by a wall of tall deep-pink rhododendrons.

She sat on the bench with the sun pouring down on her. Behind and around her the bees were noisy in the flowers that had just begun to open. Putting her books and papers aside, she leaned back with her eyes shut. So much had happened this year, and now it was almost over. She had lost James, though of course, as she knew well now, she had never really possessed him. She had lost him to Ruth. They were getting married at the end of the summer. Ruth was leaving the University and going with James down to Belfast. The resentment and silence between herself and Ruth had at last dissolved into an uneasy truce once Ruth had realized that Kate still liked her and did not take offense at her being with James. Kate had asked Ruth if she would continue toward her degree. With a helpless movement of her shoulders, the other girl had merely said, "I might . . . at Queen's. Or I might just stay at home and keep house. James would prefer that." At first, Kate could only think that it might have been herself in that place with James. But once away from Ruth, she realized how glad she was that it was not. She could never have hidden away in a darkened, narrow house in Belfast, married to a man who was so deeply entrenched in Paisley's version of Christianity that there would have been nothing but argument between them right from the start of their marriage.

Well, and what if she had "lost" James? She had found Deirdre, a girl who consistently and faithfully respected her, cared for her, and was honest with her. She knew that Deirdre, unlike Sheila, never gossiped behind her back. She knew Deirdre was completely trustworthy and constant—a friend.

Kate regretted her withdrawal from Deirdre when Liam had first come courting. Despite that cooling on Kate's part, Deirdre had still helped Kate in the Union, still attended prayer meetings regularly, still sat with her in the refectory, still invited her home to Armagh for the weekend. And Kate had learned—to her own wonder—to grow accustomed to Liam, to his teasing ways with Deirdre and, most surprisingly, with herself. Liam took her far less seriously than she took herself, one of the first people ever to do this in a kind way. Consequently, she had begun to wonder dimly if she herself took everything too seriously. She had seen in James the danger of blind obsession that cared not who it hurt or what it damaged. And so she had cautiously yielded to Liam's humor and laughter.

Yet this turned all her judgments upside down. Measuring herself against Liam, for example, Kate had glimpsed her own self-preoccupation and her own selfishness (a word she could hardly bring herself to use, and certainly not to anyone but herself). She saw not only Liam's obvious devotion to Deirdre, but also his easy generosity and his social commitment. Nor had he led Deirdre into the kind of political activity Kate had feared—the slow suction and downward whirlpool of socialism. In fact, she had noticed only the positive influence of a heightened social conscience and a greater discipline in Deirdre's study habits—something else Liam had encouraged in her, for with all his easiness, he was far more disciplined than Deirdre.

Thinking now of all the good that Liam and Deirdre had done in the town and at St. Jerome's, Kate promised herself, not for the first time, that next year she would become more involved in social action and in helping others outside the Union. Perhaps she would not even run for the vice-presidency again. With James gone to Assemblies College, Roger was certain to be voted president; and she didn't know if she wanted to work with him. If she could extricate herself from the Union a bit, she would have more time for equally important concerns.

The Christian Union. Almost guiltily, for the first time she admitted to herself her frustrations and disappointments with the organization. For months she had gone through the motions of arranging prayer meetings, mission speakers, outside evangelists . . . with few results. Though she knew that one could not measure the kingdom of heaven in terms of numbers, she was disappointed that only one or two students had come, as she said it, to know the love of Christ. She had wondered and worried all year about the influence of Communism in the University—had seen that force as the major adversary. There were several first-year students who were avowed members of the Communist party. Liam himself had openly admitted his membership in the Northern Ireland Civil Rights Association, which was well-known (at least among her

[154]

associates) as a socialist organization. She had argued with Liam about this more than once.

"Look how it is in Russia," she had accused him. "Is that what you want in Northern Ireland? No freedom of speech? No freedom of the press? Persecution of anybody who believes in God? Persecution of anybody who expresses an opinion different from the state's? Is that what you want here? Is that what you call a system created for the people?"

"No," he had said. "You're mistaking socialism for Communism, which is nothing better than state capitalism. What I dream of seeing is a community where factories are owned in common, where production of goods would be according to human needs, not according to how much money they would bring in. Any leaders in such a society would be there solely to organize. They'd be answerable to it . . . they'd not be in charge of it; they'd not be capitalist overlords."

Kate had laughed. "Ah, but government officials already are supposed to be public servants. But they don't serve the people any more than the leaders of your society would. I suppose you'll be telling me in a minute that bribery and corruption would be impossible because everyone would have access to the stockpile of goods."

"You're putting words in my mouth, Kate. But, yes, that's possible."

She had laughed hollowly. "Then I suppose you don't believe in the impossibility of reforming mankind, in the fact that man is born in sin, is born depraved, is born incapable of saving himself. You're preaching a gospel that says man can change himself."

"Yes, he can. Not by a capitalist government, but—"

"What makes you so sure," she had interrupted, "that every man would be equally interested in promoting the growth of the state?"

"For one thing, everybody would have enough to eat. People would realize it is in their own best interest to 'promote the growth of the state,' as you say, so that there would be enough to eat and so that food could be properly distributed. . . . I think things would be very different." He paused briefly. "Doesn't it make your blood run cold, Katie, when you hear of overproduction in the States

[155]

described as disaster? As a burden? When grain rots and milk is dumped and South American coffee beans are burned if too many are grown—just because it would upset the world market? Does that seem right?"

"No," she had agreed, "but I don't think in a world as complex as this that the simple socialist ideals would solve these problems. There will always be people who are lazy and greedy."

"Then what's your answer?" he had demanded. "Not capitalism, I hope."

"Oh, no! My answer is Jesus Christ."

"Jesus came once. What good did he do? He died on a cross. He was buried with criminals. What good did he do?"

"None, if that's where he'd ended. But he rose. He promised freedom—spiritual freedom. Change from the inside out. Your reform is from the outside in. It won't work."

He had shrugged finally and, in a stubborn voice she had come to recognize, had murmured, "Kate, we'll have to beg to differ, I'm thinking, since I can't agree with you about 'the faith.' Dear help us, I can't even agree with Jack about it! But I know one thing: I'll not find the truth in the Roman Church, nor in yours either. If Jesus promised freedom, why don't we have it in Northern Ireland instead of crazy Catholics and Prods shooting at each other all in the name of God?"

"Liam, you won't find freedom in any church," Kate persisted. "Because the church is just a body of fallible believers. The only way you'll find freedom and truth is in God himself, in His time."

And so she had gone on praying for Liam, and for Deirdre, that she would persist in testifying to him since she of all had the most interest in seeing him come to faith. She prayed for all of them now—for Liam, for Deirdre, even for James and Ruth—with her eyes still shut. The sun's warmth penetrated the shrubbery and the cotton cloth of her blouse. A sort of blessing.

Summer, 1970

The first two answers came easily. Within three days after her meeting with Father Kennedy, they were neatly written in blue ink and placed on the back of her desk. Not the Graham Greene reading, though. She waded through encyclopedias, handbooks, almanacs, and articles, yet still felt she didn't know enough about Catholicism to start writing. A shock, that. She kept reassuring herself that *of course* she knew about Catholic dogma, *of course* she knew "how Catholics think." But she didn't.

The two novels surprised her from first to last. Why had Kennedy told her to read novels that argued against what he had said in his office? The heat, the stench, the betrayal of Mexico; the brutal indifference of postwar London with its crude graffiti and empty social connections: both were existential visions. Nothing particularly Catholic about them. In the squalor and shabbiness, Greene was merely portraying the corruption of a world from which God was absent.

The library was empty and hushed. Only the soft soles of the librarian and the light scratch of Kate's fountain pen made any sound at all. Only she remained late on this Friday afternoon at the end of term to finish her exam questions.

Four o'clock. Kennedy had wanted the answers by four today. For the first time in two years, her work would be late. She felt no anxiety, just a leaden frustration with the network of arrows and asterisks that made up her notes on two novels and many reference works. Her brain seemed blocked until, after watching the dockyard cranes for a few minutes, she wrote:

[157]

In Greene's novels, human relationships are dramatized against the background of a cruel, changeable world. These surroundings reflect his protagonists' hopelessness.

She sat back, pleased. She could pursue that thesis without giving in to the conclusion that Father Kennedy plainly wanted of her.

She wrote more, expanding on the novels' treatment of entrapment, betrayal, failure, despair, and emptiness. The essay was taking shape well. As she consulted her notes again, however, some difficult words commanded her eyes. She had scrawled, "the paradox of pity and mercy in unregenerate 'whiskey priest,' of love and kindness in a woman who has broken moral laws." And again, "Why does Greene make God pursue Sarah, the priest, etc.?"

Irritably, she picked up *The Power and the Glory*. It fell open at a page she had marked.

> *... a world of treachery, violence, and lust ... It was for this world that Christ had died: the more evil you saw and heard about you, the greater glory lay around the death ... it needed a God to die for the half-hearted and the corrupt.*

Pity and mercy she thought. *God the jealous God, the God who forgives, loves, even pursues the lost.* She closed her eyes. It *was* a Christian vision, then. A broader emphasis. Not one all Irish Presbyterian would share. But it was Christian, and she couldn't argue otherwise. Catholic or not, it was Christian. Christ was no Presbyterian. *Nor Catholic either,* she thought in quick defense. And He was merciful beyond any mercy a Christian could bestow, pitying beyond any pity a Christian could feel. Obviously she had ignored too much of what the two novels said. Kennedy would never accept her arguments.

Then is it my vision that's deficient? she wondered. *Is it I who need to learn to have more pity and mercy? I who need to listen to some of what Catholics say?* She put her head down on the cool, worn grain of the table. *Lord have mercy, Christ have mercy, Lord have mercy.* The words beat up behind her eyelids. *From the Mass,* she realized with dull surprise. Then where had she heard them? A T. S. Eliot work? Father Kennedy? An Anglican Eucharist . . . ?

[158]

The glass door of the circulation room slammed, and she jerked up. Had she fallen asleep? Sheila, a pert smile on her face, was stepping lightly toward Kate. Feeling the usual annoyance, she tried to brace herself.

"What on earth are you doing?" Sheila rested her hands on the table across from Kate and leaned forward with her brows arched. "I thought you finished ages ago."

"Oh, n–no—" Kate was still dazed by her discovery. She would have to start the essay all over again. Greene had jolted some of her oldest prejudices—exactly what Kennedy had wanted. But how could she reframe her thinking when the answers were already late?

Sheila turned over a few books and papers, frowning. "Greene? What course is this for?"

"Not for a course. For Kennedy. He wanted an extra essay from me."

"Oh, you poor soul—how did you ever win that privilege?"

Kate sighed and didn't answer immediately. "Sheila . . . it's a long tale. And I'm late, as you can see." She straightened her back and assumed the sort of lofty tone she often used with Sheila—though less often recently. "Did you have something particular you wanted to ask me? Is my stuff in your way? I suppose you're packing."

"Heavens, no. Tomorrow maybe. Actually, I do want to ask you something. Roger and I thought we'd go over the border tonight to The Point Inn. To celebrate the end of term and all. Will you come with us? Do, Kate—it would be such fun." She gushed on. "It's a pub. You'd love it. They have folk singers—it's all quite wholesome." There was a touch of mockery in her voice. "No drunkenness. Not your typical Derry bar."

Kate began to smile at Sheila's description. "You make it sound almost as staid and safe as a Women's Institute meeting, Sheila. Thanks, but I can't." She waved her hands. "Look at this muddle for why."

"We've changed places. I should be late, not Kate."

"Late Kate. It's my turn, I suppose."

"You don't mind if we go without you, then?"

"Mind? Why should I? Since when do I go out drinking with you and Rog—or anyone?"

A shrug. "Oh, I know, but this is different. It's a celebration. A whole gang of us are going . . . Trevor, Sam, Caroline, Jack, Liam, Deirdre—" Her voice trailed off, and she stepped back a pace. "Well, never mind."

"Thanks, Sheila, honestly, but I can't."

"Good luck with Greene, then. Will you have it done before we get back?"

Kate pushed up her glasses and tucked a stray end of hair behind her ear. "I hope so. But don't worry about me. You go on. And have a super time."

The library seemed emptier than ever when the door closed behind Sheila. Kate looked wistfully out of the window again. Would she have gone anyway? She didn't like to drink, didn't like rowdy places or large gatherings. But the folk music, mournful and joyful at once, would have been a balm. In a sudden fury she ripped up what she had written so far. She would get some coffee from the Students' Union and start again.

She wrote feverishly once she had taken a break. Time was of no importance now that she had acknowledged her biased reading of the novels.

> Greene's Catholicism informed his thinking and writing. His beliefs provided the basis for his themes and fictional dilemmas. To ignore his obsession with God is to risk misunderstanding his work completely.

There. Once she had written it outright, the rest followed naturally. The negative themes, she saw now, were balanced by a presentation of redemption and grace that was no trite posture or empty creedal statement. Greene's God was larger, far more merciful than hers. He was a God who called for commitment more than perfection—which would come only from the shed blood of Christ, anyway. *That's why Christ had to suffer*, she thought. *How else could He redeem such brokenness and indifference?*

She put her head down on her folded arms again, shutting out all visible distraction as she looked, uncomfortably, into herself.

"Blessed are the merciful." Yet she had less mercy than the drunken, runaway priest in *The Power and the Glory* . Less mercy than Liam, who professed no faith except in some vague socialist ideal. And far less mercy than Deirdre, who lived her faith more than she spoke it. *"Blessed are the merciful."* Then must she have mercy even on the one who had murdered her mother and sister? *"Leave the past to God's mercy . . ."* Her prayer came slowly. *Father, I feel humbled . . . I haven't seen your love as you want me to. I've emphasized judgment more than mercy, Lord, at the risk of diminishing your mercy in my life and the lives of others. Change me, Lord. Help me to forgive that murderer. It's painful already, but change me. Change me, change me.*

Change, change, change . . . .

The words echoed across the water into the summer, pursuing Kate through the pages of Greene and Waugh and Hopkins. Pursuing, yet driving her on.

"You've changed, Kate."

Her father, grayer than she remembered him, thinner, his shoulders more bowed than ever by the weight of pastoral duty, sat with her in the parlor. Neither of them watched the television that jabbered in the corner.

"Oh?" She smiled vaguely. It was the first personal remark he had made since her homecoming a few weeks before. "For the better, I hope."

"You're harder, more assured."

Her heart sank.

"I mean, you're surer of where you stand in Christ. Less prone to shift with other ideas as you used to."

"Thank you," she murmured. It was a dubious compliment. Her gaze wandered out of the small window with its tinted glass. The garden of high summer was rife with purples, reds, and oranges. An unemployed man her father felt sorry for was trimming the shrubs. "I wonder if I am."

She had given her father a copy of *The Power and the Glory* to read. As always, she had wanted his opinions, to sit at his feet like Saul at the feet of Gamaliel. He had said, "But you don't agree with any of this gloomy nonsense, do you? Heretical, blasphemous, I'd say."

Funny, that's almost what the Catholic Church said about it at first, she thought. She surveyed his face. "You've read the whole book?"

"All I want to."

"Ah . . . ." *He isn't even willing to finish it and discuss it fairly . . . and I sound like Father Kennedy.*

"I repeat, you don't agree with this man's vision, do you? I mean, he's a bigoted Catholic."

Her eyes meet his briefly, then skipped to the window again. "I don't know." Then she smiled and said carefully, "The lecturer who wants me to read Greene's work—he's a Catholic." She trembled inwardly, knowing she had stirred up a dormant volcano.

His lips compressed into a narrow line. "No doubt some long-haired radical who says sin is salvation and talks all the time about 'paradox' and 'creative tension' and the like."

She laughed suddenly. "Colm K–Kennedy?" With the words came disgust that she hadn't even given him his proper title before her father. A small betrayal, though Kennedy would forgive her. "Oh, no, he's an old Franciscan."

Her father made a faint noise of distaste. "Even worse. Don't be listening too much to him. Weigh all this reading against scripture, my dear. The wheat is sown with tares. Remember, 'All scripture is given by inspiration of God, and is profitable for doctrine, for reproof, for correction, for instruction in righteousness, that the man of God may be perfect.' Look in second Timothy, chapter three." He sighed. "But you're not studying theology, are you." He scratched his head. "I forget that sometimes. By the way, you haven't mentioned your friend James very much. Is he—?"

The television suddenly arrested their attention. "Six people have died and 276 have been injured after another weekend of rioting in Belfast and Londonderry." The news bulletins had been the same almost every evening during this long, overheated summer.

"One million pounds' worth of damage is recorded. . . ."

"The worst terror in East Belfast since the 1941 air raids. . . ."

[162]

"Fifteen hundred British troops moved into the Lower Falls Road area today and a curfew has been imposed amid bitter street fighting that has left four more dead. . . ."

"An eighteen-month old was killed today by a sniper's bullet. . . ."

"The little girl killed a few days ago was buried today after the Provisional Wing of the IRA described her death as 'an unfortunate accident, one of the hazards of guerrilla warfare.'"

Tears rose into Kate's eyes, and a lump into her throat. Involuntarily, she said, "Oh, Lord, have mercy."

Her father looked oddly at her and, in a quick, angry leap from his chair, switched off the television. Between his teeth, he said, "There'll be no change in Ulster until the Catholics go where they belong, back to the South."

"Oh, father, no—"

"No change."

No change. Oh, Father. *O Father . . . change me . . . help me to forgive. Change me, change me. . . .* Like Saul getting up from Gamaliel's feet to lay his coat too late at the feet of Stephen, she gathered up her papers and left the library.

The lecture building was eerily quiet. Father Kennedy would be at the friary on Saturdays, she guessed. Everyone had gone for the summer, or so it seemed—Liam on his way to America, Deirdre to Armagh ("I promise to write every week, Katie."), Sheila and Roger to England. . . all of them gone.

Kate bent to slip her papers under the door, a note of apology attached. But there was a rustle on the other side; then the door came partly open. She started guiltily, straightening her back.

"Aha— *un pêcheur!*" Father Kennedy was scowling. In his brown habit, unwrinkled this time, and his severely owlish glasses, he frightened her.

Stooping to retrieve her work, she stammered out an apology.

[163]

He dismissed it and beckoned. "Won't you come in?"

"Oh, no, thank you . . . my train . . . I—"

"These answers are late, you know."

"Yes. I had difficulty with the Greene essay."

"I thought I told you to come in if you ran into problems."

"You did, but I was making progress. I could see that I would work through it in the end." Was he deliberately making her uncomfortable?

"What was so difficult?"

"My ignorance," she said slowly, not looking at him. *Ignorance?* Had that sounded affected, falsely humble?

He was turning the pages. Right in front of her he was examining her answers. She squirmed, like a wriggling creature pinned to the wall on the point of a sword.

"But did you enjoy the novels?"

"I don't know if I'd say I enjoyed them—but they certainly provoked me."

"To what?"

"To thought."

"What d'you mean?"

"I suppose you could say that I saw some writing on the wall?"

"What writing? The graffiti at the beginning of *The End of the Affair?*"

She searched his face: it was neutral, but his eyes were playing with her. She blushed. "No—I mean—as in the Bible. I found myself . . . weighed myself in the scales and found myself wanting."

"Oh. You've been looking in the mirror again, Miss Hamilton. Don't you know all that introspection is really a form of vanity?"

She opened her mouth to reply, but he held up a hand with two fingers raised in the peace sign.

"Never mind. Never mind— *Te absolvo.* Go on. You must catch your train. Oh, by the way—for penance, you can say ten *aves* and read some Hopkins."

She looked at him, aghast. He was mocking her and his religion—all at once.

He laughed suddenly. "Ah, Katherine, you're so deliciously teasable! Go on, you take everything seriously." He held out his hand to her. She grasped it after only a second's hesitation. The gulf between them was no gulf to him; this man cared about her. Though she might be confused, uncertain, she was not uncertain of that.

"God bless you, Katherine."

"And you, Father Kennedy."

She turned away, biting her lip. She had always shunned the title "Father." This time it had come of its own accord. Had change begun already, as subtly as rings of water enlarging from a thrown stone?

Friday and Saturday, October 2 and 3

The new term was a week old, almost as clean as the sheet of white paper in front of her. After a summer away, such clear ideas had formed in Kate's mind about how different this year would be. She would keep life simpler, talk less and listen more, work even harder. She wanted a First. She must be in love with books to earn it. But after only a week back, what with Sheila's late nights, some squabbles in the Christian Union, and the demands of the Irish drama in a course Father Kennedy had insisted she take, the year no longer seemed as clear and simple as she had hoped.

A sort of autumnal melancholy had settled on her today so that all she wanted was to be alone. Everything she looked at—the roan berries clustering in the shrubbery, the amber turning of the leaves in the chestnut trees outside the lecture halls—everything reminded her of "lastness." Her last autumn in Ireland, her last year at the University, her last freshers' squash, her last CU retreat . . . her last everything. "Lastness and lostness," she intoned to herself. As if her very life was slipping from her as surely as the color from the trees. She despised her own nostalgia, but it clung to her like dead, wet leaves.

Deirdre's second-year room made a good haven. It was quieter and more secluded than her own. At the top of the building, it was one of only six rooms on the fourth floor. A single bed, dresser, wardrobe, desk, and a battered basket chair—that was all under the sloping ceiling. And Deirdre had given the place to her for the night because Kate wanted to sit up and fill in the long applications for London University. The library would never have been quiet enough; the first dance of the year was going on below it

[166]

in the Great Hall. She was probably the only woman left in all of Woodburn.

A slight scent of Deirdre's perfume hung in the room. Lilac? Rose? Kate couldn't quite identify it. At first it was pleasant, but after a while the room seemed oppressive and close. She stood up to open the window, a small skylight that was above the desk. *Like an artist's attic,* she thought in vague amusement as she pushed at the catch. It was stiff and wouldn't budge. She climbed on the chair and pushed harder. Still no luck. Well, she would have to leave it shut, then, and open the door slightly.

Name. In her neat, methodical italic she wrote, *Katherine Louise Hamilton. Address: The Manse, 58, Old London Road . . . Age: 21.* She leaned back in the chair. Perhaps these forms would not take as long as she had expected. The University wanted everything in sextuplet, but so far the answers had come automatically.

Education . . . Institutions of higher learning . . . Degree(s) obtained . . . Class or division of degree(s), if known . . . Major study. . . .

At first her thoughts flowed as smoothly as the blue ink. But then she had to deliberate. She chewed the cap of her pen and stared at a poster on the wall. It was of an American cornfield. Liam had worked for minimum wage this summer as a line painter with a road crew in Chicago. He had brought the poster back with him at the end of September. Row upon row of shining green corn marched to the poster's horizon.

Chosen field of study . . . Degree sought . . . Reasons for undertaking postgraduate study . . . Career goals. . . .

She wrote *English Literature . . . Master of Arts.* She hesitated at the next question. Why *was* she intending to study further? Because Father Kennedy had flattered her into believing herself a cut above most undergraduates? Because God wanted her to? Because she could do more to serve God with an advanced degree? Yes, but how could she write that?

She scratched idly on a scrap of paper beside the long forms. Could she, in fact, do more for God with or without an advanced degree? So many avenues opened themselves to her: to closet herself with books all her life and become a teacher of other students, perhaps like Father Kennedy? But no, she would never have his encompassing vision, his blend of wit and compassion. All

[167]

right, then, to edit other writers' work: to change syntax and spellings and semicolons all her life? For what? For *God's* sake? No. Then what? To write magazine articles for a Christian relief agency? Possibly. To marry and have children? Who? And why?

She could not leave the "career goals" line empty, so she wrote, *Possibly journalism.* She smudged the last syllable by accident but did not notice immediately. The questions that followed were mechanical again: *Expected place of residence . . . Source of grants, if any . . . Expected date of completion of studies.* Her hand moved more quickly again, but then she noticed the smudge and promptly made another mistake. Frowning, she hunched forward and squinted to see how she could change the lettering to hide the mistakes. The writing looked worse, not better, and this was only the first form. There were five more to go, for she had deliberately not used carbon paper, thinking blue ink on all six would look neater.

Laboriously she began to copy the second sheet, resigned to a few small errors. The forms would still look tidy enough when she had finished. As she wrote, she happened to glance at her watch. Another frown. Twenty to one. Had it stopped this afternoon? She shook it, listened, then groaned. No, it was working.

With a sigh, she stood up to stretch. She must stay alert so that she could finish tonight. Tomorrow she had to read O'Casey's *The Plough and the Stars;* it would take all day if she did it justice. But the room was making her sleepy. The skylight must open somehow.

Standing on a chair again, Kate saw that the catch was twisted to one side to keep the window shut fast. Turning it, she found that it slid open effortlessly. Cool air slapped her face, and she inhaled deeply.

On impulse, she reached to turn off the light and then straightened up again so that her chin rested on the lower edge of the skylight. Waves of air swept her face. Inches away were the slates of the steep Woodburn rooftop, and beyond them, in a pale wash of reflected light from the city, a sea of stars. Had Deirdre discovered this marvel, she wondered? She could pull down a star if she put her hand up.

Somewhere in the world below a sound that had gone on for a

long time ceased. The silence roared in her ears until a car raced its engines on Northland Road. *The dance is over,* she thought. Deirdre and Sheila would come back to the other room, the room she still shared with Sheila. They would bring Liam and Roger and drink cocoa for another hour. Deirdre would fall asleep in Kate's bed, oblivious to all. And she herself would copy answers until four in the morning before finally falling exhausted into Deirdre's bed.

Laughter and talk mounted the steps outside. Voices and footsteps on the second, then on the third floor. She stepped down from the chair and shut the door she had propped open earlier. Deirdre had taken all she needed downstairs, but Kate wanted no other visitors either.

She wrote more carefully now, concentrating intensely. At half-past three, when the residence was utterly silent again, she finally finished. Her head felt light, and her eyes felt scratchy. As she tried to blink away the dryness, she padded across the narrow linoleum hallway to the bathroom. At last, having changed into her night clothes and laid her glasses on the desk, she slid under Deirdre's blankets and commanded herself to sleep. She was drawn up through the open skylight to stars she could see without her glasses.

"Kate, I'm sorry . . . sorry . . ."

She groaned. Who was sorry? What was wrong? Then she opened her eyes to a half-light. Was it morning already?

"I didn't want to wake you. I'm sorry." It was Deirdre, softly rummaging in the wardrobe for her clothes.

Kate turned her head. The pillow felt wet. She must have been sleeping with her mouth open. Embarrassed, she rubbed her eyes and sat up abruptly, drawing the bedclothes over her hunched knees. Her hair fell like a tangled horse's tail over the bedspread. "I don't know if you did—wake me up, I mean," she murmured.

Deirdre looked at her indulgently. "I suppose you've been awake for an hour at least?"

Kate eased under the bedclothes again, feeling rather foolish.

[169]

"No—I've not been asleep more than . . . what's the time, anyway?"

"Eight o'clock or so. It took you all night to fill in those forms?"

"Till half three." She shut her eyes again. Her body felt heavy, almost drugged.

"Then I'll let you lie in peace. I'm going up to St. Jerome's."

Kate willed herself to open her eyes again and said, "Oh—what'll you be doing up there?"

"It's different almost every time. But probably something with the weans. They need someone to have some fun with, that's all." Deirdre opened a drawer.

Kate tried to fathom her friend's rather flat tone. Was it because she had declined all Deirdre's invitations to go to the orphanage? "Will you be gone all day?" she asked. "How would it be if I came this time?"

Turning from the chest of drawers, Deirdre registered her surprise. "But I didn't think you wanted—"

"I know I said I wouldn't be able to talk to the nuns. But I think I've changed my mind a wee bit."

A wide smile illuminated Deirdre's face. "Then you'll go today?"

Kate sat up again. She couldn't read O'Casey after so little sleep, anyway, so why not?

"I'll just be gone the morning. We could come back at lunch time. There's a game this afternoon . . . Liam's playing."

"Rugby already?" She began to push back the bedclothes, still slow and sleepy.

"Katie, are you sure you'll go?" Deirdre was watching her face closely. "You're so pale—"

"Well, now, don't put me off once I decide I'll do it."

"Oh, good. The children will love you."

"I'm sure they love you, Deirdre."

Deirdre shrugged. "They love anyone who loves them. It's that simple. But they need to get love more than give it. Oh, I'm glad you'll go."

[170]

Children. Middle-class children with neatly pressed and starched green-and-white primary school uniforms. Clear skin and clean fingernails. Children who said "Please" and "Thank you for having us to tea, Reverend Hamilton." Children whose fathers were the local businessmen, teachers, doctors, pastors.

Children. Presbyterian children. Girls with neat plaits and boys with felt caps they doffed for church. Children who sat still in the pews and smiled angelically after the children's sermon her father preached each week. Children whose parents were missionaries in Haiti or Malaysia or India.

Children. Boarding school girls: little prim Victorias in stiff blue-and-gold uniforms; bored with Boer Wars, blasé about Brahms concertos, indifferent to inquisitions and armadas alike. Who under their demure veneer had crushes on the games mistress, the Beatles, and faceless boyfriends, imagined and real, in Kensington and Tunbridge Wells. Who hated each other as desperately as they were polite to each other. Who reckoned God to be no more than a word for compulsory Sundays or for cursing a mistress behind her back.

Children. Kate had loved and hated them.

But these wee Irish children . . . how could she either love or hate them? There was nothing lovable about them, and nothing to hate, either. Some hung onto Deirdre with hands still smeared with breakfast. Their noses ran; their eyes squinted. Some even had asthma, their labored and squeaky breathing making Kate herself breathless.

From the bastion of Deirdre's familiar arms (did they truly remember her after so long away?), two or three of the littlest sized up Kate. The others eyed her from a safe distance and then went on with what they were doing, which, for some, meant doing nothing.

Kate sat down cross-legged on the cracked blue linoleum of the playroom and watched quietly. They would soon get used to her. She looked around with a mixture of recognition and repulsion. The room reminded her of the empty room in the attic of her primary school where she and other little girls had taken "music and movement" classes to learn poise, balance, and grace. But that room, with its scarred cream walls and upright piano, had been

[171]

empty deliberately. This room should not be. Holes pocked the plaster walls, devoid of pictures. And this piano looked unplayable: the lid was permanently stuck halfway across the keys, and broken strings corkscrewed out of the splintered side. The Virgin, in a small framed painting, looked down through cracked glass from the top of the dilapidated piano.

With a discordant jangling, a small boy now climbed onto the keys and then onto the top of the instrument. He carefully moved the Virgin a few inches aside, then stood so that he could see out of the only window, a casement roughly level with his chin. Kate watched him. He remained utterly still, entranced by the world beyond, oblivious to the scene behind him.

And which is better for this child, Kate wondered. *To stay in this playroom, or to live in the Ardoyne?* There, he would be, perhaps, a future stonethrower, a future bombthrower with no choice for survival—or destruction—but the IRA. Here, though, he was at least loved. The love might be haphazard and spasmodic—the lick of a wet flannel around his mouth and ears in the morning, the rebuke of a nun over unfinished lunch, the businesslike, chapped hands of another as she helped him into pajamas at night—but at least it was real.

The nuns ("sisters" as Deirdre called them repeatedly). How did she feel about these women? Awed? Intrigued? Even a bit frightened by their soft, watchful eyes, pliable mouths, and spotless habits? The inner silence about them, a gathering-in of the self that was not selfishness, but repose? They had moved across the faded reed floor mats like queens in a court. Two of them, both bowed with age—one carrying a black cane as twisted and knobby as a blackthorn shillelagh—had passed Deirdre and Kate in the vestibule. In a querulous voice, the one with the cane had looked up at Kate with dim eyes, saying "How nice to see such a tall sister." Afterwards Deirdre had teased her: "Sister Patricia thinks you're one of them! She's nearly blind." Kate had first smiled, but then grieved. *They can call me a sister, but I cannot call them sisters.*

And when they had brought Kate and Deirdre to the playroom, the sisters had moved among the children with calmness and the plain expectation of obedience. They had gone, however, leaving the two young women with the listless children who roamed

[172]

randomly around the prisonlike confines of the room. No interest for them in the few broken toys that lay abandoned in the corner: a doll's pram with one wheel missing, two dolls without hair or clothes, a tricycle without pedals, a few torn books. . . .

Kate shifted slightly on the floor. Where did one begin to love such listless, hopeless children? She felt overwhelmed with pity and yet, as in a nightmare, too paralyzed to do anything. Oh, it was easy for Deirdre, who had already gathered a small crowd on the other side of the room and with pantomime gestures and exaggerated grimaces was telling a story. Deirdre could forget herself so easily.

At last a little girl, of six perhaps, with pathetically thin legs and a torn green pinafore, began to circle Kate; the child was wary but curious. Instinctively, Kate reached and drew her onto her lap. The little body resisted, pulled itself tight.

"I won't hurt you," Kate said gently. "What's your name?"

The child stared at her. "You talk funny," she said.

"Do I?"

"Not like the sisters. Not like Deirdre. You talk funny."

Kate laughed softly. "I'm sorry. I'm not Irish like you and Deirdre . . . and Sister Celestine." Not Irish? And wasn't she? Why had she said that?

"You talk funny."

"What's your name anyway?"

"Kathleen Mary Shaughnessy. What's yours?"

"Katherine Louise Hamilton."

"That's a funny name."

"Is it? I suppose it's as funny as yours, Kathleen."

The child relaxed and leaned more heavily against her. Her blue eyes fringed with long dark lashes were as quick and watchful as a young animal's, but they did not look straight at Kate, and that squint pained her. Had this child, too, seen one of her parents killed? Did this watchful innocence belie an adult knowledge of violence and inhumanity?

"What are you doin' here, Katherine?"

"Oh—" It was hard for her to answer. *Mummy, oh, Mummy!* . . . *Get down, Katie, get down! It's dangerous.* . . . The gray Belfast street faded into the gray Derry playroom. "Oh—I came to see you."

[173]

"But you don't know me."

"I'm starting to. . . . What do you like to do when you come in here, usually?"

The little girl shrugged. In such a thin body, the gesture was absurd. "Depends who's here."

"Do you like to draw pictures?"

Kathleen giggled. "I don't know. The sisters don't let us have crayons except in the school. We might make a mess." It was a flat statement, without bitterness.

Kate couldn't help a sad smile. How could the room look worse? She said, "Would you get in trouble if I lent you a pencil when I'm here? I could bring some paper and we could make pictures. Would you like that?"

"I'd like to. But I don't want a paddling."

"No one'll paddle you. I'll ask the nuns—the sisters—about it next time."

Kathleen gave her a steady look. "When—next time?"

"I don't know when I can come again. But I will come, I promise, with some things to do."

The child must have heard promises before, for she said dully, "We'll see, won't we." Perhaps she had heard the nuns say it.

Kate could not bring herself to utter reassurances that would sound insincere, so she gave her a little hug. But Kathleen pulled away, this time to inspect Kate's face more closely. She pointed to the glasses.

"What d'you need glasses for? Can't you see straight?"

Kate laughed, "I'm short-sighted. That means I can't see very far."

"I'm going to get glasses soon, Sister Celestine says. And maybe a patch on one side so this eye works harder. It's lazy." She screwed up her face in disgust. "Lazy! Isn't that silly?"

Kate nodded solemnly.

"And why is your hair like that?"

Kate looked round the room. All the little girls had short hair, she noticed. And the nuns—did the children ever see them without headpieces? No, of course not.

"In a plait, you mean?" She flicked the braid down behind her shoulder.

"Yes. A plait. A plait."

"Because it's rather long. It gets in the way."

"Why don't you cut it, then?"

"I like it long, that's why."

"That's funny. . . . Can you play on the piano?"

"It's broken."

"No, it's not. Listen." The child jumped up and pushed down several keys at once. Only one note sounded.

"I'll try," Kate said. She got up reluctantly, glancing over to Deirdre with a rueful grin.

She found that almost all the keys around middle C were broken, but the lower octaves were mostly intact, even if out of tune. The boy who had been looking out of the window turned around and sat down with his feet dangling right in front of her. Since there was nothing to sit on, she knelt on the floor. What could she play? Sunday school choruses would not be appropriate. Nursery rhymes? Perhaps something the children could all sing or dance to? *Oranges and Lemons?* —"Here comes the chopper to chop off your head . . ." No! What terrible words! *London's Burning?* No, that's an English song. *The Grand Old Duke of York?* No, so is that. What about a folk song, then? One they might know.

"Do you know *Michael Row*, Kathleen?"

"Sing it. Please sing it."

Kate called Deirdre, who had a sweet soprano voice, to sing with her. Deirdre happily got all the children, even the littlest ones, into a circle around the piano and started them clapping. The older children learned the words quickly, and soon the bare room echoed with the booming bass of the piano, the lilting trebles of the children, and ragged hand-clapping.

> *Michael row the boat ashore, alleluia!*
> *Michael row the boat ashore, alleluia!*
> *The River of Jordan is deep and wide, alleluia!*
> *Milk and honey on the other side, alleluia!*

Kate looked around with joy. The children loved the singing. She had found a way of making them all happy. *Milk and honey on*

[175]

the other side of the Jordan, she thought. *May they not be long in coming to these children.*

> *The River of Jordan is chilly and cold, alleluia!*
> *Chills the body, but not the soul, allelu–u–ia!*

Deirdre had gone now, back to the rugby game and Liam. The sisters had ushered away the little children for naps. The oldest ones had gone out to play or to watch Gaelic hockey. Kate had intended to stay only for the morning, but she had stayed on. Kathleen's wary eyes turning to laughter; the sisters' mild, kind faces; the happy singing—all had brought her a strange serenity. She would stay to do whatever needed to be done. O'Casey could wait until tonight or tomorrow.

Saturday, October 3

The day had warmed. Fog that had rolled over the lough early that morning had ascended but not yet burned away. Now it hung about a thousand feet over Creggan, over Bogside, over Waterside—over the whole city. It sieved the hot, just-past-equinoctial sunlight into fine pale-gold rays that angled down in straight rods from the clouds. The still humidity deadened sound and encased under an uneven dome the wide circle of Londonderry that Kate could see from her ladder. The sisters had sent her out to pick apples.

She was utterly happy. Her face grew hot and stray strands of hair clung to her cheeks; perspiration pricked the skin above her upper lip. The rhythm of pick, put down, reach, pick, put down absorbed her completely. She was aware of nothing except the present: the apples, round, hard with juice, warmed by the sun to a tart, sweet smell; the slight taste of salt on her mouth; the heat drenching her back; the ooze of dew, fallen apples, and damp leaves from below the tree; the high-pitched whir of invisible crickets.

Her loose peasant blouse served as a basket for the apples. As soon as the front of it was full, she cautiously backed down the ladder and placed the fruit on the corrugated cardboard storage trays given her. She was climbing the ladder after bringing down such a load when a tenor voice called Deirdre's name. The sound came from the far side of the orchard, by the convent.

She paused where she stood on the fifth rung and looked across the green and yellow trees. No one. Only apples, leaves, and damp bark. But the voice came again, "Deirdre, where are you?"

[177]

Kate turned and climbed to the top of the ladder. Cupping her hands around her mouth, she shouted, "Over this way!"

Several minutes passed. She picked no apples, but watched the broad grassy path that had brought her to these trees. A man was approaching; she heard him whistling *By the Rising of the Moon* a few seconds before the blur of his figure came into her vision. With a ladder balanced over his shoulders and an apple crate in his free hand, someone was coming jauntily down the path—Jack Monaghan.

She shouldn't have been surprised. She knew he came often to help at the orphanage. But in her fragrant, warm solitude, she had forgotten everyone and everything. He thought he was coming to keep Deirdre company, but instead he was trespassing on her peace.

She had always divided people she knew into groups: Protestants and Catholics; English and Irish; those she loved and those she feared. For some reason, she feared Jack. She wished he would let her work alone.

"Oh—Katherine. Where's Deirdre?" He looked as disappointed as she felt herself.

"She was here, but she went back at lunch time," she said. "There's a game."

"Oh, aye. But one of the sisters said she'd come out here picking."

"No, she didn't at all," Kate said flatly. "The sister must have mistaken us or not known Deirdre." She turned and resumed picking.

He watched her for a moment and then heaved the ladder onto the next tree. "You've a good idea there with your shirt," he commented. He picked up a cardboard tray. "I'll have to find a way to do the same sort of thing. Now tell me, where've you picked?"

She continued working as she answered, "I've picked these half dozen, can't you see?" Her voice sounded sharper than she had intended, so she quickly amended, "We could alternate trees on this row, if you want to."

"Fine." He climbed up the ladder, set the tray between three forked branches and began to pick as nimbly as an English

[178]

greengrocer, who with quick fingers could fill a bag exactly to the pound with greengages, plums, or apricots.

Jack did not seem inclined to talk, for which she was grateful. All the same, she was aware of him and could no longer reach for apples and climb up and down the ladder with freedom. Instead, she felt slow and awkward. She kept breaking off twigs and leaves with the apples and once almost missed her footing on the ladder.

Finally, she grudgingly asked him if he would show her how to pick more quickly. "You've done this before, haven't you?"

"Aye, once or twice. See now, this is how to do it."

They stood side by side in the ankle-deep grass by his ladder. His tone was soft, not patronizing. "You have to get your whole hand round the apple. Cradle it. Don't just jerk at the stalk. Turn it to one side—see?"

She watched his hand move to one of the low branches. His fingers were long but blunt, not thin and white like Father Kennedy's. Red-gold hair dusted the back of his hand. She reached up to an apple near his and tried to imitate the little twist he gave it before it came off with a soundless snap.

"That's right. You'll never bruise it that way. It comes off whole. No leaves. It shouldn't fall either."

She smiled suddenly. "Thank you."

He smiled back. "Don't you think that we'd pick a lot faster if we worked together? If one picked and the other steadied the tray and carried trays up and down, we'd get down the rows in no time. Take turns, we could." He glanced around. "We'll never finish anyway, but I'd like to do more for the sisters than just half a row."

She shrugged. "We could, I suppose."

They worked in silence again, only now much faster. Tray rose upon tray, filled with apples. After several hours, Jack had to fetch more empty crates from the storeroom.

While he was gone, Kate sat at the bottom of her ladder, waiting. The air had cooled now, but she was still flushed from the effort. She chewed idly on a blade of grass and stared up at the translucent sky. It was already tinged with violet, pink, and green.

Jack came wheeling boxes on a rickety wooden railway-porter's trolley. "Now we can really pick," he said. "That is, if the sun doesn't set on us."

"It will soon, I'm afraid," she said, looking up at the sky again.

"Come on, then. Will you pick this tray, or shall I?"

"If you pick, I'll hold the tray again."

They climbed their ladders and filled another tray. Kate took it down and handed up another. With his usual quickness, Jack perched the tray on a branch and had half a dozen apples on it before Kate had even set foot on the first rung. She was just starting to climb up again when Jack let out a roar, the tray went toppling off the branch, and he lunged sideways after it. His ladder swung dangerously to one side as apples and leaves rained down on Kate. She rushed to brace the ladder and stop his fall.

"Can you hold it?" he laughed.

She looked up to see that the top of the ladder was pushing hard on an old branch thin enough to bend and break. With her full weight, she leaned against the heavy wood.

"Now what?" she gasped, her teeth gritted with the exertion.

"What would you suggest?" he asked with mild sarcasm.

"Well, for goodness' sake, climb down quickly. I can't hold you much longer."

"You're stronger than you think," he said.

He was teasing her, she saw, for the ladder suddenly fell away from her as he swung off it and onto a sturdy branch. He hung there for a moment, his feet dangling a few inches from her face. Then with a warning shout he let go and dropped onto the ground, where he lay perfectly still.

Anxiously, she bent down toward him. He was shaking. "Are you all right?" She was shaken herself.

He sat up, laughing.

"What on earth happened?" she demanded angrily, irked that he had almost convinced her he was hurt.

"A wasp flew onto the apple I was picking," he laughed up at her. "What a fool! I flicked it away and knocked the apples, tried to grab them, and . . . you saw the rest. All for a silly wee wasp." He stood up, brushing the leaves and grass out of his hair and clothing, then looked more closely at her. "You look white as a ghost, so you do."

[180]

"You frightened me half to death," she snapped, "lying down there shaking like that."

He began to laugh again. "I'm sorry, honestly." He looked at his watch, his expression changing. "Ah, but look at this. It's after half four. We have to get on."

Up among the apples again, Kate soon forgot her anger. Around them the sky dimmed, the shadows lengthened, and a cold breeze came up. She hardly noticed, for Jack's fall had broken the reserve between them.

"So what did you think of the children?" he asked her now.

"Sweet," said Kate, smiling and thinking of Kathleen; but then as she heard the word she realized how inadequate it was, so she added, "I wanted to put my arms around them all. They seemed so sad, so hopeless somehow."

"Except that the sisters do love them. They're cared for here."

"I can see that," she agreed quickly. "But there's something awfully missing. It's terrible to be without a parent no matter how much someone else may care about you." She looked across at him over the apple tray.

He stopped picking and met her eyes but said no more about that. Moments later though, after she had gone down the ladder with the full tray and come up with another empty, he asked her, "And what d'you think about Father Kennedy this term?"

"In what way?"

"Haven't you noticed how thin he's become?"

"Yes, I did. But summer's a good time to shed weight. Many do."

"Shed weight?" Jack mocked. "But he had none to lose. He was so thin already."

Kate felt foolish as she tried to discern his implications. "Do you think, then, there's something seriously wrong with him?"

Jack didn't look at her. His fingers moved deftly over the apples. "Yes, I'm sure of it."

The blood beat up into her face. "What—what sort of thing d'you mean?"

"I don't know for sure. But next time you see him, just look at him. His skin is dry, yellow."

"I always thought that was just his natural coloring."

[181]

"I don't think so. I've seen pictures of him when he was younger. He didn't have that dried up look about him. He was heartier altogether."

"Yellow skin. What could that mean? Kidney or liver?"

"I think he's maybe got cancer," Jack said matter-of-factly, though his pained expression belied indifference.

"Oh—I hope you're wrong. I do hope you're wrong."

"Well, next time you see him, take a close look. Are you studying with him this term?"

She nodded, swallowing hard. "Yes, modern fiction. I thought you were in there too."

"I haven't seen you." He seemed surprised.

"Well, it's a big class. I'll try to sit down in the front on Monday and see for myself. Oh, I do hope you're wrong."

Jack was watching her closely. "You like him as much as I do," he stated.

"He's the best teacher I've ever had. And I've had some good ones. In England I had some of the best in boarding school. But Father Kennedy outstrips all of them. . . . I'm not thinking of just loss for myself," she hastened to add, "but for all the people who are coming behind us, and because he's such a—" She searched for the word. "Such a humanitarian. He loves his students. Deeply interested in others." Then, without thinking what she was saying, and without remembering that she was talking to a Catholic, she said, "Why would God end his life before time?"

"I don't know," Jack said slowly, obviously taken aback. "But I do know God gives and God takes away."

"Oh, that's such cold comfort," Kate shuddered. "I always think of that verse in material terms."

"But that's not the only way those words were meant," Jack countered.

Her eyebrows arched. Was he instructing her? He, a Catholic who had probably read no more than a few Bible verses?

He read the look in her eyes. "I've been reading the Holy Scripture with Roger."

"With Roger," she echoed bemusedly.

"He's quite an evangelist, is Roger. Wasted no time in

[182]

persuading me I needed to know the Word of the Almighty, and to know it right from the Bible itself. I've been devouring it."

She smiled in approval. "That's good. I'm glad." Then her face fell again. "But, oh, Father Kennedy—I can't bear to think he might be dying—now—before he's finished his life's work."

Jack called her on that. "How are we to know whether or not he's finished his life's work? God's given him a vocation. God doesn't turn around on Himself and undercut that." He paused, his eyes sad. "He's one of those rare priests who's almost too good for this world."

She couldn't reply; her thoughts raced: *If not in this world, where? Heaven?* How could she be sure that any Catholic would go to heaven? Even if she loved Father Kennedy and had admitted to herself that he had a faith, one that had something in common with hers, it was nevertheless one she did not fully understand. No, she had no assurance that he would be in heaven. Graham Greene's novels might have shown her that God's mercy was greater than her comprehension of it; still, she thought of that mercy as the "Catholic view," not necessarily one she herself could subscribe to.

"I saw him last summer in Belfast."

"Oh?" Her voice was noncommittal. What did that have to do with the conversation?

"It was during the flood. He and Father Michael and some of the other Derry Franciscans were down in the city as emergency workers helping clear away water, sandbagging, assisting those who were washed out of their houses. He looked terrible then, so he did—weak, working at half the pace of the others. That's when I first began to wonder about him. Now I'm fairly sure."

Kate couldn't bear the thought that Kennedy might die. Everything in her denied that possibility. And so she took up Jack's mention of the flood instead. "Just what exactly did happen anyway?" she asked. "I saw bits of it on the news and in *The Observer*, but I still don't know much. How was it that you saw Father Kennedy? What were you doing there?"

He gave her a strange look. "I live in West Belfast. . . . Doesn't the BBC broadcast that sort of thing—the flood, I mean?"

"Some. Not enough to satisfy me."

[183]

"No, I suppose not. . . . It was the rain. Terrific rain, almost tropical. And a gale on top of it. The water was four feet deep in places. We'd over three inches of rain in ten hours—what would you expect?"

"Three inches!"

"The river came up quickly. Flash flooding everywhere. Streets, houses—everything was saturated or under water." He frowned. "My family was lucky. A few inches in the cellar, and the roof leaked a bit upstairs. Nothing much. But down the street, oh, half a mile maybe, people lost all their furniture—all they'd stored in their cellars—a lot."

Kate murmured with sympathy.

"The Brits—" he smiled ruefully at her, "the Army, I mean, pardon me, were welcome in Ballymurphy for the first time. Trained for such an emergency, I suppose. And boys who'd doubtless been stoning soldiers and blowing up the customs post the week before—did you hear about that? . . . no?—well, they were all down there working away, moving sandbags, hauling out furniture, helping the old folks into rubber dinghies, and rowing to the Army canteen."

"The Army arranged temporary accommodation, didn't they?"

"Aye, I think the whole thing softened a few hard hearts, but not enough." Jack stopped picking again, his face meditative. "I remember praying over and over again that week that the flood would bring peace and knock some sense into people."

Kate nodded. She had prayed the same, though certainly in a different way.

"But there they were, the very next week, the Protestants and government argue-barguing about whether or not the RUC should have guns, the civil rights people demonstrating about an internment policy we don't have and won't, please God, and the IRA blowing up another customs post." He was shaking his head. "None of it seems right. The country's gone stark mad." And he went back to picking.

Kate said, "I suppose there's not a Catholic in Belfast—or Derry for that matter—who'd cry if the Army left?"

"I'm not sure. That's what a lot of folks think. It was specially bad at the beginning of August after that young lad O'Hagan was killed down in the New Lodge Road."

Kate nodded. Everyone in Britain knew of that controversial death: bystanders and soldiers could not agree whether the youth was armed or not when shot by the Army marksman.

"The language I heard that week! Feelings ran very high, even after his wake. And people felt the Army was provoking the riots—stirring up the Catholics in the Ardoyne and Ballymurphy to justify importing even more troops."

Kate had read as much, she said, in *The Observer*.

"But that's what I meant about the flood. People were won over then—just a bit. The flood might have been worse and done more good—along those lines."

"Don't you think they should leave, then?"

Jack turned to watch her as she set the apples in the tray. "I'm not sure," he shrugged. "If the rumors of provocation are true—yes, they should get out. Things are bound to get worse. I doubt the IRA will be content with tame wee explosions at isolated customs offices—or even more spectacular ones at the railway stations." He shivered. "But if they do pull out . . . the fighting won't stop, I'm afraid. Some on both sides seem to feed on violence." He stopped abruptly. The tray was full, so he climbed down with it and came up with another.

Kate smiled wanly at him as she took her turn picking. She was almost as quick as he now. "You sound a little like Liam. No wonder you and he get along so well."

Jack shrugged. "Violence will never solve things. You don't think so either, I'm sure."

Kate hesitated. She had silently condoned some Army tactics that the civil rights people had condemned. And she still felt that Protestant paramilitary groups had the right to hold parades and keep guns. "I don't know," she murmured doubtfully.

Jack made a noise of disgust. "Think of it, Katherine. The Army's done wrong. But others have—and will—do worse if the Army leaves. Paisley's verbal violence and provocative parades are no better, either, than the IRA's bombs and kneecappings. It won't be just your Protestants—the poor people on Fountain Street and other such places—who'll suffer if the Army goes. It'll be your poor Catholics in West Belfast and the Bogside who'll suffer too. People feel more secure on both sides as it is, at least." He heaved a sigh. "When all the troubles started, many of us couldn't sleep at night for fear the Protestant vigilantes'd burn our houses down around us—or worse."

"The burning still goes on, all the same."

"Not as much as it did. Not now, anyway."

Kate stopped picking and leaned against the ladder. An overwhelming tiredness had suddenly taken hold of her. Her head felt light, her stomach hollow and sick. She remembered now how little rest she'd had the night before and how little she'd eaten all day. Brushing hair away from her glasses, she said dully, "I'm tired, and hungry too."

"Aye, you probably are. And we've said enough about the troubles, I'm thinking. Let's rest a wee minute."

Kate looked up into the sky as she rested her cheek against the rough wooden rung. A cobalt lake hung above them: no stars and no clouds. "Should we stop?" she ventured.

"We could. You do look done in." They climbed down, and Jack put the last tray into the crate. "Here, have an apple." He tossed one to her.

"The nuns—the sisters—won't mind?"

"Of course not." Jack dropped to the ground and leaned back against a tree.

It was darker under the branches than up above among them. Kate sank onto the side of the trolley and bit into the apple. Juice spattered onto her cheeks and hand. Wiping it away, she said, "Maybe we could just fill one more tray, off the next tree. Then we'd have ten full crates."

"A good round number. But we're short a tray."

"I'll get one."

"I thought you were tired. It's too dark anyway, isn't it?"

"It's only just twilight, and walking's better than standing on a ladder. Don't you ache?"

"Only a little."

Kate ate the apple quickly and threw the core across the orchard as she went for the tray. When she came back up the wide path, a sharp-edged new moon was just visible over the eastern edge of the orchard. Luminous, tipped with blue at the top and rose beneath, it hung right above the trees.

Ahead of her in the shadows she could just see Jack standing half way up the ladder in a tree that was still heavy with apples. He had tilted his face toward the sky, and the light of the moon caught his ruffled hair and long nose. She could see his lips moving. Unaware that she stood close by, he seemed to be praying.

Saturday, December 12

Liam and Jack had been surveying Bogside together for months. They made an odd pair: the one short, with tangled fair hair partly lost under the upturned black collar of a too-long coat; the other tall, in a shapeless gray wool jacket, his hair cut square over the eyes and at the back; the one moving quickly with light, alert steps; the other striding unselfconsciously; the one turning his head from side to side, his face watchful, to scan others on the pavement; the other, his face almost blank, looking beyond with soft gray eyes. Had they not walked together, both wearing the green, red, and white scarves of the University and both carrying clipboards given them by the Commission, no one would have guessed any relationship between them.

A bus roared past them, sending up an eddy of dead leaves, cigarette papers, and stale air. At three o'clock the street lights were already coming on, cold glows in a cloudless, colder sky.

"It's getting raw," Liam muttered.

Jack pulled his scarf tighter. "Yes. Time to get home."

"We're just starting."

They were going together from the Guildhall up through the Diamond to the Protestant area of Fountain Street.

"No—I mean *home*. Belfast. Newry. I'm tired of Derry, aren't you?"

"Only till Friday, Jack. Not long. The eighteenth. Bloody marvelous."

Jack stopped briefly as he transferred the clipboard from one hand to the other. He'd forgotten his gloves, and the hand outside his pocket already felt numb. "Hmm ... the eighteenth. And

[188]

wasn't that when you and Deirdre started out together? Some time around then?"

Liam smiled. "No. The fifth. We didn't forget, either."

"An anniversary."

"An anniversary. A year, Jack!"

"Irishmen never forget anniversaries, do they?"

"Not likely." A smile curled Liam's mouth again. "Especially the Prods, now. Apprentice Boys . . . the Boyne. . . . Might as well have been last year."

"Catholics don't forget either, though."

"Yes, they do—'too busy saying Mass and making babies.' That's what Prods think; I'm positive of it." Prods. He'd hardly used the word since Deirdre. It sounded strange, all of a sudden.

They passed the Chinese resturant. Jack stared in abstractedly. "You're in a funny mood today! What about October fifth . . . Burntollet on January fourth? Does NICRA forget?"

He shrugged. "Maybe not."

"I'm surprised you're still in NICRA."

Liam flashed out a surprised, defiant look. "Why?"

"What can it do anyway?"

Liam's face darkened. "Use peaceful means to stop internment, for one thing."

"That's just party rhetoric. Even the rallies are dangerous. There's always someone who wants to fight. Then look what you've got—the IRA sniping at the troops, and more people dead in the cross fire."

"Is that worse or better than people standing silently while Stormont talks about internment? Acts on it, too, maybe? Someone has to make a statement."

Jack shrugged. "I used to think so too. Now I think, 'And someone has to wash the blood off the streets afterwards.' NICRA doesn't kill people, but if it keeps up the way it's going, it's going to be guilty of murder as much as the IRA is guilty. On goes the revenge, Liam. And people don't forget anniversaries. As we said."

They turned from the Diamond into Ferryquay Street.

"Some are better remembered. But Deirdre and I now—"

"And what does she think about NICRA?"

[189]

"It doesn't matter what she thinks." The answer came almost too quickly.

"You love her, don't you?" Jack pursued, even though he knew Liam's temper was rising.

"More than you know. . . . What is this, Jack? Catechism?"

"Then it matters."

Liam scowled. "But she's still influenced by Kate. Kate's opposed to NICRA. Thinks it's full of Communists and terrorists. She's made Deirdre afraid for me when there's no reason to be."

"I'm not so sure."

"About the Communists and terrorists?"

"No—that there's no reason for fear."

"Oh, you're sounding more and more like my father every day. Lay off, Jack."

"Sorry. I've been around this province a mite longer than you, remember?"

"That gives you license to lecture?"

Jack laughed. "No. You can ignore everything I say, if you want to."

Liam scuffed the pavement as they went along. He disliked disagreeing with Jack, whom he had unconsciously begun to use as his yardstick for judging things. Rather slowly, therefore, he said, "There is a wee bone of contention between us right now, if you must know." He tried to sound casual.

Jack knew better. "About NICRA?" was his sharp retort.

"Yes . . . a rally in January I mean to go to. But she won't hear of NICRA at all. We've been avoiding the subject now for days."

"So what will you do? Not go?"

Liam spat his answer back with a snarl. "Oh, aye, I'll go right enough. I just won't tell her . . . nor will you." He fixed Jack with an intent, determined stare. They stopped briefly in front of a shoe shop.

Jack sighed. "It means that much to you to go?"

"I'd not miss a rally like that."

"Important is it?"

"Very. There's talk of a Bill of Rights to be taken to Westminster."

"Not for the first time."

They started to walk again. Liam shook his head. "No. The Connolly Association got fifty thousand signatures for it in the summer. The secretary of NICRA urged a Bill of Rights last September—in Westminster. But nothing's been done yet."

"And do you think it will, anyway, even with a bill?"

"Oh, don't be so bloody reactionary."

"No, I'm serious. What difference will laws make? Can you legislate nondiscrimination and equal rights?"

"You'd bloody well better try, that's what I think."

"It's just sticking plaster on a dirty wound, though. Inside, people hate as much as ever."

"So you give up? Play defeatist? Do nothing?"

"I don't know. I can't see things the way you do. But I don't think passivity's right either. There's a middle way somewhere."

"Yeah. Sit on the barricades, barbed wire and all. Try it sometime. See how you like it."

"That's not what I mean," Jack answered patiently. "Not fence-sitting. I mean—" He threw out his arms. "Things like this . . . the housing survey . . . what we're doing now. Each work according to his own vision of what should be done. According to his means. In his own way. We can't change the world, Liam. We can change a small corner of it, though."

Liam's eyebrows flickered in faint derision. "Now we agree. You'll change your corner by running a parish somewhere. Old ladies crocheting blankets for orphans. The bridge club to raise money for the starving in Biafra. The christenings and wakes. That's your corner, Jack. Mine's in NICRA. Maybe in politics. Maybe in a union—I don't know."

"And Deirdre? She's in the picture too? Will she be crying by your casket while I say the Christian Burial after you've been murdered by someone as hotheaded as you but with fewer scruples?"

With a look of horror, Liam stopped dead and swore at him. "Don't you ever talk that way again! Why—"

They faced each other, still the odd pair: Jack white, his mouth unhappy; Liam red, his eyes furious. They stood tense as wary dogs before a fight. Two women passed them, throwing anxious glances over their shoulders as they hauled their children away.

[191]

Jack broke the constraint first. "Well, perhaps we'd better work by ourselves today. We're not doing too well together."

Liam's shoulders dropped into a slouch again. "No, let's just change the subject."

They went on for a while without speaking. Under the Ferry Quay Gate, the wall looming over them as gray and dark as a plug of cooled volcanic lava. Southwest under the wall, and so to Fountain Street, where the seventeenth-century Church of Ireland cathedral, St. Columb's, dominated the skyline: massive, dark, formidable. At the top of Fountain Street a crowd of small girls was clustered in a noisy argument, loud and shrill as angry starlings and magpies. But as Liam and Jack approached, they stopped to stare. A row of blue eyes, unkempt light brown heads, hand-knitted sweaters in blues and reds. No greens here. This was Fountain Street, after all.

The children spread out as the men passed. Two of them began to turn a skipping rope, and immediately a chorus of treble voices started a chant Jack remembered from his own childhood, when it had come floating over fences from Protestant playgrounds.

> *Ye Loyalists of Ireland*
> *Come rally round the throne!*
> *Through weal or woe prepare to go,*
> *Make England's cause your own.*
> *Remember your allegiance,*
> *Be this your battle cry:*
> *For Protestant ascendancy*
> *In Church and State we'll die.*

One girl skipped the rope in precise time. She was sure-footed and serious-faced. For some reason Jack thought of Kate.

Liam was bristling with indignation. "We'll do well to drown 'em out with 'The Merry Ploughboy,'" he said sourly under his breath. "What obscenity out of the mouths of wee girls."

"Aye. And they don't even know what they're singing."

"Bigotry. Something we'd never stoop to ourselves now, would we?"

Jack matched his banter. "Indeed not."

[192]

"You should see the Americans skip, Jack. Jumping rope, they call it. Little black kids of eight doing double dutch. I've never seen the likes of it."

Jack didn't answer right away; then he said, "You loved the States, didn't you?"

"I did. What I saw, y'understand."

"That's all you talk of now. America and Deirdre. Last year it was rugby and Deirdre."

"Deirdre has lasted, see?"

"Dangerous subject, Liam. Sorry."

"Beautiful subject, you mean. She'll outlast everything else that I talk about." He gave Jack a quick warning look. "Even politics. And civil rights. Though I'd not admit it to everybody."

"I'm glad to hear you say it. Even if you are contradicting yourself."

"Don't get smug." His voice brightened, the harshness suddenly gone. "I'll tell you, Jack, though not a word to anyone—"

"You're making me your father confessor? Please don't. Not yet. Not after the words we just had."

"Oh—they're gone. We're friends. And I can take it from you. No, this is something you'll be glad to hear." Liam paused. Behind them, the shrill little voices piped on.

The glorious, pious memory of William drink for aye,
Who freed us from all Popery, huzza, me girls, huzza!

"I'm after marrying Deirdre. You know that, do you?"

Jack nodded and smiled. His eyes began to smart in the cold. "I thought as much."

"Aye. There's no one else for me."

"She's a good little woman, Liam. You've asked her?"

"No, not yet. I'll wait till January—after the rally." Again the warning look. "If she can take me as I am, then we're all set. I'll wait a few days after the meeting—then—" he clapped his hands— "pop the question!"

Jack touched the cuff of Liam's coat. "You'll maybe do fine. But just be sure *you* take her as *she* is." His voice was gentle, not reproving; cautious, not wanting to offend.

[193]

Liam frowned slightly. "Meaning?"

"She's been brought up differently—her mother a Methodist and all."

"And her father's a Catholic. I don't need Freud to—"

"No, I know that. But you'll not try to press her out of her ways—into politics and activism against her will? You'll not be doing that, will you, if you do marry?"

"If we do." His mouth was grim. "But no, you needn't say that to me. I'll not do that. I love her, Jack. The way she is—that's the Deirdre I want."

Jack grinned widely. "Such wisdom."

Liam was laughing now, a shade embarrassed. "Pray, Jack. God'll hear you. That she'll take me. I couldn't bear—"

"Of course I'll pray. D'you think I've not been already?"

They stood there smiling at each other, now as warm and close as a few minutes before they had been acrimonious and angry. Jack looked into Liam's lively face and saw a kind of joy he himself had not known.

But then it was back to the present. They studied their clipboards. A few houses yet in Fountain Street. Next, on to St. Columb's Hill.

"We're making a pretty slow start," Jack commented. "Half three already."

"So it is."

"Then let's split up. What d'you say?"

Liam hesitated. "Are you sure you want to? Been working together a long time now. And anyhow—" He broke off, tapping on his clipboard. "Why did the Commission send us over here?"

"You're worried about being in a Protestant house? Why? We've never had any problems before. Know what we're doing."

"On William Street or Lisfannon Park, yes."

"But no one'll eat you. They're people, just like Deirdre's mother. Overbusy. Worried half the time about money and employment and health. They'll be as glad to see us as the Bogsiders are. Any ray of hope . . . however remote . . . some escape from their landlord. . . . Just the same as your own people, too, no doubt."

"No doubt," Liam repeated ironically.

Suddenly overhead came a distinctive thrashing, thrumming sound. They both looked up in surprise as three British Army helicopters flew from the direction of Waterside across the azure band of sky between the houses.

"Troop choppers!" Liam started and looked around anxiously as the helicopters applauded their way through the air. The downwash of their blades slapped against the fuselages, thwacking dully against the terraced houses and tunnel-like streets.

"You are nervous, aren't you!" Jack teased after the noise had faded to a distant whirring.

Liam shrugged. "You might say that."

"But didn't you notice—they had them all decorated up. I bet they're playing Father Christmas to some of the weans over in Bogside."

"Blarney, Jack."

"We'll see. They did last year. . . . But come on, let's get going. You'll do all right by yourself, won't you?"

"I s'pose so."

Jack pointed to a house halfway down the street. "You take that one. I'll go across. We can meet up afterwards and see what we've got."

They parted immediately, Jack going across the road. He could still hear the skipping girls' song coming faintly from the top of Fountain Street.

> *In ninety-eight, of later date,*
> *Our helpless sires were slain;*
> *Had Papists power this very hour,*
> *They'd do the same again.*

No past in Northern Ireland, Jack thought. Even 1698 was present.

The first house he approached looked deserted. Forty years ago it must have looked the same as every other house on the street, but now the windows needed paint, the mortar repointing, and the bricks were pitted in places as if someone had sprayed them with bullets. *Unlikely,* he thought. This area might house poor families, but it was a close neighborhood. No terrorists here. Working-class Protestants only. Linen workers. Dockers. Decent people.

[195]

He pushed the bell. It buzzed somewhere at the back of the house. From within came a man's shout, a slammed door, the sound of a child crying. Then silence.

He waited. If they only knew that his coming might one day mean a new home for them, they'd be rushing to the door. But then he smiled at his own naïveté. Things wouldn't be that simple. Ever.

The child's crying stopped. A curtain at the one front window moved an inch, then dropped. Still silence.

Somewhat disconcerted, Jack pushed the bell again. Then there was a grating of bolts and a rattling of security chains and the door opened about two inches.

"What are y'after?" A surly male voice.

For a moment, Jack wanted to laugh. The man must fancy himself a character in some old American gangster film. But the Commission people had taught him to be cautious in every interview until he knew the people were willing to talk. So he restrained himself and spoke politely and easily. "I'm from the Derry Development Commission. We're doing a housing survey and I wondered—"

"Derry, y'say?" The man's tone was nasty. He said the word explosively, like an obscenity.

"Londonderry," Jack corrected himself quickly.

"And you wondered—?" The man pursued, imitating Jack's unmistakable West Belfast brogue. He had not yet shown his face, but Jack pictured him about forty-five and heavy, though not tall, judging by the height of his voice. Perhaps with a few jiggers of whiskey down him already.

Jack shifted uneasily on the step. "If I could ask you a question or two that we've been asking a lot of people all over the city?" *Mostly in Bogside,* he added mentally.

"No." A flat refusal. Toneless. Abrupt. But the door did not shut. Was he expecting Jack to say more?

Carefully, he began, "They're questions about your house. The number of residents. The length of time you've lived here. Whether or—"

"Shut up. No questions here. Take yourself off." A loud click sounded from just out of sight behind the edge of the door. "Or

[196]

you'll be sorry." Two inches of shiny, black pistol barrel appeared right in front of Jack. The hand that held the weapon was steady. "Now take your bleedin' questions and go. We don't want bloody Taigs, students, and the like on this street." The barrel moved slightly in command.

Jack had no time to think; he could only react. He stepped back and to one side and murmured, "I'm sorry to trouble you."

"You will be, if you hang around," the man sneered. "I've been watching you and that other fellow—get out unless you want half the UVF on you." Then he slammed the door. The bolts and chains clattered again.

Jack stayed close to the wall of the adjoining houses and, half crouching, ran the remainder of the street to the corner. He stood there, shaken, and looked around. No children. No Saturday afternoon shoppers. No one. Not even Liam. Again, he resisted the impulse to laugh—it all seemed too improbable and fantastic. But all the same he was breathless, almost winded, from fright. Out of sight of the street, he leaned against the wall and shut his eyes. In the brief darkness he heard the roar of his own blood. He opened his eyes again. Would he be safe even here? His breathing slowed, and as it did he realized that the man had probably been far more afraid than he was. Bravado. The UVF was gone by now, surely. Or was it? That man feared some enemy. Hence the locks and chains, the pistol. Should he go back and try again? At some other house, perhaps?

He looked at the clipboard, which he'd been holding so tightly that it had dug a deep, bloodless line into his left palm. *No,* he thought, *a dead surveyor's no use to the Commission.* He'd better get Liam and go on to St. Columb's Hill.

The cathedral clock had chimed the three-quarter hour and passed it by several minutes when movement in the street behind him stirred Jack. Turning, he saw with relief that Liam was looking for him, so he waved and called. As soon as Liam reached the corner, he started telling Jack about the family he'd just surveyed.

Jack interrupted him. "Let's go to St. Columb's Hill."

Liam's eyes widened. "What for?"

[197]

"I was just threatened with a pistol. We'd better leave this street alone until we've talked to someone at the Commission."

"You're joking."

"No, I'm not."

Liam sauntered to an ancient stone watering trough a few feet away. He set his clipboard on the edge and slouched against the rough stones. "I don't believe it!" He stared at Jack, as though sizing him up, and lit a cigarette.

"Believe it. And we're sitting ducks out in this open area, too. He said he'd been watching both of us."

Liam scoffed. "But 'they're people just like Deirdre's mother.' You were right. In fact, I had the most cordial conversation just now. Wanted to give me tea and cakes. Told me their nephew was up at the University when it was still Magee . . . and on and on."

Jack turned away. "All the same, let's not stay here now. I'm no coward, but no fool either. The fellow warned me about UVF members on the street. Said we should both be on our way."

"Then let's." Liam picked up his clipboard again, and they jogged toward Bishop's Gate. "So much for that, Father Monaghan. Hopeless people, are they? Grateful for any ray of hope, are they?"

"Don't. You've said enough." Jack sounded grave.

"Well I'm glad I wasn't the one to go to that house. Never had a door slammed in me face, let alone a gun pointed at me. Not even by Deirdre's mother!"

Jack relaxed a little, chuckling, and they slowed to a walk.

"Oh—but wait a wee minute. I did so have a door slammed on me once."

"Oh?" Jack was only half listening. St. Columb's Hill was just ahead, and all he wanted was to get out of the wind and dark and into a warmer place. Somewhere less hostile this time.

"Kate Hamilton slammed a door on me once, I remember. A while ago, so she did."

Jack's eyebrows rose slightly; he remembered her slamming a door on him, too.

"But there were mitigating circumstances. And I've forgiven her." Liam sounded magnanimous, pleased with himself. Jack didn't pick up the dropped thread. Over his cigarette Liam gave him a sidelong glance. "But never mind it now. You want to work together? I don't mind it alone now, but after what—"

"Yes, let's stay together. I've a feeling we'll not get much more done anyway." Jack looked at his watch. "Gone four. Oh—it feels like six to me. These short days! Let's see if we can go at least three more houses."

"Right enough." They stood briefly under a streetlight to check the house numbers they would take. "This one first?"

A feeble light glowed through holes in threadbare gray curtains in the window of the row house. As they waited for someone to answer the bell, Liam pointed out the word "welcome" just discernible in white letters on the stone doorstep. One of the letters had been partly effaced so that the word read "we come."

Once again the door opened only two inches. The crack of light around it was brighter than Jack expected. "What is it?" a man's voice asked. No rudeness this time, but a note of caution.

Liam answered, "Good evening, sir. We're here from the Londonderry Development Commission—"

Ah, Jack thought, *he's wiser than I was.*

"—wanted to ask you a few questions. We're student volunteers—doing a survey."

The door jerked wider but was held fast, still not wide enough for them to go in. Jack knew by the uneven way the door had opened that the man had wedged his foot against its other side. Mistrust. Fear. What a way to live! But it was the same in West Belfast. Especially at night one didn't open a door too quickly. Especially not to men—strangers.

The head of a young man appeared around the door, on a level with Liam's. Straight, dark, untidy hair. Pale blue eyes. No smile. He took their measure with a steady, neutral scrutiny. Then he held the door wide open. "All right. Come yous in. You're welcome enough."

Jack took a deep breath of relief. While he couldn't believe that everyone in this part of the city was as antagonistic as the man on Fountain Street, he'd begun to doubt the Commission's wisdom in sending two Catholics to a Protestant stronghold. And how good it felt to get out of the wind!

The entryway was narrow and uncarpeted, the floor so marked

and gouged that he couldn't tell if it was linoleum or wood. Directly in front of them a steep, painted staircase with broken banisters ascended into the darkness of another floor. To the right was a door, its paint chipping off, from behind which came the familiar sound of Saturday afternoon soccer-match results read by an Englishman. The place looked clean but smelled damp, faintly mildewed.

Their host was deferential and apologetic. "You'll be taking some tea with us? Here, let me have your coats. The wife'll get you tea in just a minute." He opened the door to the right and led them into the living room. "You'll have to take us as we are, I'm afraid." He was slight, slim, and every movement apparently caused him pain.

Opposite the door a gas fire hissed out a dry, ineffective heat. Small red and blue jets of flame shot up all across it. On either side of the heater stood two faded chintz armchairs with 1930s wing backs. The man's wife sat in the one on the right. She smiled up at them with a round, homely face, then bent again to the baby she held in the crook of her arm. The child was nursing, her tiny fingers curling and uncurling on the soft stuff of the mother's sweater. The woman was absorbed, without a shred of embarrassment.

Coming into the room behind Liam, Jack hesitated when he saw the scene; he sent a questioning glance at the man. Were they intended to disturb the mother and child now?

The man looked uncomfortable. "You'll not mind, Vera? The wean's hungry."

Liam smiled. "Oh, aye, surely." He took the straight-backed oak chair indicated by the man and rested his clipboard on his knee. "We came at the wrong time, I'm thinking." But his easy tone undercut the formality of his words.

Jack, too, sat down. The man switched off the television and took his place again in the armchair opposite his wife. He sat on the edge of his chair, ill at ease, rolling the corner of his collar up and down. But his voice was cheerful as he turned to Jack. "So yous're up at the New University . . . Magee, that was?"

"Aye, I'm Jack Monaghan, and this is Liam Donnelly."

The man jumped up again to shake their hands. He shook hard

[200]

and quickly, as if he'd been trained by early discipline in this old ritual and still viewed it as something to get over as hastily as possible. "Glad to meet yous, I'm sure," he murmured. But he didn't look glad, only a little on edge. "The name's David MacDonald. And Vera."

"And the wee babe?" Liam asked.

"Angela." The man sat back a little, a glow of satisfaction on his face. "Angela Christine."

"Eight weeks old, she is," the mother said happily. "Our first."

"She's a lovely little lass," Jack approved, watching the smooth rounded head and fine white hair against the mother's breast. An intimate, warm tableau. Madonna and child. No sight more beautiful, even in a drab gray room whose only adornment was a coronation portrait of the Queen. No sight more full of hope, even in a city where people shot and maimed each other.

"Thank you. Oh, Davey, would you mind filling the kettle? We could plug it in here. Angela'll be content in a wee minute. Then I can make tea—oh, and there's some McVitie's biscuits in the cupboard, love."

Jack held up a hand. "Please don't fash yourselves at all. We're not hungry."

"Not at all? Yous'll take something?"

Liam and Jack exchanged glances, and Jack nodded. "Thank you. Tea'd be nice. It's bitter out there this evening."

MacDonald left the room.

"So what are the questions?" Vera MacDonald prompted. "And why are y' asking? Will it do us any good to answer?"

Jack appraised her face. Homely, yes, but intelligent, perceptive. He said simply, "I don't know for sure. I hope so. The Commission's got high hopes for rehousing and making improvements. So we have a lot of different questions."

The woman shifted the baby's weight slightly and stroked the little face with her right hand. "Well, if they'll not be too hard, we'll answer." A trace of skepticism gave her almost an impish look. "But I'm not altogether sure the Commission'll ever accomplish much. We've been hearing of it now for almost two years, and you're the first who've come to us." She smiled. "But, go on. I don't mean to be judging. It's nice of you to come."

[201]

MacDonald returned to the room carrying an old electric kettle that he plugged in behind his wife's chair. He stooped slowly, as though it hurt him to bend. He seemed still uneasy with the two men and watched Jack closely as he began to question.

Jack spoke without condescension, animosity, or suspicion. There was no harshness about him—rather, an ease and a ready smile. "Is it just the three of you here?"

"Aye." Vera MacDonald looked across at her husband with a glint of laughter in her eyes. "Just three now."

"And how long is it you've lived here?"

"Three years come Christmas. Our wedding was on Christmas Eve in '67."

Glancing quickly at Liam, Jack laughed. "So you've an anniversary this fortnight!"

She smiled back, basking in memories he couldn't know.

"And you're buying the place, are you?"

MacDonald shook his head, the corners of his mouth wrinkling down. "No. Leasing."

"And can you tell me how much the rent is?" Then added quickly with a frown at the form, "Don't, if you'd rather not."

"Three pounds a week." She said it quickly, with a sigh. "We're often behind, too." She nodded toward her husband. "When Davey's out of work, it's harder than you can imagine."

Jack turned to look at MacDonald. "You're working now, are you? I was going to ask you anyway, in a wee while." His voice was soft.

"I am now. But I've a bad back, see. Don't know how long they'll keep me. I've been out on sick pay twice this year already. Laid up two weeks both times." Jack didn't miss the frisson of desperation.

"It's been powerful hard for him, so it has. But Angela and I cheer him up. And we're managing."

"I'm down on Prince's Quay, in the transit shed. Loading, unloading. If only the good Lord—" He broke off, assessing Jack's reaction. "If only the good Lord would provide me a job as a crane operator, things'd be better. I'd not have to depend on me back so much."

Jack nodded, scribbling down relevant answers on his pad with

[202]

a well-used fountain pen in a spiky, distinctive hand. "I wish I could help you. Maybe someone at the Commission would know—"

"Don't think of it. S'none of their concern. And the Lord won't let us down. He wouldn'a given us Angela if He wasn't to provide for her through us. And when Vera weans the lass, she'll look for part-time work herself." He raised his eyes and looked directly at Jack. The hint of hopelessness had vanished. "Like she says, we are managing."

Jack went on with questions about the number of rooms in the house, sanitation, and how often they met with the landlord. Finally, when he came to the end of the form, he asked MacDonald to show him around.

In Bogside, in the Rossville area, Jack had seen squalid houses and flats into which were crowded three generations of a family, sometimes with as many as eight children. By comparison, the MacDonalds' house seemed spacious: two small rooms downstairs with a narrow hall and stairway, two upstairs, and a cellar—all for only two adults and a baby. But the deteriorating condition of the place appalled Jack when he contrasted it with the comfort he and Roger enjoyed—took for granted—at McCrea for only a pound more each week.

"But this is one thing I canna stand about the place," MacDonald was saying as he limped in front of Jack to the rear of the house. "No running water. For three pounds! It's no place fit for decent folk. Vera was used to better on her father's farm in Dungannon. But she never complains. And with a baby. . . . Look—" He opened the creaking back door into an alley behind the house. "There's our water. You canna see it in the dark, but—. Five houses down, against the wall. One cold tap for eight houses, and an outhouse. You'll see we don't wash as often as we'd like here." He slammed the door hard. "But it's not so bad for me. I can get a hot shower at work if I want. Vera, now, she has to go down and draw water if she runs out. We keep a big old churn of it in the kitchen, and bowls for washing. No sinks, you'll see. I fill the churn every morning before I go, but often it's not enough . . . when she's boiling nappies and the like. Angela's never been ill yet, thank the Lord, with Vera's nursing. But if she is . . . well,

[203]

maybe we'll have to take the bus to Dungannon." He leaned up against the door. "And that's not all, either."

"What?"

"Rats."

Jack shuddered. "Rats?"

"I never see such filth as there is out in the back sometimes, in the alley. Rubbish everywhere. What can you expect?" He opened the back door again. "There—see for yourself."

Peering out, Jack now saw what his light-adjusted eyes had not taken in before: the outlines of overturned dustbins and broken garbage bags all along the alley between the St. Columb's Hill houses and the next row; indistinguishable clumps of rotting food and other debris on the ground; pieces of newspaper rustling in the wind; and then, along an opposite wall, the surreptitious, scurrying movement of a small cat—or rat.

With an exclamation of dismay, he backed into the house, staring at MacDonald. "Oh . . . that's terrible!" But his words sounded lame. How could he express, in mere words, disgust as deep as he felt?

Again, though, MacDonald made less of it than Jack thought he himself would have. Was it just that he had become accustomed to things, or did he genuinely believe what he said: "Aye, it is terrible. We hear them—running, squeaking, gnawing—right from upstairs, though we've none up there, let me tell you. But we're trying to learn to put up with it. Make the best. We just don't go out after dark." A slight darkening of his face. "Use an old chamberpot of me mother's. And we make sure we've plenty of water."

Jack was shaking his head, not knowing what to say.

"I couldn't abide it if Vera made hard of it. But it's because she takes it all so easily that I can. And when I think of people without a roof, with nothing to eat at all, or with their families broken apart, or their wives and children killed in the troubles—then God reminds me to thank Him."

Awed, and humbled, Jack quietly met the man's eyes. Then suddenly, seemingly from nowhere, some words of Christ's that he had read with Roger a few nights before fluttered into his mind. *I tell you, nowhere, even in Israel, have I found faith like this.* Aloud, he said simply, "I admire your courage, and your faith."

MacDonald answered with a slow smile and stood up straighter than before. "If I've faith, then it's God's gift, by the Spirit. It's not of me own doing. Do you believe that, too?"

Half-expecting a rejection, Jack replied, "Yes, I believe that; I'm a Catholic." He was going to add, *And I'll be in the priesthood in a few years,* but something stopped him. No need to undercut the delicate understanding they had built across the old, bitter gulf.

MacDonald was studying him again, even more intensely than he had first done at the front door. "Aye, and an understandin' one. I see that clearly." He reached out his hand to Jack's and shook it with obvious warmth. "You're very kind to come away and do this sort of work. Now let Vera give you something before you go on your way again."

Liam and Jack had stayed with the MacDonalds until after six, when Vera had begun making the supper. (*However does she manage?* Jack had wondered, remembering the decrepit brown gas stove in the sinkless scullery that masqueraded as a kitchen.) By that time, Liam had rocked Angela to sleep in his arms with an old Celtic lullaby, and Jack had told the MacDonalds all about the Christmas he would be spending at home with his parents, his aunt, and his clutch of nephews and nieces. They had found in common a love of home and children.

"And you, Liam—what about you at Christmas?" Jack asked as the two men stepped onto the Rosemount bus and sat at the back, facing each other.

"Home, like yourself. The whole Donnelly clan. But I'll miss Deirdre."

"Will you not see her?"

"Oh, aye, a few times here and there. Her mother's still unhappy with me. But I'll win her over in the end. Persistence and patience. My old motto."

"Then you'll survive the days between seeing Deirdre, I should think."

[205]

The bus was warm and stuffy, a little hazy from the waft of blue cigarette and pipe smoke. Liam looked across at Jack, his eyes dull and a little sad now. "Survive, yes. But it's a terrible ache. When we're engaged . . . if—" He frowned. "It'll be different. More sure then." His eyes drifted toward the smudged mirror of nighttime glass as though toward the future, but then they returned to Jack's face. "And you? You didn't say anything at all to those people about Maynooth or about your own plans. You're still going down to see the rector, aren't you?"

"I didn't want to say anything about my vocation. That might have spoiled the good conversation we had going with them. . . . Maynooth? Aye, I've got to go before we come back in January."

"You were supposed to see him in the summer, weren't you?"

"Aye, Father Maurus—our pastor at home—and Colm Kennedy both wanted me to go down then. But I got involved in this and that and never got around to it. So I'll have to go right after Christmas. If I don't, Father Colm's threatening me with Europe . . . St. Isadore's or Louvaine. But for all the talk about Maynooth's being a priest factory, I'd not want to be out of Ireland for four years. I'll get to the seminary for sure this time."

Liam lighted a cigarette, all the time watching Jack. "You're talking so emphatically, I almost doubt it," he said.

Jack leaned forward, surprise and puzzlement on his face. "What d'ya mean?"

"Got to go . . . have to go . . . get there for sure. Your voice convinces me; your eyes don't. Somewhere in your complicated soul there's resistance."

Jack bowed. "Thank you, Doctor Freud."

"Not psychology, my friend. Philosophy. You can't prove something just by asserting it."

"I didn't think I was trying to prove a thing."

"There, you're getting annoyed. Now I'm even more intrigued."

Jack waved his hands vaguely and sat back again. "Nothing strange or complicated about procrastination. And these two years in Derry have gone too fast. When I first thought of seminary, it seemed far away. Three years at university—what a world of time."

Liam still assessed him. "You're quite sure, then, are you?"

[206]

"My turn for catechism, is it?" Jack answered mildly. "Yes, I'm still certain, never worry. Life up here's been a wee bit busier than I expected, that's all. I've not had the time I needed to reflect. . . . I'll make a retreat when I go down, so I will."

Saturday, February 6, 1971

Kate ran steadily down the Strand Road, her tennis shoes slapping on the pavement. The coins jingled noisily in the pocket of her heavy blue gym suit: two half crowns and four shillings—all she would need to replace the book of Yeats's poetry that she had lost. And what a time to lose it, too, when no one else could spare a copy. Father Kennedy had sent all his seminar students away yesterday to spend the weekend studying "Easter 1916," "1919," and "Meditation in Time of Civil War." Even the library copies were in circulation.

Although she was jogging slowly, Kate breathed the light afternoon air deeply. The day had dawned mild and pleasant, surprisingly warm, with no sign of frost for the first time in weeks. Along the wooded back path from the University she had almost heard spring in the twittering of the birds, almost smelt it in the brown litter of last autumn. The old melancholy of a few months ago had disappeared; even if snow fell again, the snowdrops were there to poke through its melting blanket. Buoyant optimism flooded her as she ran. She looked forward to the notice, soon to come, of whether or not London University had accepted her.

A small anxiety ate into her happiness as she neared the lower end of Great James Street. The British Army barracks seemed particularly busy today. Jeeps filled with soldiers lurched out of the gates and away. Boys of eighteen or nineteen, unnatural in their stiff uniforms, stood guard with grave faces, frightened eyes, and guns ready. The gatehouse was always sandbagged, but today extra bags were piled against the sentry post, and huge coils of rusty barbed wire enclosed part of the pavement beyond. And just next to the gatehouse, she noticed some shop windows had been broken. Pieces of brick lay on the street. She slowed her pace and finally stopped to listen. Sure enough, shouting and the tinkle of breaking glass came to her clearly over the soft air. Familiar, but horrifying. Why had she been so blind? No cars or buses were moving toward Guildhall Square, and only a few people were left at the end of the Strand, most of them shopkeepers frantically hammering boards over plate glass. And something else arrested her . . . the smell of heavy smoke. She looked up quickly. Was there a fire in Foyle Street? She squinted, trying to determine the source of the dense, gray columns pushing up from behind and to the right of the Northern Bank.

Even as she hesitated on the pavement outside a dress shop, an armored car pulled up beside her. "Don't go this way, Miss. It's too dangerous. You'd be advised not to go any farther." The voice was Cockney.

She swung round nervously. Déjà vu. *"It's dangerous. . . . It's dangerous!"* "Not even up to Shipquay Street? There was something I needed." Her head and arms began to prickle with fear.

"Not worth it, Miss, unless you want to be hurt. Which'd be a pity—" A wolf whistle shrilled from the dark interior of the car. "Stone throwers everywhere today. Some vandals set fire to the shops. The Joint Security Commission's warning everyone: Stay off the street. Here and Belfast. One of our gunners was killed on New Lodge Road in Belfast this morning. And a bomb went off on the Shankill. We're expecting riots here. Now." The words came out in staccato bursts—like rounds of machine gun fire. Then the vehicle speeded away leaving Kate motionless in dull alarm.

Only for a moment was she paralyzed. When she felt her face grow hot and her heartbeat quicken, she turned and started back the way she had come. But she would not run. Not now. A running anonymous figure in blue, running away from the center of the city, would be too tempting a target for sniper, petrol-bomb thrower, or overanxious soldier. A quick, sedate walk would be safer, less conspicuous.

Behind her the noise sounded louder, not fainter. Jeering male voices, crackling fires, blaring megaphones sounding soldiers' warnings: all came plainly to her on the breeze. The breaking of glass was now too distant to be heard, but Kate heard it in her mind, saw men and boys hurling their stones and bricks as clearly as if she stood in the Diamond. And the smoke, acrid and heavy in the bright sky, hung everywhere, an ominous shroud cloaking violence and more violence.

Relieved to be almost out of the center of the town, Kate quickly passed Patrick Street and continued up the Strand. It would take her less time, she thought suddenly, and perhaps be less dangerous, if she made her way up through Clarendon Street and onto Northland Road.

Clarendon Street was empty, too. That troubled her.

Halfway up the street, walking toward the westerly sun, she had to narrow her eyes against a flash of light. A blast shattered her ears an instant later. The air burst, ripped apart. Brick avenues of shop and factory walls echoed the sound, intensified it to a roar. She dropped down, her hands over her ears, over her head, by instinct. Then came the aftershocks. The pavement, the buildings, the street—everything shook. Glass jangled as a few windows caved in.

Then silence. No twittering birds. No moving cars. No soldiers, crowds, or megaphones. Just silence.

She lay quite still with her face on the hard concrete. Then she heard her own panting and sobbing, felt the blood ooze out of the grazes on her stinging cheeks and palms, tasted the gutter's grit in her mouth. What good would it do to move? She couldn't lift her head and didn't want to; she would lie still until someone found her. Let someone else help her.

She shut her eyes, willing oblivion. Instead came again the awful film that played itself over and over again in her mind: *Belfast. An empty gray street. Her mother screaming, "Get down, Katie, it's dangerous." Falling face down in a red pool. Her sister Jo crawling toward her, bleeding, dying, crying over and over again, "Mummy, oh, Mummy," until the four-year-old watcher and the twenty-one-year-old rememberer cried too, not understanding. Never understanding.*

She did not know how long she remained on the pavement. Sirens wailed. Ambulance bells rang. Shock passed. Horror faded. Fear swept over her like nausea. Still no one came.

She raised her head. Her glasses had broken, lost among the

other glass around her. Should she move? Should she sit up? Panic gripped her stomach like a vise. She leaned to the side and heaved. Nothing. Her stomach had solidified into leaden weight. She began to cry again, wrenching sobs punctuated by noisy gulps for breath that frightened her almost as much as the blast itself. She had lost control.

She must assert herself to escape—to live. She sat up abruptly, angry at the blurred, distorted surroundings; angry that no one came to help her. *I must get off the street quickly.* But she couldn't move yet, and so she stayed where she was, rocking slightly without being aware of it, and dropped her head onto her knees.

Someone was there to help, she realized. Christ was sitting beside her among the debris. It was in moments like this, wasn't it, that He most loved. He would never leave her, never forsake her. He sat beside her today as He had cried beside her seventeen years before in Belfast. For once again, at least momentarily, she had lost everything.

More minutes passed before she forced herself to struggle to her feet. Swaying slightly, she staggered toward the sun with her back to the wasteland. A taxi driver noticed her standing, shivering, by the wall at the top of Clarendon Street and picked her up. Her teeth chattered so hard that she could barely give her destination; her hand shook as she pressed the half crown into his hand when he delivered her right to the door of Woodburn.

The next five hours slid away in a blur of impressions. Sheila, agitated and solicitous, hovering round her as she undressed for a bath; Deirdre's voice outside the unlocked bathroom door, questioning Sheila in low tones; Deirdre bringing her a supper tray from the refectory, food she could not even bear to smell or look at as she sat on her bed, huddled beneath the eiderdown; the parade of visitors to the room suddenly hushed by the sickroom atmosphere: Caroline, Heather, Grace—even Roger and Liam.

By ten o'clock, when everyone went downstairs to watch the news, Kate's head had cleared enough for her to feel completely foolish: a heroine without heroism, who had no more to show for it than scratches and broken glasses. Her own selfishness mocked her. She had thought of no one but herself as she lay on the pavement, bewailing the lack of help.

[211]

Sheila returned to the room at eleven and sat on Kate's bed, twisting her engagement ring round and round as she recited the litany of trouble in Belfast—the soldier's death, the gun battle on New Lodge Road, the bomb on the Shankill. She said that the fires and riots were still going on in Derry; that several passersby had been killed or injured by the explosion of a booby-trapped car on Patrick Street. "Right outside a factory, on the Clarendon Street side."

Kate listened in silence. Then she put her head on her knees and relived it—the blast, the shock waves, the broken glass—but saw now a ball of fire in a dark car and broken bodies hurtling against a wall, a lamppost . . . . She wept again out of shame and sorrow. She had been wrong to think of herself at all, she told Sheila, arguing when Sheila reminded her that she had been in shock. She cried for a long time, then finally drank some warm milk and fell asleep.

Rustlings, voices, cars on the driveway disturbed her all night. She turned this way and that on the bed, and as she moved her long hair across the pillow with her hand, she felt again the sting of her cuts. A car backfired outside Woodburn. The sound bounced around the room, rocked the bed, and lost itself in the high-pitched scream of a siren. Then that grew louder too. It filled the room, bringing Kate, crying in terror, to the edge of the bed.

"What is it? Whatever's wrong?" A light came on suddenly, and Sheila was beside her. "Oh, Kate, you're drenched."

"What was that noise? A siren? . . . Oh—"

"You were babbling about a gun and a car. And I've never heard such a scream. Look, my hair's prickling." She held out her arm, but Kate could see nothing but a pink blur.

She groaned and sank back on the pillow. "Nightmare." She sighed heavily. "I've not had one for years." She rubbed her eyes. "Sorry, Sheila. What time is it, anyway?"

"Only eleven forty-five. I wasn't even asleep. You must have dropped off right away."

"But I didn't. I heard a car backfire. And a siren."

Sheila shook her head. "There were no cars. No siren."

Kate shut her eyes. "I thought it must be morning already. I was asleep so long . . . it seemed long."

[212]

"You're really upset, Kate. That 'siren'—it must have been your own voice you were hearing."

"I dreamed it all? Oh, no!" She sat up again, reaching for her hairbrush as Sheila searched in a drawer on the other side of the room.

"Here's some aspirin."

"I can't swallow it without water. Sorry."

"I'll get some. Poor Kate, you can't see a thing, can you?" She turned on the cold-water tap at the small corner basin.

"Not much." She plaited her hair slowly. "I'll have to wear reading glasses all day tomorrow and try to get new lenses on Monday. Awful. My head'll be splitting long before I get to Kennedy's seminar. And I haven't even read the Yeats poems."

"Don't think about that now. Here—drink this. And let's pray together."

Kate looked gratefully at the indistinct lines of Sheila's face. "Yes, that's a good idea," she murmured. Usually such suggestions came from her. But now, stiff with apprehension and damp with sweat, she was glad of Sheila's thoughtfulness.

Sheila reached for Kate's Bible and read aloud as Kate lay back again under the blankets. *Isaiah . . . chapter forty*, Kate thought. One of her favorite passages. The familiar, comforting words of promise washed over her, bringing peace.

> *Hast thou not known? Hast thou not heard, that the everlasting God, the Lord, the Creator of the ends of the earth, fainteth not, neither is weary? . . . He giveth power to the faint; and to them that have no might he increaseth strength. Even the youths shall faint and be weary, and the young men shall utterly fall. But they that wait upon the Lord shall renew their strength; they shall mount up with wings as eagles; they shall run and not be weary; and they shall walk and not faint.*

After she had closed the Bible, Sheila shut her eyes and prayed, "Thank you, dear Lord, for protecting Kate today. Thank you for bringing her safely back here. You know how much she has on her mind already, even without the explosion. So please give her peace. Help her to sleep, Lord. And give me wisdom to know when

[213]

and how to help, when and how to leave alone. . . . We also remember everyone who has to be out on the street tonight; protect them, too. And the families of all of those who were hurt and killed today—be in their midst. Bring comfort and consolation where there is grief." She paused, her voice sad. "And please, Father, bring these awful times in Belfast and Derry to good. In Jesus' name, amen."

Kate had no more nightmares that night.

Monday, February 8

Early on Monday, after breakfast, Kate made an appointment by telephone to see the optician; then she hurried to the library to read Sheila's copy of Yeats before her ten o'clock seminar. The sky was still dark with northern twilight, and she moved cautiously in her myopic haze.

Awkwardly lowering her things onto her favorite library table—not that she could see down to the docks today—she took out her reading glasses and began the poems. Within minutes she was completely lost in the spell of the verse. Yeats, the cunning musician who had first bewitched her at Father Kennedy's suggestion during the previous summer.

> *He, too, has been changed in his turn,*
> *Transformed utterly:*
> *A terrible beauty is born.*

Loud, clicking heels tapped down the central aisle of the library. "Kate! Kate!" came an urgent whisper.

Sheila, her face flushed and her coat hastily pulled around her, stood breathing hard beside Kate.

"What? D'you need this book already? I've only—"

"No—no." Sheila sat down across the table from Kate. 'I've bad news, Kate."

"Tell me. And don't dramatize, Sheila. I couldn't stand it," she said in her old stern voice.

"I just left the refectory. Roger and I were eating breakfast. Or he was; I didn't. He and Jack overslept—"

"Then?"

[215]

"Please, I'm trying to tell you."

"Sorry."

"There was a phone call for Jack—from the friary—you know—where Father Kennedy lives. One of the men there—friars, fathers, whatever you call them—said Jack would want to know that Father Kennedy had died over the weekend. There'll be a proper announcement this morning at the seminar. But one of Father Kennedy's friends knew Jack and thought he'd want to go over for the funeral—wake, I mean. He's gone already. Put on a tie and drove away, Rog said." She stopped, watching Kate's face. "Katie . . . dear, I knew you'd want to know. I'm sorry."

Kate sat back, dazed. No words, no tears. Not yet. She had never forgotten the warm October afternoon when Jack had talked about cancer, but it had seemed so utterly impossible that this alive, active man could be dying of cancer. Even now she could not believe it.

"Kate, for pity's sake, say something."

She looked blindly at Sheila. "Do you know any more? Did the friar—?"

"Roger didn't know anything. But Jack said the burial's at eleven."

"I'm going." Her voice sounded artificially bright. She arranged her books into a tight pile. "Will you, too? I don't even know how to get there." She knew intuitively that if she thought too much about it, she would lack the courage to go.

"Roger told me . . . in case you'd want to go. We can take the bus. I can't stay long, but I'll go for the wake, at least."

They walked out into the cold, but Kate hardly noticed the wind. "You knew he had cancer, did you?"

"No. Are you sure?"

"Jack thought so."

"So final. So sudden. . . . And you love him, don't you."

"Yes," Kate replied wearily, after a long time. "I love him." And then bitterly, "Loved him. Oh, Sheila, sometimes I don't understand anything. Death seems so arbitrary, so random. I can't see how—"

"You shouldn't try to understand, I suppose."

"You prayed for peace for me the other night," Kate retorted in a tone of accusation. "And now I have less again than I had before."

At the friary, cars were parked from one end of the road to the other. People were going in and out: some crying, some quiet, some talking as if nothing untoward had happened.

How can they? Kate thought. Her head had begun to ache, whether from the reading glasses she'd decided to leave on or from her own numb inability to react to the death, she didn't know.

A man in habit opened the heavy door for them. Kate noticed irrelevantly that he was freshly shaven, his face bright and congenial. Then she noticed the rich colors in the stained glass lancet windows around the wide hall and thought fleetingly of St. Jerome's.

"This way." The friar directed them to follow him down a long, narrow corridor. On the left side, doors opened into a newly refurbished chapel that ran the length of the corridor; she could smell the new wood of the pews and see the sanctuary light glowing red in the darkness over the altar. On the right hand, door after door stood shut until the end of the corridor, where their guide pointed into a parlor. "Father Colm's being waked in here. Please go in." And then he turned back down the corridor.

Sheila and Kate looked anxiously at each other.

"You go first," Kate whispered. Her mouth was dry, and a lump had risen into her throat. Her palms felt sticky. How were they to act?

The room was larger than Kate expected. It stretched out to their right, adjacent to the corridor, like the chapel. Rows of seats faced the end of the room, so the mourners' backs were to them as they walked in. The far end itself was a colorful blur to her nearsighted eyes.

They joined the quiet line that had formed in an aisle by the seats. Looking down the rows, she saw men and women in street clothes as well as men of the order in their brown habits. Most sat silently with bowed heads; a few whispered softly to their companions. Kate wondered where Jack was.

As if in answer to her thought, she saw a man leave his seat in

[217]

the row nearest them and come toward them. Jack. She took in his odd appearance: the dark, thin tie and neatly pressed white shirt; the old tartan jacket and faded jeans; the same work boots he'd worn that afternoon in St. Jerome's orchard. He had left the university in a hurry, as Roger said. But his face was what drew her. His eyes were heavy, underlined with deep shadows. And his cheeks . . . gaunt, haggard, pale except where broken by the night's growth of beard. Hadn't he slept at all?

He did not look at her at first, but at Sheila. "I'm glad you've come. It's nice of you, Sheila. And Katherine. I think we're his only students—" His voice trailed off. Then he looked at Kate, met her eyes. There was sadness in his voice; but she heard, too, a muted kind of joy that she didn't understand. "Before you go up," he said, "I need to tell you something . . . both of you." His eyes included Sheila again, briefly. "We've the time. The Mass won't begin for a wee while yet. Can you stay for it?"

They nodded. "But not for the burial. I have an appointment at twelve," Sheila said.

"I'll stay, though," Kate said uneasily. She was already torn between her new need to grieve for Father Kennedy and her old fear of having anything to do with Catholic ritual.

"Are you sure?"

"Yes."

"Then come over into the chapel for a minute." And he went ahead of them through the door.

Mechanically, Kate followed Jack and Sheila across the corridor. Her mind kept going back to the end of the room where he lay. And further back than that, to the small parlor where her mother and sister had lain seventeen years before. The seventeen intervening years had brought many funerals to her father's church; she had believed herself conditioned to them, able to remain emotionally aloof. But not this time. This time, the two came together in her mind, and seventeen years dissolved.

She was sitting with Sheila and Jack in one of the side pews of the chapel when she came to consciousness again, to a realization of what it was Jack was telling them in a whisper.

"You'll need to know. He did not die of cancer." He was looking

[218]

at Kate again, his face now full of anguish. "You remember what I said?" The appeal was to her.

She nodded dumbly, catching her lower lip with her teeth. The naked emotion on his face frightened her.

Sheila sat back, almost matter-of-fact in her quick reply. "Then what did happen? Heart attack or something?"

Jack paused. Kate couldn't understand why he kept looking at her, only at her. "The explosion . . . that bomb on Patrick Street."

"No." She shut her eyes. "No, no, surely not."

Sheila jerked forward in the pew. Her whisper grew to a hoarse exclamation. "You mean he was one of the people injured? And then—"

"No," Jack said softly, "killed outright. He was one of them." He addressed Sheila now, giving Kate time. "No one knew at first except the fathers here. They had to call his family first."

Kate slumped forward, her face in her hands. That blast. She saw it, heard it, felt it again and again. Nightmare become real. Twice. *Her mother crying again and again, "Get down . . . it's dangerous!" Her mother falling. Her sister crawling across the endless, surreal pavement. . . . Herself standing, survivor in bewildered terror. "The one shall be taken and the other left."* The random horror of it. . . . Father Kennedy's body, broken, hurled back by the deadly explosion.

She screwed up her eyes against those grim rehearsals but saw them all the more clearly. And then came again the ironic remembrance of her own naïve assertion: *God will not let us destroy ourselves in civil war. . . .*

Sheila's arm came round Kate's shoulders. Wordlessly, she began to cry.

"We can wait here for a minute, until you want to go in," Jack said kindly.

Sheila sighed heavily. "I don't know if we should go back into the parlor. Kate couldn't—"

"I must!" Kate broke in, but she didn't move or look up yet. Her voice was very low, tight with the tears she was trying to hold back.

Sheila turned to Jack. "Is the coffin open?" she asked steadily.

"I'm not sure—"

Jack held up his hand. "You needn't be afraid. He wasn't—he

[219]

wasn't right near the car. He looks . . . all right." His own face was worn. "At peace, believe it or not. They told me he lost a leg. And the shrapnel from the car . . . but he's—"

"Oh, don't. Don't. Please," Kate moaned.

Jack stopped. "Katherine, oh, please, I'm sorry. I didn't mean—I wanted you to know you could say good-bye."

Kate abruptly stood up, breaking away from Sheila. Her face contorted. "I would anyway," she said brokenly.

Sheila glanced up in surprise at the harshness in her voice.

"We won't go in until you're both ready," Jack repeated. Quiet movements at the altar made them all turn. Two of the friars, both in white, were preparing for the Mass. "Well, maybe we'll have to. I'll go up again with you."

Kate led the way back this time, hardening herself against her own overwrought state. She would cope. She would survive. She would live to love others and to see others die.

They had to stand at the very back of the line again. In front of them the mourners filed forward, kneeled a last time by the casket, then passed the receiving line to go through another door and across into the chapel.

The flower petals came into focus. Kate stared at them, collecting herself, willing herself to observe so that she would not forget. She would not look at him yet. Hothouse carnations, sprays of early daffodils, tulips, hyacinths, freesias. The colors blurred in her tears, but the perfume filled her nose and saturated her senses. She would not look at him yet. (Afterwards, she remembered no sounds at all. Color and perfume were all.)

At last she stood in front of the coffin. Everyone had knelt, but she had determined as she approached that she would not do so. It was as if the mourners were praying to Father Colm, not to Jesus.

But then something broke. She bent forward, a rush of grief taking hold of her, shaking her body as she looked at his hands, at the white, long fingers she had watched for three years in lectures and seminars, had held sometimes when he greeted her. Now they lay inert, folded on his chest. So uncharacteristic. So dead.

Her eyes traveled up over the brown cloth of his habit to his bloodless face. She knelt, crying as she had never cried before. Not the painful, frightened crying of Saturday. Not the bewildered,

[220]

terrified crying of her childhood. She cried the wrung-out tears of adult loss. *Is he at peace?* She began to battle with the old prejudices that were her legacy. Was he sleeping in the peace of ignorance, or waking in the peace of Christ's presence? Was he redeemed as one of the elect (James had always had so much to say about predestination and election), or was he damned as one of those misled by the Antichrist? Was he washed clean in Christ's blood and standing, pure now, justified by Jesus, among the great multitude around the Throne, or was he cast out into outer darkness, the place of weeping and gnashing of teeth, the place from which God was absent? And all these doubts intensified the burden of her sorrow, polarized her between the straightforward, black-and-white theology of her father and the intricate, paradoxical theology of Catholicism as she had encountered it in the Catholic writers. She clung longingly to the frail logs of pity and mercy that floated above the waves of Calvinist and Presbyterian dogmatism, but then felt herself drowning in her father's Protestant orthodoxy. *No, how can a Catholic be saved?*

At last she stood up slowly to make room for Sheila, who went forward and knelt without hesitation. Kate was wiping her eyes with her handkerchief when she heard someone behind her say, "Why are you weeping? Why search among the dead for one who lives?" The whisper was low, but clear.

She whipped round. Jack stood right behind her but had fixed his eyes on Father Colm. She searched his face. Had he spoken? Or had she heard the Holy Spirit, the voice within? He gave no sign, so she turned again in wonder. Father Kennedy lay among the flowers, his calm face a reproach to her doubts.

Sheila stepped back to join her, and Jack knelt for a moment, crossing himself, then straightened up and walked in front of them to shake hands with the men who were lined up to greet the mourners.

Introducing Sheila and Kate to the first greeter, he said, "This is Father Michael, the guardian of the House. He'll be conducting the burial."

White vestments. Pince-nez like Father Kennedy's. . . . Kate shot a look back at the casket. His glasses were gone. *"For now we see through a glass darkly, but then face to face."* No myopia in heaven. But *no sight or light to see by in hell, either.* . . . A round, beaming face. The friar was nodding, smiling, pumping her hand. Again she glanced around, saw only joy on the faces of all the fathers. They had the faith she lacked, then, that he was now with Christ. She wavered, ashamed of her grief and doubt.

"We're glad you could make it, John," Father Michael was saying.

Jack shook his hand but didn't reply.

"John's a regular visitor over here. Father Colm thought a great deal of him."

Kate nodded back in distraction, still not comprehending the joy.

She feared going to the Mass. Her father's pointed criticisms reasserted themselves. She resented the semidarkness, the painted statues, the formality of the celebrant's movements in the sanctuary. Her outburst of feeling in the parlor gave way to her resolution to be, as usual, carefully distant.

That resolve was short-lived. At the Kyrie she found herself shaking and on the verge of losing control again. *Lord have mercy, Christ have mercy, Lord have mercy.* Those words had come back to her over and over again during the previous summer, and along with them the desire to learn more mercy. *Blessed are the merciful,* she had told herself, as if the telling would work a miracle in her. And Greene's words: "It needed a God to die for the half-hearted." And Father Colm's words to her: "Leave the past to the mercy of God, and the present to the love of God. . . ."

Her internal struggle continued into the Eucharist itself, when the tenor voices of the friars soared in jubilation to the ceiling, reverberating round in a rich tapestry of song. The power of their music engulfed her, and the tears started behind her eyelids. The invitation to break bread here was not to her, but she watched Jack go up, glad to be with two she knew in this alien place.

Then she began to accept, at least intellectually, the form of the liturgy. It was foreign, but watching it dispassionately, she grudgingly admitted to herself that the Mass was not at all as she had imagined, not at all as her father had portrayed it. No mumbling priest at the altar, no worship of statues. All the old

[222]

Irish-Protestant stereotypes seemed wrong . . . until the final commendation.

Father Michael came down with a thurible to incense the coffin. Repeating the last prayers, he swung the incense three times. Kate shifted uncomfortably, conjuring up memories of what her father used to say about clouds of mystery and ignorance and darkness. *Superstition,* she thought coolly, vacillating back to her original stance.

Sheila left before the graveside ceremony, but Kate followed Jack and the others outside. The friars stood closest to the grave in a wide semicircle, facing the lay people. Taller than most, Kate could hear everything and would have seen everything, too, but for the broken glasses. Everyone had been given small printed cards which simply read *Colm Joseph Kennedy, O.F.M. 1905–1971.* The card fitted into the palm of her hand. She looked from it to the open grave to the friars, and back.

It was near the end of the burial rite when, after a short silence, the friars burst into a song unfamiliar to her—a haunting medieval chant—that Kate's feelings changed once again.

Ultima in mortis hora,
Filium pro nobis ora;
Bonam mortem impetra,
Virgo, Mater Domina.
Bonam mortem impetra,
Virgo, Mater Domina.

The cemetery had none of the resonance of the chapel, and the notes quickly lost themselves on the wind; but the depth of feeling carried her along. She wept openly again. Yet no one around her was crying. The singers were smiling, their eyes on each other, on the coffin, on the blowing clouds overhead. Celebration, not mourning. Consolation, not lamenting. She felt isolated, excluded.

Jack offered to drive her back to the University. As soon as he had started the car, he said, "I'll miss him."

[223]

"Yes." Kate sat quietly, staring at the dashboard. She had been in the car with him before, when he drove to St. Jerome's, but always with Liam or Deirdre, never alone. And now she did not want to talk to him, did not even know how to.

"But I think—and I don't mean to be trite—" he said haltingly, as though uncertain of her emotional state, "that it's better he died—awful as it was—it seems to me—"

"What do you mean?" she asked with a quick sidelong glance.

"Well, I'm thanking God for sparing him all that suffering. He did have cancer. Father Michael told me that when I got there this morning. And now, well," he smiled, "he's gone to his reward."

Her eyes went down. "Are you sure?"

He swerved to miss a skinny dog that was running across the road. "What d'you mean, am I sure? Of course he's gone to heaven."

She clenched her fist in her lap. "I wish I had that certainty myself."

He turned his eyes from the road briefly to give her a look of astonishment. "But why in heaven's name would you imagine otherwise?"

She gave a small shrug. "My upbringing," she said in a low, bitter voice. Her lips curled. She resigned herself to a discussion she would rather not have entered. "I was taught to believe that there's no heaven for Catholics, that God is saddened by their being so misled, but that they are not among His elect."

Jack laughed. "You can't be serious. I've never encountered that attitude in Roger. And you can think for yourself. You always do in the seminar."

Paying no attention to his encouragement, she quickly replied, "No, you wouldn't. Roger's much more . . . he's come from a different tradition."

"So far as you're concerned, then, Father Kennedy, the sisters at St. Jerome's, and I—we're all going to hell in a handbasket?"

She caught the satirical note and sighed. "I used to think so, and sometimes I still do. Oh, the sisters at St. Jerome's have made me see some things differently, but everything I learned when I was growing up . . ." She let her voice trail off.

"Can you explain?" He was frowning. "I—I don't understand."

She cleared her throat, trying to concentrate. She was tired; it was hard to think at all. "Superstition. That's one reason I always thought Catholic beliefs were twisted, muddled up, wrong-headed . . . all the emphasis on Mary. She's not part of the Trinity. All that talk about the Mass being a sacrifice . . . as if Jesus' sacrifice on the cross weren't sufficient somehow. But what kind of God is Jesus Christ if the cross wasn't enough?"

"We don't deny that it was enough," he said levelly.

She rounded on him with venom. "Now I don't understand you," she said. "You're going against all the basis for Catholic practice, like praying for the dead. . . . And another thing—" She remembered her father quoting, *No man cometh unto the Father but by me . . . but by me . . . by me.* "All the Catholics I've ever known—" she flung that phrase out, knowing she was going to generalize and that he might discount what she said, but continuing anyway, "they've all emphasized the role of the priest." She hesitated, looking at him, wondering what he would think, since he was going to enter the priesthood himself. "As if the priest has to be a mediator between man and God. I don't believe that. Jesus is the only mediator."

"That's what I believe too." He was smiling, and his amusement surprised and annoyed her. "I see myself in the role of priest—as do most of the men I know, including Father Colm—as spiritual guides, pastors. Just as your own minister is."

Listening to him, she shut her eyes for a moment and saw herself standing in the middle of a domelike glass house, a house of windows built around her by her father. The windows were warped, concave, convex; they distorted her perception of external reality; they distorted her perception of herself. One by one those windows had been smashed: by James, by Deirdre, by Liam, by Graham Greene, by Father Kennedy, and now possibly by Jack—so that through the jagged holes she had begun to see things, perhaps, as they were.

When they arrived at the Northland Road gate of the University, Jack pulled the car over to the side of the road and cut the

[225]

engine. They sat silently for a minute, the motor clicking slightly as it cooled down.

Jack had been watching her. "What's the matter, Katherine?" he said. "You're not at peace with yourself."

She resented the personal remark, the intimacy it implied. Feigning a directness and a confidence she didn't feel, she met his eyes. "And what would make you think that?"

"Your reaction to everything at the wake and burial. One minute you were crying, and the next minute you were angry." He spoke softly. "What's the big civil war being waged inside you?"

She frowned, staring at him, deciding how to reply in a cutting way that would stop the conversation altogether. But then weariness overcame her; she was tired of the old barriers and defenses. *Why not try to tell him?* she asked herself unexpectedly. She saw in his eyes nothing more frightening than compassion. He would listen, not condemn. *Why not?* But where to begin, when— aside from some hints to Deirdre—she had never told anyone in Derry.

Her voice stumbled, but she pushed herself to explain. "My mother . . . my sister . . . they were murdered by a sniper in Belfast. I was four." She wanted to cry. Even now, more so because of Colm Kennedy, she felt raw, wounded by it all.

Jack made a small sound of sympathy.

"The man was drunk. He was . . . Catholic." She looked at him quickly, embarrassed, then away. "I've struggled to forgive. My father . . ." she hesitated, tugged by the pull of loyalty, "hasn't helped. He's your typical old-fashioned Ulster Presbyterian— thinks Catholics should get out of the North and take the troubles with them. So for years I equated the Catholic Church with everything that hurt and deceived people—spiritually and physically. Irrational, I know—but I couldn't trust anyone, anything to do with Catholics."

Jack shook his head. Quickly he said, "No, it all makes sense. I had no idea . . . what you'd been through." He shook his head again and seemed to want to say more.

"I don't know why I'm telling you all this. What can you say? What can anyone say?"

"You've never told anyone here? What an awful weight to carry around by yourself."

She noticed his eyes were troubled, and she was moved. All the same, she only allowed herself to shrug and say, "No one."

"What about—" He hesitated, and his eyebrows rose.

"Sheila?"

He smiled slightly. "No, I was thinking about someone else— Mr. McQueen."

She flushed, surprised, but she couldn't be indignant. "No, he knew nothing. And I've had very little to do with James—for a long time." She compressed her lips, then went on. "He's a Paisleyite, and narrow as I may be, I'd never go that far. I'm glad I didn't tell him. . . . He just would have reinforced the bitterness. He wouldn't have understood." She wanted to add, "The way you seem to understand," but something held her back; she didn't know him well enough to say it.

"So all the time we were at the wake," Jack began slowly, "all the time we were there, you were thinking about your family—"

"And wanting to mourn for Father Kennedy," she interrupted. "Needing to." She bit her lip.

"But not letting yourself because of all that happened, all you were conditioned to think and feel?"

She looked at him gratefully. He had put into words what she could hardly express herself.

"Let yourself cry all you want to," he said quietly. "I know you loved him."

She felt the lump in her throat grow larger. *Yes, he will make a good priest,* she thought, *be able to hear others' sorrows.* All the same, she still felt a little on the defensive. "You probably think I'm limited and narrow—" He opened his mouth to contradict her, but she waved her hand in denial. "No—don't say I'm not. I am— compared, say, with Roger." She took a deep breath. "But I am trying to break out of that, and I'm trying to live and think in a way that would please God, because I love Him."

"You're very direct," Jack said. Then he smiled. "I wish—no, more than that—Katherine, that you had as much peace inside as you do a desire for truth."

She frowned again, unsure of his intent. Was he criticizing her

[227]

lack of peace? Did he question her love of God because of what he'd referred to as her own private civil war? She searched his face for a sign of condemnation. *None.* His gray eyes looked at her with steady warmth. She had exposed herself to him, but he still accepted her. Relieved and strangely glad, she leaned back against the seat.

"Katherine, do you remember that lecture a couple of years ago, when you and Father Colm were discussing *Far From the Madding Crowd?*" he asked her suddenly.

She shook her head, wondering at the seeming irrelevance of his question. So many classes had come and gone. And none of them mattered now.

"He was arguing with you about whether or not Hardy saw the universe as indifferent, man as a victim; and you were claiming that that was Hardy's view. But he was disagreeing and saying the universe wasn't totally unpredictable, wasn't fatalistic. Do you remember?"

"Vaguely."

"You said God was absent from the characters' lives in that story, and we were all arguing against you. And now you're talking as if God were absent from all that's happened here. Is He? Is that part of what troubles you?"

She looked down at her hands, knotting and unknotting her fingers in her lap.

"Intellectually, I know He's not," she countered. "But I have felt the last two or three days that He is. I felt quite abandoned on Saturday, after the bomb went off . . . even though, for a moment, as I sat there on the pavement, I really did feel Christ's presence with me. . . ." The tears rose again in her eyes, but she fought them back. *Self-pity.* "And when you told us how Father Kennedy died, I was angry with God. I still am." She stared out of the window at the cars passing by. "Death seems so random, so horrible. But I don't know why I see it that way. It's not a Christian view." She was surprised that she was confessing all this to him.

"I expect your father emphasized God as judge . . . you know, like Jonathan Edwards' sermon about the spider over the fire and the terror of falling into the hands of the living God . . . Perhaps that has just made you see death in a fearful way, instead of as a liberator, as a bringer of more peace and joy than we'll ever have here, especially in Ireland."

"Maybe," she conceded, not looking at him.

"Salvation's not a knife-edge we walk on. God's not vindictive and spiteful."

"I've never thought so."

"Then we have to believe He calls us to follow Him on earth for a reason . . . and for a certain time that *He* has decided . . . so that He can give us His love and we can share with others. Roger and I were reading something the other day that helped me. I can't quote you a reference, but it was about our being God's children. About dwelling in love, and thus dwelling in God. About our having confidence, therefore, on the day of judgment."

"First John—the epistle," she murmured automatically. She could hardly credit that she was hearing these words from Jack.

He watched her, his face tense. "Then you must believe, too, that Father Colm loved God . . . Catholic though he was . . . and acknowledge that Presbyterians and Baptists aren't the only ones with a corner on the truth. After all, remember, Jesus Himself is Truth . . . and the God we worship, Katherine, is the same God." He waited a moment, then went on gently. "But, listen, don't condemn yourself for feeling that death is random. It is painful, no matter what peace it brings the one who's gone. And you've been through an awful lot just lately. You're pretty hard on yourself. Life's hard enough, isn't it?"

Kate felt that if Jack said any more, she would agree with everything; that she could no longer think for herself. She wondered, numbly, if she had ever thought for herself. *First Daddy thought for me . . . then James thought for me.* Deirdre had challenged her to think for herself; Father Colm had pushed her to think for herself. And now Jack was doing the same. Suddenly all her old props were about to be washed away, unable to stand against the tide of reality.

She looked at him wordlessly. Her eyes had begun to ache.

[229]

Monday, February 15

On the far side of the coffee bar, money clattered onto one of the formica tabletops. Everyone was talking about Decimal Day and about the new coinage. Kate sat sipping her coffee, glad of the warmth in the room and the chance to be alone for a little while.

"This new fifty pence piece is rather grand."

"Heavy. Like a half-crown."

"I'll miss the half-crown. So picturesque. And the sixpenny bit."

"I won't miss the silly calculations in pounds, shillings, and pence."

"But those wee threepenny pieces . . . the silver ones with the rabbits on, from the South . . . it's wicked to get rid of them."

"Aye. It sounds mad to say 'two new pee' instead of fourpence for a coffee or thrupence for a bus fare." A guffaw.

Kate only half attended to the talk. She was thinking about the poetry seminar earlier in the morning. No Colm Kennedy to banter with and goad everyone. A woman had taken the class today. She had talked, and they had listened. Coming out of the room, Sheila had confided her relief that they didn't have to think so fast any more, but Kate had felt hollow and bored. She had tried to catch Jack's eye to see what he thought, but he had seemed deeply preoccupied; not once did he look her way.

Across the room, the voices had changed tone. She glanced around, recognizing a few fellows from McCrae, but none she knew. She was so relieved to have her new glasses. The dim world had become sharp and clear again. Then she caught Liam's name and began to listen more closely. Not every word came to her clearly, but most of the fragments were intelligible.

[230]

"And he's pretty relieved . . . engaged now."

". . . all supposed to be hush-hush. She wasn't supposed to know he went."

". . . thought he . . . went home for the weekend."

"So he did . . . spent Sunday in Belfast at the meeting."

"Wasn't there a riot that day?"

"Yeah . . . the Shankill. Not at the meeting."

"I heard the Communists were there as well."

". . . Lenehan said he saw him there."

"That's what I heard."

"NICRA'll not become a Communist front. Not yet."

Someone found the last remark funny. Loud, jeering laughter followed it.

With a shaky hand, Kate set down her cup. It rattled slightly in the saucer.

"McAvoy'd kill him if she knew he went, so she would."

"She might not. He got out of it all right. There wasn't any trouble."

"Not this time, but . . ."

Kate left her coffee, unfinished, on the table. Almost as a reflex, without thinking much about it, she pulled on her coat and went to find Deirdre.

Kate looked through the glass window in the door to the main reading room of the library; she saw Deirdre reading quietly, dark head bent over a book, shoulders hunched forward. Kate hesitated. Deirdre looked content, absorbed. Something cautioned her: *Hearsay. What good will it do? Why shatter her joy?* But then: *No, I have a responsibility to tell her. She said he had to give up NICRA. And he hasn't. If he cheats on that, he'll cheat on other things, later.*

Driven on by that conviction, Kate went in, looking first to see if Liam were anywhere nearby. Then she caught Deirdre's eye and beckoned her to follow up the wrought iron stairs to the tower, where they could talk in private. There they sat together, facing out over the bare trees to the lough.

"What's up, Katie?" Deirdre looked at her expectantly, pleased by the interruption.

Kate began to doubt the wisdom of what she was going to say.

[231]

She swallowed hard. "I overheard something just now ... that Liam may have gone to the NICRA rally ... that one last month."

"I doubt it, Kate." Deirdre looked down. She spoke in a comfortable voice, smoothing out a small wrinkle in her skirt.

"He went home, didn't he, the weekend of the twenty-second?"

"Aye. Home, Kate. Not to a rally."

"But there was a NICRA meeting that weekend. Sunday, in Belfast. It was on television. Don't you remember?"

Deirdre shook her head, frowning slightly. "I don't think so. And he was in Newry, anyway, not Belfast."

"NICRA was meeting with all sorts of people ... from the South, the Trades Union, the Campaign for Social Justice ... oh, and some Communists were there, too." She tried to report it in a matter-of-fact voice. "They were discussing some kind of a Bill of Rights to be taken to Westminster. Are you sure you don't remember?"

"I don't read the papers or watch the news as often as you do." Deirdre was still frowning. "What makes you think he went?"

Kate shrugged, backing off a little. "Well, now, I'm not certain of it. But some of the McCrae men were talking about it this morning. In the coffee bar."

"About the meeting?"

"Yes, and Liam's having gone." She bit her lip. "Oh, Deirdre, maybe I shouldn't have told you. But they even mentioned you ... how angry you'd be if you knew."

Deirdre's head went down. Almost whispering, she said, "Not angry. But very, very sad." She looked up, her eyes clouded now with pain. "He promised me a long time ago to stay away from that kind of thing. I can't expect him to become apolitical; he'll always be involved. But this—" She broke off, stared out through the window at the water.

Deirdre said nothing for a moment. When she began to talk again, it was in a dreamlike, distant voice. "I never knew a thing about the meeting. Nothing. And if he went, I'd never have known. Things were going so well between us. He's even started going to St. Eugene's with Jack some Sundays. Says he's not as hostile to Christians as he used to be since he met people like Jack ... and me." She faltered. "When he said he had to go home for the weekend, I thought—I was suspicious—that he was going to ask me to marry him. He'd been dropping little hints right along since before Christmas." She stopped.

Kate watched her with a mixture of anxiety and doubt. Should she have told her what she'd heard in the coffee bar? Had she meddled where she should not?

"I thought he'd be going for a ring. I knew he'd been saving all his money for something." Her voice failed. She looked at Kate dumbly. Her chin trembled, and her eyes swam. In unconscious agitation she fingered her engagement ring.

Longing to salve the wound she'd opened, Kate put out her hand. "Oh, Deirdre, I hope it's not true."

Deirdre stiffened. "Well, and if it is, then that's the end of our engagement. I'll not—I won't marry him if he's in with Communists. I decided that long ago, long before he asked me."

Behind them someone was mounting the stairs, but neither of them turned around to see who it was. Nor did they notice that the steps paused at the top. Waiting. Listening.

Deirdre's mouth had set into a hard line. "You warned me, Kate. I should have listened."

Kate was frightened. Only now did the full knowledge of what she had done break on her. She was frightened by the power she evidently had to influence Deirdre. "Wait, Deirdre. We don't know for sure that he went."

"I'll ask him straight out, so I will."

"Then ask." The voice was menacing, furious. But under the anger was fear.

Kate and Deirdre turned like guilty children caught stealing from their fathers' wallets. Kate's eyes widened. Deirdre's hand flew to her throat.

"Go on, ask." Liam paced toward them, a slow, deliberate walk.

Deirdre gathered herself to speak while Kate sat by, aghast. This time, though, Deirdre showed more self-possession than Kate had ever seen in her. The question came in a neutral, emotionless tone. "Some of the McCrae fellows said you went to a NICRA meeting in Belfast. Is it true?"

Liam shot a narrow, questioning look at Kate. Then, levelly, he said, "Yes. I was there. I don't apologize for it. The meeting was important."

"You could have told me."

"And lose you? Or drive you out of your mind with worry?"

"I'm sorry you felt you had to deceive me."

Liam's voice grew hot. He swore. "What do you expect? Haven't I changed enough for you already?" He glared contemptuously at Kate. "And for your pious friends. But no, that's not enough." He looked at Deirdre in anguish. "Hell, Deirdre, I've loved you too much. Obliterated myself to please you. But I'm me—Liam Donnelly. Not Roger whatever-his-name is. Not Monaghan. I thought you could love me as I am. But no—"

"I do, I do," she begged, crying.

"No, you bloody well don't. If I can't go to NICRA when I want to . . . or any political meeting . . . then we don't belong together. Nothing'll work between us."

"You shouldn't have gone. You promised. I agree. Nothing will work between us if we can't be open with each other."

He scoffed. "Open! Huh! Open with each other! Christian Onion talk, Deirdre, my lass. Grow up, woman. We've been open, all right. I've never pretended to be other than I am. And nor have you. My mistake, though—" he ground his heel on a small piece of gravel that had come up in the sole of his boot, "was to think you'd really want Liam Donnelly instead of some limp Protestant." He stepped heavily to the top of the stairs and began to shout bitterly, "So keep your bloody Protestant friends, and keep—"

Hurried footsteps came up behind him. The librarian's head appeared over the metal railing by the stairs. "Look here, what's going on?" He looked ruffled, nervous.

Kate and Deirdre stood up, Kate reaching for Liam's sleeve. "Wait—Liam, for goodness sake."

"All of you . . . go to hell. I don't care if I never see you again, Deirdre. Keep away from me. And you . . . Katherine . . . had better learn not to meddle in others' lives. I know you've had a part in this."

"You'll all go down from here immediately," the librarian snapped.

[234]

"And keep that ring, Deirdre. I hope it makes you feel bloody rotten."

Downstairs, applause broke out. "Go to it, Donnelly!"

"We hear you!"

"Missed your vocation . . . should have gone on stage, you case."

"Wow, what a balcony scene was this!"

As Liam pushed the librarian aside and pounded down the stairs two at a time, the librarian turned apoplectic with rage. "All of you . . . out! I've never had such a free-for-all in here in fifteen years. Out!" He turned and rushed down the stairs to find the students who had shouted at Liam.

But the entire library was in an uproar. Kate and Deirdre came down into the middle of it. The men were jeering, shouting, clapping, stamping their feet. Someone whistled. The women were laughing. Deirdre seized her books and coat and ran across the circulation room and down to the Great Hall without even turning to see if Kate followed. But Kate was right behind her, her face stained red with humiliation.

Sheila didn't see Roger until she almost bumped into him. He was coming back to the University after catching up on some reading in McCrae.

"Sheila! What's the matter. You're miles away." Kissing her warmly, he put his arm around her, and together they continued more slowly downhill to the refectory.

"Have you had lunch yet?" he asked.

"No, just got out of a theatre club meeting. And I had a lecture before that."

"You don't look very cheerful. What's happened?"

"Well, someone at the meeting told me an extraordinary story. I just don't believe it. I'll have to ask Kate—"

"What about Kate now?" he asked as they pushed through the swing doors into the refectory, but he sounded wearily indifferent. The smell of stew floated over the whole room. There was more hubbub than usual. Students were bent forward over the long

[235]

tables, laughing, arguing, and calling from one table to another. "What about Kate?" he pursued. "Heavens, has someone let out some laughing gas? The place sounds hysterical today." Roger had to raise his voice above the din.

"Not funny in the least. They're probably all telling one another what I just heard."

They waited at the back of the serving line.

"Don't be so mysterious. Tell me."

"Someone told me—two people told me, in fact—that there was a terrible argument in the library between Liam and Deirdre. Kate was involved somehow, too. They shouted so loudly that the librarian kicked them all out."

"Kate? Thrown out of the library for shouting? What is this . . . an early April Fool's Day joke?"

"I'm just telling you what I heard, Roger. The librarian had a fit. Everyone thought the whole thing terribly funny; people were egging Liam on. I can't imagine it, myself."

"But why?"

"I don't know. Anyway, the librarian turned off all the lights and closed the stacks. Sent everyone out in the end. Said he wouldn't open up for an hour at least."

"That's incredible!"

"I can't wait to find out what happened . . . but, oh, Roger—" Her face suddenly became serious. "Do you suppose Kate did something to turn Deirdre against Liam?"

Roger looked shocked. "Of course not. Deirdre's not a puppet. They're engaged. She loves Liam."

"But they said Liam was yelling about never wanting to see her again. Cursed and swore. Kate's never been really happy about Deirdre and Liam. Maybe something happened that she used against him."

"You're jumping to ridiculous conclusions."

"Am I?" Sheila's eyebrows arched in sarcasm. "She's played God with people's lives several times these three years."

"What a terrible thing to say, Sheila. Don't be so hard on her. She's been trying to do what she's supposed to do as V.P. She's been a good worker."

[236]

"She should never have agreed to be vice-president for a second year. She didn't even want to do it."

"That's beside the point. She's not a girl to do things in a hurry. Don't judge so fast."

Sheila shrugged, irked that Roger was supporting Kate against her. "If I judge too fast, it's probably because I've lived with her too long. A habit of hers, it is."

"Enough, Sheila."

Taking full trays away from the serving hatch, they sat and faced each other in a quieter corner.

Sheila retreated a bit. "I don't mean to speak badly of Kate. I do respect her. And I don't doubt her sincerity. She always wants to do the moral thing, the right thing. But she carries it a little far sometimes. She can't stop 'mixed' marriages in Ulster single-handedly, you know." She made a face as she said the word 'mixed.' She had never liked it.

"It's too easy to say that. We're English, not Irish, and—"

But Sheila interrupted him. "Of course we're outside things . . . somewhat. That qualifies us to see things more clearly, though, not less. And Kate . . . she's English, too, for all she talks about her father being from over this side of the water." Roger held up his hand, trying to stop her, but she went on, "Wait—she didn't have to grow up among Ulster's problems or go through segregated Ulster schooling. So she ought to be more careful of what she says. How can she judge what's best for others?"

"But her mother—?"

"All right, you told me about that. But you can't feed on the past forever."

"The Irish can."

She nodded slowly. "There you've got me. Too true." Her tone softened slightly. "We'll have to agree to disagree, I suppose—about Kate."

"But we do agree about one thing," Roger began in a conciliatory way, "that not everyone who calls himself a Christian around here is one. They judge others as if they had some sort of a right to do so by virtue of calling themselves Christians. And I'm not necessarily putting Kate in that camp. . . . But some of the people we know in the CU are far more preoccupied about being

[237]

distinctive Protestants and conservative Orangemen . . . or even Paisleyites." Remembering James, he shuddered. "They don't seem to know the difference between right-wing Ulster politics and faith itself."

She leaned forward. "And there are Catholics here who have far more spiritual vitality. I wish people like Kate could admit that. Look at Jack."

Roger frowned. "Yes, look at him. But don't keep dragging Kate's name out all the time."

"But what about Liam, though? Where does he stand with God?"

"How can we possibly know, Sheila? And is it for us to know? Maybe . . . if in fact she did have any part in their quarrel . . . Kate had a particular reason, a spiritual one, for warning Deirdre away."

"I still don't think it's her business. As you say, how can we know where Liam stands?"

Roger picked at his food in disgust. The stew was greasy today, and he was suddenly weary of the discussion. Irish politics. Irish history. Irish religion. Every day in the coffee bar and the refectory. "Let's drop it, Sheila. If you don't mind."

"Yes, let's. I'll hear what happened soon enough." Her eyes brightened with an idea.

"Now what are you cooking up?"

"Nothing. But I could take a tray of lunch up. I'm sure they won't have had any. They'll be in Deirdre's room."

Roger made a wry face. "Predictable, aren't you? I knew you'd think of a way to find out more details before anyone else."

Sheila looked crestfallen. "Is that what you think of me?"

"Come on, I'm teasing. Go ahead. Take a tray up by all means. Preferably before the fat congeals. Ugh!" He pushed his plate away, then leaned over the table to put his hands on either side of her face. "Let's not give the rabble any cause to cheer at another argument, all right?" He kissed her.

Laughing, they parted: Roger to a one o'clock lecture, and Sheila to Woodburn with a tray of food. Inside, the uppermost landing was dark. She found it difficult to see after the harsh white light outside. She knocked once; then, hearing movement inside but no answer, knocked a second time, more loudly.

"What is it?" Kate's voice had an impatient edge.

Sheila hesitated, hearing muffled crying. Deirdre's. Kate's voice came again from behind the door. This time she simply sounded weary. "Is that you, Liam?"

"No—it's Sheila. I brought some lunch. May I come in?"

There was a slight pause, during which Deirdre coughed. Sheila heard Kate whisper something. Then, warily, "Come in, Sheila."

Kate sat opposite the door in a basket chair, her fair hair ringed by a light behind it on the chest. Books were scattered everywhere—under the chair, on the desk, and on the end of Deirdre's bed. Deirdre herself sat hunched on the bed, bundled loosely in an old tartan blanket. Her face was mottled and blotched by tears. She stared at the wall as if unaware of Sheila.

"I came to bring—" Her voice trailed off, sounding artificial even to herself.

"Thanks." Kate's eyes looked through her, piercingly bright. The word was a dismissal.

Embarrassed, Sheila backed away, closing the door again.

"She was trying to help," Deirdre said in a flat voice. "Is it only lunch time?" She remained motionless as she asked.

"It's one o'clock."

"Seems like five o'clock to me. But I'm not hungry. You eat."

"Nor am I."

"It smells terrible."

Kate took the tray out to the landing and returned to her seat.

"Did you really think Liam would come?" Deirdre asked slowly. She dabbed at her face with one corner of the blanket.

Kate watched her with worried eyes. "I don't know. I couldn't think who else it'd be."

"Katie, you mustn't fash yourself any more about what happened." She sighed heavily. "And nor must I," she added without conviction.

"I keep feeling I shouldn't have told you."

Deirdre shrugged. "I would have found out in the end. Rather

[239]

now than. . . . And anyway, I'd always wondered what God thought of the relationship. I kept burying that thought. Not dealing with it. But it niggled at me. Perhaps it was meant to be." She sounded fatalistic.

"I don't believe the Lord wills sorrow in our lives." Kate sounded subdued.

"Nor do I. But you've said often to me that He allows it. So we learn something."

"It's very hard to deal with, nevertheless," Kate answered. Inevitably, she began to think about her mother and Jo and Father Colm.

"I'm learning something already. Something that'll sink deeper . . . when the crying part is over."

"What?" Kate was relieved at this first slight spark of liveliness.

"That what you've said all along is probably true. Mixed relationships don't usually work. And it's even worse when one of the two won't profess faith."

"You said Liam had begun to go to church—?"

"Aye. But it's a long road from there—" she met Kate's eyes, "isn't it?"

"It is a long road. But that's a beginning."

Deirdre's lips almost smiled. "Now who's Liam's advocate?" Then her face grew sad again. "Things wouldn't have worked out, I'm thinking. 'They shall be one flesh.' That's what the Bible says. What if one of the two denies God? What sort of a dilemma does that give God? Does he separate husband and wife in heaven?"

"One flesh," Kate repeated. "Not one spirit." Her lips turned up again. "And God's equal to solving that problem, I suppose. There's no marriage in heaven, anyhow."

"And what sort of a wife can cheer as her husband goes to perdition while she joins the angels?" Deirdre sounded bitter.

"No wife. No Christian wife. But I'm not sure—" She looked at Deirdre, almost afraid to go on. 'I've changed my ideas about some things." Deirdre met her gaze. "I mean . . . I used to think Catholics could never be in heaven. It was the basis for so much of what I thought and did." She turned her eyes away from Deirdre's amazed face and down to her hands. "But now . . . I believe that

[240]

God calls some of them. A few." She stumbled on. "I don't agree with my father any more."

Deirdre was shaking her head. "But you convinced me—almost—"

Kate could not bear to look up. "I know," she answered tonelessly. "That's what scares me now. My own power to persuade. And see where it led."

"You've got to stop talking that way. You're not responsible for our quarrel. That's as silly an idea as saying you're to blame for three hundred years of these awful troubles."

"No matter what you say, I feel a remorse worse than I've ever felt."

"Your conscience is too strong, Kate, if you punish yourself when you're not to blame."

"I feel like a Judas."

"Stop it. You mustn't." Deirdre hesitated. "So much was uncertain. Even the wedding date."

"I thought you'd agreed on that."

"Not for sure. And it worried me. Next year I'll be away . . . so much could happen."

"Away?" Kate echoed blankly.

"Remember . . . the third year's in France for me."

Kate nodded and passed her hand over her hair. Wisps of it had strayed out of the knot she'd wound round her head. "I always forget that."

"And there was something else—" Deirdre faltered. "Something I'll not say much about. It's too difficult—"

"What?"

"Things were getting difficult for both of us . . . after all these months together, and another year or more before we could marry . . . a long time for someone like Liam to wait. . . . He never said anything to me directly . . . or pushed me—" She began to stammer, coloring. "You know what I mean . . . he wanted to sleep with me. And he knew I wanted him, too. And only my knowing God's will kept me back—from complicating everything even further." She was breathing fast, her dark eyebrows drawing together. "Oh . . . thank God we didn't."

Kate was stunned by Deirdre's honesty. She couldn't answer.

[241]

She took off her glasses to wipe them but then had to squint up as Deirdre suddenly slid off the bed. "Deirdre?"

"I'm going to put this away." Deirdre slipped Liam's ring off her finger. "I need a paper handkerchief and an intramural envelope." She reached into the desk. "It's over, Kate. When I've sent this back to him, I'll not trouble myself again—" her resolve wavered, "except to go on praying for him."

Kate watched, amazed at her friend's courage. She found herself, not for the first time, comparing herself unfavorably with Deirdre. She had been depressed for days after her friendship with James had ended. But here was Deirdre, ending her engagement to the man she loved, crying her heart out for just a few hours and calmly going on with life.

As if to underline how unswerving her decision was, Deirdre stood still by the desk instead of returning to her bed. "And if it's over for me, then it must be for you, too. So let's pray together for a wee minute, and then I must look at my linguistics and semantics book."

"Oh—Deirdre," Kate moaned, "how can you?"

"I love that course. The most fascinating I ever took. Dr. O'Brien is so interesting." Her voice was almost carefree.

"Are you sure you're not just denying all?"

"As a way of coping? No." She shook her head, her gentian eyes positive. "I'm satisfied that God is in charge of my life. So I have to trust Him in all this, too."

Kate left Deirdre's room in a daze. After returning the untouched tray to the refectory, she wandered halfway to the Great Hall before she realized that she was following her old habit of going to the pigeonholes right after lunch. She would open her letters and then sleep for a while: an escape until she could think everything through.

Almost invariably, a letter from her father came on Mondays. It lay inside the "H" pigeonhole as usual, but there were two others under it for her; one in a long white envelope embossed with the London University emblem, and another in a square red envelope. She tore off her glove, shaking, and ripped open the letter from

London. Then she walked over to a bench and unfolded it as she sat down.

> Dear Miss Hamilton:
> On behalf of the examining committee for postgraduate applicants I would like to congratulate you on your acceptance to the postgraduate study of English Literature at London University. . . .

She shut her eyes and pressed the letter down into her lap. Joy leapt up in her. *At last.* She felt like calling out to the students who were strolling across the hall toward the library stairs. *I did it! I'll be at London! An M.A.—or Ph.D. scholarship!* Instead, she stared foolishly at them, a smile lightening her face. *How gracious of God,* she thought, *to let me get this now.*

After a moment she scanned the rest of the letter and then turned to the red envelope. Postmarked "Londonderry" and stamped with the hopeless and ironic caption "The Gateway to Irish Industry," it was addressed in black ink, the letters rather spiky and somehow familiar. She was still trembling with excitement about her news as she opened this second envelope.

A valentine card. She stared at it, her smile fading into bemusement. On the front, a red rose. Nothing more. No blurred lovers walking down a beach. No sentimental or crude rhymes. Utterly simple. She opened it in wonder. No signature.

Who? she wondered. Roger? Had she told Sheila she'd never received a valentine before? Very likely. And she put Roger up to it. Or Liam? As a joke . . . before all this upheaval? No, wait, there was writing on the back of the card. Oh, it was Yeats, "He Wishes for the Cloths of Heaven."

> *Had I the heavens' embroidered cloths,*
> *Enwrought with golden and silver light,*
> *The blue and the dim and the dark cloths*
> *Of night and light and the half-light,*
> *I would spread the cloths under your feet:*
> *But I, being poor, have only my dreams;*
> *I have spread my dreams under your feet,*
> *Tread softly because you tread on my dreams.*

[243]

The sender had initialed it W.B.Y., 1899. Then it couldn't be from Liam. He'd probably never read a word of Yeats. Sheila could have found the poem for Roger. But was it his writing? Where had she seen that black script before . . . ?

Without opening the letter from her father, Kate returned to her room. She left the unopened letter on her desk with the one from London University. The valentine she put into a drawer. Then she fell asleep.

The top of Crawford Square appeared and disappeared in a thick fog. He moved cautiously. Somewhere behind him, blue violins played a long, mournful adagio, but he stubbornly rejected their deceit, muttering, "Lies. All a lie."

A familiar shape loomed on his left: the Presbyterian Hostel. He thumbed his nose at it and shouted a curse. No lights went on, and no windows flung open. "Dead with sleep, so you are!" he bawled. He expected the echoing square to answer him, *So you are . . . you are . . . are,* but fog swallowed everything. He laughed raucously at himself and stumbled on up the hill.

He gained the wide porch at last. The frosted glass windows on either side of the door glowed faintly. He resisted an impulse to push his fist through one of them. *Too violent,* he thought, *even if they do look like windows in a waking parlor.* He found his key and grazed the wood by the lock. The key scraped and scratched but resisted him. He stooped slightly to peer at the lock. It was miniscule, ridiculous. How was he to get the enormous key in that tiny hole?

The door finally yielded to the key, and he fell forward, cursing loudly, into the dim hall. For a moment he lay still; then he felt the cold air rolling in over his back, so he kicked the door shut with his boot. Its slam thundered in the silence. The hallway, too, was now gray with fog.

"Cole's," he muttered to himself. "Not t'same as it used to be. No friends here any more." His speech was slurred, his tongue out of control. "And Castle Bar. Room full of drunks. All soused. Dead drunk . . . like meself." He sat up abruptly. His knee caught in the front hem of his old black coat. After untangling himself, he stayed

[244]

on the floor, looking up at the foggy stairs, at the polished mahogany banisters and worn treads. "No, not drunk. Just very philos—phil'sophical. Sing, man, sing."

He broke into an old ballad he'd learned years ago, singing at the top of his lungs in a gravel-harsh tenor:

> *Alas, alas, Mary Hamilton*
> *Alas, alack for thee*
> *What hast thou done with thy wee babe*
> *I saw and heard weep by thee?*

Then he stopped, chuckling, "No, that's never right."

> *Alas, alas, Katie Hamilton,*
> *Alas, alack for thee*
> *What hast thou done with my wee babe*
> *I saw and heard weep by thee?*

> *'I put her in a tiny boat*
> *And cast her out to sea*
> *That she might sink, or she might swim*
> *But never come back to thee.'*

> *Alas, alas, Katie Hamilton—*

Footfalls coming up the half flight from the kitchen. Heavy but quick. He stopped singing again, hugging himself.

"Liam Donnelly! What in the name of heaven is going on?" Clad in a threadbare brown dressing gown, Jack stood above him, his head lost in the fog. "Get up, man."

He staggered to his feet only to collapse again. "I sink, therefore I am," he mumbled. Among the first words he'd said to Deirdre, all of fourteen months before.

"Enough of the parody, you case. Here, I'll pull you up." Jack leaned down and hauled him up by the arm. "Hang you onto me. You're drunk as an Irishman."

"Funny, Jack."

Jack heaved him down the stairs and propped him up on a chair by the kitchen sink. "Plastered, so you are."

[245]

"Pickled. Good for the blood, 'casionally."

Jack didn't bother to argue. He pulled off Liam's coat and sweater and opened his shirt. "Can you see straight?"

"Never saw more clearly in me life. But for the fog, I'd been here hours ago." He waved his arms widely, wildly.

"What fog? No fog tonight, Liam. It's all in your head." Jack turned on the cold tap and filled the sink almost to the top. "This'll help." He hoisted Liam up over the edge of the sink and dunked his head under the water for several seconds.

Liam came up bellowing in protest, blowing and spluttering water out of his mouth and nose like a swimming dog. "What'd you do that for?"

"To sober you up, I hope."

Liam raised his fist angrily, but Jack's reactions were far quicker. He caught his wrists and pinned them down with a sharp warning. Liam slouched back into the chair and stared up at Jack with his head on one side. "S'all right, Jackie. I'll be a good boy now."

Jack released him, gave him a kitchen towel, then moved back to the big wooden table where he'd been sitting with a copy of Donne's poems and a cup of tea. He watched Liam sternly. "What were you drinking, anyway? You're half blind. No . . . don't tell me. I can smell it. Whiskey. Good grief, man, don't you have any more respect for your body than that? How much?"

Liam hunched forward and wiped off his face and hair so that he wouldn't have to answer right away. "Don't know. Bought a couple meself. A coupl'a fellows bought me . . . several." Moaning, he pushed himself up with the help of the sink and thrust his hand into his trouser pocket. He pulled the pocket inside-out. A two-new-pence piece rolled across the red-tiled floor. "That's all I've got left. Spent all I had."

"I thought you gave up the drinking."

"I did." He began to cough, doubling over.

"Then . . . why, Liam?"

For answer, Liam groped into his other pocket and pulled out a University intramural envelope. His fingers rustled inside it and held up the small diamond ring he had given Deirdre only three weeks before. "Surely you heard?"

[246]

Jack's mouth compressed into a line as he saw the ring. "No," he said softly. "I didn't know."

"Come on!" Liam jeered.

"I've been here all day."

"In this . . . kitchen?" It was still hard for him to talk.

"No, no. I mean in McCrae. Except for a seminar this morning." He made a small, self-effacing gesture. "Since last week I've not felt much like my work."

Liam nodded morosely. "Don't blame you."

"I'm trying to write an essay on Donne for the seventeenth-century literature course. Thought I might as well just stay up here all day." Liam gave him a doubtful look. "But that's all beside the point. Tell me what happened."

"If I do, would you make me a fierce cup of coffee?"

Smiling, Jack lit the gas stove and did so.

Liam laced the coffee with sugar and sat stirring it intently, watching it as though it might disappear. Finally, he said, "I was looking for Deirdre. She wasn't where I'd seen her last—in the reading room. I found her in the tower. She was thick as thieves with Hamilton."

Jack leaned forward slightly. "What d'you mean?"

"Talking! Found out about the NICRA meeting, she did. Somebody in this bloody place told her."

Jack grimaced and covered his eyes with his hand. "Someone was bound to find out."

"You didn't tell anyone, I suppose?"

Jack answered him with a reproachful look.

"I thought not." He swore and thumped the table with his fist. Hot coffee sloshed onto his hand and he swore again. "I'd like to get my hands on whoever did—"

"Calm down, man, calm down. You're out of yourself complete-ly."

"You would be too . . . ah, but you'd not have gone to the meeting anyway. Listened to your wise friend, you would have." Liam's tone was scathing.

"I never said 'I told you so.' I didn't even think it. I'm very sorry, Liam." Jack's reply was steady.

"Aye, so you are . . . and . . . so am I." He blew on the coffee and sipped a little. "The best wee woman." He sat shaking his head miserably. Then his face changed to flint. "But that friend of hers. Katherine the Great Hamilton. She had something to do with all this. I know she did. She's got such a complex. Thinks she can run everybody's life," he spat. "Can't even run her own. Look at that specter of a man she was in love with. McQueen. Paisleyite. Bloody ignoramus. Just her type. They deserved each other." He laughed. "Kate the Virgin Queen. Hah! Too bad he didn't take her off when he left. She won't leave Deirdre alone. Fills her head with daft ideas and—"

Jack moved swiftly round the table and caught Liam's shoulders. "Enough. You're still drunk, and you're full of bitterness. It doesn't do any good to lay all your anger on Katherine."

Liam scrutinized Jack's face, which was only a foot from his own. His eyes narrowed. "You poor bloody fool. So you're human, after all. Not the holy celibate everyone thinks you are."

"Don't mistake celibacy for sexlessness."

Liam ignored him. "I'm sorry for you, so I am. She's beautiful on the outside with that mane of blonde hair and those blue eyes of hers. Better look closely, though; they're full of ice. All that devout talk and pious posturing—it's just a gloss for her frigidity. She's mean, Jack." He swore. "A little healthy lust—Protestant women don't know how to deal with it."

Jack shook him. "Oh, you make me furious!" But his voice was more derisive than angry. "For a man who's taken . . . what? . . . nine courses in philosophy and logic, I'd say you've learned nothing here. Nothing." He abruptly loosed his grip and turned away. "What sort of an invalid syllogism is your argument based on this time?"

"To hell with syllogisms."

"And you don't know—can't see—the difference between frigidity and inexperience. I suppose you've driven Deirdre half mad yourself, pressing against her conscience. But don't project that onto me—or Katherine." Jack's voice had sunk to a growl of restrained anger. "And don't let your besotted imagination carry you away, either."

"Not imagination. *In vino veritas* . . . and all that blarney. Hang around. I'll tell you some more *veritatem*, if you like."

[248]

"No thanks. I've heard all I want to." He retrieved his book. "Some of what you've seen in Katherine is true. But I've seen other things. Things you'll never see in anyone you merely label 'Protestant,' 'Unionist,' or 'Loyalist.' Sober up, Liam, and grow up. Good night. I think you can get yourself up the stairs all right."

Jack climbed the five flights and stood outside his room on the top floor. Roger, he knew, was asleep long ago. Under the glaring lightbulb hanging above the landing, he fumbled awkwardly with the pages of Donne's poems. There was a particular line . . . there . . . *A bracelet of bright haire about the bone.*

He leaned his head against the doorjamb. He was shaking.

Saturday, May 22

"It's lovely out here, isn't it?"

Kate let her eyes range over the lawn, the trees, and the lough, then turned them back to Sheila's face to answer. "It is, surely. And I'm sorry to be leaving it." She waved her hand toward the shrubbery and the water. "Especially now. May is so gorgeous here. Look—the rhododendrons are almost in full bloom."

The two women were sitting on a wooden bench beside the ha-ha. It was rare for them to be studying together, particularly on a Saturday. But this afternoon Roger had taken a train to Belfast so that he could use the Queen's University library, and Sheila had asked for Kate's company. For once, the arrangement worked; even Sheila had no time for chattering with comprehensive examinations two days off. By half past four they had been working steadily in the library for over three hours, and Kate had suggested this break outside.

They both looked down over the gently sloping lawn to the apple, thorn, and chestnut trees, and beyond to the water below. Strand Road was invisible from where they sat; they might as well have been on a wooded hill away from any city, for Waterside, far from them on the other side of the lough, smudged the only urban dirt on the painting. But even Waterside looked clean today: a soft charcoal blur to Kate's eyes. And under the afternoon sun the water looked romantically blue, a pale watercolor mirroring the sky.

Again, only the perpetual scraping and grinding of the dredger northward in the lough reminded them of the city. Otherwise the air was still with hardly a breeze. The peace was interrupted only by the piercing scream of an occasional seagull weaving patterns over the water, or by the calls of some English students playing cricket at the bottom of the lawn. Pok! Pak! . . . the ball on the bat. "Over . . . How's out! . . . Run!"

Kate stretched luxuriously. She was tired, and nostalgic again about finishing her Irish university life, but the warm air and the green and blue panorama relaxed her.

"It's so hard to concentrate today," Sheila commented.

"The weather, and the end being so near," Kate agreed. "It's tempting just to say, 'What's the point?' After all, what we don't know now, we probably never will."

"And what we don't know now probably isn't worth knowing, either," Sheila laughed. "But still, we avoid the temptation and keep plodding."

Kate let her eyes unfocus and became meditative. "It's been hard for me to get things done, anyway. For the last few months."

"Not that I've noticed! You've been going as hard as ever. Organizing the spring retreat . . . CU meetings every week . . . and you've never missed a week at St. Jerome's."

"I mean academic things." Her voice sounded distant and drowsy, as if she were thinking about something else. "It's been hard since . . . since Father Colm died."

"That shook you, I know."

"Some of the joy's gone. . . . But then there are some mornings when I wake up exhilarated about being in London next year. . . . Then again I start thinking about leaving Ireland, or about the First—and get paralyzed with doubt."

"Oh, Kate, of course you'll get a First. If you don't, who will?"

Kate shrugged. "I don't think about the competition much."

"That's because, unlike me, you don't need to." Sheila's tone was gently sarcastic.

Kate smiled. "You think it's easy for me? That I don't have to make any effort?"

"No—I see you working. Much more than I do. You and Deirdre—what a pair of peasants. Always slaving away. . . . Where is Deirdre, anyway?"

"Up in her room. She said if she even walked to the library she'd

[251]

end up sitting out on the grass doing nothing. I couldn't bear it! She doesn't even have a window to look out of."

"But she's disciplined."

Kate's eyes shifted back into focus and met Sheila's again. She gazed at the cheerful brown eyes and hesitated. How could she phrase the question carefully? "Do you ever—?" She began. "I mean—have you seen Liam at all whenever you've gone up to McCrae with Roger?"

"Oh—he's sometimes with Jack. And so occasionally even in Roger's room. You've seen him here and there yourself, I'm sure."

Kate nodded, directing her eyes away again. "Almost every day. Sometimes in the refectory or out in front of the library. He sometimes nods. And sometimes he says 'hello.' But he never looks straight at me. And if Deirdre's with me—" she broke off, frowning, "then he doesn't acknowledge us at all. Averts his face and walks past as fast as he can."

"It's painful for him to see her, I suppose."

Again, Kate shrugged. "Perhaps. But he looks angry more than hurt .... Deirdre's coping well, though. Or seems to be. She doesn't like to talk of him. Says she's better off without him. And she seems content to study and get on with her life."

"She's not interested in anyone else yet?"

"No. Not that I know of. Sam asked her out." Kate's lips curved into a smile. "Remember when you thought I was interested in Sam? . . . But she turned him down."

"And I've not seen Liam with anyone else, either. Have you?"

"No, but I doubt if I would, anyway. In a way that makes their parting even sadder."

"You've never quite forgiven yourself, have you." It was a statement, not a question.

Kate wondered why Sheila was so interested, but saw no reason not to reply. She shook her head. "No. I still dread being judged for interfering deliberately. But perhaps I do invite some justified criticism."

"We all do, Kate. Oh, sometimes I wish there were no such thing as perfectionism. It's a curse."

"It is. I always wanted everything just right." She sighed. "As

[252]

right, as black-and-white as Daddy made it all seem. So straight-forward! But that's not truth, I'm learning."

"We're very serious today."

They both laughed; however, Kate then went on. "In the beginning, with Liam and Deirdre, it still seemed that way to me. Dangerous, yes, and wrong—even though I pretended not to think so. But it wasn't long before my sympathies got divided."

"How was that?"

"Well, I couldn't help liking him—his teasing ways."

"Of course not. He's so full of life. As Deirdre is, in lots of ways. You were bound to like him. Who wouldn't?"

"Remember, I wasn't accustomed to Catholics. I didn't expect to like them. Heard too much preaching against them. But I can't blame everything on my father. I've done that too long . . . I'd hardened my heart myself. But things got complicated when—" She stopped, remembering. "It threw me off balance. Father Colm, Jack, even Liam—none of them fit the old stereotypes, so some of my old Protestant advice fell by the wayside."

"And now you've changed your view about their relationship?"

Kate clenched her hands and lifted them to her eyes. "Oh, Sheila, I'm not sure. It was the whole idea of mixed marriages in general. Well, no—" She stopped. "More than that. How can a Christian marry a non-Christian? Liam's not even . . . much of a Catholic . . . though I know he's gone to church now and then. . . . And I've counseled other girls against—" She took a deep breath. "You probably know why I did that, I suppose?"

Sheila caught her lip under her teeth, nervously. "You mean the views you took from your father?"

"Yes, but—you know what happened, do you, to my mother and sister?" Only now did she finally find herself able to ask that question of Sheila.

Sheila nodded dumbly.

"The man who murdered them was a Catholic. He was drunk. But his being drunk didn't make much difference to me for a long time. I associated danger and death with Catholics. Not with drunkenness. Another stereotype."

Sheila was still nodding. "I only found out recently. You told Jack, didn't you."

Kate looked away, breathing out a small sound that was half laugh, half sigh. "Yes. Of all people to tell!"

"I understand why you told him, though. He's so terribly kind. But why didn't you ever tell me? I don't mean to accuse, but honestly—"

"I couldn't talk about it for a long time. It was too hard, went too deep. Everyone at boarding school knew. But not here. I decided I wanted to find one person—just one—to tell."

"What about Deirdre?"

"I almost did tell her. I even hinted about a bit. She knows now, of course. But her own sympathies would have been divided. Her father, and Liam—"

"Ah—yes."

"And it had colored too much of my life already. When I came here, I wanted to start fresh."

"Colored your whole life?"

"Yes. Colored. Past tense. I've finally been able to forgive that man—to pray for mercy for him. So now I can begin to forget. And I don't see everything as I used to. The old attitudes are changing." She laughed. "Isn't that curious? Who could have forseen all this! We've all changed, in lots of ways. And all will." A smile played on her mouth; she was content to close the conversation there. She stretched again. With the movement, her fair hair started to come unpinned; one strand escaped down her pale dress.

Like a lean, gold cat, Sheila thought. She watched Kate with affection only slightly tinged by jealousy. But then when Kate resumed her hunched-over sitting position, she could plainly see the tiredness on her friend's face: the furrows over her eyes, the drooping mouth. She asked if Kate was ready to walk down to supper.

"Already?" Kate looked at her watch, her eyes widening now.

"It's almost five. Not worth going back to the library."

"No, not now. But right after supper . . . I think I'll study in the room tonight."

"And fall asleep? You're looking so tired."

Kate raised her eyebrows. "Am I? Perhaps I am. All this reading! I just feel as if I've reached saturation point. Yeats, Synge, O'Casey, Shakespeare, Wordsworth, Coleridge, Hardy,

Keats, Milton, Chaucer, Donne . . . Oh! It's all too much. They all begin to sound the same to me."

Sheila smiled. "And to me! Come on, let's go down for supper. All that work . . . I'm hungry."

They strolled along by the ha-ha and down the leafy hill to the Students' Union. But when they entered the refectory, they saw only a few students they knew. Five o'clock was early for most, and many had gone home. Kate looked around for Deirdre, but she was not yet there. "When's Roger coming back?" she asked.

"Late. He thought we should both get as much as possible done today so that we could relax for the last Sunday here."

With full plates, they turned away from the serving hatch. Sheila led the way to the table where she usually sat with Roger. Kate followed, preoccupied, until she noticed that Jack was already at the table. She suddenly felt warm.

"Come on, ladies," Jack urged, looking up as Sheila set her tray next to his. His smile included both of them. "You'll surely take your supper here?"

"Of course we will," Sheila murmured. "Won't we, Katie?"

Kate slowly lowered her tray on the opposite side of the table, facing the serving hatch. "Thank you. I don't see why not." Her voice was formal, no longer the relaxed, comfortable tone of a few moments ago.

Around them, everyone was talking about the examinations, leafing through notes, and—as ususal—arguing.

"How are you getting along with the Irish literary renaissance, Sheila?" Jack asked. Long dimples appeared next to his mouth. He knew she disliked that particular lecture course.

"Not very well," she grimaced. "Kate and I were both studying it this afternoon. We're tired of it, all of it." She glanced at Kate, who had lowered her head briefly to say grace. "But Kate's forging ahead anyway. Ask her. Ask the brains of Britain."

Jack turned his gray eyes toward Kate. He took in the weariness, the look of strain around her eyes and mouth. Softening his voice, then, he said, "And you, Katherine, are you going to make it until Wednesday?"

She didn't smile. She did not want—yet wanted—to meet his eyes. "Oh, we'll all manage fine." She looked down and moved her knife in clean, sharp cuts through a piece of chicken. "The last

[255]

days before the exams always seem worse than the exams themselves." Neutral territory: they could always talk easily about studies.

Sheila groaned, "Oh, not for me."

"Even in Irish literature?" Jack pursued.

Sheila's head turned. She was surprised at how freely Jack could talk to Kate. All the visits to St. Jerome's must have given them some common ground.

"I hope so," Kate answered. She began to relax again. "I am tired of reading . . . as Sheila said. But the renaissance is fascinating." She smiled slightly. "Father Kennedy lit a fire for all of us." She had unconsciously lowered her voice as she said his name, and this time she managed to look at Jack. The mention of Father Colm in his presence always recalled for her their long conversation after the wake. Kennedy was one of the few real links between them. Dead, but real. She struggled to concentrate on what she had tried to say, and so repeated herself. "He lit a fire for all of us."

"He did, aye." Jack turned to look at Sheila. "For most of us anyway."

"Except me," Sheila said laconically. "He was good . . . but too good for me."

"Too good for all of us," Jack said.

"I would never have read a word of some of those writers but for him. Wouldn't even have taken the course," Kate commented. "Daniel O'Corkery, Sean O'Casey, Frank Gallagher . . . I doubt if I'd have read any of them."

Jack picked up on her list of names. "Sean O'Casey, now there's a man after my heart." He smiled. "Did you notice those grand lines Seamus Shields says in *The Shadow of a Gunman?*"

"Which?" Sheila wondered.

"I memorized them so I could tell them to Liam sometime. He'd approve." He paused, shooting a questioning glance at Kate, but then went on. "'It's the civilians who suffer . . . they don't know where to run. Shot in the back to save the British Empire, an' shot in the breast to save the soul of Ireland. . . . I believe in the freedom of Ireland . . . but I draw the line when I hear the gunmen blowin' about dyin' for the people, when it's the people that are dyin' for the gunmen!'"

[256]

Kate had put down her knife and fork during the recitation. "Aren't those grand lines?"

All Kate said was, "It's true. He was right." The reminder stung her.

Realization leapt into Jack's face. "Oh—I'm sorry—I was thinking of Kennedy, not your—"

Meeting his eyes, she murmured, "That's all right. I know you didn't.... I think I've had enough to eat." She piled up her half-emptied supper dishes and stood up.

"You're going back to the room now?" Sheila looked up anxiously.

"No, I'll get my books first, from the library. But I do want to get to bed early." Her direct gaze added meaning to the words.

"Then I'll be quiet, I promise. I'll probably stay up until midnight at least—until Rog gets back."

It was an old agreement by now. Kate nodded. "Then I'll see you later." And she vanished among the tables, only her fair head marking her progress toward the door.

"I said the wrong thing," Jack muttered, frowning.

"No, she's exhausted. And I don't think she meant to be rude, either. She just doesn't like to admit how tired she is."

"You don't need to apologize for her ... we all need some sleep ... but let's talk of something else." He straightened, looking around at their nervously chattering neighbors. "Everyone's got exam panic. Let's talk about the summer, instead."

"All right. You first."

"No you. Your plans are much more exciting than mine."

Sheila moved her shoulders in a self-deprecating shrug. "Oh, I don't know. An awful lot of what goes on before a wedding is so mechanical and bothersome. And my mother has so many ideas of how everything should be done that I've started to tell her she had better marry Rog herself."

He chuckled. "Your father might not approve."

"Maybe not. But you'll see what I mean at the wedding. Oh, I wish it would just be August the fourteenth next week, and that everything were done...." She laughed suddenly. "Although it wouldn't work too well, I suppose. We both need to earn all we can to pay for the honeymoon. And Rog has to look for a job.

[257]

Membership in the Young Conservatives won't pay too well, I fear."

"He's already talked about that. I think he'll find a good job. Some Westminster politician'll be lucky to get him."

"If Rog can get organized a little."

"He will. Wait and see. With you behind him, I predict he'll become one of the most noted political secretaries in England." Jack's voice was overlaid with amusement.

"Or notorious." She laughed. "His ears should be burning."

"Whose ears?"

Jack and Sheila both looked up at once. Deirdre stood beside them, supper tray in hand.

"Deirdre!"

"Aye. May I join you?"

"Surely. You just missed Katherine," Jack said.

Deirdre slid onto the bench opposite them, sitting where Kate had sat, facing the main part of the refectory. "No, we passed each other. She's looking very drawn. Did you notice?"

"She's tired, like the rest of us," Jack answered. He was looking at his plate, trying to get peas onto his fork. "However, we're not going to talk shop here. We're talking about this summer. If you want to talk exams, go over there." He waved vaguely at the other tables.

Deirdre giggled. "Not at all. I'm almost cross-eyed from studying. What a relief to stop."

"Well, then, Jack, it's your turn," Sheila said. "What'll you be up to? Reading all summer for Maynooth?"

He frowned. "No–o. I'll be assisting a priest in Dublin. Not with any formal ecclesiastical work, though."

"Oh, what?"

"Parish work. It's a sad parish. He needs extra help with the social service end of it. I'll be helping with a housing project."

Sheila and Deirdre nodded. "Anything like the work you've done for the Commission up here?" Sheila was going to add "with Liam," but stopped herself.

He shook his head. "Not really. It's helping people renovate run-down housing for reoccupation—places that've become un-inhabitable by most standards. But what I've done up here may be useful. And my carpentry, of course."

[258]

"It sounds just right for you," Deirdre said. "Will there be other seminary students doing the same thing?"

He shrugged. "Very likely. But I'm doing it independently. I wanted time to take a look at what parish work involves—outside the liturgy." He now turned his eyes on Sheila. "Roger's been a good friend to me, Sheila. You know that, don't you?"

Sheila was puzzled. She had lost the connecting thread of what he was telling them. "Well, of course I know. And you to him, too. But what—?"

He smiled, interrupting her. "I'll explain . . . wait a minute. He's done more for me than probably most people, even you, realize."

Deirdre, too, was listening intently, wondering at what almost seemed like hedging from Jack.

"He's helped me think about things I never questioned before. You know how dogmatic the Church is . . . I don't mean that in a derogatory way, necessarily. But all the emphasis is on the Church's dogma, and tradition. And most of us, especially in Ireland, accept it. Some blindly. Some grudgingly. Some joyfully." He broke off, his eyes creasing into a smile. "I've been in all three categories at one time or another. . . . But now I don't find the Church tradition means as much as it used to to me."

Sheila registered dismay. "Jack Monaghan! What on earth has Roger done to you?"

"Done to me? Nothing. But with me. He's got me reading the Bible systematically. Threatened he would, at the very beginning. I laughed and teased him at first. But then he read parts of it aloud. And soon we were reading together . . . every day. I'm sure he told you that."

"Probably mentioned it when you started. But I don't remember—"

"That's marvelous, Jack," Deirdre interrupted, observing his enthusiasm. "And, Sheila, Roger's a good man."

Sheila laughed, "I know he is." She made a slight bow of her head, an acknowledgment for him.

"Anyway," Jack went on, "it seems more important to me now to find out how the truth of the gospels can be applied to twentieth-century Ireland. All the argue-bargue about apostolic succession and transubstantiation and the real presence and birth control and

Papal infallibility and celibacy and Mass in Latin or Gaelic or English—*ad nauseam*—all those things seem beside the point." It had come out in a rush. He leaned back with a small, breathless laugh. Then his face sobered again. "Has Roger talked to you about me lately?"

Sheila looked even more puzzled than before. "Yes," she stammered, "certainly he has. We talk of you often."

"No, that's not what I meant. Did he tell you, did he—?" He faltered for a moment. "That I'm not going to Maynooth after all next year?" He blundered on, eyes down now, suddenly awkward. "I asked him not to tell anyone. But now I suppose it doesn't matter."

All three were quiet for a moment. Then Deirdre said softly, "I'm amazed, Jack."

He looked up quickly. "Now don't you good women misunderstand. I'm just going to take a year and get some experience first. A kind of internship. Then I'll be ready, I think. It's a decision that's come slowly."

Sheila's eyes were piercing. "You have doubts now about your calling—vocation? If you do, no one would have guessed."

"He hasn't said that, Sheila," Deirdre murmured, cautioning her.

His eyes swerved to the other side of the room. "'Doubt' is a strong word, Sheila. But if wanting to take longer to start my work . . . to find the will of God . . . is 'doubt,' then I 'have doubts, as you say." He sighed.

Sheila chewed her lip unhappily. "I don't mean to question your convictions. Sorry."

"That's all right. You're not. Everyone'll wonder." He raised his eyes to the ceiling. "Especially my poor, suffering mother. . . . But I've prayed about this for months. And I'm sure it's best . . . this year off."

"Though it doesn't sound as if you'll be 'off' exactly."

He smiled. "No—I don't want to be."

"And Roger—what did he think—when you told him?"

Jack pushed aside his empty plate and leaned forward on his elbows. "It was my own decision, y'understand . . . even if he did sow some ideas in me . . . and he thinks a year away is a good idea. But, listen, it doesn't make much difference what he thinks. It's something between the Almighty and myself." He stopped, moving his arms. "Well, it's hard to talk about this, even with you and Roger. But I wanted you to know. We'll not be having a great deal of time to talk, I'm thinking."

Sheila and Deirdre took deep breaths simultaneously. "No," Sheila agreed. "Probably not. Exams until Wednesday. Then we'll be off home. And at the wedding we won't—"

"You'll have eyes for no one but Roger then," Jack said warmly.

Sheila flushed, glancing first at Jack and then across to Deirdre. "It'll be a grand day!"

Deirdre was not looking at Jack or Sheila. Facing away from the center of the room, they focused on her and on the wall behind her. She, however, could see all the students as they came in for supper, and her attention was now riveted on one in particular. At first, Sheila did not notice her distraction; then it became too obvious to ignore. Sheila turned, following Deirdre's gaze.

Liam was walking away from the hatch. He wore the inevitable rumpled jacket, an opened packet of cigarettes protruding from the pocket. His beard had grown thick, and his hair was long and tangled. Sheila had observed these changes in him week by week as she had seen him in McCrae, but now, as she saw him in Deirdre's presence, she looked at him differently: with pity and with a poignant consciousness of what Liam had lost in Deirdre. He had needed her to steady the course of his life. Not that there was anything wrong in his disheveled appearance, but that his carelessness symbolized, perhaps, a return to old patterns that might prove destructive: a drifting back toward old drinking companions, possibly Marxists or IRA men?

Inwardly, Sheila groaned, but aloud she only said, "Oh dear, here's Liam."

Jack also swung round; then he looked back at Deirdre, whose naturally high color had deserted her. She shrank down, as though hoping he would not see her.

Liam seemed unaware of all the attention directed toward him. Staring into middle distance as if he were still thinking about Kierkegaard or Pascal, he was moving slowly in their direction.

He saw Jack first and made an ironic face, lowering his eyebrows in mock disapproval. "Deserted your books early today, Monaghan, haven't you?"

[261]

"Late enough." Jack's reply came after only a second's delay.

Then Liam saw Deirdre on the other side of the table. He had begun to set down his tray; now he wavered. Sheila watched as their eyes met: Deirdre's pained and uncertain; his surprised, a little suspicious.

"Won't you eat here with us, Liam?" Jack asked gently, not expecting him to stay.

Still looking at Deirdre, Liam did not reply. His expression was now one of reproach and bitterness. Without taking his eyes off her, he put his tray next to Jack's; but instead of sitting down to eat, he remained standing and reached into his pocket. Green eyes stared into dark blue.

At last he found what he wanted. Something small, round, and white spun across the table to Deirdre. The ring? Deirdre blinked. No. It was a Polomint.

"A token of peace, Deirdre." The same, familiar, harsh voice. Rough but not rude. . . . He retrieved his tray and turned his back on all of them to sit alone at a table in the far corner.

Deirdre sat, stunned. The mint lay untouched by her plate.

"It had to happen sooner or later—that he'd have to say a word or two to you, or you to him." It was Jack who broke the uncomfortable silence; he spoke hesitantly, as though he understood her need for a moment to collect herself.

A small, speechless sound passed Deirdre's lips. She formed the word "Yes," but it stuck in her throat. Her hand closed over the mint.

Each holding a pile of books, they stood close together under the weak sodium lamp that illuminated the bottom steps up to Woodburn. It was past curfew and the red front door was locked.

"I missed you today," she said.

Roger smiled, but the smile was lopsided. He was lightheaded, he had told her, from working so late and then trying to read under the poor lights of a Belfast-Derry railway carriage. "I missed you, too. But the Queen's library was such a help."

"I'm glad."

"I really must get back to McCrae, darling, or I'll never wake up for church."

"You were going to St. Eugene's with Jack, to the early Mass, weren't you? A sort of final fellowship hour?"

His face contorted. "Was going. I hate to let Jack down . . . but eight o'clock is only—" he squinted at his watch, "five hours away!"

"Try to go. He told me Liam was going as well. And, oh, I forgot to tell you—"

Roger shifted with slight impatience. "Better make it brief. I tell you, I'm falling over with sleep."

She leaned over, took his books from him, and dropped both hers and his onto the steps so that she could put her arms around his neck. "I'll hold you, love. It's important news."

The crunch of gravel under boots and the jingle of keys warned them that the janitor was on his way. They had called him from the Students' Union to let Sheila in.

"Quickly, then," Roger said into her ear.

"It looks as if Liam and Deirdre might get together again."

He drew back in quick surprise. "What makes you think so?"

The janitor appeared out of the darkness. His gait was uneven. He passed them doggedly and went up to unlock the door without so much as a grunt of acknowledgment. Sheila smelt wine on his breath as he descended past them again.

"Yous'll lock that door again," he grumbled.

"She will," Roger assured his disappearing back. "Now, tell me. And then I must go."

She described the little exchange between them in the refectory. He listened with a neutral expression. "He wasn't just making fun of her?"

"I don't think so."

"Poor little Deirdre."

"She's far more crazy about him than she lets on."

"I think so, too." He rested his hands on her shoulders. "And I am about you. But sleep calls me—" He kissed her, then bent down for their books. Piling hers into her arms, he nudged her up the steps. "Goodnight, love. I'll see you at St. Augustine's?"

"I certainly hope so."

[263]

"Go on and shut the door. I won't move till you're inside." He stood looking up at her, his face soft with love and weariness.

She closed the door quietly and locked it. Woodburn was silent. After groping for the hallway light, she trudged wearily up to the second floor. Kate had left her the small light on the stand between the beds. Sheila tiptoed around, undressing slowly. She, too, was tired now. Lecture notes and books were strewn all around Kate's desk and bed. Sheila was surprised at this disorder; Kate was usually so meticulous. But comprehensive exams had a way of changing everyone's study habits. Cramming. Even Kate had done it today.

Just before she turned off the lamp, the gleam of Kate's glasses under the light caught her attention. Curious to see what Kate had been studying, she leaned over softly, careful not to knock anything down. Kate had borrowed her copy of W.B. Yeats's poems again. She had been reading "He Wishes for the Cloths of Heaven," but her glasses rested on her well-thumbed Bible, which also lay open. Sheila smiled. How typical of Kate. Matthew. *Judge not, that ye be not judged. For with what judgment ye judge, ye shall be judged: and with what measure ye mete, it shall be measured to you again.* The words caught her eye as she reached for the switch. They made her shiver.

She turned and looked at Kate, asleep on her stomach without a pillow, her face turned away from the light. Her thick hair tumbled over the near side of the bed, and she had shielded her eyes with her right hand. *"Tread softly because you tread on my dreams,"* she thought. And wondered, *Does Kate have any dreams?*

In that moment, Sheila pitied Kate more than she had envied her only a few hours before. She saw forlornness and vulnerability in the sleeping form. It was a new feeling for Sheila. Destined for London and for the highest class of degree the New University awarded, Kate had often aroused jealousy in her, not pity. But Sheila would not have changed places for anything. To her, Kate's future seemed suddenly joyless and empty.

Sunday, May 23

Kate came up through the deep green shade of evening, up through the woods at the back of the Students' Union, climbing the hill slowly, looking through the tissued canopy of leaves to the May-blossom white of a northern sky. She stopped for a minute to observe the great variety of dappled greens: the lush radiance of the chestnut leaves, the shrill intensity of new beech leaves, the darker shine of a few holly sprigs. Going on up the path, she became increasingly conscious of her need to notice everything around her, since this was her last Sunday at the University.

An early curfew for the entire city had brought all the Protestants, including Kate, hurrying back from church. And as a final celebration or pre-examination jamboree, the folk club had booked the coffee bar for the whole evening. She was to meet Deirdre, and together they would go down to sing and laugh and listen.

Deirdre already stood at the steps waiting for her as she rounded the side wall of the building. Kate had expected to see Roger and Sheila, too, since they had gone to church at St. Augustine's with Deirdre, but neither was there.

Anticipating Kate's question, Deirdre called, "Come on, it's starting now. Roger and Sheila have gone down already."

They hurried across the dingy hallway that led to the refectory, then turned down the well-worn stairs to the basement. From below came the excited talk and laughter of over two hundred students and even a few lecturers, all packed into the coffee bar, filling every table, chair, windowsill, and available floor space. At the back of the room, French windows opened to the trees that

[265]

Kate had just passed through; below them the path seemed to drop away into a leafy green abyss.

Picking their way over legs and shoes, hands, sweaters, jackets, guitars, flutes, and fiddles, they managed to find a place on a corner windowsill which allowed them to look both ways across the L-shaped room. Uproar. A tumult of loud voices, plucked strings, and scraping violin bows. If there was one thing that united the University students—Catholic and Protestant alike—it was folk music.

Opposite Kate and Deirdre a student neither of them knew was practicing a poignant lament familiar to both of them by melody, but not by name. Turning to Deirdre, Kate said, "It's sad, isn't it?"

"The song?"

"Yes—but I mean that this is the last real Irish singing I'll hear until who knows when."

Deirdre smiled. "Och, no, indeed it's not. You'll be back over the water soon, won't you?"

Kate returned the smile. "I hope so." Her voice was wistful. She looked away to see where Roger and Sheila were sitting. She did not find them immediately, even though they were only about ten feet away, Roger lounging in a chair and Sheila cross-legged on the floor, leaning her back against his knees.

Deirdre, too, looked around, her eyes searching for the face she had most wanted to see since yesterday. At last she found him. Liam stood in a recess toward the front of the room where the evening's performers were clustered with their friends; Jack was with him. Not wanting to betray the direction of her gaze to Kate, she kept looking around the room, intermittently coming back to him for brief moments.

The crowd fell silent as one of the lecturers, a young Spanish teacher, moved to the center of the room and began to play, not an Irish lovesong, as everyone expected, but the forceful chords and rhythmic rolls of a flamenco piece. The music sounded a strange contrast to the haunting melodies of most Irish ballads, but the man's students roared with delight and began to clap in time. His hands flashed over the strings until he played so fast that no one could keep up with him, and the clapping subsided to ripples of admiration.

Finally, when applause broke out, he handed the guitar to his wife and took up a banjo. Equally at home with this instrument, he plucked out the driving, frenzied rhythms of American bluegrass: *Orange Blossom Special* and *Foggy Mountain Breakdown*. The syncopated sound danced round the room and bounced out of the French windows into the mellow light of late evening.

When the flamenco and bluegrass were over, some of the McCrae men began to call loudly for Irish music; their complaints were raucous but good-natured. In response, one of the most popular singers stood up and gave them an old ballad, *The Lass of Loch Royal*.

> *"And who will build a bonny ship*
> *And set her on the sea,*
> *That I may go and seek my love*
> *My own love Gregory?"*

> *O up and spoke her father dear*
> *And a wealthy man was he*
> *And he has built a bonny ship*
> *And set her on the sea.*

Deirdre smiled with pleasure and swung her feet to the rhythm of the song. The music brought no sadness to her as it did to Kate, who had leaned forward and was resting her chin on her palms.

The next musician was a fresher from the Mourne Mountains who, as a child, had learned traditional ballads from her great-grandmother. She first sang *Sir Patrick Spence* in a clear, high voice that was untrained but beautifully pure.

> *The king sits in Dumferling town*
> *Adrinking his blood red wine*
> *"Sir Patrick Spence is the best sailor*
> *That ever sailed the brine."*

[267]

The men in particular loved her and cheered her on between songs. But when she sang, always without accompaniment, the room was absolutely still. She did *Lord Thomas and Fair Eleanor, Lord Randal,* and *The Elfin Knight.*

Kate turned her head to look out at the trees once more. Nostalgia about leaving Ireland crept up on her again. The conflict—the deaths and the daily horror of headlines—would leave a bitter flavor on her tongue, but the memory of the Irish landscape, the music, and the people—some in particular—would remain, too. She would go from Ireland, but Ireland would stay with her. . . . *They* would stay with her.

When the girl had finished, the room lay hushed for several moments before anyone applauded. Deirdre inclined her head toward Kate's. "That's Ireland for you! Someone sings a lament that's older than all the strife by centuries, and everyone listening can forget the troubles."

A bawdy song, *Maids When You're Young Never Wed an Auld Man,* followed, sung by Steve Lenehan and two others Deirdre didn't know. The audience swayed back and forth, clapping boisterously and guffawing in all the right places.

Knowing how much she disliked such songs, Deirdre stole a glance at Kate, who now sat with head down, legs moving very slightly, eyes focused on the floor. Her lips, though, curved into a half-smile, as though in spite of herself she could not ignore the comicry. Deirdre felt torn between Kate's silent criticism and her own natural inherited appreciation for all Irish music. So when the song ended, she leaned over again and whispered, "And that's Ireland for you, too."

Then came the moment Deirdre had waited for with dread, with longing, and with a kind of quiet joy that she could not have explained had she tried. It was Liam's turn to sing. Deirdre noticed that Kate was watching him, her hands clutched tensely back around the sill at either side of her. Taking courage, then, Deirdre also turned her eyes toward him, intent on every move he made.

He was almost the old Liam of two years ago, wearing a grubby aran sweater, frayed jeans, and old brown boots. She noticed the familiar spots of yellow paint still left on the boots from his time line-painting on the Chicago highways. But his clothes were even more untidy than they used to be, his hair more unkempt than before. His face was still the same, however: lively, witty, alert, sensitive ... he seemed totally unconscious of her watching him.

All his songs came from the sea. The first, *Irish Rover*, sent the room rocking with laughter, though everyone had heard it countless times and could anticipate its every joke.

> *We had sailed seven years*
> *When the measles broke out*
> *And our ship lost her way in the fog.*
> *Then the whole of the crew*
> *Was reduced down to two*
> *'Twas meself and the captain's auld dog.*
> *Then the ship struck a rock*
> *Oh, Lordie, what a shock!*
> *And nearly tumbled over.*
> *She turned nine times around*
> *And the puir auld dog was drowned (ah-ooo)*
> *Now I'm the last of the Irish Rovers!*

Next came the lilting melody of the modern folksong, *Shoals of Herring*. The students hummed with Liam, "And I used to sleep standing on me feet, And I'd dream about the Shoals of Herring."

Liam then plucked the opening bars of *The Water Is Wide*. Deirdre's heart quickened, and she held her breath, compelled to stare, and yet fearing he would look up at her with eyes full of the shared knowledge that this was one of her favorite songs.

As she expected, he suddenly lifted his eyes toward the windowsill where she and Kate were sitting. She heard the sharp in–drawing of Kate's breath. He did not shift his gaze as he sang.

> *The water is wide—I cannot get o'er*
> *Neither have I wings to fly*
> *Give me a boat that can carry two,*
> *And both shall cross, my true love and I ...*
>
> *I put my hand in some soft bush*
> *Thinking the sweetest flower to find.*

> *I pricked my finger to the bone*
> *And left the sweetest flower behind.*

When the song ended, there was a slight, uncomfortable pause before the applause. Some rustling and fidgeting. The University was too small to be without gossip, and the breakup of Liam and Deirdre after the argument in the library had not gone unnoticed.

Seeing Deirdre's head drop in anguish, Liam apparently could not resist the impulse to push her to tears. He put down his guitar, clearing his throat. A few of the Irish students, those who knew him well, whispered among themselves, "*Carrickfergus,*" as he began to sing in Gaelic without accompaniment.

The audience did not have to understand Gaelic to know the words. All had heard the song in translation many times.

> *I wish I was in Carrickfergus,*
> *In Elphin, Aoidtrim, or Ballygrind,*
> *Now I would swim over the deepest ocean,*
> *The deepest ocean, my love to find.*

> *But the water is wide; I cannot swim over,*
> *Neither have I wings to fly.*
> *I wish I had a handsome boatswain*
> *To ferry over my love and I.*

Electric emotion ignited the air between the singer and the one for whom he sang. Tears began to fall down Deirdre's pale face; where she gripped the windowsill, her knuckles blanched. She and Liam stared at each other as if no one else were in the room.

For a moment the coffee bar became utterly silent. Deirdre leaned forward on the sill, pressing her heels back against the wall. In a dreamlike half-awareness she saw Liam hand his guitar to Jack, his eyes still on her. Almost mesmerized, she slipped forward. Kate gripped her elbow to arrest her fall.

"I'm going!" Deirdre cried, her face frenzied. Kate released her arm. She dodged, jumped, and stumbled round all the obstacles in her way until at last, painfully conscious that all the students saw her confusion, she gained the bottom of the stairs. Up she ran.

"Let's all sing *I'll Tell Me Ma*," one of the folk club sponsors shouted, ending the awkward silence below. Clapping started again, and the sound of a guitar.

I'll tell me ma when I go home
The boys won't leave the girls alone
They pulled my hair, they stole my comb,
And that's all right till I get home.
But he is handsome, he is pretty,
He is the beau of Belfast city . . .

Deirdre hurtled across the empty hall. Was it Liam playing down there? Was he only baiting her, punishing her?

"Deirdre!" His voice echoed behind her, distraught. He was running after her.

She turned, breathing hard, her hand over her mouth. He slowed to a walk so that as he came to her, she was able to take him in again: the uncombed hair, the intense eyes . . . she stopped there. Nothing else mattered.

The noisy singing floated up from below them.

Let the rain and the hail and the snow blow high
And the winds come whistling through the sky
He's as nice as apple pie,
And I'll get my own love by and by.
And when I get a love of my own
I won't tell me ma when I get home . . .

Without a word, he took her hand and led her out of the building. At the top of the outside steps, they stopped. He swung toward her, almost sprang on her. Grasping her shoulders with his hands, he stared at her for a second; then he pulled her into his arms. The movement was almost savage, so abrupt that they both began to topple down the steps. But he caught her tightly with one arm and grabbed for the iron railing with the other.

They remained as they were, halfway down the steps, clinging to each other with a kind of hunger. Deirdre began to weep.

"Oh, don't, don't," he whispered.

[271]

"No, I'm so glad." She was breathless, laughing and crying at once.

Frantically he brushed the tears off her face and bent his head to kiss her, but he crushed her more than kissed her, and her whole body began to shake. She sank so heavily against him that they swayed, dangerously near to falling again.

Steve Lenehan and a girl came running down the steps behind them. Steve made crude smacking noises with his mouth as he passed; then in the blue twilight he saw Liam and paused. "So you're at it again, Donnelly?"

Liam swung around with his fist raised. "Get lost, Lenehan!" he shouted. Then he turned to Deirdre, more gently this time.

"I think . . . since we seem to have a penchant for falling off things tonight . . . that we'd better find *terra firma* before—" Not even bothering to finish, he caught her hand and led her down the steps and up the hill toward Woodburn.

"Not there," Deirdre groaned. "Nothing's private. Let's go over there, on the bench." And she led him through the failing light to the same seat from which Sheila and Kate had looked out over the water the day before.

"It's a bit hard," Liam complained.

"But it's so lovely out now. And you can lean on me. I'm not hard."

"That's not all I'll do if you talk like that," he raised his eyebrows suggestively. "Come here."

Arms round each other again, they rediscovered each others' mouths, eyes, hands . . . . At last Deirdre pushed him gently from her. She was laughing, and her teeth had begun to chatter. He moved back to her immediately. But he was calmer now, and they sat with their foreheads pressed together, breathing each others' warmth.

"We'll get married," he said. She nodded, the movement shaking his head, too.

"I've thought of nothing, no one else for three months. And I've waited for this, thinking what we'd do if it ever happened. But I didn't think—"

"Nor I."

"You seemed so cold and hard, Deirdre."

"That's how you seemed to me. Indifferent. Hateful."

"But I wasn't."

"And I wasn't, either."

"It was Kate's fault, wasn't it. That cold b—"

She stopped his mouth with his hand. "No!" she cried, her voice ringing with desperate emphasis. "Don't ever—ever—ever say it. Kate's been the best friend I've ever had. And she's been almost as hurt by this as we have. She cares for both of us."

"Then the world's a bloody funny place these days," he scoffed, his voice skeptical, but also amused.

"Believe me, she's not as you've imagined her. Some things have changed."

"Well, thank God for that."

"I do thank Him."

He laughed. "And I do, too. For you. Are you sure about this?" He broke away, indicating with his hands his hair and clothes. "Are you sure about me? That you want me after all?"

"Yes." The word ricocheted back without the slightest pause.

"I let myself go. Drank too much, smoked like a chimney, stopped going to lectures. . . . But I promise to reform."

"Oh, love, I don't want those foolish promises again. They don't mean anything to me. I want you. You were right that day. I did want you on my own terms." She waved her hands wildly as she rushed on. "We'll both have to change, Liam . . . I suppose it'll be difficult." She frowned fleetingly, then continued, "But I fell in love with the Liam Donnelly who joked around and—" she laughed suddenly, "gave me peppermints and wanted to know what my friends thought of you when really you didn't care and danced like the eighth wonder of the world." She held her arms open and he came to kiss her again.

Stroking her hair and neck, he smelled the familiar perfume. Their embrace was all the dearer because of this familiarity. She pushed her fingers into his hair and cradled the back of his head in her hand.

He shook his head free with a sound of disgust. "Don't. My hair's awful. I will change that. It was an adolescent desire to get back at you that made me let it get like this. Teenage stuff."

She smiled. "It doesn't matter."

[273]

"It matters a little, but—" He took both her hands in his and rested them in his lap. His face, clear to Deirdre's searching eyes even in the half-darkness, became grave. "We have to be practical for a moment. That's usually your job. But I've had a lot of time to think . . . about everything. As I said."

Her eyes widened eagerly. "What. Tell me it all."

He looked down. "You're right. We'll have to give and take a lot. Remember, you're going to France at the end of September."

"I don't want to. I couldn't bear to be away from you again." Her voice wavered.

"Shh—no, you won't have to be. I'll take a year off. We could get married next month." He held up one hand as her mouth opened to speak. "Wait. This is one time in my life when I'll not be patient. Better to marry than to burn, Deirdre. A quotation from Father Monaghan himself."

"It's from Scripture, Liam." She smiled a wry smile at his laughing eyes.

"Not surprising. He's turning Protestant by all accounts, anyway, reading the Bible with Forbes . . . but that's beside the point." He held her eyes with his. "There's no reason to wait. No reason to be apart any more. I decided I might not even finish the degree anyway. You've become a much better student than I am, and I'd like to see you finish. So we'll live in France for a year, and then back here for another, if we can stand Derry after being away . . . and if we're not expecting by then."

Her face flushed a bit. "You really did work it all out!" Then she laughed gaily. "But what good is Gaelic in France?"

He gave her hands an impatient shake. "You're not turning me down, are you? That I can't speak French is never reason to wait. Is it now?" He was sure of her but needed her assurance.

"No reason. And I don't want to wait, either."

Leaning over to give her another quick kiss, he suddenly wrested his hands from hers and undid the top buttons of his shirt. She watched him, her eyebrows drawing together. He said, "Then, *cushla mo croide*, joy of my heart, you'll take this back. Don't you ever take it off again."

She watched him fumble with the small clasp of a gold chain

that held the ring. "Here, I'll undo it," she murmured. "I never knew you were so sentimental."

"Yes you did. You've forgotten too much. But I'll remind you."

Above them, black, wadded clouds radiated like clumsy spokes from the hub of a lambent moon, their uneven undersides outlined in blue and silver. And the moon's light left a bright wake that whirled down to the city and the lough in a trail of amber, white, turquoise, and cobalt. But Liam and Deirdre saw none of this. In the darkness, they did not even look up.

Thursday, May 27

Roger came for Sheila just as she and Kate were beginning their packing. He wanted to take pictures of her, he said, down by the docks and on the city wall. And since she needed little to distract her from the dull business of fitting all her belongings into a trunk, she went right to the wardrobe for her raincoat.

"We should have done this last weekend," she grumbled. "The weather was so perfect. Just look at it now."

Bent over her shelves, Kate pushed wisps of hair out of her eyes and looked past Roger out of the window. Gray drizzle and fast-moving clouds. Leaves bent backward by the rain and wind. "Awful," she agreed, and went on pulling out the books and piling them onto her bed according to their size.

"It doesn't matter," Roger said cheerfully. "In half an hour it'll change again. And I have a good umbrella."

"So be it. I hope your camera likes gray days," Sheila said.

"It'll do. Hurry up."

"All right, all right. I'm coming." She began to brush her hair.

Roger turned away from the window. "Kate, you look as if you're getting along pretty fast."

"Not too badly, thanks." She didn't look up, but she did smile. "I wish I'd booked the crossing for tonight, though, like you."

"We should swap tickets. At the rate Sheila and I are going, we'll miss the train and the boat without any trouble."

"Not if I can help it," Sheila laughed. "Though you might miss it."

"No I won't. I'm almost packed. Now hurry up!"

"I'm ready."

[276]

"Then let's go." And with a look of pretended despair, Roger opened the door for Sheila, and they were gone.

Kate was glad to be alone for a while. Sheila had been prattling on about weddings, her own and Deirdre's, and now she could do so to Roger. Kate would rather think about sorting books and clothes than about weddings that were still weeks away.

The shelves stood empty. She stared at them as if seeing them for the first time: the scratched brown paint, the thin streaks of dust showing where the books had stood. And though she had emptied the shelves twice before, in two previous Mays, they looked different this time. Empty of her books for the last time. In October someone else's books would be arranged on them: Goethe, Schiller, Kant, Hegel, Nietzsche, and Liebniz instead of Tennyson, Eliot, Shakespeare, Brontë, and Yeats. Someone else would sleep in her bed, perhaps not always alone; someone else would work and dream at her desk—not of literary criticism, but of logic and history, not of Liam and Deirdre, Jack and Roger and Sheila, but of others she did not know.

She sat down on the vinyl padded chair by the cold mantelpiece and debated about leaving the packing until tonight. It was only half-past nine. She would have the books and clothes arranged in the trunk before eleven; and even her untidy desk drawers, the one place she'd allowed herself to cram things away in no order at all, would not take all day. And what would she do, anyway, in an empty room for a whole day with everything packed and her friends gone? She would think . . . too much. She would stand at the left bow window and look north to the cloud-covered blue slieves and grow sorrowful about leaving Ireland. Or if the sun came out, she would wish herself beyond those hills on the white sands of Fahan, the Lough Swilly beach where the students loved to go on fine days and where Roger had proposed to Sheila two years before. She would dwell mournfully on how quickly the three years had passed in this country to which she had always wanted to return.

How quickly . . . and how unsatisfyingly. Not that her intellect was unsatisfied, but her soul. She was being wrenched away before she was ready to go. She hungered for an understanding of this land, these people. An understanding she had not even realized she

[277]

lacked, listening all her life to her father's pronouncements. Brief return trips for the wedding of Deirdre and Liam and for the July commencement would not satisfy. If only she had more time.

From her weekly trips to St. Jerome's with Deirdre and Jack, she had learned more about the power of love than she had from years of her father's sermons. And tasting afresh the mercy of God's love, and watching the joy of human love, she wanted more time to absorb it all for herself. Perhaps she should go to St. Jerome's just once more, tomorrow morning, before she left for the Larne steamer. She started. Yes, that would be a much more constructive way to spend Friday. But then she leaned back again. No, she had already said good-bye to the sisters and to the children. To go up again would only prolong the sadness.

Strangely irresolute, she glanced around the room. Sheila had left a litter of papers, notebooks, photographs, and records lying all around her trunk; she would examine them, talk about them one by one before she packed them. Perhaps she herself should pack Sheila's trunk for her. She and Roger would never be away by the 12:45 train.

A knock at the door roused her. Glad of an interruption, she called, "Come in. . . . Deirdre!" Her eyes brightened. "It's you!"

"Aye. I came to see what on earth you're doing now that you haven't to study any more."

"Come and join me. Nothing! I'm just sitting down."

Deirdre appraised her face. "Contemplating again . . . I've come to help you."

Kate threw out her hands. "Oh—I've little enough to do as it is. Where's Liam?"

"Drinking coffee. He's packed already. And so am I."

"I wish you weren't all going this afternoon."

Deirdre stepped nearer and laid her hand on Kate's shoulder. "Don't fash yourself. The Irish Sea's a puddle. I know you'll be back."

"And you'll be on the other side of the Atlantic by then."

Deirdre laughed. "One day. Not yet. The English Channel first."

"*Vive la France!*"

Deirdre pirouetted round, her eyes radiating happiness. "So

[278]

romantic! To live in Paris for the first year. Poor—in a garret. With a great philosopher. Like *La Bohème* or something."

Kate smiled at the fantasy and gave Deirdre a hug. "Just don't die of consumption like Mimi! Be happy, Deirdre."

"I am!" She sat down abruptly, looking Kate straight in the eye. "Well, now . . . never mind me. Please let me do something for you."

Kate pulled a face. "Honestly, there won't be much to keep me busy anyway. Oh, I suppose you could get me some coffee, or look in the pigeonhole . . . if you're really hard up for something to do. But wouldn't you rather be down with Liam?" Her voice sounded somewhat wistful.

Deirdre smiled at her. "Don't look so woebegone! I'll be with him happily-ever-after, I hope. He can do without me just now. I'll say hello to him when I get your coffee."

"Coffee might wake me up. Thanks."

When Deirdre had gone, Kate began to work steadily again. She folded her winter clothes and wedged them into the trunk. The summer clothes, except what she would need the next day, went into her suitcase. She began to enjoy the sense of completion, of closure, and forgot for a while her longing and regret. Visualizing Deirdre rushing down to the coffee bar to find Liam, Kate sighed with the relief of no longer having reason to berate herself. She was thankful for the mending of her friendship with Liam. She had even enjoyed his bantering, his cajoling and teasing for the past two or three days.

As if materializing out of her mental ramblings, Deirdre reappeared with a steaming cup of coffee in one hand and an envelope in the other. Kate put down the dresses she was folding and took both from her.

"Thanks. And you went to the pigeonholes as well, I see."

"Yes. It's only an intramural letter."

They sat down again, across from each other by the fireplace. Kate took a sip of coffee and glanced at the front of the envelope. *Katherine Hamilton.* She frowned. That writing reminded her of something . . . what was it? Something important from some time ago. The words were written in black ink in a spiky hand she had seen before. A vague recollection stirred at the back of her brain

[279]

but then was lost like a drop falling into moving water. She shrugged. She would remember as soon as she opened it.

She split the envelope with her fingernail and unfolded the small piece of lined notepaper inside. Looked first at the signature at the bottom. *Jack.* Again she frowned. What was it about that writing?

Looking up with a small smile, Kate caught the interest in Deirdre's face and realized that her curiosity had been aroused by all the staring and frowning. "It's from Jack," she murmured. Then she looked down at the letter, her face beginning to feel warm. The writing was familiar, of course; she had seen it in seminars repeatedly when he sat near her taking notes.

"From Jack? That's funny. Why would he write you a note?"

"I don't know." Kate scanned it quickly.

> *Dear Katherine,*
> *Roger and Sheila tell me you won't be leaving until Friday, and since there are some things I'd like to talk with you about and to ask you, I'm wondering if you could spare Thursday afternoon for me? If so, please meet me outside the library right after lunch, say, about one o'clock. I'll understand if you can't come. Suggest another time if you'd rather; I'm in no rush to go home.*
> *Sincerely,*
> *Jack*

She handed the letter to Deirdre.

"Strange! I wonder what he wants? Will you be meeting him? The rest of us'll be gone by then. But I thought you might like to come over to Waterside with us in the taxi."

"It's the same train you'll all be on, isn't it?"

"Aye. We didn't plan it that way. Liam and I could have gone any time, for that matter."

Kate gestured helplessly. "I'd rather go to the station with you." She grimaced. "In fact, it's annoyed me all morning that I've got to wait around until tomorrow. . . . I should have known how quickly everyone would vanish."

Deirdre took in her look of frustration. "Well, don't fret. You might as well have an early lunch with us and see us off from here." She smiled. "And it'll be good for you to talk to Jack. He's always good company."

Kate shrugged. Her mind moved ahead quickly. "I suppose I could. But I'm puzzled. Why all the mystery? He doesn't even say what he wants to talk about. And we've had weeks of going up to St. Jerome's. Why couldn't he have talked to me then?"

Deirdre pulled down the corners of her mouth and raised her eyebrows. "I don't know. He's quite a private person. You can't always tell what he's thinking."

"Did he say anything to you about wanting to see me?"

"No, nothing."

"Or to Liam?"

"I don't know. Liam's not said anything if he did." Deirdre stopped, her face suddenly relaxing. "The only thing I can think of is something he said the other day to Sheila and me."

"What?" Kate heard the snap in her own voice and repeated the same word more softly. "What?"

"He's not sure about the priesthood any more."

Kate's eyes widened. "He said that?"

"Not in so many words." Deirdre winced. "In fact, I probably shouldn't have said that. He said he needed a year off to think more. He's going to do a sort of internship with a priest in Dublin. Didn't you know that?"

"He told me he was working down there this summer. But I thought he was going to Maynooth."

"He was. Said he didn't want us to misunderstand him. He just needed time to think, that's all—" She bit her thumbnail. "But I don't recall all he said. It was Saturday . . . the same time Liam came over and spoke to us. That put it all out of my head."

Kate groaned, covering her face with her hand. "Why couldn't he talk to Roger instead? Sheila told me Rog has been discussing theology with him for two years."

"You think he wants to ask what you think of his doubts . . . or whatever they are that he's not calling doubts?"

Kate did not look up. From behind her fingers, she lamented. "I don't know. What else could it be? And I'm no wellspring of spiritual knowledge. He's deeper than I am in lots of ways."

"It's good to hear you say that," Deirdre commented gently.

[281]

"Because it's true, Deirdre." She raised her head and looked at her to emphasize her point, then looked away again. "I have the greatest respect for him, for his calling. I'd dare not say a word about it. Who am I to give advice? Perhaps I will go to the station with you after all."

"Oh, no, you won't. If Roger could have helped him, he would. You have a reputation for being wise. And don't argue." She laughed suddenly. "It's a compliment to you that he wants to talk with you."

"He could go to his mentor in Belfast. Or someone in Maynooth."

"They'd be biased, Kate."

Kate sniffed. *And so would I,* she thought silently. But she left the chair, folded the letter, and placed it on top of the muddle on her desk. With her back to Deirdre, she said, "Then I'd better go. Perhaps you're right. Provident timing and all . . . maybe I will have something to offer him."

Sheila came back a few minutes after Kate and Deirdre had resumed Kate's packing. Her cheeks were red from the wind and her hair tangled. She panicked when she realized how little time remained for her to get everything ready; so Deirdre and Kate helped her. Soon Liam came in to find Deirdre and offered his help, too.

They chattered away as they worked, but Kate was quiet, her mind traveling ahead. Not to all the good-byes after lunch, but to her meeting with Jack. Already her mouth felt dry and her hands damp. What should she say to him? She would scarcely have time before one o'clock to be alone and pray. Perhaps after the others had left she could come back to Woodburn for a few minutes to collect herself. But no, he would probably be outside with her, waving good-bye as the taxi pulled away; if she ran off, he might think she did not want to talk with her. And besides, some of the best ideas came to her when she was least prepared to make an apology for her convictions. *So I'll not worry about it now,* she thought. *Que sera, sera.*

They all went together to lunch in the refectory for the last time.

[282]

Roger and Jack came in after them, from McCrae. Jack sat at the other end of the table from Kate. He neither looked at her nor spoke to her. But she watched him now and them from under her lashes, watched his hands moving, watched the changing nuances of his expression as he and Roger discussed details about Jack's journey to England for the wedding. What was he thinking? Deirdre was right: it was hard to tell. She picked at her food, not caring whether she fasted or tasted. *His hands,* she thought. *Picking apples. Lifting up Kathleen at the orphanage . . . a priest's hands . . . blessing someone, anyone, not me. His face . . . a priest's face . . . caring for someone, anyone, not me.* What was he thinking?

At quarter past twelve, two taxis pulled up outside Woodburn. The three men lifted Sheila's and Deirdre's trunks down the stairs with a lot of good-humored complaint about all the lead Sheila had packed. Roger grumbled about sexual segregation, since the second taxi was to take him and Liam over to McCrae for their own luggage. And Kate, standing in the driveway outside, hugging her cold arms against the wind, watched all the proceedings as though in a dream: distant, detached, numb to the sadness of parting.

The drivers grew impatient with the length of the farewells. Suddenly there was so much to say and to remind each other about. Kate clung to Deirdre with tears in her eyes, and Liam, seeing the tears, kissed her laughingly on the cheek and told her to "turn off the waterworks."

"It's well for you to say that," she murmured, holding his arms and smiling into his green eyes. "You look after her, Liam."

"I will. And you after yourself, Katie Hamilton." He leaned toward her for another kiss, this time on the mouth.

She looked at him in surprise, catching her lower lip between her teeth. "Away with your blarney, Liam Donnelly. Save it for Deirdre."

"You'll miss it like the devil, Kate."

"I'll miss you both, terribly." She looked behind him to Deirdre, who was climbing into the back of one taxi with Sheila. "Now go. You'll hardly get to Waterside. Roger and Sheila'll miss the boat."

Roger was shouting to Liam over the noise of the engines. "Come on, man, for pity's sake. Enough chatting up Kate, now."

[283]

Liam gave her hands a final squeeze, then shook Jack's hand, and, with a wink and a terse "Good luck," he ducked in beside Roger. Kate backed away to the bottom of the concrete steps, by the lamppost, and through a film of tears looked at Deirdre's bright face pressed to the glass window of the other taxi. Jack, too, moved aside and stood next to her, waving as the taxis swung from the curb and turned back toward the Northland Road gate.

Kate, still rubbing her arms, raised her eyes to Jack's. "Do you still want—?"

"You have time this aft—?"

They both spoke at once, then stopped, embarrassed. She waited for him.

"You do have time this afternoon, don't you?" He looked anxious, wanting her to say yes.

She cleared her throat. "Aye. Right enough." Unconsciously she had dropped into her father's Belfast accent. Hearing herself, she made her voice crisper again, adding, "But you said one o'clock, at the library. Was there something you needed to do first?"

He consulted his watch. "I didn't know whether I'd be up here or over at McCrae. That's the only reason I suggested one. It makes no difference to me."

"Then if you don't mind . . . I need a few moments upstairs first."

"Fine. I could wait in the reception room."

"We're going to the library to talk?"

He smiled. "No . . . that was just a central meeting place . . . our usual stamping ground. . . . I didn't know where you'd be either. But my car's over there. I drove Roger up."

A frown flickered over her eyes. "Your car?"

He took a breath. "Yes, would you mind if we went somewhere else to talk, out of the University altogether?"

"Of course not. I'll get my coat."

"We could go to Fahan."

Looking up at the blustery sky, she laughed. "Today? Though I was thinking about it just this morning."

"It's probably sunny over there," he urged. "We're in the lee of the mountains here." He raised his hands and let them drop again.

"But if you'd rather not, we could just sit in Woodburn . . . in the reception room, I mean."

Again she laughed. "That's no choice at all. Let's go to Fahan." She ran upstairs and shut the door of her room. It looked deserted already: mats rolled up for summer cleaning, the sink empty of Sheila's toothbrush and toothpaste and shampoo, one bed stripped to the mattress, and all except her night things packed away for the next day.

She stood in the middle of the floor feeling an alien in all the emptiness, glad after all that she could leave it tomorrow. But then, recalling Jack waiting for her, she began to shake.

She knelt by the bed and put her hands on the eiderdown, dropping her head on them. She clenched her teeth against their chattering and tried to pray. No words would come; her thoughts were too tangled and disconnected. And so she rested there, listening to her own uneven breathing and to the steady thrum of her blood.

As she became still, she began to see things more clearly. She was torn between the reality and the dream. The reality was her responsibility to speak her testimony without demur. And was that so difficult, especially to someone with his insight? She had done it before, with others. The dream was her desire to hear him answer warmly to that testimony. And even to hear him say other words . . . but those were the stuff of romantic half-dream wanderings in the dark, and in anguish she screwed up her eyelids against their impossibility.

Finally she got up and pulled on a cardigan and her white raincoat. White? It was turning gray now. Then she found a green scarf in the top of her suitcase and stood in front of the mirror. Even if it were sunny at the beach, it would be windy and cold. She tied the scarf over her head, but it slid backward immediately; so she brushed out her hair again and retied the bright silk as tightly as she could. The eyes watching her from the mirror were blue, flecked with green because of the scarf. They were also flecked with fear.

[285]

When Jack rolled the Morris to a halt at the Barney's border checkpoint, a British soldier stepped forward. Bending, searching the inside of the car with his eyes, he rapped out the usual laconic questions.

"Destination?"

Kate sat forward a little to see the soldier's face, and Jack said, "Just to Fahan."

"Bit cold for the beach, ain't it?"

"A bit, yes."

"Got anything in the boot?" The soldier eyed the back of the car.

"Nothing except a spare tire. Want me to open it for you?"

"No, stay inside the car. . . . And what's under those blankets?" He jerked his thumb toward a bundle of faded tartans on the back seat.

Jack reached over the seat to move them. The soldier raised his gun quickly. "No, don't lift them. Unlock the back door, please."

Jack did so, and the man stretched into the car with his left hand and moved the blankets himself. "All right, mate. You're on your way." He slammed the door again, leering through the windscreen at Kate. "Nice girl."

Jack only grinned, but Kate was piqued. "I won't be sorry to say good-bye to the British Army," she muttered as they drove away.

"Your own countrymen? I'm sorry for the poor lads."

"They're not my own countrymen, remember?"

He smiled, his eyes not leaving the road ahead. "Ah, nor they are."

She looked around to the stony circle of Griannan of Aileach on their left—an ancient fort—and to the sides of Asdevlin rising on the right into the low clouds. Dark rain was driving against the hillsides ahead of them. "Where's this sun you promised?" she accused.

"Shining on Fahan, naturally. Have you ever seen it rain on Fahan?"

She laughed. "Of course not. But I've never gone there in the rain, either. So I wouldn't have." She stared out at the drops beginning to patter against the windows.

And rain was falling on Fahan.

Jack drove the car off the road into a level, sandy area dotted with tussocky grass, about ten feet above the beach proper; a gently sloping bluff separated the car park from the sand. There were no other cars in sight, except for those swishing past behind them on their way to Buncrana or Derry. The rain drummed over their heads on the metal roof; the tide was in, whitecaps foaming in the wind only thirty yards away.

Kate looked out at the gray water and grayer sky, at the purple clouds obscuring all but the foot of the mountains on the other side of Swilly, and at the leaden arrows of rain pelting the beach. Her heart sank. "I'm disappointed," she said. "It would have been so good to get out and walk." Her voice sounded forced.

He toyed with the car keys, then stuffed them into his jacket pocket. "It'll blow over. You know how quickly the weather changes here."

"But it's been miserable all day."

"In Derry, aye . . . but you'll see."

She stared at him. He had not brought her here to discuss the weather. He fidgeted slightly under her gaze, turning so that he was facing her directly, his back against the door and his long legs stretched toward her feet. Behind his head the rain made rivulets down the window and the glass began to mist over. They might as well have sat in the car outside the library, for all they could see of the beach, she thought.

They were both stalling, neither knowing how to move from the inconsequential. Finally, he said, "You do know why I wanted to talk to you?"

Her eyes went down. "I think so. But go on, tell me yourself." She heard him take a slow breath.

"I've been learning a lot about the meaning of love," he began, his voice unsteady. "And I had to talk to you before we went our separate ways."

She looked up, her eyes shining. "I'm glad you felt you could talk to me about it." She gestured, a small nervous movement of her right hand. *He must have come to some deeper understanding of the love of God,* she thought. "And I'm glad I was still here this afternoon—" She smiled wanly; her jaw felt tight. Overhead the rain still babbled on the car. "Even if it is raining." He looked pleased, but uncertain of how to go on, so she picked up the thread again. "But I don't understand why you didn't say all you wanted to say to Roger. You've talked with him about theology, haven't you?"

Jack seemed taken aback. "Yes—we've talked about that, too."

Observing his surprise, she began to wonder what Roger had said to him. Had he advised Jack to forsake Catholicism altogether and embrace evangelical Protestantism? *No, Roger would never suggest such a thing,* she thought. *And yet . . . what was it Deirdre said . . . "He's not sure about the priesthood any more . . . he wants to hear what you think of his doubts. . . ."* Inwardly, she began to tremble. *He's deeper than I am in lots of ways . . . deeper . . .* and so she stumbled on the question: "Surely you don't mean—surely you're not going to give up your vocation?"

Jack blinked. "Well . . . I don't see how I could join the priesthood and still love—"

Frustrated, Kate broke in. "Of course you can love and serve God. Just as well in your church as in a Protestant church."

"What do you mean?" His eyebrows knitted in bewilderment. "Don't you have any idea of what I'm trying to say to you, Katherine?"

Except for the wind bursting on the glass and the water dripping, there was silence in the car as they watched each other. She saw his face change from bewilderment, to doubt, to something akin to despair. The balance of their relationship, such as it was, was somehow shifting, now, even as they failed to understand each other. That much she understood, but no more. Once she had needed his comfort. Now he seemed to need hers.

"Come on, Katherine. You're never so slow in the classroom as you are now. Don't tell me you didn't receive what I sent you in February—" He stopped. "And that you didn't recognize the handwriting."

"What you sent me—?" Bewildered herself, and growing uneasy, she unconsciously edged toward the door. "Please, I'm sorry—"

In reply, he only looked at her with eyes full of a dark emotion she hardly dared name to herself.

And then, she remembered. *The valentine. That distinctive writing. The red rose and the Yeats poem. "I would spread the cloths under your feet: But, being poor, have only my dreams."* And she had put it away in her desk and almost forgotten about it ... lost in her own private dreams: of Father Colm, of Liam and Deirdre, of London University ... and of Jack himself. But she had forgotten the valentine.

He saw the knowledge break over her: a wave on the beach. His long-fingered hand came toward her arm, but dropped into his lap as he looked at the amazement on her face. "I've been in love with you since last October. That first day at St. Jerome's ... in the orchard." The reproach had gone from his voice, his gray eyes now vulnerable and candid.

The sound of her heartbeat was louder to her than the dwindling rain outside. "Oh, Jack." Her eyes filled, and she took off her glasses so that she would not have to look at his agonized face any more. "I've been completely blind. I thought I was beginning to see things clearly. If only you had said—"

Bending toward her, he reached into his pocket and gave her his neatly folded linen handkerchief. "How could I, now tell me. Surely, surely, you knew."

She shook her head, buttoning and unbuttoning the hem of her raincoat, struggling with her emotions. "No."

"But I thought everyone must know. You filled my mind. Became an obsession. How could someone ... something ... so present to me not be real to others? Why did you think I wanted to talk to you if not to tell you this?" His urgent voice commanded her to look at him, but she couldn't—not yet. "I was surprised by how quickly you agreed to come today, but—"

She covered her face with one hand. In a small, weary voice, she said, "I thought you wanted to discuss your beliefs with me. Ironic, isn't it."

He laughed. "My beliefs! Dear Katherine! Oh, not today ... it's not faith but another of St. Paul's three 'great things' that I've got on my mind today."

"But ... you're going to be a priest," she spluttered. "It's always been a *fait accompli,* ever since you came here. And you said yourself once . . . God doesn't reverse a calling. . . . How could you possibly start thinking of—?"

"Don't be so utterly heartless." He mocked her innocent question in a falsetto voice: " 'How could you possibly start thinking of women?' " Then, reverting to his natural tones, he went on. "Listen, don't you have any feelings at all? Don't you have any understanding of what celibacy might mean, what its problems and temptations are?"

Hurt, she said coldly, "No. I suppose I don't."

"Well, I've been fighting against it for eight months. You're wrong about me; I'll never be a priest. I can't love in mind and spirit alone." He struck his chest with his hand. "Something called 'body' gets in the way . . . my eyes . . . when I look at you—"

"Oh, don't—you mustn't say those things. Please—you're tormenting—" She began to ache inside.

"And my hands that want to touch—this." He reached out suddenly and lifted a handful of her hair from her shoulder. "I've looked at this in lectures until I thought I'd go mad."

Her breathing quickened, and honey, not blood, began to flow through her. She could have pushed his hand away, but she didn't. Shaking her head slowly, she murmured, "Forgive me. And don't put me on any pedestal, either."

He let her hair go as suddenly as he had touched it. "No, I don't think I will. I think I understand you better than you do me."

"You probably do." Her voice was petulant. "I told you a great deal . . . one of the first times we sat in this car together." She longed for him to touch her hair again, but, perversely, she gave no sign.

He watched her. She sat twisting his handkerchief between her fingers and biting her lower lip. "I'm glad you told me all those things." His voice softened again. "I thought then . . . half thought . . . that perhaps you could learn to love me, too. I've seen how you can love, Kate, at St. Jerome's. And with Deirdre and even Liam. And at Father Colm's wake. And you did share a lot that day. I took it as a sign that you liked and trusted me."

He had always called her "Katherine" before, never "Kate." "Oh—I did—I do." She turned her face toward him again. "Will you believe me?"

[290]

He looked at her uncertainly for a moment. "Then . . . the valentine? . . . You really didn't know?"

She swallowed hard. "I didn't know . . . I finally thought Roger must have sent it . . . with a little help from Sheila. I never dreamed—"

"What could I say to you without using worn-out words? I borrowed Yeats. I knew you liked his poems. It was a way of making myself take some action—forcing a decision. If you didn't give me some kind of response, I could either forget all about it, bury everything . . . or I could try to do this . . . what we're doing right now. Talk to you." He looked at her steadily. "I had to."

She put on her glasses again and saw hope in his eyes.

"What else could I do, for heaven's sake?" he went on. "Talk to Sheila?"

She shrugged, outwardly composed again but inwardly in turmoil. "You might have talked in a general way to your priest at home?" It was a question, not an answer.

"Father Maurus! He would have dismissed what I told him as mere infatuation . . . late adolescent romantic nonsense . . . the pre-seminary jitters of all would-be celibates. And the one person I might have talked to is dead." His voice fell lower. "He would have been very sympathetic, knowing you."

She did not know how much she could trust herself to say, but after a moment she pleaded, "You had so many opportunities on our way up and back to St. Jerome's."

He shook his head. "Not really. Deirdre was usually with us. And you were absorbed in the children, the work, your studies . . . always afraid to talk of anything personal. Always afraid to be intimate." His tone was bitter again.

It was her turn to remonstrate. "How could I, now tell me?" she echoed.

He twisted his mouth into a grim smile. "And always ironic. But you didn't deceive me. I saw again and again . . . at the wake . . . even last Sunday, that you weren't as hard as you pretended to be. It's just your way, your defense. I'd also begun to realize at St. Jerome's that you could only be aware of me as a co-worker. You were never aware of me as a man, sexually."

His emphasis on the last word made the blood rise into her face

[291]

again. "Then you were wrong," she said steadily. "Wrong from the wake onwards." She did not look at him, but out at the drizzle, hardly able to get the words out. "I was more and more aware of you. But I became terrified. Me . . . falling in love with a Catholic—a priest. So I prattled on . . . too much, as you said. It was a cover-up. And you think you had no one to talk to? What could I say, and to whom? Jack, I . . . I didn't even understand what was happening inside me. I tried to dismiss it as no more than physical attraction. I had no idea how to deal—"

"And that frightened you? That you were . . . falling in love with me?" A smile began in his eyes.

"I didn't say that."

"Yes, you did."

She looked away.

"Kate—you're wonderful!" His voice was full of amusement now. "You've poured everything into your books. You've lived your life vicariously—through them. Never allowed yourself to love with all you've got. Your soul and your brain . . . are they all of Katherine Hamilton?"

She turned on him furiously. "You—a priest!" She spat out the word. "How can you talk of sublimation—and that's what you're driving at, isn't it?—when you've been subverting your own vocation for months by eyeing me up and down in lectures!" She flung her head back. "Don't throw those kinds of judgments at me if you understand me as well as you say you do."

She saw, though, that her anger meant nothing to him. His eyes were direct and warm and full of fun. With an exasperated exclamation she shoved open the door and swung her legs out.

Laughing, he called. "Kate, wait." She stalked off into the rain. "Don't be so stubborn." Grabbing a blanket from the back seat and shouting again, he followed her over the bluff and down onto the sand. "Wait!"

The green scarf blew out behind her, a flag of fair hair underneath it. She stopped, and he caught up with her.

"Please listen," he begged.

"Let's walk," she said savagely.

"In this?" Even though the rain had eased to a light drizzle, the wind and waves still swirled and rolled in the loud air.

"In this."

"Then put this blanket over yourself. You'll be drenched."

She took it ungraciously and covered her head and shoulders with it. But after going a minute, she taunted him, "Where's yours?"

"I'll have to go back for it, or share that one."

"It's not big enough for two."

Ignoring her, Jack pursued, "But you said it. I heard you. Deny it all you want to. You were beginning to love me."

She hurried on relentlessly until he caught her arm. "No more games, Kate!" They stopped still, facing each other, ankle deep in gritty wet sand. He was shouting over the wind. "I was trying to tell you that I've found other ways of serving God than in the priesthood. And I don't want to do it alone." He pulled her toward him, his hands on her wrists.

She let her arms go limp, and her face crumpled. "Don't. We've said some awful things to each other. We need to amend them first. So don't think I don't know how to respond to you. I do. But you're going too fast. Saying too much." She shook one hand free and covered her face again.

He moved closer, bending his mouth to her ear. "Let's go back to the car. Please. Or we could go up and sit in the hotel lounge for a while."

"No—I'd rather stay in the car. I'm sorry."

He put his arm around her. She did not pull away this time but leaned against him as they walked.

The relative quiet inside the car sounded deafening after the wind and waves outside. They sat staring at each other for a long time, each wondering at the freedom with which, suddenly, they could do that.

"I don't mean to push you," Jack said, very softly. "I was trying to see if I could break down your—" He waved his hand, searching for a word. "Your wall of . . . whatever it is. And I wanted you to know that I've never been surer of anything I've said to another person than when I say I love you."

She nodded slowly. "And I've loved you, too. From the day Father Colm was buried." Her eyes dropped to her coat hem, but

[293]

she didn't see it. "We've both learned so much from him. . . . But I wasn't conscious of everything all at once. Were you—?"

He shook his head. His gray eyes were warm.

"I never stopped to analyze why it was so important to find you at the wake . . . and to come back with you." She smiled at these admissions. "Never considered, at first, why I didn't enjoy going to St. Jerome's so much unless you were there." She took a deep breath. "There was so much I didn't see."

He took her hand. "That doesn't matter any more. Just thank God we're saying these things to each other. We might not have. And I don't know what I would have done if you'd not come—" He reached across and with one finger traced a light curve under her eyes and back to her wet hair.

She saw that his eyes were moving from her eyes to her mouth, and the old warning voices whispered in her brain. *It's not wrong exactly, but pretty dangerous. . . . Two unequally yoked don't pull well together.* But she rejected them absolutely. There was nothing unequal here. *Leave the past to the mercy of God, and the present to the love of God, and the future to the benevolence of God. . . .* She turned toward him.

He slid away from the steering wheel and lifted her onto his lap. In the cramped space, he held her in the circle of his arms, kissing her as he had never kissed before and as she had never been kissed: his warm, wide mouth on hers, and his hands on her wet hair, her back. She let herself drown in his kisses.

Outside the car, the drizzle stopped and the clouds rolled away, south, toward Strabane. Above the rough water, the blue iris of the sky cleared and widened. Walking together along the edge of the lough, they could see to the other side of the water—to the mountains that the rain had obscured only an hour before.

A Note About the History

Ireland, it is often said, has no past; all its history is present. The civil rights march in Londonderry on October 5, 1968, introduced many British students attending the New University of Ulster to the Irish Question. But the "troubles" in Northern Ireland began long before that march and its subsequent unrest and violence.

At the beginning of the seventeenth century, James I of England organized Scottish Presbyterians to plant Ulster. His action was one more in a long history of attempts by English monarchs to suppress the island's inhabitants; for James, that meant the suppression of the Irish Catholics. His plantation policy allowed English overlords to confiscate land from the Irish and then to rent it to Scottish and English planters. As a result, by the end of the seventeenth century, only fourteen percent of all Irish land belonged to Irish Catholics; in Ulster itself the percentage fell to only five.

The dissension and mistrust between Catholics and Protestants deepened as two societies evolved with separate languages, cultures, and forms of worship. The displaced Irish, driven from the fortified Protestant strongholds, were forced to eke out their existence by farming the thin topsoil of the bog lands and mountains. Those who returned to the cities toiled as servants or unskilled artisans for Protestant employers. And whether they labored on the farm or in the city, they were universally suppressed; they were deprived of the right to practice law, to join the army, to own a gun, to own a horse worth more than five pounds, and to lease land. They were even massacred by Oliver Cromwell in 1649 at Drogheda and Wexford.

Division between the two groups was not, however, confined to Ireland. The Protestant King William of Orange (popularly known as King Billy) landed in England in 1688 and claimed the

[295]

throne from the Catholic monarch James II. James fled to Ireland, where he raised an army of Irish and European soldiers to combat William. He led his Catholic followers to the walled city of Londonderry but was locked out by the now famous Apprentice Boys. For one hundred and five days, he laid siege to the city as thousands within died of famine and disease. William raised the siege and subsequently defeated James at the Battle of Boyne on July 11, 1690. On July 12, 1691, James's defeat was made final at the Battle of Aughrim, and to this day, the Protestant Orange Order celebrates July 12th with marches, rallies, and parades.

The Anglican ascendancy of the eighteenth century imposed penalties on Presbyterians and Catholics alike, bringing about a brief reconciliation between the two. But extremist Protestant vigilantes continued to strain that tenuous alliance by persecuting Catholics.

In the nineteenth century, English politicians and landlords saw the political advantages of dividing these groups and contributed to antipathies by awarding privileges to "Loyalist" Protestants and by playing up to Unionist fears of a Catholic rebellion— tactics that led to the continued suppression of Catholics. The polarization of the two communities became even more extreme during the potato famine of the 1840s in which the Catholics suffered most severely.

Irish nationalism grew under the influence of Charles Stewart Parnell, the Fenians, and later the Irish Republican Brotherhood (the nineteenth-century forerunner of the Irish Republican Army). The Protestant majority in Ireland feared the revolutionary and nationalistic fervor of the Irish and formed the Ulster Unionist Party, which, backed by the English Conservatives, opposed Prime Minister Gladstone and his pro–Home Rule English Liberal Party.

At the beginning of the twentieth century, with Home Rule still the object of political juggling but not a reality, the simmering tension turned into boiling violence. Private sectarian armies massed in both the north and the south. Republican revolutionaries staged the 1916 Easter Rising and organized a campaign of guerilla activity. The establishment of an Irish Free State in the south in 1921 did not end the violence, either, since the political boundaries drawn around British Northern Ireland's six counties assured the continued discrimination, directly and indirectly, by a Protestant majority against a Catholic minority.

As late as 1969, many Northern Irish Catholics were excluded from local elections by laws that gave votes only to property holders and gave extra votes to those with more than one property. The Unionist majority thus maintained the status quo, unofficially backed by such paramilitary groups as the Ulster Special Constabulary (the "B" Specials); the Ulster Volunteer Force (UVF), which was declared illegal in 1966; the Ulster Protestant Volunteers (UPV), formed in 1966: and the Ulster Constitutional Defence Committee (UCDC), formed in 1966 by Ian Paisley, self-styled Moderator of the Free Presbyterian Church.

Reforms aimed at moderating the Unionist position and increasing the government's credibility began in the late sixties; among these were the disbanding of the "B" Specials, the establishment of an "integrated" force called the Ulster Defence Regiment (UDR), and changes in the voting laws. But Catholic and Republican groups such as the Northern Ireland Civil Rights Association (NICRA), formed in 1967, and the People's Democracy (PD), formed in 1968, mistrusted and challenged the government's actions. In January 1969 civil rights marchers led by Bernadette Devlin were brutally ambushed by militant Protestants at Burntollet Bridge. The battle that ensued has become a symbol of the violence in Northern Ireland. By the summer of 1969, British peace-keeping troops had been stationed in Belfast and Londonderry, but the political and economic forces had already set the stage—three hundred years before—for a continuation of sectarian warfare.

Acknowledgments

"The Patriot Game," words and music by Dominic Behan. Copyright © 1964 and 1965 Clifford Music Ltd., London, England. TRO - Essex Music, Inc., New York, controls all publication rights for the U.S.A. and Canada. Used by permission.

"The Patriot Game," words and music by Dominic Behan. Copyright for UK, Eire and all territories under PRS/MCPS jurisdiction held by Westminster Music Limited. Used by permission.

"Lucy in the Sky with Diamonds" by John Lennon and Paul McCartney, and "Within You Without You" by George Harrison. Copyright © 1967 Northern Songs Limited. All rights for the U.S.A., Mexico and the Philippines controlled by Maclen Music, Inc., c/o ATV Music Corp. Used by permission. All rights reserved.

"The Water Is Wide," traditional folk song, as sung by Joan Baez. Used by permission of Miss Baez and Ryerson Music Publishers, Inc.

"Shoals of Herring," by Ewan McCall. Oak Publications, New York.

Other folk songs quoted are traditional.

Excerpt from *The Power and the Glory* by Graham Greene. Copyright 1940, renewed © 1968 by Graham Greene. Reprinted by permission of the author, Viking Penguin Inc., and Laurence Pollinger Limited.

Excerpt from *The Shadow of a Gunman* by Sean O'Casey. First edition 1925, first issued in St. Martin's Library, 1957. Used by permission of St. Martin's Press, Inc., New York, and Macmillan London Ltd.

The "Ultima" used by permission of Fr. Salvator Fink, O.F.M., Director of St. Anthony's Guild.

DOUGH SWILLY

Dunfanaghy

Buncr

Griana
of Ailea

Letterkenny

St

TYRO

FERMANAGH

REPUBLIC OF IRELANI

| 0 | 10 | 20 | 30 | 40 miles |

| 0 | 10 | 20 | 30 | 40 | 50 | 60 kilometers |

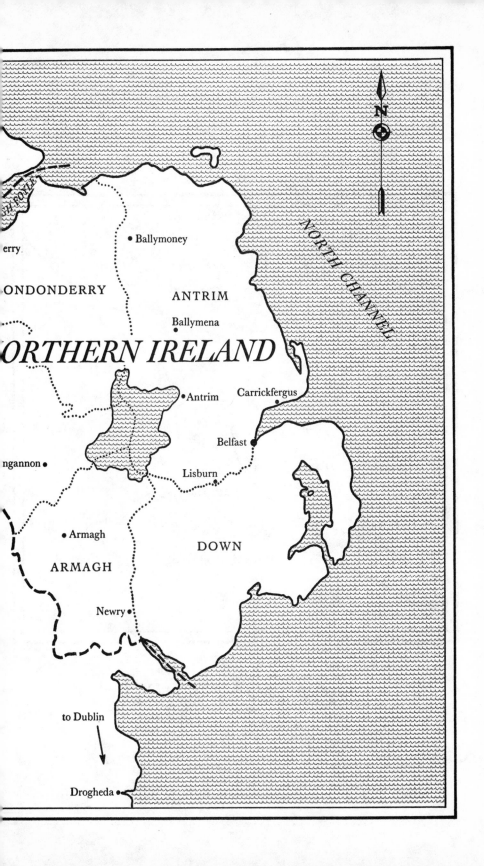

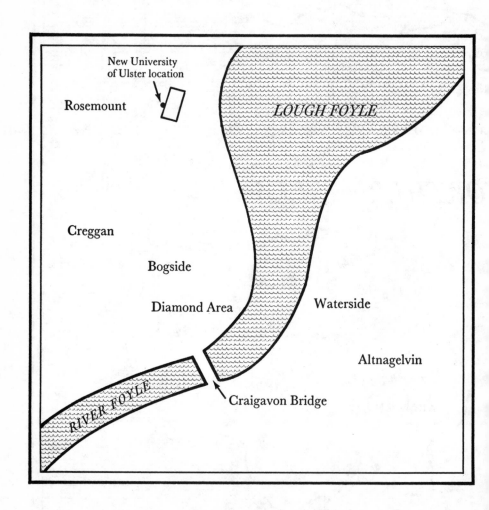

LONDONDERRY

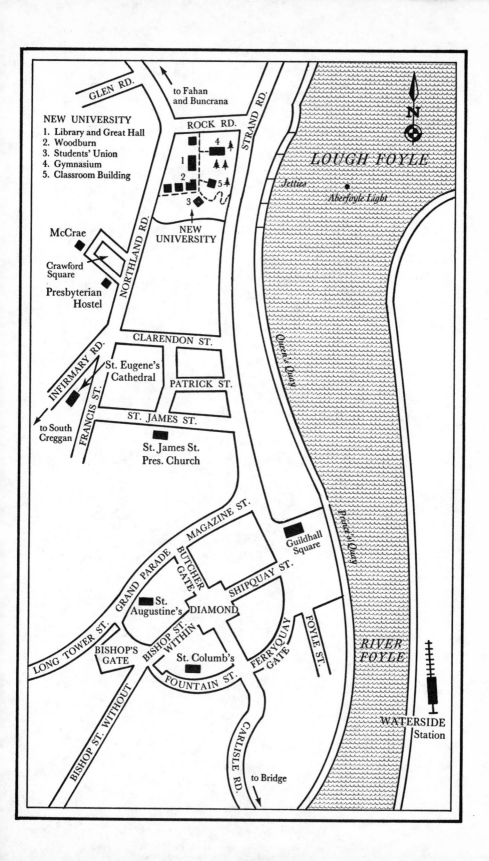

NEW UNIVERSITY
1. Library and Great Hall
2. Woodburn
3. Students' Union
4. Gymnasium
5. Classroom Building

GLEN RD.

to Fahan
and Buncrana

ROCK RD.

STRAND RD.

LOUGH FOYLE

Jetties

Aberfoyle Light

NORTHLAND RD.

NEW
UNIVERSITY

McCrae

Crawford
Square

Presbyterian
Hostel

INFIRMARY RD.

CLARENDON ST.

St. Eugene's
Cathedral

FRANCIS ST.

PATRICK ST.

to South
Creggan

ST. JAMES ST.

St. James St.
Pres. Church

Queen's Quay

MAGAZINE ST.

GRAND PARADE

BUTCHER GATE

Guildhall
Square

SHIPQUAY ST.

St.
Augustine's DIAMOND

BISHOP ST. WITHIN

Prince's Quay

LONG TOWER ST.

BISHOP'S
GATE

St. Columb's

FERRYQUAY GATE

FOYLE ST.

FOUNTAIN ST.

RIVER
FOYLE

BISHOP ST. WITHOUT

CARLISLE RD.

to Bridge

WATERSIDE
Station